WILD AS THE STARS

KERRY CHAPUT

Black Rose Writing | Texas

ISBN: 978-1-68513-620-8
LIBRARY OF CONGRESS CONTROL NUMBER: 2025930162
PUBLISHED BY BLACK ROSE WRITING
www.blackrosewriting.com

Printed in the United States of America
Suggested Retail Price (SRP) $23.95

Wild as the Stars is printed in Minion Pro

*As a planet-friendly publisher, Black Rose Writing does its best to eliminate unnecessary waste to reduce paper usage and energy costs, while never compromising the reading experience. As a result, the final word count vs. page count may not meet common expectations.

Cover design by Asya Blue @ www.asyablue.com

Dedicated to those who struggle with mental health.

There's beauty in the darkness, even when you can't see it.

Step inside for the show of a lifetime.
Welcome to the world of enchantment and magic.
Welcome to the Luminaire.

CHAPTER ONE

1928 Seattle
Eleanora Cleary

My legacy is to sling magic onstage, so naturally, I decided to scrub dishes alone in a dingy underground bar. Sure, the dish soap ruins my hands, and the rags smell of sour booze, but the perks at the Milk House can't be denied. The dancers at our speakeasy warm the room with cinnamon-scented mist. Their jazz hands drop amethyst gems into a sea of grass, and nothing sets my skin alight quite like our belly dancer spinning halos of gold.

Living adjacent to a dream will have to be enough.

"Eleanora, stock is dwindling." Lady bellows from the kitchen where I stand with empty bottles of "milk." Everyone knows there's gin in those bottles, and no one knows what Lady's real name is.

"Yeah, yeah." While I wash dishes and restock her speakeasy, my mind spins a tale of what my life could have been, if fear and frenzy hadn't yanked everything away. Gone are the nights of sweat and heat and fire. I've become a scullery maid who sweeps up remnants of another girl's magic at the end of the night.

At the entrance to this crumbling theater is the word *Vaudeville* painted in red on a splintered piece of wood. Lady deemed her establishment worthy of the famed theater circuit, though I can assure you, it's not. The Milk House is nothing like the glittering shows at legitimate theaters across the country. No, we feed the hungry underbelly of Seattle streets with what they can no longer legally consume—gin and magic.

"Eleanora!" Lady snaps from behind the bar. "Stop dawdling."

I throw the rag over my shoulder and cross through the theater slower than is necessary so I can watch our burlesque dancer shoot diamonds from the cones over her breasts. She moves like a celestial dream.

I'm lucky. Too many of us are homeless or locked away in institutions. Here, the beat of the band drowns out the overwhelming sadness. Lady is part of my speakeasy family—for better or worse—and I can't avoid her instructions much longer.

"Why are you in such a hurry?" I ask. "Our belly dancer hasn't even arrived yet." And there's no show without her.

She checks her scarf. A sure sign she's hiding something. "Listen, something big is happening tonight."

"Is the police chief asking for a peep show again? I'll get the baseball bat."

"No." She reaches for my arm. "A theater director will be here. He's on the hunt for a dancer."

"Like you'd give up one of ours." My laugh doesn't seem to crack a smile from her. "What's going on?"

She steadies her gaze. "He's from the Luminaire."

The way my chest seizes. I could spit fire from how hot my throat burns. "I see."

"This must be difficult for you."

"Not difficult." Don't cry, Eleanora. Don't you dare cry. "That's just life." After I slink from her touch, I push open the blackened door that leads up a staircase that leads to another doorway that leads to a makeshift theater on the ground floor as a front for hidden deeds downstairs.

Under the sallow light of an old lightbulb on a chain, a player piano groans an out of tune version of *Oh! Susanna* while mechanical farm animals spin in circles. A man in the audience yawns. Another lowers his hat over his face for a nap. Lady pays them in coins and all the "milk" they desire, so there's never a shortage of volunteers in this sad establishment. Prohibition, where off-duty policemen drink our hooch and dance with our magic girls. What a joke.

One patron snores with such gusto that he wakes himself from a drunken stupor. My hands smolder with hidden fire, and my eyes wander to the burn line where I once scraped my fingernails along the wall when no one was looking. Lady welcomes any girl who dances with abandon and although I adore the shows downstairs, I keep my elements where they belong—locked up tight.

Out in the enclosed alley, the moon pours regret over me in a pool of light. The stars once twinkled their whispers above me, but they've been silent for years. And my past is about to land in my present with a sickening thud. I busy myself by filling crates with bottles wrapped in brown paper.

I try to stop myself, but my mind wanders to darkness, to the traumatic sweet spot that both shocks and soothes my insides. The memory welcomes me to its ugly depths. A gorgeous jazz dancer with crystals in her auburn curls slicing open her arm with a razor blade, elbow to wrist, not caring that I watched in horror as her skin blossomed open like a bloody flower.

One person always shakes me from my unease under the night sky, and I prepare myself for Aria's squeaky voice. "How are the girls looking?"

"Magnificent. As usual." Poor kid. She's spent all twelve years of her life at some orphanage in the city. Lady has kicked her out more times than I can count, but the scrappy little girl hung around until she gave her a job. "You should go home. It's cold out here."

"No way! I won't let Lady down." Her smile offsets her scrawny limbs and patched jacket two sizes too big for her bony frame. "Someone has to guard these milk crates." Her defiant nod fills me with sadness, as if this is the most important job in the world. If any cops come snooping around, she flips a switch that lights an underground lightbulb to alert the speakeasy. She gets a nickel every night and all the real milk her heart desires. Not a bad hustle, I suppose.

"These alleys are better than the ice box orphanage."

How strong her optimism must be. "It's dangerous here, kiddo." I slip a pair of gloves from my pocket, trying not to stare at her pale blue fingers. "Someone left them behind last night."

"It's nothing." The gloves are three sizes too big, but she slips them on anyway. "Aren't we lucky? We get to work near the best dancers I've ever seen."

"They're the *only* dancers you've ever seen."

She giggles. Her happiness is like a shield against this bitter world, and I envy the hell out of her. "Think I can perform one day?" she asks.

I fix the misaligned buttons on her coat, straightening out the collar to cover her exposed neck. "I think you can do anything your little heart wishes."

"Except spin magic like you." She sits on a turned over bucket. "To think, one of our girls could make it into the Luminaire, with legal magic above ground, with spotlights! Boyfriends waiting in the wings and a huge audience throwing roses. Swoon! Do you think the Star Girls levitate in their sleep? I bet lipstick spins in the air and birds sing to them as they dress."

I can't help but smile at her overexcited imagination. "Magic Dance isn't like that. We're just women who bleed a bit of magic when we dance. We aren't witches or anything."

Estimates say we're two percent of the population. The fire dancers, the rarest of all magic, stoke the country's most irrational fears. Most have been locked away, so anyone left hides in their homes or swallows their fire until they go mad. And some of us wash dishes for safe keeping.

"You should dance for the director tonight! You can become a Luminaire Star Girl just like your—" She catches herself before saying the thing I beg her not to talk about.

Dance for the director. Fat chance. Every girl like me produces pretty elements like water, flowers, rainbows, and gems. If anyone saw fire spurt from my palms, they'd haul me to the closest institution. The theater is closed for restructuring after calls to shutter their doors. And this guy shows up looking for new talent?

"All those regular Vaudeville shows with no magic?" Aria says. "How boring. What's the point of dance if you can't spin rubies and gold? The legal ones just dance and sing and make silly jokes," Aria scoffs.

"Vaudeville performers are some of the highest paid women in the world. We would be too if Prohibition hadn't ruined it for us. No riches for the feral performers who spit diamonds in the middle of a grand jeté."

"Come on, wouldn't you like to perform at the only theater that allows magic?"

Desperately. But I gave up on that dream five years ago. I toss the stinky rag at her. "When will you stop pushing me?"

"Never."

Aria's starry-eyed visions for my future keep me holding on by the thinnest of threads. Somehow, she keeps this tiny hope inside me smoldering.

My best memory was the Milky Way twinkling as my mother danced around me on a clear summer night. Of course, I didn't know the name of the constellation then, but I sensed somehow, we were connected. That was before I learned of our bloodline and the destiny to dance bright and die young.

I still find myself on our rooftop under a blanket of stars, hoping I'll hear the universe's whispers again. I never do, but a useless dream is better than no dream at all.

"Eleanora!" Aria throws the rag back at my face without losing her sweet smile. "The show's about to start." I lift the crate with a grunt as the bottles clank inside. Aria's excitement warms the piercing worry in my chest. "It is awfully cold out here," she says with a shiver.

"Fine, you can watch."

She shrieks and opens the door for me. I might need her to pick me up off the floor when that director shows up. She tucks into my shadow and follows me through the winding trail of creaking stairs and rusted doors. Once inside the speakeasy, light blasts us as the girls warm up for their big night.

Aria rubs her eyes after the flash. "They're so glamorous and shiny."

"Eleanora—"

I spin to face Lady. "I know Aria shouldn't be down here, but it's a big night. I'll hide her in the kitchen and scoot her out when the dances are done."

Lady sighs. "Fine. Just restock my bottles. The director will be here any minute."

Our belly dancer sits hunched at the bar. Her lipstick is smeared like a deranged clown, and she yanks a rosette from her hair to cover her mouth as she burps.

"Are you okay?" I ask, and she responds with a dry heave.

She's coming down from a nasty hangover. I can't let the patrons see her like this, so I help her to the bathroom. The Milk House has somehow managed to avoid the country's disgusting purity raids. Lady must hold some kind of power in this city.

The saxophone player noodles out a jazzy tune as I neatly arrange the gin and whisky bottles behind the bar. The whole basement frizzles like fat popping in an iron pan. Aria tucks herself in an alcove and watches me. "You sure you don't wanna be out there?"

"Positive." Lady has never let go of the idea that I could carry on my mother's legacy. In a different world, I'd be spinning fire like a golden web around my tap shoes. In this one, I'm Eleanora Cleary, twenty-one-year-old-dishwasher who speaks to silent skies. At least my magic won't land me in an institution for wayward women. I cringe so hard my teeth ache.

A blaring horn crashes me back to reality. I poke my head into the bathroom to find scattered faux blossoms and a pair of scuffed scarlet-red court shoes tossed to the floor. Her head is in the toilet. "Get it all out." I motion to the closest dancer. "Get her water, will ya'?"

Another day, another performance. More booze. Layers of guilt and shame and crawling toward the safety of their beds with magic spent and souls weary.

The blackened door opens. The music stops. In walks a young man in a jazz suit with a starched collar and a fedora slanted low over one eye. A ponytail holds a wavy mass of golden hair and his Adam's apple bobs in place with what appears to be a nervous swallow. His two-toned Oxfords gleam like a waxy apple.

Lady elbows me. "That's him. The director."

"I couldn't tell." Lies. Not only can I tell he's not the usual Milk House patron, but I also notice the not-so-subtle way my stomach dips when he meets my gaze.

"Welcome, welcome." She gestures to the best seat in the house, where the table isn't sticky, and the bartender is only a snap away. She scrapes the back legs of his chair along the floor while I watch his graceful moves.

Aria tugs at my sleeve. "Let me see."

"No." I lead her back to the kitchen. "We'll watch through the service window. We settle in for the show as Lady laughs at everything the young man says.

They discuss something and both turn back toward us. His dark eyes bore through me. I instinctively drop to the floor and pull Aria down with me.

"Why are we hiding?"

I shush her and quietly curse Lady for bringing the Luminaire director here without warning. A reminder of my failed life dropped right here like a slap in the face, and I can do nothing but watch him evaluate the non-Fire Girls for a spot at the theater I once dreamed of headlining.

Lady bursts into the kitchen, hand on her hip. "We have no waitress."

"She's sick. I wouldn't get near her. I bet it's influenza. Or diphtheria. Possibly tuberculosis."

"You really need to stop reading the obituaries." Lady rubs her eyes and growls. "Get off the floor."

"Why?"

"Because you're all I've got." She grabs my arm and lifts me to standing.

I don't like this at all. "I wash dishes, alone in the protected kitchen. I don't serve patrons." My stable life is already tenuous, with hysteria hovering around my every move like a screeching threat. "I know what you're doing."

"The only thing I'm doing is keeping my business afloat." She tugs at my sleeve. "You serve tonight."

Lady, with her lacquered makeup and her gray curls tucked under a silk scarf, could pass for the most eccentric grandmother in the city. Her bony fingers hold my arm with care, but she whispers in my ear, "Get him drunk and keep him there. And pretend to be pleasant. Perhaps he'll choose the hand walking ice queen or the metal twins."

So named for the woman who walks on her hands across a sheet of ice and the twins who dance together in a spinning silver and gold ring. More metals and elements, just as everyone expects. Nothing out of the ordinary here, like rings of fire or shooting stars.

The term magic dancer isn't wholly accurate, but when is anyone ever accurate about anything? We produce different types of elements, and not everyone dances. Who cares about labels? The women with magic are just grateful to move our bodies. Most of us dance in basements just to get the magic out of our bones. The country lumped us in with booze as the downfall of society, turning Prohibition into a war on girls.

Outside my kitchen, serving the director, oh-so-close to the stage that glitters with magic potential? Not terrifying at all. Dammit, Lady. I slide my body against the bar as I approach the man with golden hair.

I plaster on some version of a smile as I stumble toward his table for one. He turns to me as I catch a glimpse of his face without the fedora. His deep brown eyes have rings of gold. Good grief, even his eyeballs look rich.

"Are you one of the dancers?" he asks.

"No." I consider adding more to the story but stop myself before I unload my life story. "No."

He stands and stares into my eyes with unnerving interest. "Are you certain?"

"Excuse me?" I cross my arms, but Lady is there to bump her hips into mine.

"It's just, you could easily light up the stage. Lean arms like willow branches. Black sleek hair and gray, foggy eyes with a beautiful long neck."

My breath catches at the word beautiful as it leaves his barely parted lips. "I'm not a piece of art to gawk at."

"I'm sorry, I didn't mean to um—" He searches the room. "Is the show about to begin?"

He leans forward, so close I can count the freckles on his nose. I stare at the ends of his thick caramel hair I could run my fingers through. Holy hell, Eleanora. He's just a man.

I want to say something sharp and acidic that will force his gaze away. But I can't find the words, so I panic and point to the bar. "Drink."

"Oh, um. Whisky. Neat."

"Yeah, okay." Lady snarls at me, so I turn back to him and curtsy. *A curtsy, Eleanora? Really?*

Lady pours the drink, forcing a controlled smile. "Get it together, girl."

"I'm not accustomed to all this. It makes my skin itch to stand this close to people, and all those spotlights. And Jesus Christ, that man might be the most handsome thing I've ever seen. It's terrifying."

"Are you certain you're Fiona's daughter?" she says with a laugh.

"This is what living at arm's length of your dream will do. Make you hate it for loving it so much."

I grab the drink, grateful not to spill more than a few drops. With a plunk, I serve the whisky to the man with fire eyes. "Enjoy the show." It's not his fault I want what I can't have. The way he looks at me makes my earlobes burn.

Aria watches from the service window, laughing at my expense. I stick out my tongue to make her snort laugh. When I glance back at the man from the Luminaire, he's smiling at me. I duck back into the kitchen and rush to the sink, exposed and very uncomfortable.

Back with the dirty dishes, away from the stage, I can breathe without worry of dance taking over my body or fire shooting from my hair. When you risk exploding fire from every part of your body, you learn very quickly to avoid bystanders. A wayward flare could burn someone's eyebrows and land me in some hellhole—an institution for the insane and unwell. Sure, this safety also fills me with immeasurable sadness, but such is life when you're labeled illicit goods.

Lights dim. Music taps a jazzy rhythm. Girls shimmy in a line, turning the stage into a pool of silver water. They take turns stepping forward. Some spin and flip through rainbow mist, others swing from the golden ropes they spin with pirouettes. These girls have accepted the danger of it all, or maybe they don't know any different. I admire the hell out of them.

Lights bounce across the director's gleaming hair as he examines the girls with the boredom of a tax man. What if I were up there taking my shot? When he looks over his shoulder to meet my eyes, I retreat behind the wall, swallowing any notion of stardom.

Through the show I focus on dishwater. Light and rainbows and gold shoot from the stage as laughter and applause ripple through the speakeasy. My heart aches, but I force a steely glare and draw my fingernail through the soap suds along my skin, back to the painfully comforting image of that dancer's fileted arm all those years ago. Her eyes turned desperate as she tried to bleed the magic from her body. A reminder of what Magic Dance would do to me... if I let it.

"Eleanora, it's over. You should have been up there." Aria's sad smile fills me with guilt. I should have watched and cheered for their moment of underground glory.

I force a crooked smile, hoping she won't pick up on my regret. The Luminaire makes monsters out of stars, and if I were braver, I would have blasted the man with an epic fire dance. I would have begged him to make a monster out of me.

She hugs my waist before ducking out the back door toward her orphanage.

I'm certain Lady will tear into me for disappearing tonight, so I stay for an hour after all the noise dies down, drying glasses until they gleam. Back in the hidden dance hall, it's dark and quiet and cold. Just as I like it. Five years ago, I jumped onto this stage to debut my tap moves, full of hope and retribution about to explode. By sixteen, our elemental responses are fully developed. They're fresh and bright, and a little unwieldy, making a girl's debut a thrilling risk for underground party seekers. I had practiced for months, dancing the routine in my sleep. But I bombed. A literal explosion. Fire shot from my hands, and I fell to the floor in a panic. Both my eyes were bruised purple for weeks.

My chest tightens with the memory and my head dizzies like an old, unwelcome friend. I want to scream until the panic recedes.

At least I'm alone.

My body launches into yet another episode, where I'll either fall face first onto the tacky floor, or claw at my hair until my mind once again connects to my body. "No, no no," I yell to my feet. Forget the failure. Remember the shine. That's what Lady tried to teach me. It never stuck.

For some odd reason, my body listens, and panic recedes. I pick up the broom and pretend to waltz with it. I sneak out my tap shoes from their hiding place behind the bar. Okay, they're tattered Oxfords with pennies taped to the soles, but late into the night when I'm alone in these shoes, I'm the world's most famous dancer.

I hold the broomstick across my chest and slide my foot across the stage. Tap, tap. One, two, three, four. A silent, lonely bar reassures me. Toe heel shuffle. Buffalo. Slide. My limbs hum with energy. I spin the broomstick until it becomes a pinwheel of fire. As my feet ground to the stage, my top hat takes shape, and I barrel roll with everything I have. I dance free and happy and wild, as if I'm not about to panic and set the bar on fire with my toes.

I remove my top hat with a twirl and allow the warmth that spreads through my chest to flow down my arms, to my hands, and out my fingers in a flash of fire. Releasing heat from my core lightens my mind, filling an almost ancestral need to watch something burn. Flames grow tall, creeping to my legs in wondrous danger.

How desperately I want to levitate for just a moment.

"Stunning."

All the fire disappears into the hollow of one spotlight. The only sound is the broomstick as it knocks onto the wood stage. He saw my flames.

Mr. Luminaire steps into the bar, eyes alight. "I haven't seen a fire dancer in years."

I kick the broom aside, hiding how the dissipating heat stings my belly. No hiding my identity now. "You can thank the purity raids for that. Those of us who remain do our very best to stay hidden."

"What's your name?" he asks.

I always dance at night, dipping my toes into the magic pool for an empty house. I should have skipped tonight. "Hey, Mr. Luminaire, the last thing I need is some director reporting me for illicit dance."

He steps close enough to smell mint and vanilla. Like he's a damn peppermint cookie. "I'm not going to report you."

I click the kitchen door shut and continue cleaning. "Why don't I believe you?"

He tucks his golden hair behind his ear with such softness I wonder what his skin feels like. "I don't believe that nonsense that fire dancers are unstable." He catches my eyes, seeming to will me into enchantment. "You're incredibly beautiful."

Time stops and I worry my throat will collapse like a flattened straw. "Are you unwell?"

"Aren't we all?" He clears his throat with a nervous rattle.

I want to run my fingers along his neck and chin. But touch is dangerous and wanting painful. If something inside me senses lust or love or any version in between, a swell of magic can take over and I'll have no control at all.

We stare, neither of us willing to look away. He's around my age but seems so mature and worldly. "You had no right to watch me."

"No, I didn't."

"And yes, my dance is stunning." Fire burns in my blood.

He laughs, more out of intrigue than humor. "Want to know what I think?"

"I'm certain I can't stop you," I say, as if I'm not dying to hear more from him. Anything, really. I want to hear his honeyed voice.

"These performers were all lovely. But there's something special about you. It's in the eyes and the way you move. I hung around here tonight, hoping to see you. Call it a hunch, but I sensed you were holding in some fierce magic. It's bursting inside you, isn't it? The desire to levitate?"

I bite my lip, wondering if he sees how much I look like my mother. We shared everything. Gray eyes, black bob. Dance, unsteady fire, magic, fear. The difference is, no way in hell I die in a sanatorium.

"I like my feet where they belong… firmly attached to Earth."

"My name is Miles," he says. "My father owns the Luminaire, and I want to build it back stronger than ever."

Mr. Price's son shows up here out of the blue? My belly aches with so many memories, I can't even pick one. To many, that theater means magic, and magic is the gilded gateway to moral corruption, where the devil waits to devour your soul. To a girl born with magic burning in the deep, dark cavern of her heart, the Luminaire is a summit I've longed to reach, knowing a crash awaits me on the other side.

"What I'm asking is terrifying, I know," he says. "But we could change things."

"Why would I want to expose myself?" I mean, of course I've dreamed of the gowns and the spotlights, and the glittering gems I could toss onto the balconies like hail. I reel my excitement back in.

"We're closed for a few months to create a new show. We can prove Magic Dance isn't dangerous, and you could be just the woman to make it happen."

Me, Eleanora Cleary, headlining the Luminaire. My crimson lipstick would match the roses the audience throws at my feet. I'd be dipped in gold and unafraid, shooting all the fire and stars my little tapping feet desire. "This dishwasher is not your girl. Find a real performer." I hold the door open.

"I know who you are, and I want you to audition for me," he says. "Come to the Luminaire and dance."

Of course. He wants my name. A Cleary could create a sensation to shock audiences. He's out to use me, not knowing I won't even dance for the mice that scurry through here at night. "Go home, Miles."

"Don't you want a better life than scrubbing dishes? Fire dance is your legacy."

I don't answer as I'm too busy slamming the door in his face, along with any hope I could ever take center stage. The only spotlight on my body will be in my dreams.

CHAPTER TWO

Eleanora

Once I've screwed my head on straight, I retreat to the protection of my attic, cursing my bad attitude and Miles's high cheekbones. I had to go shooting fire, didn't I? Hell, I practically held a solo audition for the man instead of retreating to the rooftop where only the stars could watch me shoot fire. Now I have to muster the strength to walk away from the opportunity of a lifetime.

There's nothing luminescent about my room above the Milk House. A mattress on the floor, a pitched roof so steep I can only stand in one corner, and one tiny window that faces the alley.

"Price's son. Really?" I talk to myself, pretending my mother might answer back with some sort of sign. Raindrops slide down the attic window in rivulets, obscuring my view of the sky. I trace one winding drip on my dry side of the window. "He wants a sensation to prey on everyone's trauma from the last time a Fire Girl reined the stage." They call us that like a breed of dangerous dogs who need eradicated for public safety.

I imagine a real Vaudeville stage with an orchestra and decadent outfits of crushed velvet and beaded bodices. Where a stained-glass ceiling scatters colored flecks of light over golden goddess statues.

A knock on the door startles me. "Eleanora, open up."

"Lady?" I open the door. "What the hell was that tonight?"

She shrugs. "Young Price wants a performer. He asked about the pretty server."

I withhold an eye roll. "And what did you tell him? That I scrub lipstick stains with the best of them?"

"I didn't tell him who you are, if that's what you're worried about." She pushes her way inside.

"He already knows who I am."

Lady's silver hair is wrapped in another scarf. She wears a new one every night, inhaling cigarettes like she might die without them. Her flailing business took off the day the country went dry and dark, when she converted the basement into a forbidden bar. And then we arrived. Fiona the Irish fire dancer and her terrified daughter.

Smoke trails from an exhale through the side of her mouth while her cigarette crackles between her fingers. "He asked why you don't dance."

"Nosy man!" Who's pushy and handsome with perfectly clear eyes. I tap my toe on the warped wood floor. One, two, three, four. "He wants me to perform a levitating tap dance that will single-handedly restore love for fire dance to this magic-fearing city."

She blows a ring of smoke in my direction. "Sounds a lot like your dream, no?"

I wipe off my useless makeup. "I burned my face at that embarrassing attempt at a debut." I tuck my hair behind my ear. "Since I can't have anything I really want, I will live life my way. No performance. No more heartbreak."

"Tall order." She inhales one deep breath of her cigarette. I can practically hear her lungs crackle from here. "It was one bad night years ago. Besides, hiding away and avoiding life doesn't prevent heartbreak."

I untuck my blouse and sigh. My heart aches all the time. I don't think I could handle much more. "It's more than that one night." It's the laws that label us as subhuman. The little girls who hide in their homes because their magic appeared during ballet class. Teenagers harassed by policemen, kicked out by their parents for something they can't control. Everyone hopes they don't have the little girl with fire in her soul.

I've never warmed to Lady. I can't forgive her for her part in my mother's downfall. Sure, she's kind of like a grandmother who'll never leave me, but some things are unforgiveable. I kick my shoes off into the corner by my bed. "I'm not going back on stage."

Once again, she inhales before she speaks. "I've seen stage fright with dancers before. It always passes."

Stage fright. My entire life is a fight for solid ground. It grows intensely worse on stage, like concentrated fear about to pop me open.

"You just want me to bring Fiona back. Like the glory days." Or the hell days as I like to think of them.

"Or maybe, I just don't believe anyone needs to change who they really are." A curl bounces from under her scarf, refusing to remain with the others. "Someday this country will accept Fire Girls."

How I ache for my mother. Just one more smile, I often beg the universe, as if the stars can gift her back for a short time. I'd even take her in her unwell state, near the end, when she terrified me.

"I believe we make who we are," I say with certainty.

"And you chose to wash dishes in a speakeasy?" She always knows how to cut down my confidence.

Dream-adjacent. It's the only way I can tolerate all the loss. "Good night, Lady. And don't surprise me like that again."

She throws her hands up and swooshes her way out of the attic. Once my door is locked, I stretch my tired body and stare at the starless night. Tap, tap, tap with my toes, I let my mind lean into what it felt like to spurt flames tonight. For a director to admire me.

Until my throat tightens and I gasp for air, certain the floor will swallow me into darkness. Just the thought of performing makes my body revolt. Like a panic-wielding god pointing his trident at my throat.

I brace myself on the cool window and count the raindrops that patter on the sill outside. I was fine before that silly man showed up. Hidden in the kitchen, I can stay away from expectant eyes, should any errant fire spit from my hands.

Alone. Just as it should be.

***

Another night as Milk House support staff. I carry the girls' laundered costumes to their dressing room as they laugh and plaster their makeup, guessing who might snag the coveted Luminaire audition. And I have to listen without falling apart.

This speakeasy has been my only home since Chicago. The closest thing to the great theater life that's never loved me back. At the Milk House, familiar disappointment lulls me into a sense of numbness. Where performers bloom shining metal from their hands and where dancers plunk ice over sweaty bodies who sway together in shared debauchery. I've been close enough to taste the elements without stepping foot on the stage that stole my dreams.

Who needs the Luminaire when I have the safety of failure?

"Eleanora, you should be up on stage with us." Our diamond Charleston dancer wraps a feather boa around my neck, but I slide it slowly away until the red feathers fall to the floor in a heap.

"Please. I hold the important role of cleaning crew and dish scrubber. You'd be lost without me."

She spins me toward the mirror. Of its own accord, my foot points against my other ankle, and the position causes a trail of smoke to poof from my hands. For a flash, my body opens. A channel from the depths of me opens to the outside world. Until fear claws at that happiness with one massive swipe, and I'm just me again. I wipe my palms on my slacks as if clearing away dust.

She brushes my hair and speaks over my shoulder to my reflection. "Fiona made history at the Luminaire. She'd be so proud if you made it there too." The memory squeezes my heart hard enough to sting. Mother taught me how to summon magic and dance free, something she could always manage, despite the monsters closing in.

"And look at me now." Luminaire royalty terrified of the spotlight. If I could go back in time, I'd force my mother to dance softer and control her fire. I would stop that sure-footed sixteen-year-old who stepped on the Milk House stage expecting magic to fulfill her legacy.

She tucks my hair back with a star pin and drags a fingertip across my lips, coloring them with deep crimson lipstick. "Listen, no one can decide your life for you, kid." She leans her chin on my shoulder. "Especially not some men in government who are neither women nor magic."

As if deciding to be a starlet would be enough.

"Doors are open!" Lady yells between puffs.

The room clears but I stay behind to stare at my reflection. How I once coveted tap shoes of gold. I called myself Diamond Nora with an act of fire rings and a galaxy of light. My dance was free and wild and spun by the stars. I'm a brilliant performer when I'm all alone.

"At least I'm all dolled up for my shift in the kitchen." Tears well in my eyes but I swallow them back down, doing my best to force a smile.

Back in the safety of dirty dishes and mops and brooms, I can't shake the off-putting dizziness deep in my brain. Memories bite at my heart as if they have fangs. Holding mother's hand. A harvest moon dangling overhead, vermillion in color and enormous in size. My bare toes teetering on the rough corner of the rooftop, scratching the bottom of my feet until my skin sprang with blood droplets.

"We're going home, baby." She smiled with such sincerity, such belief that the stars would catch us. I knew we would both die, or worse, break many, many bones, but I couldn't let her jump alone.

Shot from my memories back into the stuffy, gin-soaked washroom, I wipe my eyes hard. I've messed with destiny and now I'm paying for it. Before I can stop the rush, my arms tremble, rigid and painfully tight. My mind shoots into orbit. Spinning in a tornado of the worst panic imaginable. I hate this place my mind goes. I repeat *I hate it I hate it* until the tornado stops spinning and pressure builds in my chest. Back in my body once again.

"I'm here." I open my eyes to see Aria, holding my hand and smiling. "You're okay."

The rush of fear that rises like a tide in my brain instantly slows when she sticks her tongue out at me. I laugh through tears, though my body explodes with heat. I can feel every pore, every strand of hair. Everything hurts.

"Want me to sit with you?" This kid has been around long enough to know that I won't step foot onstage. The harder everyone pushes, the deeper I resist.

I nod, embarrassed that I need a twelve-year-old to quell my panic.

We sit in silence, but she taps her feet together, wiggly as ever. Finally, she says, "The mush at the orphanage was extra pasty tonight."

And just like that, my body no longer hurts. The poor kid eats mush, and here I am complaining about failed dreams. I lean my head back, grateful for the calm in my body and for Aria's steady smile. "I'm sorry."

"Welcome back." She squeezes my hand once more and jumps to her feet, proud that she knows how to yank me back to reality. "Back to my post!"

I drag myself up as the music starts and elements fly into the air. Gold light and emerald dust splash across the walls, while beaded mercury skitters across the floor. I watch through the service window, grateful for my post-panic stability. The only calm my mind knows is the space after an episode, after the fear explodes. Nothing yet to wash, so I search for something—anything—to take my mind off the ache deep in my magic body.

Lady kicks open the kitchen door. "You have a visitor."

"Oh, come on."

She shrugs and disappears. I shake myself together and exit my kitchen, through dancing couples that sway to the beat of our trumpet player. Skirts find their way up thighs by wandering hands while straps dangle off shoulders like beaded cobwebs. Orchids bloom from the horn and flit through air, vanishing just before they land on patrons' heads.

Miles leans his elbow on the bar. With no hat, and his hair tied back in a low ponytail, he exudes the casual confidence of a Stetson ad. "You." I intend to smile but my face doesn't seem to cooperate. "I told you I'm not coming to the Luminaire."

"Please, just listen. This hiatus is make or break for us," he says. The music thumps over his voice. I grab his collar and drag him toward the kitchen. "You don't need to be aggressive about it," he says.

God, he smells good. Out the kitchen door and upstairs to the alley, I take in a deep breath of crisp, misty air. "Listen to me, Miles Price. I've made clear I won't audition for you. I have no interest in being the next Fiona Cleary."

Aria isn't guarding the crates, and I wonder if she's hiding somewhere, listening to this conversation.

"Okay, I get it." He tips his head subtly, like the movement of the hour hand on a clock. "Will you tell me why?"

Fire Girls are as rare as different-colored eyes, but the country seems hysterically worried that we'll take over and turn their souls black. Men drown in hooch. They beat their wives and still, women are to blame. Magic girls don't tend to bother with things like marriage and coddling the men who tame us. No one seems to appreciate that.

"You mean beside the obvious? We've all seen the stories in the paper and watched dancers dragged away. The rest of the lucky few remain hidden, and for good reason."

He rubs his neck, considering how he wants to proceed. "The Luminaire has made some mistakes. Big ones. We've used our performers and not protected them."

My mother was the country's biggest star who crashed from stardom. I wince inside every time someone mentions her, like an unrelenting cramp.

I fight the urge to look away from his wide jaw and sculpted lips, as everything in me screams not to trust him. "Performers absorb all the risk. The audience would have me tied up and dragged off stage."

"I don't think they will." He smiles with those high cheekbones and my knees threaten to give way. "Seattle wants something new. So do I."

Aria peeks out from behind the crates. I can't focus with her little ears listening to everything I'm saying. "Come talk to me up here." I take three steps up the fire escape toward the rooftop.

"Up there?" His voice shakes.

"Yes. What's the problem? Afraid I'll spit fire at you?"

He grabs the railing and takes one step but returns to the ground. "Nope. Can't."

An extreme urge to touch his hand takes over. *Don't you dare ask him about his feelings. We don't care about rich boy problems.* I shake away the bothersome sympathy like a sticky cobweb. "Listen, I dance for myself and that's enough."

"Will you walk with me?" He extends his hand.

"Walk?" I ask.

"Yes. It's where you put one foot in front of the other to move your body to another destination."

I roll my eyes but find myself opening the lock to the outside street. "Fine."

We walk with ease under a cloudy sky and silver crescent moon. Another starless Seattle night gleams under a hanging mist, the city's lights reflected in pools of water gathered in the streets. Hands in his pockets, he splashes through the puddle with a pas de bourrée.

"You dance?" I ask.

"I used to," he says with a shrug. "Long ago."

Every step away from home reminds me how far I could fall. He smiles, his head tilted sideways, a softness in his eyes. My forehead warms in a swell of attraction. My golden halo just appeared above my head. I usually hide it by avoiding situations like these.

"This is stupid." I turn back toward the Milk House. "Sorry to waste your time."

"Don't go." His voice holds a hint of begging, and I lose all sense of reason. He stares over my head with a smile. "Please?" He leads me around the corner toward the lighted marquee of the Luminaire. My hand slides from his as the neon lights warm my cheeks.

There's no use denying my emotions when a misty crown hovers above my head like an advertisement. Tonight only! Awkward magic dancer longs to kiss elusive director until her lips burn.

"Do you know what that plaque says?" He points next to the door into the theater, where a gold-plated sign lures potential patrons.

"Step inside for the show of a lifetime. Welcome to the world of enchantment and magic. Welcome to the Luminaire." I've memorized every word.

He's still holding my hand. "Everyone's against us despite having packed houses every night. My father wants to tighten his control, but I want to let your wildness breathe. I'm going to fight the city and their ridiculous laws."

I can see in his eyes he has big plans, and he dreams of changing something he never will. His optimism is inspiring, really. "We're just like gin, Miles. The city dives into secret bars to taste danger while they curse us in the daylight. 'Lock up the magic dancers! They're cursed with boobs *and* magic.'"

I think he'll laugh or run away, but instead, he leans close enough to set my heart thumping. "That's exactly what I want to change. Our hiatus gives me time to structure something better than we had before."

My eccentricities usually offend people, but not him. My desire to push him away is dwindling, so I resort to the worst thing in the world: the truth. "I can't dance, Miles."

"Sure you can. I saw you."

"No." I rub my eyes hard enough to sting. "I have… episodes." *Don't say too much.* "I blackout when I step onstage. My brain and body fight against each other and fear always wins." I don't know why I tell him this, so I shrug out of sheer embarrassment.

"What's your stage name?" His gaze is soft, and kind, and I hate it.

"Diamond Nora."

He bites his lip, poorly concealing a smile. "Okay, Diamond Nora. Come to audition for my father tomorrow night. Let's show him what it looks like to give power to the dancers."

"Did you not hear me, Miles?" I step back with a stumble. "I can't do it."

He pulls me back under the marquee and points to the gold sign again. "The only reason we have a magic theater is because of women like you."

Gliding my hand over the plaque conjures memories of Mother's decline. I watched her unravel until she became unrecognizable. As broken as she was in those years before her death, forcing herself onto legal, non-magic Vaudeville theaters after Prohibition was worse. She tried to perform on the legal circuit, knowing that's where the money was, but without magic, mother seemed to writhe in pain. Manic, on the verge of tears.

"You want me to tap dance when I've never performed for an actual audience, risking the most embarrassing moment of my life. I'll fail miserably."

"Or you'll take the theater by storm."

"You have dozens of better dancers to choose from. They're beautiful, their magic is refined and they're willing to learn every move you teach them. My magic is like a feral cat, cornered and hungry."

"That's exactly why." His smile is bright enough to blind me. "You won't take orders from anybody, that I can tell."

"That's not usually a selling point for a dancer."

"For the show I'm trying to craft, it's exactly what I want. And I need dancers like you." He clears his throat. "I'll make sure no one will hurt you while you're inside these walls."

I keep my halo under wraps by sheer will. "What happens if I want to leave these walls?" The wet air turns the tip of his nose red, which I keep focus on to avoid my gaze wandering to his lips. "Look at what happened to my mother."

He nods, a moment of solidarity. "People love a lie. Especially one that points at those who are different."

I pull away to stare at the framed posters of the Star Girls. An entire troupe of women just like me. A place of protection where I could break the panic that holds me like chains to all the darkness in my life. I like the sound of that. At least, I think I do. This idea just hatched itself a few seconds ago, and I'm curious to see how far I'll take it.

"You can call me Eleanora."

"Miles Price." He bows. "Flailing director and disappointing son of the most famous theater proprietor in the country."

The Milky Way dropped stardust on my eyelashes and lit the ground under my feet when I danced with mother on rooftops, but now all my elements live in the dark. Wild joy once seemed possible.

Every emotion swirls in me, and I'm not certain which will land. Surprisingly enough, fear retreats, and bravery finds its way to the surface. "I think this is a very bad idea." As soon as the sentence escapes, I want to swallow back the words. What the hell am I doing? My mind and mouth live in two separate universes.

Miles flashes me a cheeky grin. "Does that mean you'll do it?" His joy is strangely contagious.

Two minutes to change my life. An opportunity that didn't exist before today, and certainly won't ever come again. "I don't have real tap shoes."

"I can fix that. And together, we could fix the stage fright too."

"What do you know about that?"

"Not now." A half-smile tugs at the left side of his mouth. "I'm trying to impress you, Diamond Nora."

He's doing one hell of a job. "Listen, I can't walk onstage tomorrow and become a different person. I'll panic and faint, and possibly set your stage curtains ablaze."

"Or, you'll remember the spark that ignites fire from a shuffle ball change. And then we can make a case to my father as to why you deserve to be one of our troupe."

"What do you get from this, Miles?"

He squints and looks up to the sky as if the stars shine too brightly in his eyes. "Performers are hard to come by. All the sensational ones are locked up or hiding. The Star Girls we have are great, but they've been taught to subdue their wildness. If we don't fight, there will be no more magic and no more Luminaire." He centers his gaze back on me. "I'm creating an empire to fix where my father failed. That starts with giving the stage back to the ones who built it."

The blurry red dome lights from the marquee frame my vision, my eyes misty from the moisture that gathers in the air. "What happens when I fall apart on stage?"

"*If* you fall apart, then you return to the Milk House, back to dancing alone."

The image burns a hole in my gut. Once you imagine a moment of possibility, falling back down to a lonely basement sounds terrible. "I won't get arrested?"

"I'll throw myself in shackles before I'd let anyone take you away. And I'll work with you to overcome your panic."

A protected home where I could unleash magic without fear of being attacked. The notion is tempting enough to make me wonder if that's what I've been missing. Besides, I wouldn't hate being close to him.

Against everything inside me screaming for normalcy, for a comfortable silence in a cold Milk House Sunday evening, I want this. I want the spotlights for one moment before I burst into flames, because I could feel that joy again—the kind I only felt while dancing with my mother, flames alight around us.

CHAPTER THREE

Eleanora

At five a.m. as the city sleeps off hangovers, I slip down to the Milk House stage to face the empty chairs in the deathly quiet speakeasy. Only a few hours left to prepare for the day that could change my life.

I stand tall at center stage, in my scuffed heels, pushing down swirling thoughts of everything that could go wrong. Broken ankle, the stage collapsing under my feet, head injury, hospitalization, a painful death. Christ, Nora, you really can get distracted.

A warmup of plié and relevé wakes my tired body. I stretch longer than necessary, avoiding the inevitable fire that may explode if I keep dancing.

"You look pretty."

The tiny voice breaks my concentration. "Aria. It's not even daylight yet. What are you doing here?"

She rests her chin on her hands. "Watching you." She wears a powder blue dress with a faded ribbon in her hair, same as always. Required orphanage attire, I assume.

"Lady will haul your butt back to the headmistress if she finds you sleeping in here."

She shrugs. "She's all talk."

"I can't practice with you staring at me." I'm dying to tell her. "I have an audition."

She leaps up, arms out. "That's so exciting!" Her face beams with light. "You're finally doing it!"

I grab her thin, bony hands to steady her as we share smiles.

"Tell me everything."

My neck tightens, realizing I'll need intense honesty with her and myself. "The Luminaire."

"Oh, this is so exciting." She crosses her arms and squeezes herself into a hug. I wonder how often she does that. "Your destiny."

What if destiny got it wrong? I sit next to her, abandoning the overwhelming worry over how this day will unfold. "The orphanage is that awful, huh?"

Her fallen face might be the saddest thing I've ever seen. "They want me to stay quiet and I want to talk! They tell me I'm a naughty girl who'll never find a family, but I don't listen. My family lives right here, at the Milk House."

Helping me wash dishes in a secret bar is her idea of a family. Suddenly, the audition doesn't seem to hold the same importance it did. I rub my neck hard enough to burn. "I wish I felt that way."

"This place isn't so bad."

Loss oozes from every crack of this crumbling building, but I keep that thought to myself. "My name means shining light. Did I ever tell you that? As if I'm fated for a dance with the stars."

She twists her face. "See? You should be in a beautiful, dreamy theater like the Luminaire. You deserve all the spotlights."

I wish I was the success she sees me as. "I've earned nothing."

"Who says you have to earn it?"

"There's no point to any of this if the world still fears women like me." Sometimes honesty slips out when I least expect it, leaving me all squishy and vulnerable. I wish my mouth and mind would find a truce.

Aria nods in understanding. "The headmistress tells me I would do well to shut up. Nobody wants the truth, and that's all I seem to say."

"I love that about you."

Her cheeks redden and plump as she smiles. "You do?"

Aged far beyond her years, I sometimes wonder why she hangs around me. "The world could use more truth."

"Thanks." Her admiring gaze lowers my boiling fear to a simmer.

Even if I could perform today, what if I open the door to a part of myself that doesn't belong out in the world? I could welcome the fire that would eventually burn me. I don't tell her about the magic girls lost to purity raids over the years, only to see those same lawmen back in the speakeasies the next night, pawing at magic dancers as if their bodies are for sale. I don't recount Mother's teachings to prepare for early-onset hysteria due to my fire.

Aria nibbles on her fingernails, deep in thought. "If I get to watch you dance to a waterfall of roses—" Her breath catches. "I'll believe that someday I can step into the light too."

And that's all it takes to commit to this moment. Aria's stifled tears and a healthy dose of guilt. "I better rehearse my number then."

***

My mind is a war zone.

Possessed by the promise to Aria, I don't turn back. I don't head upstairs to my attic room and sleep for days as my mind begs to do. Instead, I've dressed in beaded shorts and a blouse borrowed from the dressing room, and pinned my hair in finger waves for the audition.

The great unknown of the Luminaire awaits, like an evil magician beckoning me with clawed fingernails and a promise of fame. My fear is solid. It's known and real and deep inside me, like a root system.

On my way out the back door of the theater, Lady hollers at me, cigarette in hand. "Hey, Eleanora."

I didn't want to face her, but she's got a way of hooking me. "Yeah?"

"Look at you, all gussied up. The Luminaire will be lucky to have you." She inhales from her cigarette, deep enough to cause one eye to wink.

She's good at selling lies. Even I believe her. "Why do you keep me around?"

"My business flourished during Prohibition, and I needed someone I trusted to help me run this place. You were what, thirteen when your mother dragged you in here?"

My ribs tighten. The day we became illegal rests in my memory like barbed wire. The final dance on our Chicago rooftop before all hell broke loose. I went to sleep a normal girl and woke to Mother's panicked eyes. "Yes."

She flicks her ring finger against her thumb, her long fingers holding the cigarette steady. "You were so shy and timid, and all you wanted was your mother. And beautiful Fiona. So wild." She hesitates while studying my reaction. "I know you resent me for sending her to the big stage."

"I resent myself for failing her." I didn't speak up when she'd drink booze for breakfast. Or when she became a household name as the dangerous fire dancer whose next performance could blow up the theater. "I never tried to stop her. I was too busy needing my mom."

"Fiona was a tornado. You couldn't have stopped her if you tried. I've seen plenty of her kind, but your mother breathed magic, as if she were her own galaxy."

I don't have my own galaxy as I'm too busy living in my untamed, swirling mind. Why didn't I get her wild? "All those years after she died, preparing for my debut to make her proud." Tears sting my eyes, but I don't let them fall. "What if I fail her today too?"

Lady drops her smoldering cigarette to her side. "You know what I think would be incredible?"

I'm not certain I want to know, but I respond anyway. "What?"

"Step onto that stage today and take back your birthright. Prove them all wrong for making laws against your magic."

I pull away from her intense gaze. Not that I disagree, I just hate the pressure of being nominated to change the world.

"Do it for you, not your mother," she says with a smile.

Perhaps her little talk worked, because a flutter of excitement taps at my belly. Outside the gate of the Milk House, Aria awaits, eyes lit up like the sun.

"It's time, Eleanora." She claps quietly under her chin.

She walks beside me on the same path Miles took me last night. Late morning under the Seattle mist, the city loses a bit of its allure. But I'm certain magic brims inside the Luminaire at all hours of day and night.

"I can't wait to see you up there, shining and dancing."

I stop walking and with a wince say, "Aria, you can't come in the theater." I decide to keep moving. *Don't look at her.*

"They lock me in the dark room when I misbehave."

My legs halt of their own accord. I can't hear this right now. It's enough to break my heart before the biggest moment of my life. Don't turn around, don't turn around. But what do I do? Yes, I turn around to face her teary eyes and can only focus on her sadness instead of the looming audition.

"They punish me for escaping and wandering the city. I hate that dark room." She shivers.

I walk back to meet her tiny frame with legs so bony I wonder how they hold her up. "Why do you risk punishment just to spend time at our rundown speakeasy?"

"Because I won't let them break me."

The bustling city fades to silent next to this tiny girl's big feelings. "What do you want, Aria?"

She smiles, her mouth carving a giant grin across her face. "I want to sing."

"Can you sing?"

She props her fists on her hips. "What a dumb question. Of course I can. I mean, I think I can. Yes, I'm certain. As soon as I try it, I know I'll be enchanting."

With an exhale, I hang my head. "Your confidence is impressive, kid."

"If I don't believe in myself, who will?"

Her hazel eyes glitter in the filtered sunlight. I want to protect that fragile little ball of light before the world slices one giant, deep cut through her core, the kind that never fully heals. "Fine. If you hide in the wings, you can watch my audition. Silently."

She claps her hands and squeals with delight.

"Just don't let anyone know you're there."

And here we go, off to the most magical theater in the world, where elements glimmer in the spotlight. An aspiring tap dancer with her pesky little optimist hiding in the wings.

A crowd of well-to-do ladies chant at everyone who walks past. They thrust signs in the air that read *Purity Now* and *The Devil Lives Here*. I step between the pearl-clad women and Aria, trying not to meet eyes with any of them.

"Why do they hate this theater?" she whispers to me.

"They think magic and booze are the reason their men can't control themselves. This place allows both and they're hell bent on shutting it down."

A woman clicks her fancy heels towards us and shouts, "Lock up the wicked women!"

I turn from her and help Aria focus on the glimmering plaque on the wall.

Step inside for the show of a lifetime.

"Even the sign is shiny," Aria says.

As I stare at the plaque next to the glossy oak door, a deep thump bangs through my belly.

"You're the best dancer in the whole world," she says. "I know you are."

Every sharp comment I want to make remains silent, overrun by those hopeful hazel eyes. "Thanks," I choke out.

"Let's go. These women scare me."

"No, wait—" The moment is too big to jump right in, but Aria has already knocked and rang the bell.

Just breathe. My ribs tighten like steel, but Aria simply flashes a toothy grin.

The door flies open as a woman greets us with a southern accent and bouncy blond curls. "Yeah? What do you want?" Behind her a red carpeted staircase unfolds like a soft beach wave. Sconces and chandeliers scatter prismed light on the mahogany-paneled walls.

"I'm here to audition."

Her brow crinkles and the slightest wheeze whistles in her voice. "We don't hold auditions." She moves to close the door, but Aria slams her foot in the way and elbows me.

"Miles invited me," I say.

The petite blond with the big voice slides the door back open. "He invited you? Well, well. That's rare."

"I'm a tap dancer." She stares, waiting for the second half of that sentence. Our identifier within the community acts like a handshake. "Fire dance."

She lifts her head, eyes wide and focused. "Fire?" An uneasy silence crawls around like a creeping vine while she examines me head to toe. "Around back." She slams the door before we have a chance to respond.

"Did you see that staircase?" Aria's voice is an octave higher than usual and cracks with excitement. "And the crystal chandeliers?" She swoons, eyes rolling back in her head.

"The lobby is magnificent. Can you imagine what the stage looks like?" I imagine my mother bouncing behind the curtain as the orchestra greets the audience, billboards of her face plastered at the entrance, and men dressed in three-piece suits saying *Step inside for the country's greatest show.*

We approach the plain door in the back alley. I stare at the black metal as my mouth goes dry. I've never seen inside. Only imagined.

"Go on," Aria says.

"Today will change me. One way or another, I'll never be the same."

"Is that so bad?" she asks.

"Yes, it's terrifying." I widen my eyes and nod my head with certainty, so she understands the world is much more complicated than she realizes. Though I assume she already knows that deep in her bones.

"Remember when you met me?" she asks. "I was so cold all the time. Until I pickpocketed from that man I told you about who turned me into the cops, and they forced me into that damn orphanage."

"You're not making a great case for change here, Aria."

"Sure, that place is dirty, and the people are mean, but my hands aren't freezing, and I have a bed. Most of the time," she adds as an afterthought. "And best of all, I have you." Her fragile hand reaches for mine.

I want to pull away, but her giant eyes guilt me into squeezing back. I don't like touch. Most days, I can hardly tolerate the air on my skin. "I'm not sure I can do this."

"Yes, you can, Eleanora. I believe in you."

"Are you sure you're only twelve?"

The door flies open. A frazzled woman with smeared lipstick squints against the cloudy daylight. "Christ, it's bright out there. You the tap dancer?"

"Yes." I reach for Aria's hand. "I'm here to audition." The woman shields her eyes and waves us into the black cavern of backstage.

"Hurry it up, girl!" The woman's voice beckons from inside the darkness.

We step inside as the door bangs shut. I hold Aria's hand, mostly so she won't wander off and I can cover her mouth if she squeals in delight. We follow the woman through dark walkways and past showgirls in beaded headdresses. An errant spit of gold from one of their mouths lights the path toward stage left.

"Wait here." The woman digs through a bag resting on the floor while a cigarette balances on the side of her lip. "We're nearing the end of rehearsal. You're up after Zelda. Here." She hands me a new, shining pair of tap shoes. "Young Price insisted we give you some decent dance shoes."

They're heavy and cool to the touch. I tap my fingernail on the sturdy steel under the toe. Unlike pennies, these taps clang, sweet as bells. "Who's Zelda?"

The woman puffs on her cigarette and blows a ring of clove-scented smoke at Aria and nods toward stage left. "That's Zelda."

The stage turns dark. The organ blares. A piano and violin enter softly. Once the drums begin, the curtains slide open. A giant blood moon illuminates the stage as beaded strings drop like fall leaves. They flicker amethyst and emerald and sway to the music. Pointed stocking feet appear.

Descending from the ceiling, one foot and one hand wrapped around a shining gold rope, a Star Girl glows in a diamond bodysuit.

"Midnight Zelda," the woman says.

Thick thighs, round belly. Fat by all accounts. All the things you don't expect from a headliner at the Luminaire. Zelda arches her back as the rope spins slowly. She extends her arm and drops her head back, the spin accelerating. My heart races, unsure what comes next.

Drop.

She releases her grip and falls backward, her one wrapped foot catching her dangling body. She arches her back until her heel touches the top of her head, arms splayed, red lips in a glossy smile.

Zelda lifts to grab the rope, unraveling her foot. She hangs freely, pulling her legs into the splits over a field of illuminated flecks. Gold covers the stage, like a sea of shimmering light. Her legs maneuver gracefully with one pulled close to her head, the other extended towards the stage. The rope begins to spin, slow at first but speeds up to a dizzying cyclone.

When my heart races with the thrill of performance, it teeters precariously on the sensation I might explode. I don't know what will burst forth—beams of light or blood splatter.

It's exhilarating.

She dazzles with flips and spins, her giant breasts defying gravity. When she rises to the roof of the theater, the music crashes to silence. She heaves for breath, a wicked smile revealing pearl-white teeth.

The moment she leans forward in a swan dive, a collective gasp lifts the room like a wave. No wonder the basic men of the country want to purify us. Zelda glows confidence. She personifies the beauty and brightness of the elements that burn in our souls. It's too much for the average man to consume.

She plummets, coming to a thudding halt splayed out mere inches from the stage. The swoosh of her body sends gold flecks fluttering into the air where they hover like an exhale. She winks, then throws herself into the air, spinning as she did earlier, only this time, magic holds her.

My heart aches for the world I've never been a part of. Zelda performs twelve backflips in a row and lands with a quiet thud on her sea of gold. Applause ripples through the theater.

One squeeze from Aria's hand reminds me why I'm here. "Your turn," she says.

"I can't follow that!"

"Yes, you can." Her messy hair and eyes like green moons only add to her ability to guilt me into believing in myself. She makes me want to step onstage and blow the crowd away.

I swallow what feels like star anise in my throat as I click across the stage in my shining black tap shoes. My legs follow, though I'm not sure how because everything below my waist is numb. My heartbeat trembles in my ears, broken only by a high-pitched ring.

"Your name?" A man's voice bellows from the audience behind the spotlight. It isn't Miles. More like a growl, his voice is gruff and deep and impatient.

"Diamond Nora." The words come from outside my body. My eyes adjust to the blare of the stage lights. It's all happening so fast.

Scattered through the audience are Star Girls. Luminaire headliners draped across chairs in shimmering bodysuits and makeup of fire and ice. They're so beautiful, it's like watching the Milky Way on a clear night.

"Take position," the invisible man says.

My brain instructs my feet to move but my body revolts. *Why must you make such an ordeal out of everything?* They're just people. This is just a lacquered wood stage like every other theater. You're just a dancer.

A shiny, pale arm slit by a precise silver blade in a manic plea to end the magic. I shake away the image. Years ago, one of us slit her arm. Get over it, Nora.

As I contemplate throwing up, I catch eyes with a slender woman. Her hair is a puff of auburn ringlets shooting out of her head. She holds a fiddle at her hip and a bow in her hand. She smiles at me. With a slow nod, she indicates to take a breath, so I do.

Better.

Silently, she seems to speak to me, reminding me I'm not competition. I now have two sets of eyes cheering for me in this dark space. I point to the piano and just as the notes start, I find Aria, hiding behind the thick velvet curtain.

Tap, tap, tap. I set the beat with one heel. My calves quake but they'll work themselves out. Two minutes to a new life. Two measly minutes to change everything.

Shuffle ball change. Shuffle ball change. Darkness creeps into my belly, but I talk myself through it. Magic swells inside, growing and thumping and taking charge of my mortal body. Gems and rainbows and fire swirl in my chest while light flutters in my forehead and still, I dance. I hold the fire inside, putting a cork on its heat to control the burn. My fingers and lips grow numb, my eyesight blurry. I hang on to this tap dance by my fingernails until, the explosion occurs.

Panic reaches its claws down my throat as fire shoots from my tap shoes unprovoked. The stage flames with a sea of crimson and orange. I no longer hear the piano. I can't open my eyes, because I'll fall into the depths of this theater and my dream will disappear forever. I claw at my hair, grabbing hard enough to distract from the thumping. The world tilts, and I'm afraid I'll drift away to nothingness.

My cheek hits the floor with a disheartening thud. The fire has been snuffed.

When the episode passes, I hear nothing but quiet and shuffling feet. Lights flicker off with a thud.

The softest calm my body ever knows. It's like all the fear has thundered through me and out my fingertips. The numbness in my body dissipates. Relief and failure all in one. Just as I anticipated.

CHAPTER FOUR

Eleanora

As I emerge from the hazy afterglow of fainting, the girl with the fiddle touches my hand. "Are you alright?"

No, I'm very much not alright. "Yes. Just embarrassed."

She helps me sit up. "Don't be. My first time on this stage, my notes were more offensive than a dying cow."

Despite my mortification, I find a smile.

"My name's Ruby." Her red freckles give her a girlish look, but everything about her deep brown eyes speaks of an old soul.

Aria is gone. The spotlights are off. I see no director in the audience, but a few Star Girls watch from the forestage. "How long was I out?"

"You stared in a daze for about a minute before you hit the ground."

Bitter devastation finds me again. "I lost my chance, didn't I?"

She doesn't respond, and I know it's over. Tears threaten to fall, but I'm too tired to cry. She helps me up, her hand soft on my arm. "The Luminaire isn't everything you think it is."

Gold candelabras stand like sentries at stage left and right. Carved into rose stems and dipped in metallic paint, they reflect the stage lights, and drip gold wax like knobby fingers. Elegance and intrigue, opulence with the mystic. "Looks like a dream to me."

She helps me off stage as the other girls quietly clap. Ruby whispers, "Hey, before you fell you really had something."

What an incredibly naive, stupid idea this was. I let the man with gold eyes talk me into the promise of an impossible dream. Hope is dangerous and painful and now I need air.

I climb to my unsteady feet and search the curtain for Aria, but instead glimpse Miles and who I can only assume is his father, the infamous Winston Price.

"What a waste of my time," Price barks.

"She's got something."

"I told you, I don't want her here."

What I have is much worse than a case of jitters. I want to scream that panic devoured me years ago. Set a course for my life. Since I can't climb out of the darkness, I live in dreams and fear and fractured memories of things I don't understand. Lady says I exaggerate worse than a melodrama.

Ruby tugs at my blouse sleeve and lowers her eyes, embarrassed for me. "Don't listen to them. You're already magic, Diamond Nora." She winks and disappears back onto the stage, but I can't stop from listening to the two men who'll decide my future.

"I want her here," Miles says.

"Her dance was good. But the fire." He shakes his head. "Too risky. She panicked and went unconscious."

Nothing like recounting your worst failure in detail as men discuss your worth.

"Miles, stop bringing home strays. Send her back to whatever failed stage she came from."

"We can't turn away Fiona's daughter," Miles says. "Give her another chance."

Hearing her name, in this theater, after the disaster I just unleashed, it's all too much. I can't be here.

Through the dark tunnel backstage, I grope my way to the alley door, which I only find when a showgirl blows rings of yellow light as she stretches. Out in the searing daylight, I catch my breath, alone.

My body thuds, heavy and useless against the brick wall. How I want to crawl back to yesterday, scream at Miles for flashing me that perfect smile, and yell a resounding *No, I will not embarrass myself on your stage.*

Lost in my visions of could have and should have, I don't notice the door fling open. "Eleanora."

Oh no. Not the gold eyes and caramel hair again. I don't dare look up for fear that he'll convince me to levitate right here in the alley. "I told you I couldn't do this."

His sigh just adds to the heaviness on my chest. As if I let him down too. "Did you hear my father back there?"

"Yes. My audition was a waste." Sums up the hope I've carried around for years quite nicely. My shoulders slump. I wish Aria was here. "I can't produce another Celtic Fire. Not that I want to anyway."

He lifts his hand as if taming a wild horse. "Okay. I came to the Milk House to find Fiona Cleary's daughter." I growl and turn away, but he jumps right in front of me again. "Fiona's legacy will get you in the door. Your dance will keep you here."

"You wasted your time with me."

"I see something special in your dance." He keeps his gaze on me, despite my head rolling in all directions to avoid those eyes. "You dream of a world that's just beyond your reach and convince yourself that nothing and no one can change the things that hold you back."

"You got all that from me serving you one drink?"

He shrugs with surprising modesty. "I got that from the longing in your eyes and the tightness in your shoulders. I understand you."

There's a story there but I have no space in my heart. That's not true, I have a gaping giant hole with plenty of room, but I'm too stubborn to let him in.

"You want Fiona's daughter to shatter society's fear of fire. It's poetic."

He shrugs. "You're so much more than her daughter. Fiona unleashed fire, but you're on the cusp of something more. I can see it."

Mother both craved and cursed the fire that's in our blood. But like soured milk, magic turns poisonous with time. She succumbed to her power, and I've spent my life trying—and failing—to protect us.

I want to say all of this, explain my precarious situation and why this entire day is proof I'll never be good enough. But all I say is a quiet, "I only find joy when I dance for myself." Limit risk. Control of the highest order.

He nods in understanding. "It must be hard. Your mother is a legend."

"Which one? The mother who held me and laughed as we danced barefoot under the stars, or the mother whose magic leaked from her body like a slow bleed, until nothing was left but haunted eyes." I know which legend I choose to remember.

I don't mind telling my story. I quite enjoy watching people squirm when they start to understand how magic beats the holy hell out of us.

To my surprise, Miles tightens his lips into a serious and thoughtful expression. "If anyone understands the pressure of living in your parent's giant shadow, it's me."

Those soft eyes. Dammit! What is it about this man? His strong jaw, chiseled cheekbones, how his lips curl down and still exude charm. Maybe he's right. I've been Fiona's daughter more than I've ever been Eleanora.

"You can try to fight it, but you can't hide yourself forever. At least, that's what I tell myself."

"I know what awaits me here. Dance until magic swallows me. Then I'll own nothing—not my body or my mind."

The air is cold down here in the depths of despair. Where magic dancers cleave off a part of themselves. Just a slice to let the magic ooze out. But I knew dancers when their eyes were clear and dance was pure, before the hysteria. We're all at risk of mental collapse, but Fire Girls burn out faster and brighter. I can't help but close my eyes to remember the moonlight, the Milky Way, and Mother's smile.

"What does the stage do to you?" he asks.

"I was always more of a backstage dreamer kind of girl. But I trained at the Milk House, ready to debut my act. Diamonds and gold and an explosion of stars and fire. I convinced myself I could finally step into the spotlight."

"Sixteen. You wanted to dance at peak fire."

"It's a lie, you know. My mother hit her brilliance at thirty. Sixteen is when we're most vulnerable and pliable. That's why they think we're the prettiest." The words hurt to say. "I wanted to show the people we aren't tawdry whores. We're joy in dance form."

His breath catches. "I knew I was right about you." I shove his arm playfully. "What happened?" he asks.

"I fainted. Face smacked into the floor of fire, just like today." I slap the back of one hand on the palm of the other. "I burned my legs and bruised my face. I never tried to perform again. Until today."

Miles flashes a disarming smile. "You know what makes a good dancer great?"

"No, actually."

"Neither do I." He looks up to the sky and breathes out a puff of white air. "That's the real magic. The intangible thing no one can explain, but we all know when we see it."

He looks at my hand as if he wants to reach for me, but I cross my arms against the cold. "I want you here," he says.

Those four words lighten every inch of my body. "My episodes own me."

"Nothing owns you, Eleanora. You simply haven't felt safe." He bites his lip. "Can I show you something?" he asks.

Run far and fast and never look back. Dive back into the soapy dishes at the Milk House and hide away until you turn gray and sassy like Lady. This is what my mind screams, but what does my mouth say? "I suppose."

I follow Miles back into the theater, past a hall of doors, down a dark staircase which twists ninety degrees every four steps, and through curtains and doors, we arrive at the entrance to a basement dimly lit and humming with electric air. "Where are we?" My mouth goes dry, but I ball my fists and demand that my body behave.

"This is your new rehearsal space. If you'd like it to be." Miles opens the double doors. We step into a cavernous basement five times the size of any rehearsal space I've ever seen. Remnants of magic touch every corner of this giant gymnasium. Blackened walls seared by bolts of fire, cracked glass stained with blood. Divots on the floor from powerful shoes and warped baseboards from floods and melted ice.

"How am I going to overcome this thing inside me?" I motion to my chest.

"With my help. And our troupe. We all understand the pressures of this world."

Each moment is another step farther from my safe kitchen. "Your father agreed?"

His grimace doesn't match his head nod. "Not really, but I'll win him over. So will you."

"You're serious about this? Me, here?" Multicolored chandeliers dangle from the gymnasium ceiling, each crowned with a decorative molding of stars.

"Quite serious." He grabs my hands which makes my heart race, and not in a panic sort of way. In a, please touch me until I die, sort of way. "I want this show to be free where dancers choreograph their own acts and craft their own magic world. Where we aren't afraid. Where the ridiculous laws of Prohibition don't limit you." He squeezes my hands. "None of you deserve to be shunned."

I'll pull away any moment, but right now, his touch fills me with excitement, and I find myself craving this world. Against all reason, I want to become Diamond Nora.

"Your first show will be a New Year's Eve showcase. That's three months to work toward your debut. If you succeed, Seattle will fall in love with you."

"And if I fail?"

"Then I fail with you." He slides his fingers from mine. "This place needs to be reinvented, and so do I. We've had the one magic exception in the country, but we've not done enough with that power."

The magic. I can see it on the walls and feel it in the air. Surrounded by girls like me who've risked it all and won the most coveted of spotlights. If I step outside, this opportunity disappears forever.

A whirling, dazzling light spins from the ceiling in a rainbow of glitter like a dust storm. A woman lands in a spin, her toe shoes made of rubies and spitting light into a watery scarlet pool around her feet. Nearly sixty, her gorgeous lean limbs hold a ballet line as graceful as anything I've ever seen. She comes to a stop in a soft plié. Her dark brown skin shimmers like gold.

"My name is Iridessa. Welcome to the family, Eleanora." She glides across the dance floor like a color-filled cloud.

"Iridessa is our best instructor, and she'll help you sharpen your skills," Miles says. "I'll meet with you regularly to help with your transition. We'll give you every chance to succeed."

I look up to the twenty-foot ceiling covered in gem panels. Wall sconces cast metallic light on worn oak floorboards stained by smoke. "Three months, huh?"

"I knew Fiona," Iridessa says. She looks at my neck as I swallow the lump in my throat. "She was magnificent. And you will be too, once we work with your fire."

Spotlights bring all kinds of attention, which is why I've remained backstage. My mother danced here, and breathed unrelenting fire inside these walls. A side of her I could never access.

Miles leans close to my ear, shifting his gaze to my reflection in the cracked mirror. "Three months to find your wild."

I miss her so much I can't breathe. But here, I feel her presence. Her dance. For my mother and her mother, and probably her mother before her, and for every woman who's lost themselves to a world that will never understand them. For little Aria who deserves hope. For myself.

"Let's dance."

CHAPTER FIVE

1919, Chicago
Fiona Cleary

There's one moment I live for. I thirst for it. The flash of time between my final pose and the eruption of the crowd. When the lights obscure my vision, and the flames heat the stage, my mind goes silent. It's only a beat—shorter than a breath—but my body prepares for the rush of adoration and love.

As always, I let this moment inspire me just before I step on stage. My skirt shimmies with the handsewn beads that glitter under stage lights. Silk stockings hug my legs, and I shift side to side in my laced peep toe heels. Fire and energy course through my veins, waiting for the emcee to announce the closing act.

"And now, the moment you've all been waiting for. Please welcome the country's finest dancer," he announces into his microphone. "The brilliant, beautiful, Chicago-famous, fire-starter goddess, Celtic Fire!"

I don't burst onto the stage. Tonight, I stroll, allowing space for the crowd to lean into their excitement. If there is a better sensation in this world, I've never felt it. Their applause digs into me like fingers through soft sand. Their screams set my body alight, igniting the fire in my gut that never fully extinguishes.

I allow the silence to settle. I scan the crowd and flash a smile as my right foot slides out to a point and my hand slides up my throat. Seduce them, hold them hungry and mesmerized, then blast them with the flames they've all tried to snuff.

The music quickens. Magic turns my outfit into a plain white leotard, hair pinned like a society lady. Balls of fire twirl like tumbleweeds between my open palms. I withhold a howl as fire escapes my body. The Orpheum's owner stands at stage right, warning me with his usual scowl. His favorite four words are "Don't frighten the patrons." I ignore him and blow flames into the air as a ring drops from the ceiling.

The audience gasps. Good. They should be afraid. They adore me on stage and shun me in daylight. I cartwheel my way into a backbend, leaving one foot in the air flickering like a sparkler. The ring descends and I hook my knee. It carries me up, up toward the mirrored ceiling. I blow out my flames and swing from the hot metal circle to squeals of delight.

From deep within my memories of hurt, I think of the offended glances, the newspaper headlines that call me wicked. The threats from policemen who want to appease their churchgoing wives. And I dive off the circle toward the stage. A trail of blue flames catches my foot, swinging me over the audience as a fire wall blasts from my hands. I release myself and backflip, landing on the stage in laced Irish Dance shoes, and turning the heat into diamonds that shower the audience.

Their fear is palpable. For a moment, I was the god who could end them with my power.

Breathe.

And then they erupt.

After a show of gratitude and a stage of roses thrown at my feet, I smile and kiss the air, walking offstage and shoving my shoulder into the owner.

"Watch it, Fiona." He straightens his jacket.

"You don't write the rules here, John. I do." I motion to the crowd who still roars, begging for more. "I could take my act elsewhere."

His face reddens, somehow appearing rounder as he grows angry. "This is my theater!"

I shove my finger into his sternum. "You need to grow a spine. Did you see the protestors out there tonight? They're gonna hurt the performers one of these days."

"You're dangerous, Fiona. We're all terrified of you burning someone."

"I haven't burned anyone yet." The crowd's thunder ripples through the floor under my feet. This coward bows to the growing hysteria of Magic Dance—but not enough to let me go. I make him too much money. "You know, John, every time you try to hold me back, I just want to burn a little brighter. Stop telling me how to perform."

"The entire city is in a frenzy over your magic. You're lucky I let you stay here." I flip my hand toward his face and walk off just as he yells, "And my name is George!"

I don't bother wiping off the soot that dusts my arms and neck. It gives me a smoky scent and reminds everyone who I am. I burst through the heavy doors to the icy Chicago night, tapping my way next door to the Elephant Bar. I step inside and open my arms. "Who's going to dance with me?"

Several men remove their hats and slide close. They're all handsome and shiny with excitement. I push past the eager men toward the off-duty cop in the corner. He's young and dangerously handsome, but I've got words for him.

He rolls his cigarette between two fingers, watching me strut toward him. "Look at you. Beautiful as ever."

I bite back my rage. "Hey, Billy. Dance with me?"

He puts out the cigarette in a glass ashtray and reaches for my waist. He presses my chest to his. I lick my lips to make sure they remain glossy and plump.

He nuzzles my neck, groaning like he wants to bite my skin. "I want you, Fiona."

"You didn't want me yesterday. Remember?" I glide my fingers through his hair to watch his eyes widen. "When you walked past me by the newspaper stand? When the group of men called me a filthy bitch. Remember?"

I drag my hand down his thigh. He doesn't pull away. They never can resist a woman's touch. "I was working, doll."

"Working for who? Certainly not me." I grab a fistful of his hair. "You let them threaten me."

"Can you blame them? You're out here throwing flames while the country is losing their damn mind over magic. They're afraid of booze too, but I'm still here with a magic girl in one hand and a bourbon in the other." He attempts to wink. "Come on. It's not my fault you Fire Girls won't listen to reason."

I tighten my grip on his hair. "What reason?"

He chugs back his drink, losing every bit of handsome appeal. "You've burned audience members! You've turned Vaudeville into a circus."

I step toward him knowing I'm a twig of a thing but have fire bubbling under my skin. "I've never hurt a soul."

"Your kind has. It's the same thing." He takes a step back, not wanting to admit he's frightened of me. It's been part of our attraction. "Just dance without fire. Jesus Christ, Fiona. It's not that hard."

He has no idea how impossible that is.

"Do people tell you to stop blowing smoke in people's faces? Do they tell you to stop being a loudmouthed cop who thinks he's the most important man in Chicago? No, they just let you be you. That's all I ask."

He lights a fresh cigarette and blows a puff of smoke in my mouth. "You're trash. Always have been. But you're a good lay." He reaches for my thigh with a squeeze so tight I wince.

I yank his fingers back so hard I hear them crack. He pulls his hand to his chest with a scream, forcing the bar to a halt. "I don't need you, Billy. I never have. You were nothing but a pretty face." He was more than a pretty face. He was the angry mob I subdued in bed every Friday night. The laws they've passed in cities all over the country that I undressed and had my way with.

He reaches up to slap me, but I begin dancing. A hip roll and smack of my hands at my pelvis. Once I shimmy my hips, my halo appears.

Warmth glows from my forehead. Rage, love, lust. The extremes that live at the edges of emotion prompt the gold ring, a warning to us both of what I'm capable of.

"Hit me," I say. "See what happens." I glide my hands up my legs as I whip my hair sideways, and come up with balls of fire in my palms. I won't hurt him, but he can think I will.

He drops his hand. "Wench." With a strut, he spits a fleck of tobacco on the floor. "Plenty of guys go slumming, but now we all have to answer to the law."

Once I stop shaking, I smooth my hair back in place. I flop myself at the bar, ignoring the eyes on me. "Hey," I ask the bartender, "What's he talking about?"

She rests her hand on mine with a firmness that says I'm screwed. "The cops have been in here three times this week looking for magic girls. They've dragged a few out by their hair."

I drop my shoulders. "Why haven't I heard of this?"

"You've been busy with your show. By the time you come in, it's late. They haven't done any nighttime roundups yet."

"Shit."

"Yeah." She shrugs one shoulder and turns toward a couple begging for a few Rickeys.

The theater owner appears in the doorway. John or George, or whatever his name is, never comes in here. The music stops when he walks in. Everyone knows he's not fond of the magic this bar protects.

He comes straight for me. "You're fired."

He says those two little words with such ease, I wonder how he sleeps at night. "You can't fire me."

"I just did." He slaps a newspaper on the bar top. "In a few hours, the papers will run this headline. It's all across the country. You're done for."

I spin the paper so I can read the words.

January 16, 1919.

Temperance Wins: 18ᵗʰ Amendment ratified, prohibiting the production and sale of liquor and magic.

"They finally did it." I can't believe they made us illegal. "What do they expect us to do?"

"Stop slinging magic that contributes to the moral corruption of America." His nostrils flare.

"You made buckets of money off this moral corruption, you jackass."

"A guy's gotta make a buck." He slaps the newspaper once. "Your time is up, Fiona. Get out of my theater and never come back."

"I never liked you, John."

His face reddens again with beads of sweat popping to the surface of his temples. "Forgive me if I don't pay you for the last two shows. You aren't a citizen any longer. I owe you nothing."

I jump off the stool, towering over his slight frame. "You let your uptight wife turn you against the performers who made you famous. I guess that's what happens when you marry an heiress. You're nothing but a servant in her world of riches."

He tightens his fists in a fury so pathetic I almost regret insulting him. Then I remember how he let hecklers throw mud during performances and allowed cops to harass us outside his theater as he looked the other way. This betrayal has been a steady train that left the station years ago. "Go to hell, Fiona."

"I'm already there."

He stops at the doorway, looking around the bar. "Magic is finally outlawed and so is booze. You all better find yourself a place to hide."

I meet eyes with everyone at the bar. Every one of us is a magic dancer or loves a magic dancer. The police will be here in a matter of hours to blame us for society's problems. They'll shut down every bar and every theater.

And I'll be the first one attacked. The most recognizable Fire Girl in the country, with a daughter who hides the same talents.

***

The clock reads two a.m.

The sky, a dark splash of stars, drops a flutter of snowfall over the city. I slip in quietly and click the door shut. A plate of cold dinner sits on the table with a heart carved in the mashed potatoes. My sweet girl.

I scratch my scalp with both hands and slump into the ripped green loveseat I picked up on the corner one day. "This isn't happening." But of course it is. The country has been trying to contain us since my grandmother stepped off the boat from Ireland. Outsiders are always the target.

I remember his hand gripping my thigh, and stand to shake the sensation away. I thought he'd protect me. What a fool I've been.

I tiptoe into Eleanora's room and watch my beautiful daughter sleep. She's tucked up on her side, hands gathered under her chin like she did as a child. At twelve, she's smart and careful, and the best thing in my whole world.

My chest stings. They'll come for us. Legally, they can do that now. The grocers who refuse to sell to us are nothing compared to what's coming. Many hospitals already turn us away, afraid we'll burn their staff or unleash witchery. Will they round us up? Send us to prison? One intrusive image of lawmen tearing her from me is strong enough to splinter my heart into shards.

I rub the backs of my fingers on her cheek and over her silky-smooth locks. I keep my hair short so the audience can view my neck. Eleanora braids hers. She doesn't care what everyone thinks, and I adore that about her.

She pulls her heavy gray eyes open. "Mama," she says with a relieved smile.

"I'm here, baby." My love for her overtakes me. I swoop her in my arms and squeeze her close. She doesn't say a word. She simply rests her head on my shoulder, as if I can protect her.

"Is everything okay?" she asks.

No, nothing is okay. My daughter's fate is the same as mine—dance hot with fire until she dies young. None of us have lived past forty, the fire turning us mad. How do I teach her to dance anyway, despite the terrible end that awaits? I just do. I gather myself and pull her shoulders back so she's looking straight at me. "Get your shoes on."

"What, now? I'm tired."

"Please, now. The moon is bright and low."

She groans but agrees. She slips on her shoes and a cream silk robe. Her long braids trail down her back, her eyes shining like a stormy sea.

We make our way up the stairs outside our apartment and onto the balcony. From here, the city glows like fireflies below and the river gleams with silver moonlight. Snowfall covers our hair and eyelashes as goosebumps pepper our bare arms.

We begin with arms up, hands reaching toward the stars. We step in rhythm, a dance I've never taught her though she knows in her soul. I danced with my mother in secret in the dark, just like this. As we sway and spin, a ring of fire surrounds us, warming our bodies. An orb of warm yellow heat forms in each of our hands. We kneel and bow, holding space for the light.

Eleanora smiles, a beautiful wide grin. Glittering stars frame her face as the orb lights her cheeks. She's so ethereal and timeless, I choke on a sob as it rises in my throat. We glide along the inner ring of fire, locking eyes and spinning our orbs until it appears.

We've summoned fire, and with it, every woman before us who dances under a dark sky, allowing the history of Magic Dance to flow through our earthly bodies. The Milky Way appears like a welcome friend. "See?" I tell her, "The sky speaks to us."

The fire disappears and snow falls once again, as we hold hands. Tomorrow we must run and hide, but tonight, we are Wild as the Stars.

CHAPTER SIX

Eleanora

The Luminaire is more than magic. It's a Victorian theater with carved angels in its molding and diamond chandeliers. It's a show of wealth and opulence in the belly of the city where Magic Dance found a home. This haunted theater holds the potential to break me free from the cage I've built. The protection of a Prohibition exemption could change the fate of this Fire Girl from early death to a long, mystic-filled life, just like our dance instructor.

"Girls, please welcome Eleanora Cleary." Iridessa guides me into a dressing room with walls of feather boas and strings of pearls. Each Star Girl sits at her own mirrored table crowned by jars of makeup and perfume, feathers and beaded hair pins. They all turn to look at me. Most smile, yet I focus on the ones who don't. They could be serious people, or they could hate me, this girl who fell on her face and still earned a spot in their prestigious theater.

Ruby jumps to her feet, her hazel eyes shimmering with delight. "You did it." She wraps me in a hug. She smells of lavender and lemon, and her freckled cheeks shine like stardust.

"I'm not certain I belong here, but I'm ready to try."

"Of course you belong here." Ruby calls over a girl with fluffy blond curls. The one who opened the door earlier today. Her wheezes are more pronounced.

"I'm Sadie, resident water dancer." She checks her pale lips in the nearest mirror. "We decided long ago there's no such thing as earning your place. If you live with us, you're a Star Girl. Welcome to the troupe."

"Fiona Cleary's daughter. You got fire, I assume," an acrobat asks.

"Yes." I attempt to say it with gusto and not the fear of burning myself bald. "When I'm not passing out on stage, that is."

The room falls silent, filled with confused glances. I want to scream that yes, I see the irony. A tap dancer full of pent-up magic in a magic theater, who isn't even sure she can stand upright in front of an audience.

Iridessa claps her hands together. "Ten minutes to warmup." Her dancer's neck seems to elongate when she looks at me. "Prepare yourself for a long evening."

"I'm ready."

I say this with cracks in my confidence. All I have to do is think of the panic that consumed me and fear rushes through my chest. But I *want* to be ready, and that will have to be enough.

The acrobat snorts. "We've turned down some of the best dancers in the world and Celtic Fire's offspring gets a shot because of her last name."

Sadie knocks her hip into her. "Get to your tumbling and leave Eleanora alone." She walks off but not before shooting a rigid, disapproving glance in my direction. "Don't worry about her," Sadie says. "It's been tense around here lately. We're expected to make this new show something that will get the protestors off our backs."

Ruby leads me to an empty makeup chair. They fuss with my look, brushing my bob until it shimmers like a black pearl. She holds up a deep maroon palette. "This would look amazing with your complexion. Too bad we don't get a say in such things. Old man Price says only approved colors from now on."

Approved colors? My mother designed her own costumes and yelled at the directors if she didn't like a number.

"Young Price must like you," Sadie says with a wink.

"Stop it."

"I'm serious!" She runs a charcoal pencil along my upper eyelid with great focus. "He's kind of grumpy, but still handsome."

"Miles seems to think I'll add something to this troupe."

They drop their arms and stare at my reflection. Ruby cocks her head. "Miles?"

"That's what he said his name is."

"Oh, Eleanora," Ruby says with Southern sass, "You must be one of those girls who doesn't see how pretty you are." She rubs oily pink blush over my cheeks. "It seems our director has noticed."

I push her away. "I didn't make my way in here because the director thinks I'm pretty."

"Of course not."

"Don't dismiss me as a talentless harlot who sleeps her way to the top, because that's not me." I'm not exactly sure who *me* is, but it certainly isn't a floozy. My voice has grown loud, as the girls look at each other. Shit. I've overstepped.

Ruby rests her hand on my arm. "We don't think that, Eleanora."

"Yeah, forget I said anything." Sadie flashes a giant smile.

I want to grovel at their feet. Apologize for being so terrible at vulnerability. But I bite my lip instead. "It's fine."

I duck into the gymnasium and don't dare look back. My anger has always kept me from making friends. Except for Aria, and she hardly counts. She's more like a little admirer I can't ever shake and don't understand. What have I done to make her look up to me? I join the troupe in warmup like the outsider I am.

Pliés, relevés, synchronized stretches. I've never followed a routine, but my belly fills with excitement as we move in a collective rhythm. *Together.*

Iridessa, gorgeous and lean, leads us from the front of the room. "Everything you need to be the most powerful dancer in the world is already inside you. You *are* magic—your breath, your body, your heart. Dig deep and let your true dance light up our stage."

She directs us without one hitch in her breath as she moves through arabesque and holds firm on pointe. Her black leotard and pink toe shoes change color in the flash of lights; red, blue, yellow.

"Your bodies are works of art." Her voice, clear with power, seems to lift the girls off the floor as some begin to levitate. I've always been too afraid to leave the ground. "Push yourselves. Allow your talent and strength to pulse through your limbs. Movement is the cake, magic is merely the frosting."

Their timing is impeccable, and their lines strong. Gold dust puffs around us, emanating off several dancers like a whisper. We come to position in a deep back bend, hands lifted toward the ceiling. Iridessa eyes her troupe. She locks gaze with me and winks, rainbow light shooting from her eyelashes.

"To your stations," she says.

The group disperses. Iridessa glides over to me. "You can move. Lovely lines. Good posture."

"Thank you."

"But you're far too invested in everyone else."

I catch myself staring at the acrobats, using a cloud of mist to catch and toss bottles of sparkling wine. Sadie produces water droplets and dances to form them into shapes, a notable disappearance in her wheezing. "How can I not? Look at how beautiful they are."

"Mr. Price didn't bring you here to be like everyone else. He brought you to discover something unique and special."

"Can't I do that and still admire their talent?"

"I don't know, can you?"

The young women around me move with color and life. "How do I find their confidence?"

"Come." She leads me through a door into a small rehearsal space. Hands behind her back, she walks behind me and stares into the mirror at our reflection. "I've spent my life teaching dance, but what I really do is show people how to quiet the noise of the world. How to summon the best of yourself and use it like armor. Those voices of doubt didn't come from you, Eleanora."

I clear my throat of the sandy remnants of embarrassment and stare at my reflection with tears glistening in my eyes. "How do I make them go away?"

She walks toward me, her feet in turnout and her spine tall. "You start by focusing on what you were put here to do. Every time you start to break, go back to what you know."

I take position and begin the warm-ups I've watched my mother do so many times. I try not to look back at her for reassurance.

She walks away and I'm left with my reflection, and a stream of memories that threaten to turn to rapids. All I have is myself and the inexplicable belief that I am right where I belong.

***

I retreat to the rooftop where I can breathe. The sky looks the same here as it did from the Milk House. Cloudy with whispers of struggle.

"What are you looking at up here?"

Over my shoulder, I see Ruby and Sadie. Hesitant, they tighten their fur jackets and wait for my reply.

Listening to the whispers of my dead mother, but no one needs to hear about silly dreams. "I like to watch the stars."

"Oh." Sadie's cheeks glow pink in the cool night. "Can we join you?"

"Sure." No fur coat for me, so I wrap myself in a blanket I found on the sleeping porch.

Ruby looks empty without her fiddle. "How did your first rehearsal go?" she asks.

"Fine." I nod to convince myself. "Good. Tiring. Overwhelming." Shut up, Nora.

"Iridessa is tough, but we trust her. She'll do right by you."

"I can tell." I've developed a raw talent for reading faces and energy and body movement. I can tell who a person is by how my body reacts. With Iridessa, my chest warmed.

They lift their gazes to the sky. "All I see is clouds," Sadie says.

"Typical Seattle night. Give it time and the black sky will explode with specks of light."

"I've never met a dancer who's into astrology," Sadie says with a smile.

"It's not so much astrology as—" Memories flood back to me. Dancing under the silver moonlight. My little toes sinking into the soft, cool mud as a kid, and sleepy dances as a teenager. "They make me happy."

Ruby's giant hazel eyes flood with moonlight. "I'm the resident medicine girl from the woods of Virginia. I use herbs and oils to heal sore muscles, cuts, and anything else the Star Girls experience. If something hurts you, you come find me."

Does she have a potion for a lonely life? A liniment for courage? I want to smile and thank them for seeking me out tonight. Instead, I simply nod. "Thanks."

We lean back to watch the clouds glide across the sky as stars appear like freckles.

"I'm sorry we hurt your feelings earlier," Ruby says. "This must be very overwhelming for you. We're happy you're here."

Ruby elbows Sadie. "Yes. I'm sorry I'm such a bigmouth."

I tighten the blanket around my shoulders. "The thing is," I hold back for a beat, unsure how to communicate. "My mother was called a slut." I don't dare look at their reactions. "People said awful things about her." I sit up and force myself to look at them. "I shouldn't have snapped at you. I'm sorry."

"We all get those comments for showing our bodies. I mean, what do they expect, dancers in flour sacks? Zelda gets more hate than the rest of us." Sadie shakes her head. "She just likes men. Is that such a big deal?"

"Yeah, exactly. Why do the men have all the say in how the world views us?"

They smile and exchange glances. "Welcome to the family, Eleanora. We're all fighting similar battles here, but we do it together." Ruby slides her hands in her pockets.

"It seems like your lives are a dream. All the Magic Dance you can spin, with a packed house every weekend."

The girls look every which way. Ruby shoves her hair poof away from her forehead. "Inside this theater is the only place the laws can't reach us. But there's not much freedom anywhere for our kind, is there?"

"It's like I always tell the kids that hang around the theater," Sadie says. "We all breathe the same air." She inhales a high-pitched whistle. "Some just do it easier than others."

How awful it must be to struggle for air. Her lips hold a sheen of blue and her chest muscles seem as strong as her biceps.

Kids around the theater. Shit. I forgot about Aria.

***

At midnight, I doubt I'll find her, but I still can't rest until I try. I haven't seen her since that horrible audition two days ago. Sneaking out was easy, as it doesn't seem anyone leaves the Luminaire but Price. Too dangerous. By the time I arrive in the alley, my heart is racing and my fingers prickle with nerves.

Nothing cracks the illusion of success like forgetting the one person who's always been by your side.

She isn't in the alley. I consider knocking on the orphanage's window or scour the streets around the theater. I drop against the makeshift fence and stare at the door to the speakeasy's kitchen.

"Nora?" Her hopeful, tiny voice appears from behind the milk crates.

Relieved, my hands stop tingling. She runs to me and throws herself into a hug. "You're alright. I was so worried about you."

Her thin arms dangle like ropes around my waist, but her cheek warms my belly. "What happened at the Luminaire?" We sit on two overturned buckets. She locks her arms at her sides, her face lit up like a Christmas tree. "Tell me everything."

"What's the last thing you saw?"

"Oh, you looked nervous and your eyes kind of rolled around in your head and your face turned pale. Then you hit the ground."

Leave it to her to give it to me straight. "Right."

"The Star Girls rushed to help you. I hid in the curtains. I kept my promise! I wanted to run to you and shake you and tell you to get back up and try again, but I thought you'd be mad if I did."

"What happened after that?"

"Some old lady kicked me out. Gave me a hunk of bread though. A group of kids gather in the streets and beg for food along with all those magic girls begging for an audition. She must have thought I was one of them." She kicks the pebbles at her feet. "I was worried about you."

"You don't need to worry about me." Secretly, I love it.

"Of course I do. You're my best friend."

My chest squeezes around my heart until it aches. I'm her only friend. "I made it in, Aria. I'm a Star Girl."

Her eyes fill with tears and it's the first moment I've let myself absorb the joy from the wild day I've had.

"You did it. The big dream you thought would never come true."

Her pride fills me up like a swell. "They'll train me for my debut on New Year's Eve." I choose not to breathe life into the worry of another episode.

Aria nods with confidence. "You're going to be the best Star Girl that stage has ever seen."

Her optimism is too much. "Aria, can I walk you home? It's late."

"I am home." She smiles, obviously refusing to talk about the orphanage. "Can I watch your New Year's Eve show?"

"Of course you can. I couldn't do it without you." And I mean that at the core of my very being. She's one of the few people who has ever seen me through the throes of an episode.

Her face drops. "I won't see you for three months?"

This poor kid is begging to be part of my journey, and her big eyes are like a test to my soul. "I'll visit you still. Just like tonight."

"When? Where? I need a plan, Nora."

I laugh, appreciating her tenacity. "I tell you what. A fire escape at the Luminaire takes you from the alley to the rooftop. I'll meet you there every Wednesday night at sunset."

"Yes!"

"I can't get you into the theater without someone throwing a fit, but I doubt anyone will go to the roof except me."

"Thank you, Nora." She squeezes me in a tight hug. "The moment I see you on stage, I'll know I can do anything."

No pressure.

I tighten her jacket. "It's cold out here. You ask Lady to give you a blanket, okay?"

"I'm fine." She waves me away. "See you on the rooftop!"

I begin to walk away but glance over my shoulder. She's smiling, eyes closed, dreaming of something happy and hopeful. Someone, someday soon, will break her little spirit. I say a wish to the stars that it won't be me.

CHAPTER SEVEN

Fiona

City Bans Alcohol and Magic
Fire Girls are First Target

The sun hovers below the horizon, casting a blue haze of twilight across the city. The view from our third-floor studio makes the cramped eyesore almost worth it. I brace myself on the exposed brick as weakness spreads through my knees. My world is about to bottom out. Eleanora is about to learn just how dangerous our gifts are.

I need to get myself together and find us a safe space to hide out until the magic hysteria dies down—however long that takes. All that effort to make a tiny percent of the population go into hiding.

Eleanora walks out from behind the partition, sleepy-eyed from our night dance. Her one suitcase probably holds a few dresses, undergarments, and tap shoes. "How long will we have to leave for?"

"Oh, sweetheart." How to tell her it's all already gone? "We aren't coming back."

Her shocked face may as well be her step into adulthood. She's learning the wicked ways of this world right in front of my eyes. "Never?"

"I'm sorry, no." I walk into my bedroom, swiping my stage jewelry into a cinched bag and sifting through only the clothes that don't dangle with sequins.

Eleanor marches in and drops her case on the floor. "Why do we need to leave? You can just take a job on the Vaudeville circuit. They're allowing regular dancers to stay. That's where the money is, anyway."

"Regular dance without magic? No way. I can't do one without the other." Most of my closet won't come with me. Knockoff alpaca fur that looks like the real thing, evening gowns I beaded myself to glossy perfection. All useless now.

"Just take the job with the money, Mother," she says.

"If I cared about money, we wouldn't be living in this dump." I kick the loose baseboard back in place.

She grabs my arm. She seems to have grown taller since she walked from the other room. "Just dance!" She's never yelled at me before. "Who cares what stage it's on?"

"Pretending to be someone I'm not. Is that how you want me to live?"

"Yes!" She drops her hand from my arm as her halo appears with the faintest glow. "Dammit." She swipes at it, but the light does not respond. It only grows brighter. "You dance for serious money and use the rooftop to blow off magic steam. You can still get your standing ovations, and all the handsome men you want."

I don't fight back. I deserve that. Performing is such a high that I deal with an insatiable hunger. Human touch cures my loneliness and makes me forget the miserable morning light to come. "We can fight about this later. Right now, we have to go."

She crosses her arms. "I'm not leaving."

She picks now to stand up to me? "Yes, you are."

"You can't just take me away from my life. I like my bedroom and the bakery on the corner. How the fire escape lets me stand in the sky and how summer smells like perfume." Her eyes well with tears. "I don't want to leave."

I drop the clothing to the floor and reach for her hands. We sit on my bed as I look straight into her eyes. "They've made us illegal. The entire country is about to break bottles and close bars. Anyone with magic will be rounded up and forced from their homes. And I'm the most famous magic girl in the city."

"We haven't done anything wrong."

I hate this. Every second of it. "They don't care. They blame us for all the trouble."

Women hide bruised cheeks with blush all the time. Married men slink into the bar after a show looking for a taste of magic, complaining of their boring lives. We are forbidden fruit no one wants in the daylight. They soothe their wounds with alcohol and beautiful dancers. It's no wonder their wives fought back. Too bad they chose the wrong targets. The problem is not the booze or the magic, it has always been their men.

"I haven't hurt a soul." Her big gray eyes turn icy blue. "I don't even have friends."

I place my palm on her cheek. "Some women are meant for greatness, and their experiences of living a lonely life teach them something most will never understand."

"I'm not destined for greatness."

"Oh, darling, yes you are. You just haven't seen it yet." I force a smile to cover the bleeding ache in my heart. She doesn't see her gifts. Her beautiful dancing and her ability to see truth. The way she will change people someday. I ache for all the learning she still must endure. "You are more than this world handed you."

"Please. Just try to take a job in a regular theater and we'll just dance in secret."

I place my hands on my thighs with a slap. "Never."

"Even when they want to hurt you for it?"

"Especially then." I lift my suitcase and tuck my jewelry bag under my coat. "It's time to go."

She looks down at her feet, tapping them in place with the speed of a hummingbird's wings.

My beautiful, brave girl wipes her eyes and lifts her suitcase. Though her knuckles whiten and her jaw pulses, she agrees to move forward. It's our only choice.

With winter clothing of gloves and hats, we may just escape unnoticed. As we step out the door of our apartment, I remind her, "Don't look back."

The morning snow has fallen. The sun rises in the hazy sky. Papers flutter in the breeze carrying news of Prohibition. Quiet still, but the air hints at a brewing storm. We hurry down Michigan Ave, heading north toward the pawnbroker. His shop is closed so we walk around back. I knock until my knuckles burn.

The man finally throws open the door. "What the hell do you want? I'm drinking my coffee."

"I'm selling my jewelry."

"We open in an hour. Now beat it." He tries to shut the door, but I slam my boot in the doorjamb. He looks at me with a snarl. "Lady, listen—"

"I'm Fiona Cleary. In a matter of hours everything I own will be useless to me, but you can make a killing."

"Celtic Fire?" He examines my face and glances into Eleanora's sad eyes, then reluctantly opens the door. "Come in."

The storage room is cluttered and musty with one table in the center of piles of junk. We step through the curtain into the store where glass cases display pocketknives and jewelry, postcards, letters, and watches.

The man runs his hands down his suspenders. "What you got?"

I pull out my velvet bag and uncinch the strings. "Pearls, ruby earrings, diamond hairpin. It's all here." Everything I've pilfered from shows that now means nothing.

He can't hide the glimmer in his eyes, or the excitement in his hands as he reaches for a string of pearls. "You wear these on stage?"

"Every one of them." Instinctively, I wrap my arm around Eleanora. They're just jewels. Things. "As of today, everything related to magic becomes illegal. I am the face of a time gone. Give me what they're worth, or I will take everything down the street to Arty's."

His snarl indicates I've hit him where I intended. "I hate Arty. Swindler."

As he examines the jewelry, Eleanora turns toward the window. "Look at the people," she says with a strained voice.

Groups of joyous people pour into the streets. Women clap and hold up newspapers in triumphant shouts. Joy pours from their hateful eyes over their hard-fought win. Years they've been gunning for us, turning magic dancers into villains. Eleanora watches them stomp through the snow. Right here, the light fades from her cheeks like a sunset. Her eyes tremble under tightened brows. They've made my daughter fear and I'm powerless to stop it.

A woman in a baby blue cloche hat examines the window display, dragging her gloved hand across the window to clear the frost. My stomach thumps. An achy, nauseous, boom in my gut. We stand very still, tracking her eyes as she examines her reflection and adjusts her hat. We know the type. A churchgoer, demanding and ruthless, controlled only by laws that identified us as citizens with rights. Until now.

"Mama?"

The woman looks beyond her reflection and catches my eyes. It takes her a beat while her eyes struggle to place me. "Is that a Fire Girl?" As couples and families gather at the window and door, the sunlight filters away. We stand in this darkened room watching them slam their fists against the shaking glass, these churchgoers suddenly fueled by the frenzy of vigilantes. "Get her."

The pawnbroker rushes to lower the shades. He looks at us with frantic worry. "You need to leave." As he rushes to open his cash register, I grab Eleanora's hand, forcing myself to remain calm.

"What do we do?" she asks.

The man shoves a wad of cash in my hands. "Out the back door." He guides us toward the storage room as he looks back over his shoulder. "They've been gunning for this moment for years."

I divide the money, with half tucked in my bra and the other half shoved into Eleanora's interior pocket. "Button up."

He pushes us out the door. "Go. I'll distract them out front."

I grab her hand in mine with far too much force, leading her toward the end of the alley. "It will be fine, baby girl." As we near the opening between buildings, a man catches sight of me. *Billy.*

He lifts his cigarette to his mouth, unbothered by my presence. He's still wearing a suit. Off-duty.

"Billy. Please let us pass."

"Why would I do that? You're prime meat for the slaughter."

My palm grows damp with sweat as Eleanora readjusts her grip. "Because you don't want us to get hurt. Now let us slip by."

He sucks a drag, releasing a snide glance at Eleanora. I never mentioned I was a mother. He flicks the last of his cigarette as the smoke sizzles in the snow. "She's back here! I get a bonus for rounding up trouble."

"Sick bastard." We turn and run, hands clasped. "Don't look back. Just run." The snow crunches under our boots. We both slip on a portion of ice hidden under the top layer of snowfall. As I lift her back to standing, three people approach. Shit.

Everyone stands still for one quiet moment. Then the woman yells, "Get her."

I shove Eleanora toward the wall. "Run."

"No." She shakes her head. "No."

I pull them away to the other side of the alley. One woman grabs my hair, throwing my hat to the ground and stomping on it. The one in the baby blue cloche shoves me, but not hard enough to knock my balance. Then she reaches for Eleanora. She grabs her jacket and shakes, forcing her to drop her suitcase. Her head bobbles, hair flying in her face.

Fire instantly burns in my palms. I march over, yank the woman back to look at me and land a solid punch right in her eye socket. The remaining couple rush to her side.

"I said run!" I guide Eleanora toward the ladder, which she finally climbs. I guard her legs as the man slaps me hard enough to turn the world blurry. Eleanora screams, but I don't turn lest he knock me unconscious with one slam to the base of my head. I kick his shins and launch another punch at the woman.

One I can handle. Three is a losing battle. They all pounce. I fight off hands all over me as they rip my coat and tear my blouse at the buttons. Off in the distance, Eleanora screams for me through strangled sobs. I fight harder. I land one claw at a face and yank someone's hair.

I give up on fighting and fall to my side, arms up to protect my face. Curled in a ball with stomach clenched, I hold tight against hands as they pummel my back and ribs. I no longer hear Eleanora scream.

Suddenly, the hands lift. I'm still huddled, when I hear a man yelling "Go on!" I look up, head shaking. An image forms of the pawnbroker pointing a gun at the fleeing threesome. I fall to my back and watch the snowfall over my face. Am I breathing?

"Hurry up." He helps me up, but I can't stand upright. "Get in here."

I try to yell for Eleanora, but I see her lifting her tap shoes from the snow and placing what she can grab back in her suitcase. She rushes to over, arms out, afraid to hug me.

The man slides open a garage door and shoos us inside. Eleanora helps me onto a sofa in the corner. I catch my breath, trying to smile but finding it difficult. She holds my hand as tears stream down her face.

"It's all over."

The man drops his shoulders. "I'll heat some water so you can clean up. I think my ex-wife left some clothes around here." He looks sideways with cheeks aflame. I look down to see my top ripped open and my bra exposed. The money is gone.

He putters in the next room while Eleanora sits in front of me. "Why did they attack you?"

"The church ladies have hated me for years. Corrupting their men or some such nonsense. They finally got their chance to take a few hits." I gather what's left of my top and clutch the fabric with an aching fist. "I told you to run."

"I won't leave you." After all these years, she still trusts me. "I'm scared," she says.

I sit forward though it bites, and smooth her hair back. Suddenly nothing hurts. The money doesn't matter. "We'll start fresh. Somewhere far away, okay?"

She nods, looking down to catch her breath. "A normal Vaudeville life now?" When I reluctantly nod, she breathes a sigh of relief. "I love you."

"I love you too, baby." I watch her stand, a renewed faith in me, and a promise I'm not certain I can keep. I stumble up through a sharp pain in my side. I make my way to a cracked mirror against the wall.

A rip in my skirt reveals scratched skin underneath. Red fingernail marks swell against my white thigh. A purple bruise has already started on my ribs. My lip is swollen on one side, and my eye pulses in a pink shiny lump.

Above my head, a faint gold halo flickers in and out as desperation consumes my insides. Me and my fire blood are now illegal. People can attack us without recourse. And it's all to save the morality of a country who's been protecting the devils all along.

"They loved me once." I say this to myself, to my reflection. Eleanora steps into view behind me.

"But Mama, if all they wanted was your performance, they never wanted you at all."

CHAPTER EIGHT

Eleanora

For years I've fallen asleep to the sound of my own breath, and occasionally, mice nibbling in the walls. My first night on a sleeping porch with dozens of girls all in a collective state of slumber may as well be a bed in the center of an orchestra.

I rub my gritty eyes as Ruby points a glass spray bottle at my face. "Close your eyes." A floral mist kisses my face. "Rose water. My granny called it the wake-up splash."

"It's nice." I keep my eyes closed and inhale the sweet scent of roses. "What's your cure for red eyes?"

"Coffee." She yanks my arm, and we join the river of girls flowing down the stairs toward the dining hall.

"Woah." My usual breakfast of toast and orange juice seems pathetic next to this feast. Freshly baked muffins and pastries fill the room with the dizzying scent of butter and sugar. Bowls of fruit and silver platters of sliced ham. Goblets of juice in gem shades of orange and pink. Glass carafes filled to the brim with steaming coffee.

Sadie bumps into me. "Local bakeries supply us with the freshest pastries in exchange for tickets. One of the perks."

Iridessa approaches the door. "Good morning, ladies. Eleanora, grab a quick bite and head to the main stage."

"Just me?"

"Just you." She turns to walk away but not before straightening Zelda's posture.

"Rehearsing on the big stage already? Get that dream, Eleanora," Ruby says with a wink. Her morning hair is full and wild.

The old stage pops under my feet. Unlike the stages I've been on, this one hums with potential. I can practically hear the applause from the walls.

"Hello? Iridessa?"

I slide my toe across the stage in a line, arm extended to the balcony. Did my mother trace these steps? Can I fill her spotlight? My hopes dangle by a thread, but here I stand in an empty theater, dreaming in real time.

"Don't speak." My heart lurches at the sound of Miles's voice behind me.

"I don't take orders," I snap.

He steps closer. "This isn't an order. It's just a little trust exercise." My fingers tingle at the tenor of his voice.

"Interesting, seeing as how I barely know you."

"Your debut is around the corner." How his confidence rises and falls intrigues me to no end. "Iridessa will work on form. I am here to work on this." He points his finger to his forehead.

"Who says this," I point to my own temple, "needs attention?"

He glances to his feet then up through the top of his eyes. "Something ruined your audition. And it wasn't your body."

The goose egg on the back of my head reminds me how deeply I failed. Mother is the reason I'm here at all, and I worry what Miles wants. "Celtic Fire was Fiona's. I can't bring it back."

Miles exhales. "Who says you need to be like her?"

"I'm guessing your father does."

"My father doesn't see what I see." He stands shoulder to shoulder with me as we stare at the balcony decorated with gold cherubs and silver stars, framed by freshly steamed crimson curtains. The entire theater looks like a three-tiered decadent cake to be sampled by the rich.

"What do you see in this theater?" I ask.

"Firelight and gems might be why people come, but performance and art are why they stay. Father focuses on tonight. I focus on our future."

"And you think I'm key to that future?"

He shrugs. "I do."

I can't tell if he believes in me, wants to exploit me, or just likes a challenge. I suppose I don't care. Miles gave me the keys to the kingdom, and the rest is up to me. "I'll do your little trust exercise. But you owe me something in return."

"I owe you nothing." He seems amused, intrigued by whatever might pop from my mouth next. "But go on. I'm curious what you want."

His deep stare makes me want to look away, but I'm locked in his gaze. "You said you understand fear. What did you mean?"

He doesn't flinch or recoil like I expect him to. He leans closer until I smell peppermint tobacco on his jacket once again. He rubs his chin, as if to consider how much he wants to reveal. "I left here two years ago to join the human curiosities in Astley's Traveling Circus of London. Father didn't approve."

I glance around the theater, counting the seats so he doesn't realize how deeply I'm invested in this story. "Go on."

"My life here was suffocating. Everything in the Price world is about money and status and power. I was bored." He takes a penny from his chest pocket and flicks it up in the air, catching it and slipping it back in. "I trained with some of the most magnificent creatures alive. Daredevils and acrobats. Some with magic and no rules to hold them back."

No Prohibition in England. "What was your curiosity?" I ask.

"Rope dancer." He does a quick jig, part tap and part ballet.

"Where does the fear come in?"

He focuses his attention, eyes straight on me. "I dropped my partner. She broke both legs."

"Jesus." Suddenly, the theater grows dark. I don't notice the glittering statues or rich velvet walls because his blank eyes take over, fighting any speck of emotion.

"Is that enough for you?" he asks. "Can we dance now?"

His unexpected raw honesty cracks a bit of light from my dark insides. We share the silence, as both of us seem to hide the pain just below a cracked surface. To avoid one more word on the matter of breaking bones, I force out a word. "Yes."

He pulls something from his pocket. A crimson scarf. He drags the soft corner along the space between his thumb and forefinger. "May I?"

Against everything in me screaming *no*, I find myself nodding yes, like a fool.

"You don't trust me yet, but I hope that will change." His breath tingles the back of my neck as he ties the scarf around my eyes. "The trick is to make your mind think you aren't performing." His voice whistles like a summer breeze in my ears. "Stage fright is your mind preying on fear. We take back control."

My hands want to shove him away. But my body lights with excitement, overriding everything else. "Okay, I can't see anything. Now what?"

He slides his hand across my stomach. His chest rises and falls against my shoulder blades. "Follow my lead."

Following only my intuition and the warmth of his body, I move with him. Our feet slide across the floor, keeping perfect time. Our hips and torsos fit like spoons stacked atop one another.

"You find the beat inside you, instead of looking at the audience." He runs his hand along my shoulder and down my arm until he's holding my hand. "Tap."

Toe, heel, shuffle. His shoes slide like fine sandpaper across the stage. We tap together, Miles matching my moves like a silent shadow in my dreams. He pulls me close, lips resting against my cheek, which sends my heart racing.

"Forget the crowd. Forget the past." He spins me three times then pulls me into his chest. "You're a dancer in the moment. Nothing more."

"Nothing less," I say.

Our chests rise and fall together. His thumb drags along the curve of my waist, turning my mind into a hazy fog. "What do you want?" he asks.

I hold tight to the performer inside, kicking her way free. "I want to dance wild."

The silent theater seems to whisper and buzz. The energy of the elements runs through my veins, and hysteria grows like groundcover under my skin. But I am more than what this world handed me. That's what Mama used to say.

"You hesitated," Miles says between sways and dips.

I see things in shades of truth and secret seasons. A hidden meaning only my intuition knows. "Fear. It tells me I'll end up ruined, just like my mother."

He guides me to a stop but still holds me as he removes the blindfold. "I don't think you'll be ruined."

His mouth upturns naturally like a permanent smile. Those glass eyes of gold reflect the stage lights. All of it leaves me weak. He spins me as I gasp. I come to a rest facing the nonexistent audience, as Miles's fingers glide down my arms. Behind me he whispers. "Take a bow, Diamond Nora. You just performed at the most magical theater in the world. And you did it without a speck of panic."

"I didn't spin any magic though."

"That comes second. First, we take back your spot on the stage. We remind you that you belong right here, where your mother warmed the air and made history."

A smile fights its way past the fear. I enjoy every silent second of this triumph. Somehow, she's close as a shadow. But I look around to see an empty stage. Just me and the odd warmth of a partner's touch still on my hands.

I'm just one dancer, but maybe I can change the world.

I spin, arms out, withholding a deep, joyful laugh. As I whir to a stop, the beauty of the Luminaire eludes me as all I notice are two angry eyes and a thin, curved mustache. Standing on the balcony, Mr. Price glowers. My arms drop and my smile fades.

"Miss Cleary, my son is delusional. And so are you. You may have danced under the protection of a blindfold, but you'll never be what Fiona was. No one can."

All the hope of Miles's touch cools and fades. Mr. Price stands like a devil warning of his evil powers. He stares at me the way those people stared at my mother. The ones who beat her the day Prohibition landed in our lives like a bomb.

CHAPTER NINE

Eleanora

Three rehearsals a day. Morning technique work, afternoon group rehearsal, and all day trying to impress Iridessa. Evening is when my weary legs fight the fatigue aching in my bones. I'm not sure I'm succeeding.

"It's been five days," she says while examining my posture. "This is where your body wants to give up, but your mind must persevere."

Despite my trembling limbs and knotted hips, I manage to elongate my neck and keep my expression calm, leg extended in arabesque but dropping ever closer to the ground. Iridessa taps the underside of my ankle. "Lift."

A grunt escapes me and sweat beads on my forehead. Through sheer will I raise my leg against the stabbing spasm in my side for three whole seconds. Then I collapse to the floor like a worn dress.

Iridessa glides and moves as soft as a dream. She never seems to tire. "You must commit fully, despite all that holds you back."

My face smashed into the floor, I manage a garbled, "I thought I was."

She taps her cane next to my head. "Stand."

I roll to my back and count the panels on the ceiling. One, two, three, four. "I've never been this tired." Or perhaps, I'm delusional. Mr. Price's snarl still scratches at my mind, sharp and angry. I drag myself up and face the mirror, eyes shadowed by dark purple moon slivers.

Every time I want to give up, I remember Aria and how much she believes in me. "I'm ready."

"Young Price sees your potential."

I stare at our reflection, battling the insecurity that swims through my head. "But you don't?"

"I didn't say that." Her face is so taut by her hairline pulled into a bun that her skin shines. Glossy and clear, her cheeks glow like bronze in the sun. "Stop looking outside yourself for approval." She points to her sternum. "You find that in here."

Her sheer black skirt turns rainbow as she glides in circles around me, leaving a trail of primary-colored dust.

"But we dance for applause. You and Price decide if I'm good enough to stay. None of that is up to me."

"Your moment onstage is yours." She pirouettes on pointe fast enough to turn her image into a mosaic of metallic light. She lights the room with color which settles in a glowing pool at her feet when she lands in third position. "The only place of true freedom."

"Can I really spin magic on that intimidating stage?" The words leave a bitter taste in my mouth. I can't differentiate my wants from the things I need.

"I believe you can." Her colors fade and she turns to face me. "The key is to dance fully and deeply inside yourself." She faces her reflection as her cane appears back in her hands.

"You're not mad, or in a sanatorium, or accused of having the vapors. Do you hold some arcane secret to the universe?" Her face still glows with light. I worry her secret is that she's played by the rules and remained quiet about all the tragedy that happens outside these walls.

Her posture never wavers, but her eyes gloss over with a sheen of worry. "I've made difficult choices."

"They hate us. Even when they adore us."

She repositions her turnout. "There you go, thinking of everyone else again. How do you plan to perform when you're looking in the wrong places?"

"Iridessa, why do you only ask me questions when I can barely stand?"

"When you're tired, you're the most honest." She taps her cane, indicating I'm not finished here. I hold position, prepared to collapse as soon as she releases me. "Begin leaps."

I withhold a groan. All I can imagine is my soft bed and one of Ruby's evergreen ointments slathered on my sore legs.

Iridessa rolls out a trunk of costume accessories. As she digs through, she throws a handful of hats behind her. I move past the beret and the cloche. A top hat shines among the rest, just like the one my magic conjures. I reach for its rim. Black and sleek, the plush cools my hands.

I place it on my head and check my silhouette. Confidence surges through my limbs with complete ease. With a spin, I flick the hat in the air. It floats in place, suspended by gold mist. Sticky, effervescent bubbles spurt with flames from both hands. Magic swelled too easily. Like this hat is some conductor of inner stars. My chest balloons with pressure, but pure fear sucks the flames back in. The top hat falls to the floor, my taste of free magic evaporated as if it never happened.

Iridessa turns to find me gasping. "Are you alright?"

"Y–yes." I shake my head and kick the spellbound hat aside, though I ache to reach for the rim again. "Starting on leaps."

Point. Smile. Step, step, step, leap across the stage with everything I have, ignoring the terrified voice inside my head that felt unruly magic in that top hat beckoning me to set it free. *What the hell was that*?

***

When the hard work of the day is done, evening rewards us with champagne and cake in the first floor Sapphire Bar, a performers-only place to celebrate. With its mirrored walls and cobalt frosted sconces, the room resembles a sea of Star Girls multiplying for infinity.

The girls welcome any man or woman they choose for the evening, often a secret lover from the outside world. Through clouds of cigarette smoke and puffs of gold ash, the Star Girls dance freely in blissful freedom. I wonder how many understand what a thin shield stands between their party and a purity raid.

Zelda dances on the bar to admiration from several young men. She blushes when the one in glasses smiles at her, causing her halo to glow and fingernails to turn to shining glass.

"Is that her boyfriend?" I ask Ruby.

"We don't really have relationships. Too hard. But yeah, he's got it bad for her."

Ruby sways to the music, a longing in her eyes. "Do you have someone from the outside?" I ask.

"Me? No. I mean, no." She hesitates then shakes her head. "The outside doesn't understand us. Out there, we're witches and misfits. Oddities to be teased and laughed at. But in here," her glittering eyes reflect the blue light from the chandelier. "We're stars."

"How long have you lived here?"

"Three years."

Three years barely leaving these walls. I couldn't do it. Makes me wonder if people are right about Fire Girls. We're wild, like the fiery temperament of orange cats.

The Star Girls dance and laugh and kiss their dates under the twinkling sapphire ceiling, but Ruby stares with a longing I understand. We both lean against the cool glass mirrors, watching everyone else live for the moment.

"What happened back in Appalachia?" I ask.

She forces a smile. "What always happens. Mountain people looking for reasons to mistrust." Before I can ask more, she elbows me. "Look at them. We've made a family here where we aren't shunned for our oddities. We're lucky, really."

Lucky. If we can resist the fate of unruly magic dancers in the solitary halls of asylums. Panic flares in my chest. The room tilts like a sinking ship. I'm sitting in a sapphire fog of worry, spinning out of control, going under. Stop. Stop.

"Eleanora, stay with me." Ruby's voice echoes.

I rub my eyes hard with the heels of my palms until my black lids turn into a cluster of stars. "I'm fine." The words come from outside, where the remnant of myself is tethered to Earth.

"Come on." She lifts me, though I can't tell from where, as my numb body floats weightless and seemingly heavy as lead.

I can't breathe.

I can't breathe! My mind shouts but no words escape.

I can't see.

Make it stop.

I try to push through tears, but only strangled whimpers tumble out. "Ruby?"

"I'm here." She grips my arm. A moment of truth in this hellish freefall. No Aria to bring me back, but now I have her.

A wall supports my back. Blackness recedes to a blurry view of the Luminaire lobby, empty and scarlet red.

"No one can see you," Ruby whispers.

I slide to the ground, pull my knees to my chest, and dig my teeth into the bony skin near my kneecap.

Minutes pass, possibly years, when the panic recedes like a wave. There it is again, that calm blanket of a worry-free body.

Ruby rests her hand in mine. "Better?"

I recoil, desperate to run away. I stand on weary legs, and catch myself on the wall, dizzy with every emotion pouring through me. "I want this to stop."

"My mother had the fire too. It's hard to live with that pressure."

Her bright green eyes hold me in a trust I'm not familiar with, where I don't need to look away. "What happened to her?"

"I'm not sure." She leans her head against the wall. "We lived on the eastern edge of Appalachia, where Virginia meets North Carolina. The neighbor boy kissed me." She flinches. "He fell ill that night and the family marched toward our shack with torchlights."

"They thought you made him sick?"

"Yeah, by casting a spell. Mama breathed fire and her wicked daughter controlled the world with her fiddle. Our house partially burned."

I should reach for her like she reached for me, but the moment is tenuous. Like either of us could break.

"Mama sent me packing the next day. Gave me all the money she had and told me to come to the Luminaire. Thank God they took me."

"Doesn't seem fair." My legs find strength enough to stand tall. "You didn't ask for any of it."

"But have it I do. From the fiddle to my mother's magic, it's who we are. Religious folk decided we were of the devil, what with our spells and herbal medicine, but we're just mountain people spun from folklore."

"Doesn't it scare you? This thing we have inside?"

She turns to me with a solid smile. "Magic can heal. It creates smiles and laughter. Just because it's different, doesn't make it wrong. The people who hate us frighten me far more than a little elemental magic."

"You haven't seen your Mama since?"

"I like to think she's hiding in the woods of Virginia, dancing under the moonlight with the other hidden witches in the world. Silently free."

Silently free. What a lovely image. A fire dancer who escaped the punishment.

"Thank you, Ruby." I push off the wall, hesitating long enough to consider a hug, but the idea makes me squirm. My palms are sweaty, and my hands are still numb.

"You're welcome. Do you want to come back to the Sapphire? The drunken magic shows usually start about now."

"I have something to do."

***

While the Luminaire oozes glitz, the Milk House screams disenchantment. I walk through the grimy alley, back to the place of my nightmares. The door bangs shut behind me. How soon I forgot how feet stick to this floor.

"Eleanora, you're back." Lady stops polishing her milk jars long enough to notice my makeup and long, swishy dress. She throws a towel over her shoulder. "And all made up." Her tired eyes have aged her more than I realized. "Is the Luminaire everything you dreamed it would be?"

The sad stage still holds an out of tune, dusty player piano. "Not sure yet."

"If there's something you'd like to say, can you get to it? My old bones would like a rest."

"You can give me room to someone else." I have no idea why I say this. I needed to step in here to prove that I've changed.

Lady lights her long, thin cigarette. "You've been at the Luminaire for less than a week. Why the rush?"

"I'm trusting my choices." I step closer, willing my tears to stay locked up. "Isn't that what you always taught me?" I'm bolstered by my post-panic calm and Ruby's story. It's the outsiders who ruin us.

"Why are you really here?" She seems exasperated, but her saffron turban over her gray curls serves as a reminder that Lady might live forever.

I bite the inside of my lip to buy time. "The Luminaire is something."

"It's your new home, kid." Her sass is as blatant as ever.

I spin a loose jacket button between my thumb and middle finger hard enough to pinch. "You know things."

"Yes," she says with a smile. "I do."

"The girls tell me it's like prison." I pause but of course, she gives nothing away. She's going to make me work for it. "But I see gorgeous outfits and a grand theater. Expensive booze flowing like fountains, and any partner a girl could want."

"Sounds like a dream." She lights another cigarette.

"Price doesn't want me there. He seems to hate me."

"Winston Price will use you and toss you aside when you no longer serve him. That's theater life."

"He hasn't even given me the chance to be used. I'm slightly offended." I shake my hair from my face as if I'm brimming with confidence.

"To succeed there, you'll need two things." Her necklace pendant is a vile of booze. One shot's worth. She throws it back and lets the empty glass dangle at her chest. "Thick skin and the ability to say, *Yes, sir.*"

I withhold the scream that claws at my chest. "His rules won't dictate my dance."

"And that's why he doesn't approve of you. Fiona once threw chocolate pudding in his face when he told her what to wear." Lady puffs on her cigarette, her eyes never leaving mine. "Nobody likes a woman with troublesome things like opinions and a voice."

"I'm tired of that label. *Fiona's daughter.* My name is Eleanora and I want to tap dance for myself, not for some money-obsessed owner with a creepy mustache."

"The Luminaire is big business, and magic is their goods. Price may have all sorts of terrible things in the works, but I guarantee his son is no victim."

I straighten up. "What terrible things?"

The door opens behind me where a wide-eyed Aria steps inside. I gather myself so I don't frighten her. "Hey, kid."

"Hi." She's hesitant, but happy to see me. We both look at Lady with scowls.

Lady sighs. "Aria. Again."

"She's not bothering anyone." I force my anger back in like a screw top on an overly filled bottle. "Aria, I need you to go home. I promise, I'll see you on Wednesday."

"Are you alright? You look sad."

I squeeze out a smile. "I'm great. Just catching up with Lady."

She looks between us. "Okay. But Lady, be kind. Eleanora is our big star now." Her child-like grin suggests she believes that fairy tale. She agrees and slinks back outside.

"Come on, Lady. She's just a kid."

"Aria is your shadow, not mine." She exhales. A momentary break in her crusty exterior. "Word on the street is Price is planning something more than a reinvented show. I don't know what."

"Will you tell me when you find out?" I smooth out my dress.

"Of course. I wouldn't send you there if I didn't think it was right."

I glance back at the pathetic farm animals in the worst front for a speakeasy this town has ever seen. "You really think I can do this?"

"I know it deep in my heart. You were meant for this."

Follow the rules and swallow my big opinions. I can force myself to do that.

I think.

CHAPTER TEN

Eleanora

Iridessa pushes me for hours. My mind conjures all the things Price might be planning, and I repeat *follow the rules* so many times the words become the background to my thoughts.

Tap, tap, tap. She keeps time like a metronome while I glide and stomp, beating out tap moves within an inch of their life. My feet ache, a thumping tenderness climbing up my shins.

"You need a break," she says.

"No, I don't." I conceal a wince as my cracked toes seep blood into my stockings. "I need to be magical." A dash of Fiona, with a healthy dose of me.

"Look." She spins me to face the mirror. "Pushing yourself too far is dangerous. Your body can take the heat, but there's no telling what will happen with your fire. I don't want you chasing Fiona's ghost."

"I've been chasing her my whole life."

Iridessa elongates her torso. Her chaînés create a whirling spin as a tornado of clouds envelops me in primary-colored light then softens around my arms and chest. When the cloud clears, Iridessa extends her arm in a révérence. A bow reserved for student to show respect for teacher at the end of our lesson. Today, she turns the tables.

She winks and prances off toward the gymnasium where rehearsal is in full swing.

Our first magic swell appears in childhood, usually at pivotal moments in hormonal shifts or our first attractions. We release gold, like an aura above our heads. Studios and theaters have strict rules since Prohibition. When mist halos over a dancer's head, she's deemed unstable, kicked out, reported to the police, and will spend her days releasing steam in speakeasies or alone by candlelight. Unless you're a Cleary. Our fire dance becomes a political matter.

It's best not to release it in the first place, but that never works out well. I tried to swallow mine. Wrangle the flames back inside. That only made me burn from the center of my core, and it makes my panic worse.

"What are you staring at?" Miles watches me from the doorway, and I snap to attention.

"How long have you been standing there?"

"Long enough to watch you daydream your way through something intense."

Damn my distracted brain. It too often forgets about the body it inhabits. "Why are you here?"

He crinkles his nose in a playful surprise. "It's time for our rehearsal."

"Since you don't stick to any sort of schedule, I can only assume you decide to find me whenever you're bored."

"I am a very busy man, Eleanora." He puffs out his bottom lip to resemble his father. With a low grumble in his voice, he adds, "I make stars out of magic girls and sell gin to their admirers."

"You must have made a killing, Mr. Price."

"Yes, well, this lousy son of mine wastes his time behind stage when he should learn the family business." He bows, one hand behind his back.

His easy smile doesn't match the sentiment, so I don't react.

"Right." He straightens and clears his throat. "I share too much. It's always been a problem."

"Says who?"

"Mr. Winston Price the third. I made my mother laugh, but she died years ago and now the mansion is so dull and serious." He holds his finger up. "There it is again. Sorry."

"You don't need to apologize." He seems nervous. Bumbling, almost. I quite like it. "The pompous man I met at the speakeasy had lots of opinions. I prefer this version."

"Sometimes I wonder which version of me I'll keep around." He turns me to face the mirror and rests his chin on my shoulder. "Moving on. You still have a long way to go, Eleanora. Your moves are stunning, but your confidence needs work."

"Iridessa tells me not to push myself." I flick his nose to get him off me.

Miles rubs his nose. "That's better. Use some of that anger. And don't worry, this exercise won't push you. We're going to find your dance voice."

"Dance voice?"

He tilts his head, smiling at my reflection, which cause my neck to flush pink.

"It's your unique sound, your thumbprint," he says. "Find the dance you were born with."

"Your father would not approve of free dance."

"Then let's not tell him." Gold rims glow in his marble eyes. Rings of fire I could jump through, if only I wouldn't get burned.

Men smile at me. Some even try to flirt. Until my cheeks redden, and my gold aura shines above my head. Once they know I'm a magic girl, they recoil. Miles hasn't turned his eyes from me once.

"Why did you look for a new member of the troupe?" I ask.

He shrugs. "We had to shut down. The threats were getting intense. In the restructuring, father demoted a few performers to the showgirl line and screamed that no one was sensational enough. He let slip that Fiona's daughter lived at a speakeasy around the corner."

How did he know? "That's a lot of pressure for a girl who passes out every time she stares at an audience."

He extends his hand. "Dance with me."

Just me and him, director and dancer. I'm nervous to stand cheek to cheek again, so I walk around the room and run my fingers through the props stacked on the far mirror. I gulp air behind a waterfall of gem-colored feather boas, staring at his easy gait, his sandy hair falling over one eye.

He spins past me as his shoulder brushes mine like a whisper. My breath hitches. He's teasing me to make me want him. Too late. That first act is already in full swing, begging for intermission. My forehead warms and there goes my halo. I swat at the air, but the gold crown remains, just like always.

I step out from the boas, letting one drape over my shoulder. "Give the crowd what they want, yes? Flirty and fun, just like Celtic Fire. Well, before she set the place aflame."

Miles pulls the boa in front of me as it flutters along my neck. He drops the mess of feathers to the ground and stands toe to toe with me. "Don't let the crowd decide. You choose who stands on stage."

My throat tightens, but I swallow hard against the pressure. Say something. Anything. "I'm trying." It's not eloquent, but it's true.

Miles extends his hand, palm up.

"What do you think you're doing with that?" I know exactly what he's doing, and I want nothing more than to touch my palm to his, but I'll be damned if I let him know that.

"I'm asking the most beautiful woman in the room to share a dance with me."

"I'm the only woman here, Miles."

He winks, the scoundrel. "You'll always be the most beautiful woman in any room."

A rush fills my head so full and dizzying I allow my hand to float to his. I bask in his eyes and arch my spine when his hand slides against the curve of my low back. His fingers draw a soft swirl on my skin.

A waltz. He lifts and lowers me like a wave, gliding me across the floor in a simple box step. Our steps move together as natural as smiling. My arm remains stiff. My gaze past his ear. His soft, luscious earlobe.

Alas, his peppermint scent and gentle touch shatter any pretense of my toughness. I want his touch. When I accept this rush, my halo disappears.

He pulls me close, cheek to cheek until my breath turns to a sigh. A sigh! Like I need a fainting couch. I allow my mouth to wander toward his neck. Bellies pressed together, our hips sway like tall grass.

Maybe I need that fainting couch after all.

He spins me, soft as a dream. He grips the back of my thigh and lifts, lowering me into a dip where I arch back to expose my neck.

I lift my gaze to his lips as they silently call for me, like a faraway birdsong. I've kissed men, but more out of curiosity. Miles's lips hint at something dangerous and thrilling. Our cheeks brush, our lips nearing like hands in the dark.

Suddenly, I remember who I am. How this swell of affection will turn my magic loose. My chest tightens like a loaded cannon. I can't breathe. No more lights and no more laughter. I wheeze through an episode unlike any I've ever felt. Like I want to scream but my tight throat won't allow me.

"I can't see. Everything's black." Panic thunders through me. I ball his shirt in my fists and shake, too terrified to cry. Although an episode hasn't killed me yet, it feels like it should. Like my heart can't possibly take the stress.

Miles holds his hands over mine as the light returns to my hazy eyes. "My legs hurt." It's all I can say.

"I'm right here." He pulls me close, and I collapse into him. Feeling rushes back into my body, but all I hear is the thumping of my angry, tired heart. Disappointment ripples through me. I grab my hair and rock in place, wishing I could be somewhere else. Something different than a Star Girl hurling toward an asylum.

I can't move forward, and I can't go back, which means I'm stuck right here in the thready hope that I can stop the hysteria. Fight the ridiculous purity warriors. Dreams of stardust tap against the sky while my life is tethered to the ground. Born inside me like a fireball raging, the wicked winds of an approaching end stare me down. A destiny I can no longer outrun.

I storm out of the rehearsal space as tears gather in my eyes. Miles rushes after me. "Eleanora, wait."

"No. This is exactly what I told you would happen and now I'm mortified." I turn to face him, so he sees my rage, then I continue stomping down the hall to the staircase.

He grabs my arm. "Our dance was beautiful."

"I see you, Miles. Push the tap dancer to her limits. Make her swoon. Force her to swell with magic. Who cares if she blows up in the process."

He jumps in front of me, hands up. "Just listen. If you want to run away after I speak, then fine."

"I want to run away now."

"Eleanora, we danced. And it was perfect. I understand your fear, I really do, but if you'll just trust me, we can get through this."

Flashes of my top hat send chills through my mind. The prismed floor, Miles's hands on my waist. It's enough to send me unconscious. "You want Celtic Fire."

"Wrong." He lowers his face eye to eye with me. "Metals, gems, lava, or whatever the hell else you spit out matters little to me. I just want you to find your moment."

"I panicked again."

"You think too much."

"Oh, well. Problem solved. Thank you for curing me, Mr. Price the Fourth." I roll my eyes, but he reaches his hand out again. When he looks at me like that, intrigue shoves all the hesitation aside. "How can I overcome the fear when I'll die young because of this thing inside me?"

He lowers his eyes. "I don't know."

"Fire has cursed me with a flash of brilliance that will only end in hysteria. I'll lose my mind just like my mother." Honesty hurts my throat. "And every other Fire Girl this world has ruined."

"I have something to show you," he says.

Hesitantly, I follow him through the dimly lit halls of the empty Luminaire to the entrance of the main theater. He leads me by the hand to a red velvet seat in the center back row. "Watch."

The orchestra hums to life with a flute. Stagehands carry out a trough of water. Sadie flutters with the music. Eyes closed, she holds her hands as if a snow globe sits between them. Her fingers wave and water droplets ascend from the tub, each one shining with crystalline light. She sashays and glides through ballet positions as her hands summon the illuminated water.

"Stunning," I whisper.

Miles watches me take in the show. Sadie bows, performing cartwheels on a wave of water as it carries her offstage.

The stage falls black and quiet. A shadow walks to center stage and takes position.

Ruby's fiddle starts soft as a whisper. Spotlights rise and settle on her tall, thin frame. Her wild hair is tied back under a silk scarf. She closes her eyes when she plays as magic inhabits her.

"Nothing scary about this," Miles says.

Ruby's body sways to the rhythm of her music. Haunting and dark, her fiddle seems to start a conversation. Mr. Price scowls at her with arms crossed.

"Why does your father look like his face might explode?"

Miles leans sideways to whisper in my ear and when his breath touches my neck, the swell of magic threatens to swallow me whole. "That's his warning face. He's going to kill me if things get out of hand. He wants control and I want you all to let the magic fly free. We've settled on somewhere in the middle."

Ruby pulls every note like the one time I saw a man making taffy on the boardwalk. The lights flicker, then shut off as Ruby quickens her pace, and the tune grows deeper, richer.

A stage bulb floods her with silver light. Set decorations flutter from every corner of the room. Smoke rises from her feet. String lights dance through the air and encircle her, bouncing to the rhythm as her head sways. A witch's hat spins over her head, shining light over her billowing black gown. Vines and roots from backstage maneuver their way under her shoes and lift her from the ground. They cradle her and she swings through the air, silver metallic dust spitting from her bow.

Her song is poetry without words. Lights drop over her head, a sky of illumination, and Ruby finishes her performance suspended in air like the magical woodland creature she is.

Miles leads me out to the lobby by gentle fingers pressed to my hand.

"Wait, I want to see what's next. They're amazing!"

He smiles, a hint of mischief in his eyes. "That was women performing a show for my father, where they practically bite back their talents to meet the image of a Luminaire star."

"That's what you saw? I thought they looked confident and strong. Not at all afraid of the magic that might explode from their fingernails or the hysteria that might chomp them bite by bite."

"Can you imagine what they could do if they actually let go, like I'm pushing them to do? If they danced for themselves and just tore the roof off this place?"

"The only one I've ever seen do that is my mother. And look how that turned out." Miles's exuberance falls every time I remind him we are little more than star creatures led by fear. I step close, my heart pattering high in my chest. "Why do you need this? What sort of question are you trying to answer?"

"If it's possible to be born with a fracture in your heart, like a bone that never heals." The honesty in his voice breaks a little something inside me.

I flash back to our last night in Chicago. I stood on that fire escape as strangers beat my mom bloody. I would have let them attack me too if it wouldn't have killed her to see it. After that, we jumped from town to town, both of us crumbling a little more with each stop. "I don't know, but if there's a fracture, it means you loved something so hard it broke."

"Sounds like you need this show as much as I do." He steps back, slides his hand from mine. "Goodnight, Diamond Nora. Until we dance again."

"Miles?" He glances over his shoulder, hesitant. "I don't think you share too much. I think you share just enough to make you human." I like that he spits out every thought in his head. I don't need to guess what he's hiding.

"Did I really make you swoon?" he asks with a smile.

"Go to sleep."

He nods. Hands in his pockets, he descends the stairs of the lobby and out to the brisk night drizzle toward his lonely mansion. And I let the memory of his touch swell excitement through my neck and up to my shining gold halo.

CHAPTER ELEVEN

Fiona
6 months post-Prohibition

Another town. Another Vaudeville theater.

It's my third show of the night. New Orleans reminds me of a ghost story come to life with statues that seem to watch my every move and moonlight that shines like chrome. Words hold spells here. It all makes my skin itch.

As the emcee calls my name, my insides sting with bottled heat. A glass canister about to crack. Nothing about the uninspired dance routine warrants applause, yet there they go clapping for my step into the spotlight. I hate every stage now, every three-minute jig like a slow death to my soul. Normal dance, just as my girl begged for. And it's killing me from the inside.

My gut tightens. My head throbs. Every step and shimmy compound the pressure in my core. Fire presses against my skin like a swollen foot in a shoe one size too small. Still, I dance. I force a smile and shake my tits. The director eyes me with a warning so I give everyone what they want: a peek at my knickers. One of these days I won't be able to control the pressure. Fire will shoot from my palms, and I'll land in prison. One thought of leaving Eleanora alone straightens me right up. I bow and shoot the crowd a cheeky wink before strutting offstage past the director.

"Hey, Fiona," he says with a breathy whistle. "You want to have some fun tonight?"

Nothing about this performance gives me a high. In fact, I've never felt so low. "Can't. Kid at home."

"Come on." His eyes drag over my heaving chest as I catch my breath. "You really killed out there tonight. Let me thank you." He licks his lips. "Properly."

"You can thank me by handing over my paycheck. And don't stiff me this time."

The director never glances at the tattooed man or the singing twins, but the dancers are constantly smacking hands away. He flips the tassels of my skirt. "You know you want me."

I flick his hand away from the top of my thigh. "I've been groped by a great many directors. Every one of them has lived to regret it. I bite. Hard."

He slaps a ten in my palm and places a toothpick between his teeth. "You're a tough broad."

I slip the bill in my bra. "You have no idea." I swallow the heartburn that stings my throat and shake the smoke from my fingertips. Once a director gets too comfortable, I'm done for. We'll be on to the next town by tomorrow morning.

I gather my belongings and head out the side door into the alleyway. Thick, wet air sends a bead of sweat down the back of my neck. We're renting a room one block away from the theater and I only need to leave Eleanora for a few hours at a time. She's tough but doesn't see it yet. I worry she'll never use that voice of hers though I know she can roar.

Once inside, I find her asleep, her tap shoes tucked next to her abdomen. No teddy bears for this kid. I sit on the bed, trying to pull them away, but she grips them in her sleep. Her eyes peek open. "Oh, I thought I dropped them."

"You love those shoes, don't you?"

She rubs her eyes. "Yeah. Taps on a wood floor is the best sound in the entire world."

I lie in bed next to her and tuck her hair behind her ear. "Maybe someday we'll find you a stage to tap on."

"No way." She unties the ribbons and ties them again. Knot. Bow. "I've seen what it's done to you."

"It isn't the audience that hurts me." Come to think of it, the audience may be what saves me. Nothing is more exhilarating than when they see me in my whole, real state of fire. "This magic ban is temporary, Eleanora. You should do what you're made to do... perform."

"But my magic." She sits up, eyes still fixed on the shoes. "Every time fire spits from my palms something happens."

I pull from my own well of knowledge. "The heat in your belly?" She shakes her head. "Smoking fingertips?" We've talked over the details enough times. "What still scares you?"

Her eyes spring with tears. "I think there's something wrong with me."

"Nothing is wrong with you, Eleanora. You're gifted, just like my grandmother, and years of women in our family. It's our job to keep history moving. Dance and fire."

"Even when the country makes laws against us?" She yanks the shoes and wraps the ribbon around her finger.

She's always been so quiet, but this moment gives me a rare glimpse inside her heart. Don't mess this up. "Yes. Even then."

Her entire body recoils. "My chest."

"What's wrong with your chest?"

"It seizes." Her breathing grows rapid and shallow. "When flames appear, my heart beats so hard it rattles my bones. My chest hurts like someone has punched me, and I can't breathe. The stupid magic is going to kill me. I'm certain of it."

"Oh." Her words unlock a memory I'd long forgotten. The year of menstruation where magic causes a halo for the first time. My body felt foreign. Blood and the intense need to dance with fire. A sense that I held something special, yet the world told me I was wrong. "It's fear, baby. Nothing more."

"Nothing less." Her gray eyes hold such hope, though they appear bloodshot and glassy.

"You won't hurt anyone."

"I know that." She digs her fingers into the toe of the shoe. "But everyone threatens us."

"Yeah, that's life as a magic dancer. We've always been okay, haven't we?"

"Those people beat you, Mama." The tip of her nose glows red. "The kids back in Chicago called me wrong. Dangerous. Ever since these new laws, I just can't make the magic feel safe."

"We've always been alright on our own. As long as we have each other—"

"I want more." Every sentence she speaks shocks me deeper and deeper. "I want friends. I want a family who doesn't pick me up and move me every three days."

My instinct is to snap *You want another mother, is that it?* but I know she's hurting. "I'm sorry. I don't think you understand." I won't tell her how men corner me. How they grab my thigh even when I fight them off.

"Let's just pick somewhere and stay. Please? I need friends. I don't know how to talk to people. I sit here and will myself not to dance, but my limbs seem to need movement like my lungs need air. I'll die if I don't dance. Then I tap and the world feels right, you know?" She wipes her under eyes with the sleeve of her nightgown. "Then the flare of my chest starts. The fire always comes with panic."

She's afraid she'll become me.

"Oh, sweetheart." I reach for her, desperate to hug the doubt away, but knowing I can't. She turns from me, arms crossed. "Do you want to perform?"

"Of course I do!" She flops to the side of the bed, looking up at me with giant, stormy blue eyes. "I've watched you bring every stage to life. The way people stare at you, like you're made of golden light. I want to be like that."

"Are you waiting until Prohibition lifts? Hoping one day we'll be welcomed to every stage in the country? It's not going to happen."

She rubs her fingers with force along the shape of her eyebrows and down her cheeks. "Why does life have to be this way? Even before we left Chicago, we were outcasts. Shunned for our stupid halos and shoes of fire."

"That's why I chose Magic Dance, even though the pay was barely enough to live on. I'd rather be poor doing what I love. Besides, if every law out there says that I can't sling magic, I'm still going to because… fuck 'em."

"I'm not as strong as you. I'll never be good enough or pretty enough. People will hate us, they'll abuse us, and your legacy will die with me. I can't do it!" She buries her face in the blanket, her breath hitching between sobs. I've never seen her like this.

I rub her back with a soft open palm. "We can make ourselves smaller, but the fear won't go away." I move her hair and lean down to catch the corner of her eye. She sits up, face puffy and eyes rimmed red. "Baby, the world won't be kind. All you can do is find the thing your heart wants and go grab it."

"What if my heart is lying to me?"

"Oh, well. That's part of the deal. Falling in love with someone or something just opens another type of heartache. You can't run from pain. Living a lie is its own type of hurt."

Silent, accepting tears fall down her cheeks, but no sobs or strangled breath. "How do I dance for an audience when the fire will only cause me to die young?"

"The performance doesn't kill us, the fire does. And I believe you'll end that cycle."

"I will? How?"

"I don't know, I saw it in the stars." I can't explain it, I just know she's meant to live a long life and change the world. I've always known. I hold her chin in my hand. "Don't fight who you are and never apologize for being different, you hear me?"

She nods and throws her arms around me. Nothing can break us when we're like this. Together, alone, and bonded by fire. I hold her and tuck her in, rubbing her forehead until she drifts back to sleep.

At the tiny window, I stare at the moon as a black shadow shades its silver light. Fire builds in my core. Sometimes, the need is so great I lose all sight of reason. I spin and breathe fire into the dark kitchen, leaving a trail of soot across the yellowed wallpaper. It's not enough. The hunger grows. I need to perform.

I leave a note that says *Went out for an hour.* I slip out the door, double check the lock, and slink down the stairs toward the street. The secret bar calls me. I swear I can hear it whistle. Speakeasies have popped up all over the country. I've dipped in a few here and there, but tonight, I can't resist the promise of a shot of gin and a spinning ring of fire.

At the door in the alley, I knock three times. A man peers out a sliding grate no larger than my head. "Yeah? Password?"

"I don't know. But I fire dance, and I can give you one hell of a show."

One glance down at my show dress makes his decision, and he glides the door open. The smell of musty booze and body heat lure me down the dimly lit hallway and a flight of stairs. The faint tap of a jazz rhythm sets my heart thumping. Through another door a whoosh of hot air blasts my face. Sweat and gin and magic welcome me home.

Two women dance the tango, sliding their feet along the floor in glorious extensions. Their backs bend and limbs extend as their crimson dresses spark with diamonds and citrine. Their hair sparkles with gems that tinkle to the grounds as their legs wrap around each other. Not quite as dangerous as fire dance, yet their elemental sexual heat still turns patrons feral. They've been pushed underground with us.

"What can I get you, doll?" The bartender winks. My body reacts to his warm smile.

I lean over the edge of the bar close to his face. "Shot of gin."

He raises his eyebrows. "Alright." While he glugs the booze into a dainty glass, I can't help the wiggle in my hips and the fire deep in my belly. He slides me the shot. I grab the glass and shoot the liquor back in one swoop. Hot, burning, forbidden juice snakes a trail down my throat.

As the tango dancers take their bow, my feet carry me to the stage. I don't care if I'm allowed. I need applause. I extend my arms to silence, take a deep breath, and sigh. "Good evening, friends. I am here to bring you the delight of Chicago. The best fire dance you've ever seen. My name is Fiona, and I am the fire starter goddess, Celtic Fire!"

My flames erupt instantly. A swallowed heat that's exploded toward oxygen. Orange fire sizzles from my feet. I start with my hips and add my arms, drinking in the goodness of fire coursing through me. My head spins, and my cheeks burn through delicious, sensuous dance.

A fire ring descends around me and lifts me from the ground as I spin balls of flames in my palms. The fire doesn't burn me but grows hot enough to threaten that it might. The danger of it all leaves me hungry for that bartender with the strong chest and amber eyes.

I leap from the flames and land in the splits, spitting fire from my heaving breath. Then, the moment. Blissful silence. Pure calm. Cheers erupt. Their praise and approval feed my fire until it retreats. I drink it like a river of gold.

Men stare at me open-mouthed while women stare in awe. I've won them over. They love me. I could swim in this forever.

Back at the bar, I lay my hand on the barkeep's arm. "Don't worry, I won't burn you."

"Yeah, you will." He smiles, though I catch a hint of disdain.

I pull my hand away. What does he think of me?

"You're beautiful," he says. "Sexier than any woman in here." I don't respond. "But I don't date your kind."

"Who said anything about dating?" I only need him for a few minutes. I never let them stay any longer than necessary.

"I loved one of you before Prohibition. Your fire makes you unpredictable. I'll never get tangled up with another as long as I live."

Unpredictable. Please. "You think all Fire Girls are the same?" The heat in my belly cools.

"Yeah, I do. I've seen enough of you in here the past six months. You set the place on fire and search for some lonely fool to use for the night. You're floozies. You ruin everything you touch."

The heat in me long gone, I place my hand on my hip. "If she left you, perhaps the problem was you."

He wipes the already clean bar top as his cheeks burn pink. "This place wasn't enough for her. She had to take her shot at stage life again. The way your kind needs a spotlight has never made sense to me."

I don't get it. "No above ground theaters allow us anymore."

"There's one."

I don't know this woman, but I already understand her. She followed the spotlight we were made for.

"I see it in your face. You want it too, don't you?"

"She must have lied to you. Prohibition made us illegal."

He reaches under the bar and comes up with a newspaper article from *The Seattle Times*. I spin the paper and read the headline:

Famous Luminaire Fights the Law.

Theater owner Winston Price refuses to follow the new Prohibition law. He touts freedom as a tenet to theater life. Some say he needs money. Others say he's using the Star Girls. One thing's for sure, Winston Price knows people in government. He lawyered up, managing to create an exempt zone in his theater for booze and magic. The caveat? The Luminaire isn't controlled by the government. It's a lawless land inside those walls where anything could happen to the performers or the audience. Attend at your own risk.

By the time I look up to meet the bartender's eyes, my decision is made. "Good luck here, pal. You won't be able to resist these women.

Their curves, their laugh. You'll return to them again and again until you can't live without our heat."

"Enjoy Seattle," he says.

I smooth my hair. My fire has settled, my body is calm. Enjoy Seattle. That is just what I intend to do.

CHAPTER TWELVE

Eleanora

Control the bleed.

Now that I live inside the walls of the Luminaire, my new philosophy isn't the words on the gold plaque out front, but the need deep in my body. The remembrance of what my mother felt and how she believed in me. Today, I'll let the blood of fire drop from my skin as a slow burn.

As I wait for Iridessa, the top hat releases a band of light from the prop trunk. I turn my back, ignoring the whispers of Magic Dance tempting me like a drug. I won't be seduced by the promise of magic glory.

Toe, heel. Tap, rock. My feet take on their own rhythm, guiding my body through dance with bent knees, rooted to the sound of metal clinking against wood planks.

Halfway through a dozen barrel rolls, Iridessa's voice appears. "You look different."

I won't tell her about my burst of magic or how Miles held me like we were born to move together. How our dance left me with a warm buzz on my skin that beckons the fire inside. "Settling in, I guess."

"Good. You deserve to be here." She glides over to me. "Let's begin."

Iridessa taps a rhythm, and I follow through warmup. Always ballet. Always controlled. Just like her. She rubs her hip when she thinks I'm not looking. During a water break, she winces.

"Are you in pain?" I ask.

"Growing old comes with many surprises. I do not recommend it."

"You still dance beautifully."

Iridessa lengthens her neck, watching herself in the mirror. "While you're fighting to find something, I dance to hold on to everything."

She holds position, waiting for me to join. "You've done it," I say. "You dance like a meteor shower while your mind stays clear as glass. How do you do it?"

Her jaw pulses. "I just dance."

I still haven't taken position. "What's the secret?"

"Eleanora, there's a protocol here. I teach, you follow. Now stop talking. The answer is always in your movements. Dance first, magic second. Understanding comes last."

"Please—"

Before I can let the frustration settle into my body, an older Star Girl pokes her head through the door. "Eleanora, Mr. Price wants to see you."

This can't be anything good.

I memorize the wood grain at Price's office, willing myself to knock but finding it nearly impossible. Price opens the door, his teeth clanking on a wood pipe. "Are you just going to stand there?"

"That was my plan, yes."

"Come in." It's an order, not a request. He gestures to a green leather chair with nail head trim. I tuck my skirt behind my knees, remembering to keep my back tall like Iridessa has taught me.

"What did you want to see me about, sir?"

"It's no secret I don't want you here, Eleanora." Like a punch to the temple, he took me out in the first swing. "You're a liability, just like your mother was."

While words elude me, my body has no trouble finding rage in every fiber.

"Something happens to magic dancers when they reach a certain age. They push until they can no longer control their abilities."

Breathe, Eleanora, or you may do something brash like toss the closest paperweight at his face. "We all know our fate, Mr. Price, you need not remind me I will lose my mind and die young."

I suddenly realize every woman in this place is under twenty-five. He keeps them young and compliant, adding to the country's fears over aging magic girls. Toss them out before they become a problem.

"You're right. I let them go when they become unruly. That usually happens around thirty. Sometimes later, depending on how compliant the woman is."

Compliant. What a word. What a stupid, stupid word. "I have my problems, but you know I'm half Fiona. You can't control me."

"Fiona wasn't like the rest of you." He shakes off what appears to be a moment of regret. "If she would have just let me direct her, she wouldn't have fallen apart."

Once again, too stunned to speak. Wait, no I'm not. "I've been in this chair for all of two minutes and you've managed to insult me, my mother, and every performer in this building."

He bites his lip, seemingly both irritated and impressed by me. "Your mother was brilliant for a short while. Truly spectacular." He leans back in his chair and puffs on his pipe.

"What is it you want from me, sir?"

"He tosses a pile of letters to the desk in front of me. "See that? It's my daily threat from the city and the damn churches who own them. They'll do anything to ruin our exemption."

"That's not my problem."

"But it is." Price tucks his bottom lip under his teeth and glides it back out. "Magic only flows here because of promises and lots of money. If you go wild, it will prove we can't manage you."

I swallow what I really want to say which is, *no, you'll never tame me*. This is why I shrank away in a dark underground kitchen. At least that was on my terms. "What will happen to us if the city wins?"

"You know exactly what would happen."

Of course I do, but I need to hear him say it.

"You'd all become homeless or imprisoned," he says. "Institutionalized. Purity sweeps like we've never seen. We keep magic in front of the public, reminding them you have a place here."

"You don't think I can tell when I'm being manipulated?"

Price smiles. "My son struggles with focus and drive. He's paid little interest to our family business since coming home from that ridiculous circus, but when you arrived, he finally seemed to care, so I agreed." He inhales so loud the air whistles through his nostrils. "You have danger in your bones and an inheritance of fire."

Weak men with power and money. This man is nothing new. "I'm here to keep your son invested in the Luminaire but the moment I step out of line, you'll have me arrested."

"Not arrested, but I will do *anything* to control this theater," he says with a dark gleam in his eye. "Miles will fix your stage fright, and I will protect you from the monsters. Just don't explode like Fiona did. We need your fragile little mind to cooperate."

When you go head-to-head with the ringleader, prepare to have your skull cracked. "I know you're planning something."

"We're done here, Miss Cleary." He waves his hands to dismiss me, but I don't move. I'm both frozen and defiant, wondering which will triumph.

"I don't think we are."

"Really?" He stands, looking down with doubt at my veneer of momentary confidence.

"I've been on my own long enough to know I don't need your protection." I rise with purpose, staring at him with every ounce of anger I carry, before turning to walk out through trembling knees.

"But that depends on your episodes, doesn't it?" I hold the door still, palm gripping the knob. "Sadie's depends on her strangled breathing. Ruby is a mountain witch, and that makes her a perpetual outsider." He slides his hands in his pockets, as if he isn't one bit bothered about crushing me once again. "Every one of you is already a prisoner in your own body."

Miles insists I let my magic loose while his father warns me to rein it in. "I know this theater is nothing without us, and you know it too."

The realization hits me. We all struggle with ourselves. But what if we've merely been miseducated? What if the world is full of liars, and we're the only honest ones?

CHAPTER THIRTEEN

Eleanora

Iridessa looks down on Second Avenue as we eat our breakfast. I'm still knotted up over my meeting with Price yesterday, so I don't notice the muffled screams outside.

"Those women think they're saving purity." Iridessa crosses her arms.

I join her at the window to see four women in bustled dresses buttoned up to their necks. They're holding signs that read, "Eradicate Sin" and "Magic Welcomes the Devil."

"They don't care about saving anyone," I say. I know this, but she stares with fear washed over her eyes.

Iridessa's cheeks pull as taut as rubber bands. "We have double the sin. Alcohol *and* Magic Dance."

I can't imagine this ballerina intimidated by these frail women with hand-written signs. "Celtic Fire loomed over me like a curse, and I still wanted it. Well, so did working as a dishwasher, but hey, we all make stupid choices, right?"

She shoots me a side stare, head cocked. "What?"

"I'm just saying, I'm not above making stupid choices. I would gladly take out a few teetotaling broomsticks."

She breaks a smile. "They aren't worth it." Her face doesn't move, yet I sense her worry by how her eyes shift.

"Iridessa," I place my hand on her wrist. "We're safe in here, right?"

She turns to glance at the room of Star Girls with a motherly concern that makes my stomach seize. "Finish up, ladies. It's time for rehearsal."

Sadie links arms with me, her labored breathing wheezing in my ear. "I heard Price gave you his little welcome talk."

"There was nothing welcoming about it."

Zelda knocks into my other hip. "You're a liability and lucky to have this amazing opportunity before your life implodes in a few years when you're over the hill. Is that right?"

"Sums it up."

"And he probably threw in some guilt about your family and all the things that make you ill-equipped for the big, bad world of Prohibition, but the Luminaire will give you a soft place to land—as long as you do what he wants."

We move to single file as we hurry down the stairs to the gymnasium. "I wanted to punch him," I say.

"Yeah, we all do," Zelda says. "Think of all those Star Girls kicked out of here before they hit thirty. Some were still in their prime, but Old Man Price didn't want the liability."

"Miles practically licked his father's boots before you came along." Sadie breathes into a paper bag for three quick breaths. "We wanted to punch him too."

Zelda tucks her hands under her chin and with an eye flutter, says, "Oh, Eleanora. Your tap dancing makes me weak! I want to thrust you against a wall and kiss those full, red lips until I forget all about my stuffy, boring, rich boy life."

I can't get mad at Zelda, she's too lovely. "Stop."

"But I can't stop." She grabs me by the shoulders, her eyes wide. "I need you, Diamond Nora. Without you, I'll just be another kid trying to prove to daddy I'm a big boy."

"Miles is more than that. He's been through some hard times."

"Please." Zelda swats the air. "We've all been through the wringer. Miles stands by as his father berates us. He wants one thing: his inheritance."

"Oh." I'm not sure if I want to scream or cry or run away. Perhaps all three. Of course that's why he sought me out that first night. Money. Any excitement I had deflates like an unknotted balloon.

"You alright?" Ruby asks.

"Fine." Other than this deep ache in my heart that spreads through my chest, I'm fine.

Iridessa claps several times. "Annelise, you're up."

The shy singer I've noticed but never spoken to shuffles to the center of the room. Annelise breathes a cloud of white from her pale coral lips. Her chest heaves and fingers fidget with her dress.

Ruby whispers to me. "Our blind singer Annelise can belt a tune like you've never heard."

The stage becomes a variegated web of color. Jewel tones flicker under our feet as we gasp. Annelise smiles. "I feel the color." She sings. A smooth, rich tone of soprano that reminds me of chocolate mousse.

Annelise leans into her voice, belting notes into the old gymnasium. Her voice comes from somewhere ethereal deep in her soul. The room transforms into a light show of rainbows. Raindrops appear, fat in the air above her head. Bouncing and rattling to the tenor of her voice, the droplets evaporate with a plunk.

Sadie turns to me. "I can always breathe better when she sings."

With a burst of light, snow flutters from the sky, but not a flake is white. Flurries of gemstones the same color as the stage flutter from the ceiling, which has now turned emerald, like the aurora borealis. In the distance, a flickering Milky Way winks at me.

Her performance leaves us mesmerized. Transformed. Magic doesn't seem haunting. At this moment, it seems like the one thing that can lift us to the stars. And I've been hiding from it for years.

Annelise can feel color. It's brilliant. But just as soon as joy lifts me, reality crashes me to Earth with my favorite painful vision.

While Annelise sings beauty into the world, I sit in the memory of a slow, precise blade splitting a magic dancer's forearm in two.

***

My second Wednesday at the Luminaire. I all but forget Aria again, until the cook brings a tray of cookies outside for the beggar kids, and I glimpse her in the swarm.

Like a balloon who never loses air, she bobs around my life, waiting for a speck of attention. It feels as if she's always been there. It wasn't long ago that I, too, slept alone under a rain-splashed awning, dreaming someone would care.

I pull her away from the other kids, a jacket covering my elaborate gown. Aria's dark braids bounce against her shoulders as we run down the alley. "Did you see those cookies? Big as my fist!"

I reach into my pocket and pull out another sugar cookie. "Here, I snagged another one for you."

"Careful, I'll never leave this place." She devours it in three bites.

"Are they feeding you enough at the orphanage?"

"All the mushy oats my heart desires." She licks the buttery crumbs from her fingers. "I get enough. It's just always bland. And mushy."

Her orphanage life cuts straight through to my sympathy bone. I can't believe I've left her alone at the Milk House where Lady seems to ignore her. I don't get why she's so cold with her.

"Thanks!" She props her hands on her hips. "Are you the biggest star of the theater yet?"

"No. Not by a longshot." I crack my knuckles, a sweet shot of release through my tightened hands. "The Star Girls are incredible. I don't know what I'm doing here."

She twists her hips, a giant grin lighting up her face. "I do."

"I can't wait to hear. Go on."

"You're not here for them. You're here for you."

Instead of the expected answers of glitz and glamor and the performance of a lifetime, she knocks me over with a bomb of truth. "I should be."

"I believe in you. Lady believes in you. That director picked you out of hundreds of magic girls. The only one who doesn't believe is you."

I stretch my stiff neck to examine the hazy sky. Light from the neon marquee swallows any glittering stars from sight. "My brain is different from yours, Aria. It's different from everyone's."

"How so?"

I scratch my fingers along my scalp and settle my hands on my shoulders while I think of how to describe the frenzied circus that is my mind. "Well, I have this intense, deep knowing that no one will ever break me, yet here I am, constantly cracking. The tension between the two makes me unstable at best. Panicked at worst."

"But I still love you, no matter what." She throws her arms around me. As if a hug from her can fix everything. I don't know, maybe it can.

A blast of fire throws us against the wall. Two men tumble like rocks down the alley. Once my head stops spinning, I hear a woman scream. Aria pulls me up, seemingly unfazed by our knock into the bricks. "Someone's in trouble," she says.

She jumps over the men curled on their sides moaning. I run after her, worried what she'll find. "Aria, wait." I manage my way to the corner where she stares in shock.

A speakeasy dancer cries as two men rip off her tap shoes. She kicks one in the stomach. He's so enraged he balls his fist back as if he might punch her.

Not while I have fire in my palms, he won't.

I throw Aria back and stomp until tap shoes appear on my feet. They all turn to watch the sound. I throw off my jacket, tap and spin until my palms produce fire. The men snarl at me. I think they may turn away, but then I see the dancer's face. Streaked black eye makeup and a ripped dress. The darkness in me explodes, bursting forth as a fireball.

Balls of flames roll in my palms, and I keep dancing. Keep tapping and leaping. The girl recoils, knowing what's about to happen. With a leap, I throw my hands toward the men. Their skin blackens with powdery soot.

Their screams almost turn my anger to regret, but the girl grabs her shoes back and places them on. "Thanks."

We watch them roll and groan. "What did I just do?" I ask.

"You saved my ass." She shimmies and twists and the shoes appear back on her feet.

"What happened? Did they do a purity raid?"

"No." She looks over her shoulder. "I shouldn't tell you."

I grab her before she can run away. "I just burnt two men to save you. Now talk."

"The burns are minimal. They'll be fine." She pulls her silk gloves to her elbows. "I work for a group of men. I don't know who so don't ask. They hire us out to parties and dinners. Magic and dance with a little extra show of leg. No big deal."

Aria appears behind me. I wrap my hands around her ears. "Go on."

"Tonight, I ended up dancing for the mayor."

"The mayor? The one who upholds laws that deem us illegal?"

"The very one." She reaches for her crumpled velvet cape and wraps herself to cover every inch of her crimson fringe dress. She rubs her temples. "I'm still all worked up." She shakes her feet as the tap shoes morph into regular heels. "That's better."

The men stop groaning as their faces clear and the soot disappears.

"Come on." We follow her through the streets, back to a stairwell leading below an Italian restaurant. "Those men followed me when I left the party. They tried to grab me and force me into their car for a private show. It's just how it is. I'm trying to make money, you know?" Her shaking hand lights a cigarette from her purse. "It's a cat-and-mouse game out here. I'm sure you get it. It's not like we are some of those lucky broads from the Luminaire."

"You better get inside," I tell her.

"You, too. Hey, thanks again. Too many of us get sent away for nothing. Thanks to you, I get to dance another day." She winks. "Careful with that fire. That's why they're afraid of us."

Aria yanks at my sleeve. "I'm heading back to the Milk House. Lady said I could wash dishes in your absence." She holds my arm. "I'm proud of you, Nora."

In five minutes, I'm back in the safety of my rooftop, listening to policemen comb the city. I presume they're looking for another speakeasy dancer and not one of the well-behaved Luminaire starlets. I've never used fire like that before, though I wanted to that terrible morning back in Chicago. Damn, it felt good.

The door clicks open as my friends stumble out wrapped in blankets.

"We brought wine to warm you while you stargaze." Zelda pops a cork. Sticky bubbles flow over her hand. She slurps them up and hands me the bottle.

"I think it's kind of lovely that you lie out here at night." Sadie wraps herself in a fur blanket, her lips outlined in pale blue. "Even if it's to a background of police sirens. Did you hear? A Fire Girl burned a few drunks."

I swig from the bottle as the sweet liquid dances on my tongue. "They probably deserved it." I can't believe I burned them. Is my decline starting already?

Sadie releases a thready cough. "I heard Miles tell his father you'll be the hit of New Year's Eve."

"I know what Miles wants out of me. I'm not certain I can deliver."

Sadie forces a deep inhale. "The city will want to see what raw, unfiltered magic looks like, but Price will prove he can tame you like a lion in a cage. Just like he's done to us."

These three incredible women exchange glances as I hold back tears. "I saw your rehearsals. You're amazing." I'm jealous as all get out, and now I'm worried I could hurt everyone I care about. Mother's hysteria didn't begin this young and here I have already burned two men.

Zelda gulps from the bottle and stops to catch her breath. "I want to shine while I can. We can push back against Price, his rules, and the terrible laws outside this place. And won't it be a wild ride?"

"A little fun before we crumble and have nothing left for the world," Ruby says.

I stare fruitlessly at the sky for any glimpse of the Milky Way. "Our lives are like shooting stars." I want to believe that magic can be more than a blaze across the sky. Maybe it's the answer to everything.

CHAPTER FOURTEEN

Eleanora

I practiced all night in the gymnasium, tapping until dawn flooded the stained-glass windows with jewel-colored light. I withheld every speck of magic and danced through aching feet and bruised toes, just as my mother did in those months before we landed in Seattle. She was right, holding fire at bay makes my insides revolt.

As I walk out to morning light, I hear Miles behind me. "Cleary. Get some sleep and meet me at noon." I don't look back. Too tired and weary.

Hours later, a bird wakes me by tapping on the window next to my bunk. Twilight casts a hazy blue darkness, and I don't care that I ignored Miles's orders or missed my session with Iridessa. I'm too worried and questioning what the hell I'm doing here.

I stretch my sore limbs and yawn before stepping into a coral satin blouse and sleeking my hair with Brilliantine. A puff of makeup powder and pink rouge reminds me I am a dishwasher no more. The older I get, the more I see my mother in the mirror. Her icy blue eyes and her deep black locks. I'm taller though, presumably a trait from my father—whoever he is. All I know is he's the man who first took my mother's heart and initiated a magic swell that led to a tsunami.

"They don't understand us, Nora girl," she used to say. "Love makes us magical, and men want to dull the shine when they can't handle the brightness."

Miles's touch made me want to fly. But I don't need a man to break my heart. Life has done that enough already.

I step onto the sixth-floor fire escape to take in the crisp fall night as the city comes to life below. My mother loved to dance in the partial illumination of the blue hour. Mostly, I think she loved the downtime between shows where she could swig booze and bring me to the rooftop to dream about dance wherever we wanted, in the cities or in the woods, on stage or in the middle of any city street.

A future she wouldn't live to see.

And just like that, the blue hour dissipates.

An impatient knock on the window doesn't surprise me. "Eleanora?" Miles's voice rattles with impatience. "I'm opening the window."

"Fine." Possibilities swirl. If he angers me, could I lose control and hurt him? The thought reminds me why I withheld my fire this long. Too bad that only created a ball of panic looking for something to release the pressure.

He clicks the window open, holding it at arm's length. "Good grief. What are you doing out here?" He looks as if he may faint.

"Taking in the city lights." I'm building a scaffold on sand, as people I care about climb up the rungs. When it all comes tumbling down, they'll realize I never had the skills to build anything.

"No. It's too high. You could fall."

Why is he acting so weird? "I'm sitting on a fire escape."

"You missed rehearsal. Are you alright?"

"I needed sleep."

"Oh." He tries to step out to meet me but goes pale. "Please, come inside." He groans between every utterance, grimacing like it hurts. "Your feet. They're just—hanging there."

I turn to stare at his narrow brow and pulsing neck. "Are you afraid of heights?"

"Don't be ridiculous. I'm *terrified* of them." Beads of sweat gather on his temples.

"Then go inside. I love to sit high above the city in the crisp night air." I yank off a loose button from my jacket and hold it over the edge of the railing. I drop it and count for five long seconds until it clangs on the pavement several stories below. "I can think out here."

Miles clears his throat and steps one foot through the window to the fire escape. "I'm coming out there." He stops to breathe, reciting something over and over with eyes closed as he hesitantly crawls his other leg out.

"You don't have to."

"Yes, I do." His voice raises high, like a warbly flute.

"If you're going to faint, put your head between your knees. Don't make me save you like a damsel in distress."

He does as I say, his face white as snow. He slides to all fours and groans. "How many stories up are we?"

"Six."

"Oh, God." He flattens onto his stomach and turns his face toward me. He grips the metal grate hard enough to bleed. "Is this close enough?"

"I guess."

"Good. You might need to peel me off this thing before the storm rolls in."

"Why are you out here if you're so scared?"

He closes his eyes, breathing rapidly. "Why did you skip practice today?"

"I told you. I was tired." Can't he see how terrified I am?

"You're pulling away, and I don't understand." He catches a glimpse of the alley far below and swallows with a grimace, as if he has a swollen tongue. A window across the alley slides open and his entire body jumps. "Has the grate broken?"

"You're useless." I stand and step over him.

"Please, wait."

Watching him face down on the grate, trying to help me, forces my deepest worry to the surface. "Are you using me to get your inheritance?" He doesn't mutter a sound. "Miles?"

"I can't move." His voice quivers in between whines. "Is this how your episodes feel?" He buries his face in his arm, shaking his neck back and forth.

A spark of sympathy catches fire, snuffing out the digging claws of fear that always seem hooked into my chest.

I roll him to his back. His eyes are wide and terrified. "Come on. The incoming storm could start shaking the metal."

"Very encouraging." His lips quiver.

I sit him up and wrap my arms around his waist. His back muscles are tense, and his breath beats against my neck. "Bend your knees," I tell him.

"I can't."

My episodes steal all control and safety. Like the world is spinning so fast I want to disappear. I wouldn't wish that on anyone. "Okay. We'll wait here until you're ready."

The world slows as the city quiets to a hush. My chest thumps against his as if my heart is knocking on the door to his. Thunk. Thunk. He buries his forehead in my shoulder and his hair tickles my neck. I pull him closer. Tighter. If anything should give me an episode, it's this. The director's lips on my neck. But somehow, an episode is the farthest thing from my body right now.

"Okay," he mutters. "I'm ready. But can I keep my cheek against yours?"

"Yes, you can." I help him stand, his legs trembling. "You keep surprising me, Miles. I didn't expect you to be like this," I say.

"Like what, weak?"

"No, human." Rain patters the fire escape, settling moisture into our hair and shivered faces. "Did this fear start after," I pause, "the fall at the circus?"

He nods.

My arms wrap tighter around him of their own accord. There's a specific pain to having your destiny yanked from your grasp. I know it all too well.

We stand together, his arms draped over my shoulder blades, under the quiet hum of the Luminaire's neon lights. "I'll help you," I say.

I step backward and wait for his foot to follow, like the world's slowest dance. When I pull back, he pulls closer. I forget he's Miles Price, and we become just two frightened souls holding each other under a slate-colored Seattle twilight.

We scramble inside the window as he catches his breath. Once he shakes off the fear, he stands tall and lifts his chin. "I hate when I panic like that."

"I know the feeling."

His hand still on my hip, our eyes locked in a frenzy of emotion, my damn halo lifts from my hair. All this vulnerability. His tenderness.

His arms dangle at his sides almost asking for another embrace. "To answer your question, no, I'm not using you for my inheritance." His glistening eyes stare at the sky before rolling his gaze back to me. "I'd give it all up to keep you safe."

"No one can keep me safe, Miles. I'm staring down a bitter end to this ride, and the only armor I have is what my mother tried to teach me: Don't fight who you are and never apologize for being different." Oh, how those words twist a deep ache into my chest.

He glides his finger across my cheek, wiping away the moisture under my eye. "I'm sorry for asking you to risk so much."

"You gave me the opportunity, but being here is my choice." His fingers still graze my cheek. His eyes set on mine. I take his face in my hands and raise up on my toes, pressing my lips to his as a different kind of fire shoots though my limbs. Eyes closed, soul ablaze, I kiss him until the want forces me to catch my breath.

I'm not fighting who I am, but she still scares me.

CHAPTER FIFTEEN

Fiona

In the two months we've been in Seattle, I've hit up every speakeasy and hidden saloon this city has to offer. Same as New Orleans or Philly or any no name town we've passed through, the laws keep magic hidden while purity raids grow in frequency. But Seattle has twinkling lights reflecting off puddled rain, and the sea breeze cools my skin with briny lightness. Eleanora hasn't fallen in love quite like I have, and I'm about to hit her with a brand-new world.

I can only hope my choices are the right ones.

"What's this?" Eleanora asks, staring at the splintered boards of the saddest little ice cream parlor.

"It's our new home."

If anything can knock my confidence, it's her skeptical eyes. She takes a frustrated breath. "Great. You leave me in this rotting malt shop while you sling fire in all the speakeasies in the city." Her head snaps back. "Yes, I know you've been doing it."

I'm a terrible liar. Always have been. "How did you know?"

"Because you've been coming home calm at two a.m. You haven't been pouring booze in your coffee and blowing fire on the ceiling."

"Oh." All my daytime window shopping with her and people watching over laughs haven't hidden a thing. "I've just, I'm—"

She holds up her hand like the wise soul she is. "It's fine. You were a mess withholding the fire."

"Right." We stare at the crumbling door with the sideways sign that once said *The Milk House* before it lost the last two letters. "A room is available upstairs with a shared kitchen. The owner is nice."

"It's a speakeasy, isn't it?" She doesn't look at me.

"Yes. In the basement. But the top floor sells ice cream and sodas. You can have all you want."

"Great." She drops her bag on the street, her teeth clenched and lips tight.

"Baby, we can stay here. A home for longer than a few nights. A family."

"*Your* family." She crosses her arms.

"Yours too, if you want it." I gently tug at her sleeve. "These women are your elders. They've lived with the same struggle and leaned on each other. Please, give them a chance."

"And the owner? Is she one of us?"

"No, but she's a character." Lady offered a space for me and my kid. And beyond reason, I trust her. I worry where this life of mine will take me. Eleanora needs someone stable.

"It's not like a have a say in any of this, so let's have at it."

We walk through the doors into a once thriving theater. Where once there were seats there is now empty space and folding chairs. A man cleans glasses, as two drunks sleep the night away face down on the bar.

"Where's the ice cream?" she asks.

Lady appears, hair as always hiding under a colorful silk scarf. "Fiona! I've been waiting for you. And this must be Eleanora. Pleased to meet you, my friend."

"I am not your friend," she says.

Lady doesn't look away. I appreciate her for that. "Alright then. Let me show you to your room." We follow her through a skinny door and up a flight of stairs, past a second floor full of crates and bottles of booze. Up on the third floor, she extends her arm to a sitting area. "Use this space as you please. The kitchen is behind me, and your room is right there."

Eleanora follows her finger toward our bedroom. She opens the door and looks at me over her shoulder. "It's bigger than the places we usually stay."

"Yes. We can stay here, Eleanora. For a long while."

"As long as you perform for her, right?"

A heavy silence lingers between us. Lady clears her throat. "I'll let you get settled."

Eleanora paces the room. Small but cozy, the attic space has a window view of the skyline. She lowers herself to the bed by the window, staring out at the sunlit rooftop next door. She's so wise for twelve. Like all the knowledge of the world lives inside her. If only I could take away the fear that comes with it.

I lower to the bed next to her. "Are you angry with me?"

Her gaze remains steady on the rooftop. "I knew you couldn't do it. Magic means more to you than I do."

She's smart, but she's still a child. "Nothing means more than you." She shifts but won't look at me. "I need you to understand. I am fire dance. Without it, I become angry and volatile. You will too if you keep fighting who you are."

Finally, a glance over her shoulder. "I'm already angry."

Perhaps that's my doing. Why did I have a child in a world where I will die young from the fire inside me? Grandmother lost her marbles by age forty-five. My first mentor hit her decline by thirty. Mine's coming any day now. "You're just scared. And we're always in a fight."

Eleanora can break me with her smile, so when the corner of her mouth tips up, my chest stops aching. "I want to be like you," she says.

I'm not certain that's a good thing. "You're a better dancer, with more talent in your toes than I have in my entire body."

"But you make people love you. Entire crowds scream your name. Men want to date you. Every stage wants your name on their marquee. How do you do it?"

I don't want her to live for attention like I do. It's a hunger that's never satiated. Life offstage carves out a hollow cavern inside me, and I want to live in the applause. I came to Seattle for the Luminaire, but so did every other terrified woman. I can't get through the front door through the crowds of desperate magic girls. So, I landed around the corner at a speakeasy with a real stage. One step closer to the stardom I crave.

"You need to dance for you. All else happens naturally."

She tucks her hands under her thighs, elbows locked and shoulders tight. "I'm afraid to let myself believe."

"You will when you're ready." I stand and place my hands on my hips. "Come on, meet the girls."

She considers the offer. "Okay."

We leave our bags and head down to the speakeasy. Once inside the red door, the familiar smell of booze hits us, but more important is the heat that clings to the walls. Peppered with glints of gold and smoky remnants of fire, the air beckons me. I suspect Eleanora senses it too.

"Eleanora, this is Lady's speakeasy. She's built a saloon where we can dance how we want. Where we're protected." I've danced here enough times to know the performers are top tier. Lady got one into the Luminaire recently and I'm holding out hope I'll be the next.

The jazz dancer who spins sparklers from her hands races over in her bare feet. "Oh, you are darling!" She grabs Eleanora's hands.

"She's a beautiful tap dancer," I say with a smile.

"Well, we must see you dance. Those legs!"

For all her fight with me, Eleanora smiles at the dancer and agrees to see the stage. Lady appears beside me. "Is she as good as you?"

"Better." I shrug. "She just needs time."

"Well, she's too young still. I can't have a breakdown on my conscience." Some girls don't ever make it to the stage. Some can't handle the magic that blooms from their dance. The stress drives them mad. I'm going out in a blaze on some sort of stage, preferably a famous one.

"Thank you for giving us the room."

"Sure thing. It's getting dangerous, though. Just had an officer poking around upstairs last night. I protect my girls where I can, but those bastards are coming for all of us."

"Until then, we best dance." I wink and spin as my palms warm. "Hey, do I have a shot at the big show?"

She takes a deep breath as we watch Eleanora show the girls some of her moves. "The Luminaire? Maybe."

A tingle creeps up my spine. "I've seen the marquee and the posters." Every day. I check them obsessively for any openings. "Booze and an entire theater of Magic Dance? They've done something right."

"Ah, well. Resistance comes with a cost."

I push down the excitement in my belly. "I want it."

Lady's eyes light up. I expected her to balk. I've been here less than an hour and already have my sights on more. But she sees possibility. She must get something out of it. Her array of silk scarves and pearl necklaces tell me she is one savvy businesswoman.

She smooths her skirt. "I'll see what I can do."

Eleanora taps through a blast of fire, stopping to check herself for burns. When she finds there are none, she smiles as big as I've ever seen. The magic girls clap and smile. She runs over. "Did you see that?"

"I sure did."

"It's not an audience, but I spit fire, and it didn't hurt." Her halo flickers on, casting a gilded glow across her cheeks. "Maybe we'll be okay here."

Her fire didn't hurt because she let herself feel the adoration. The love. "Yes, I believe we will." My halo hasn't appeared in years. Not since I've gained control over my emotions. I worry Eleanora never will.

She runs off to share in the adoration. As she sets off a few barrel roll flares, she laughs with the performers. She's never looked that free with me. Not ever. For the first time, the panic Eleanora describes settles into my chest like poison.

CHAPTER SIXTEEN

Eleanora

One month to the unveiling of the new Luminaire show, where Star Girls push to new limits and Price fights to keep his Prohibition exemption. One month to learn how to command the spotlight. Something is brewing, but I can't seem to figure out what Price has up his sleeve. I suspect keeping us wild things gnashing against our cage maintains the excitement. Like a dog fight.

Mr. Price paces the stage, face tightened and sour. The troupe watches from the seats, but my attention remains on Miles whose elbow rests propped on his knee in complete focus.

"We are all here with the same goal. Reinvent our show and fill these seats with theatergoers who can't get enough of our magic." Price rubs his chin for an uncomfortably long pause. "We need new and big. Something unexpected."

Ruby exchanges a glance with me. "The only thing Price needs is filled seats and dollar bills. Who cares what the city does to us in the process."

Some days it feels as if we are ants scurrying at a picnic, avoiding the stomp of shoes on our tiny bodies.

"We must be better. Bigger," he says. The girls sit at attention. "Be prepared for a spectacular show. Or you'll all be out on the streets, left to the mercy of an unforgiving city."

Sadie mumbles, "He thinks he can replace us while he returns to his thirty-room mansion on Millionaire's Row."

He catches the grumblings. "Magic girls line up, just waiting for their chance to step into our spotlight." He pauses, scanning his eyes across the theater. "Without me, this city would eat you alive."

Miles catches my gaze, but I purse my lips. He's allowing this.

"Soar across this stage. Fly color and snow and rainbows. But the moment you show signs of hysteria, it could all be taken away, like that." His snap echoes around us. "Miles?" He gestures to his son. "We've curated a program to highlight each of your strengths. Tell them."

Miles clears his throat. "I believe we have the troupe that can shatter conventions." He stares straight at me as my stomach tumbles and flips. His father seethes next to him, watching me for reaction. "We can change the country. Rewrite the narrative that you all are witches. I'll do everything in my power to help you."

"Miles." Price practically barks his name. "We aren't here to change anyone's views. We're here to produce the grandest show of our time."

"Yes, of course." Miles drops his gaze. I wrangle the sudden urge to run and hug him. If I understand anything, it's the power of larger-than-life parents.

"Now." Mr. Price claps once. "Prepare for a new and improved show. New outfits, updated moves. Controlled elements to dazzle the crowd."

"Does he not hear himself?" I mutter to Ruby. "Allow me, a very unmagical man, to control you and make the most money I can from your banned bodies."

Ruby grimaces. "When you say it like that, it makes the speakeasy life sound pretty good."

I tilt my head. "Except for those purity raids and the mice that scurry across your feet." Bleeding arm. The woman's smile as she sliced. She thought she was saving herself.

"Everyone off to the dressing room. We need updated measurements for your costumes." The seamstress and set designer lead the girls out of the theater and into the hallway.

I stay behind to watch Miles and his father in some sort of disagreement. Miles looks to his feet, lips tightened. When he looks up at me, my entire body warms. My mouth grows numb as the room darkens.

The only thing worse than an episode is having one where people can see. I slide my back along the wall, turning from his smile while panic rises inside me. Why now? No, no, no.

I pace in circles in the hallway, rubbing my throat. It will stop. Just keep pacing. Surely, I would pass out by now from lack of oxygen? My lips grow tingly. What if I die, right here in the hallway by myself?

It's too much, worrying about my body, my mind, and what I might look like to people who don't live with this monster inside them.

I force my way down the stairs and burst open the gymnasium doors. Not a soul here. This giant, empty room hums with possibility. Tap, tap, toe, heel, shuffle. Ball change. Come on, Nora. Get a hold of yourself.

But my skin is hot as fire. My magic has crawled out like spiders, and I can't put it back in. I'm in this world now and must decide between acceptance via Miles or obedience via his father. Both unacceptable options.

I think I see Aria but blink hard and rub my eyes, seeing that she isn't here. It was only a shadow.

Through the doorway to my private rehearsal space, the top hat dazzles from the trunk, calling me to its sleek rim. I could tap in a dazzling suit and top hat. A slight break in my airway. Relief. I tap, soft as wind chimes.

The top hat glides to the air with a slow spin, lit with a silver glow from the dying flames against a dark room. What if Miles is right? What if my magic can change perceptions? Little girls won't have to be afraid of their powers. They won't need to hide away when their magic swells, protected from the prying eyes of the world that scorns them. They could be proud.

Free dance will fix this. Alone. The hat bounces toward me and lands on my head. The moment it touches me, my lips come alive.

I flick my wrist and music begins. Piano notes plunk themselves, moved by only an intention. Tap, tap, tap. My boots morph into heeled tap shoes. I flutter my feet as pools of light ripple across the shining wood floor. When I snap, my hat somersaults and lands in my hand. Flames spurt from the inside of my top hat, blowing my hair back with every blast. Dance washes away the fear. Magic soothes every regret, every bite of pain in my heart.

I can breathe.

"It's just a performance," I whisper to the mirror. "One month and a fight for the world's approval." Stomp time step. I place both hands to the cool glass of my reflection, the only partner I've ever truly trusted. With a hard blink, the piano plays in time to my feet. Beckoned by the stars that flutter in my heart.

I press with straight elbows away from the mirror into a cartwheel as my legs scissor through the gold dust that puffs from my fingers. I throw my top hat into the air as my body spins tight and fast. When the hat plops perfectly situated on my head, my dress turns into a suit, silver and black and beaded. My lips are fire red, and my eyelids icy blue like morning frost. Flames surround me in a protective ring.

All my panic gone with a whoosh.

"Woah." The image takes my breath away. And just as quickly, I'm back to Eleanora, tap shoes planted on the ground, fitted dress swishing at my calves.

That felt… electric. Powerful.

I throw the top hat across the room, heaving for air.

"Eleanora, what are you doing in here?" Ruby stands at the doorway, examining my stunned face. "I know that look. You did magic."

I turn to face myself in the mirror. Remnants of blushed cheeks and burgundy lips remain. A memory of the beaded suit zips excitement up my spine.

Ruby joins me, her trusty fiddle always in hand. "How was your little adventure?"

"Like I've fallen out of the sky and into another universe." I blink hard and my face returns to normal. "Ruby, your performance has been in a silver evening gown and witch hat. Teardrop earrings with a beaded head wrap."

"Yes."

"That's what the theater wants." I close my eyes. Wide leg pants swish against my leg and the tuxedo jacket I created with my magic hugs my curves. A diamond encrusted star pin on my lapel is still imprinted on my mind. "What do you want to wear?"

Ruby bites her lip. She closes the door behind her and exhales. "I don't show anyone."

"Why not?"

"They'll kick me out of here. Everyone will mock me."

I didn't know the rest of us felt fear like I do. "I want to see the real you."

Ruby hesitates but lifts her fiddle. She closes her eyes and with one controlled glide across the strings, her wild curls grow vines of greenery and pink flower buds. Her legs turn to moss as green as a fresh cut pine. As her music fades in and out, moss-lined rocks lift under her feet.

The walls bead into droplets that collect into a giant waterfall. Water splashes to the rhythm of her notes and she sways with the ceiling that now shines pale blue light.

I can't help but cry at the sheer beauty of it all. Her music, her body. Her mind. Ruby has had an entire world hidden inside her all this time.

She hangs onto her final note as a fine mist settles at our feet.

"What is this place?" I ask.

"This is the safe place in my mind. When I'm alone, I play with freedom, and this is what comes out."

The mist is cool on my hands. Birds chirp from the dense trees. "It's so real."

"It's the most real thing I know." Green butterflies circle her wild vines of hair. "Price controls our performance. What we wear, how we smile. Every note has been curated to fit their vision."

"Why can't you give them this? This is amazing."

She drops her fiddle and bow to her sides. "Because this is mine."

My mother left everything onstage for her audience and her directors, leaving only a shell of a woman who loved her daughter. "Tonight, I danced for me." I swallow the heaviness that rests on my throat. "I let go for just one moment, and my dress turned into a tuxedo with a dazzling star pin on the lapel."

"Don't think too hard about it, Eleanora." Ruby snaps away her entire forest world. Once again back in the creaking, windowless rehearsal space, a touch of emerald mist glides across the floor. "Just let it breathe."

"I can do that?"

Ruby laughs. "Of course. It's yours." The last pink blossom fades from her hair. "Just don't show anyone or it won't be yours anymore."

If I don't show what's deep inside, how can I ever truly perform?

CHAPTER SEVENTEEN

Eleanora

Just let it breathe.

Ruby's message is clear. Hide away your true self if you don't want the world to ruin you. As we sit through a torturous rehearsal, I search Price for clues. I need to discover what he has planned for New Year's Eve.

"The world will adore you!" Price's voice booms through the theater. "Higher. Brighter. Give me your best dance."

Zelda heaves for breath from the center of the glass stage lit by spits of icy light. "I am."

"It isn't enough."

Miles tightens his lips. "Father."

Price simply waves him away. "You're all holding back. Every one of you!" He kicks a candelabra on its side as it clangs down the stairs. A rigid hush grips the theater. "Amateur!" His face pulses tomato red. "You're all more than you're giving me."

"We aren't allowed to give ourselves," I say. "You're telling us to be spectacular but don't shine too bright. Be more. Be less. It's exhausting."

"I've given you everything." He stomps across the stage. "The only legal alcohol in the city. Any partner from the outside to dance the night away with in your private bar. Here you are adored." He drags a finger in a trembling line across the room. "Out there, you are feared."

I lean forward, but Ruby and Sadie push me back to the chair. "Don't," Sadie whispers. "You'll only make it worse."

Miles coughs to get his father's attention. "I think we could all use a break. Father, won't you join me?" He guides him backstage.

"They don't get to discuss our future while we sit here like voiceless dolls." I slip backstage behind the heavy curtain that hides the lighting scaffolds. Through a slit between two panels, Miles whispers to his father. "Yes, I know they're holding back. But you're not helping by screaming at them."

"They've been protected by their instructors," Price groans. "Treated like fragile glass figurines, when they should be pushed toward greatness."

Bastard.

"They're afraid of hysteria," Miles says. "They know you'll turn them away the second they burn a hole in the wallpaper."

"This is on you, son. You brought Fiona's daughter here and promised me something new and spectacular. She needs to dazzle."

"I'm working on it." He rubs his forehead.

I grip the curtain hard enough to make my forearm cramp. I'll never fill my mother's spotlight. Ever.

"Work faster. New Year's Eve is a month away and if we don't bring out the best these girls have to offer, we're all done. This is bigger than us both now."

"I know."

Price storms off. In the sliver of light, I watch Miles drop his head, his chest thumping hard enough to tremble his club collar.

My halo presses through my scalp. Without realizing it, I pull back and knock my head into a standing light. It crashes into a metal bar then bounces to the floor. I motion to the lamp as if I could instruct it to be silent.

Miles pulls open the drape and meets my eyes. "Eavesdropping?"

"Research," I snap. I push past him, a little harder than intended. "Sorry about the mess."

He laughs with restraint, biting his lips together while his cheeks redden.

"Something funny, Miles Price?"

"You make me smile." His face flattens. "Sorry. I won't let it happen again."

In one stupid, charming moment, he's trimmed the barbed wire cutting into my mind that warns danger is everywhere. I now desperately want him to kiss me until the ache disappears.

"I don't trust you," I say.

"That's probably wise." He glances in the direction his father walked. "You're up next."

My neck tightens but I don't dare shift my eyes. "He begs for more but won't let us dance how we really could. What the hell does he want?"

He stares past me toward center stage. "What he always wants. Control. He'd burn down this city trying to hold on to this place."

"He'd ruin you too?" I slip my fingers through his.

He turns to me, eyes glassy with tears. "I may be beyond repair, sweet Nora, but you still have a shot to make things right."

I force my body to move toward center stage. Breath rattling in my ears, all I can see are the faces of Star girls. Some hopeful, some tearful. Zelda nods slowly one time. Sadie exhales and grips the chair rails, and Ruby narrows her eyes, sending me a message.

Let my dance breathe.

Price steps to the orchestra section, arms crossed. "Well, Eleanora, let's see if you've got any of Fiona's magic dust."

My vision turns blurry around the edges. Conjure one image that gives me strength. I think of my mother. The time we swam in the river at midnight and went on a scavenger hunt in the city. No, none of those seem right. Only one thing settles my heart.

Aria.

Her unshakeable belief in me and her hopeful eyes watching me shine.

"I'm waiting." Price sniffs in agitation.

"I'm ready. Start the music."

Miles plunks a short tune on the piano. "I'll accompany you." He winks. "Whenever you're ready."

I force a hesitant nod.

With trembling fingers and cramped arches, I dance my approved routine. I thud and tap and shuffle and throw my arms in windmills as the piano rhythm grounds my feet to the stage. My dress swishes and floats as I tap my way through every beat. Determination flows through me, and somehow, I ignore the finale staring me down like a dead end.

I keep my eyes on the girls, who smile and clap. I set my feet into a fury of taps, creating their own music and drowning out the piano. Sweat moistens my upper lip. My legs burn. I force the flames from my hands though this is not how they want to appear. It hurts too much. Pressure like a corked bottle.

I make the mistake of glancing at Price. His disapproving scowl almost sends me to the floor. A dam to the confidence that rushed through me just moments ago. Don't think of our blindfolded dance alone. Just do what's asked of you.

Miles isn't beyond repair. Neither am I.

Unable to think straight, I throw my hand in front of me as gold foil flies from my palm and settles in the shape of a staircase. This isn't part of my routine. To hell with Price and his stuffy rules. I run toward the starry stairs I created. With a lunge, I somersault backwards and tap upside down on the sea of gold near the stage's ceiling. My dress doesn't fall over my head like I think it will. Feet on the stars, I dangle like a bat as a stream of fire burns from my mouth. I summon Aria's smiling face to carry me home.

My body curls like a pill bug, spinning so fast fire shoots from an orb around me. As my tap shoes hit the floor, the entire stage goes up in a carpet of flames.

All my fire retreats as my hands grow cold and blue. The girls erupt with defiant screams. Price's cheeks redden and his eyes narrow.

Out of breath, I can't slow my heartbeat. All these eyes on me, all this attention. All that *magic*.

I think I bow, but my body moves outside my control. I walk past Miles without a glance into the dark backstage and into the dressing room. Mirrors everywhere. Twenty images of myself stare back at me as I teeter on an attack of some kind of stage fright that occurs offstage more than on.

Miles opens the door. "Eleanora, that was incredible."

I brace my arms to a table, willing myself to remain standing. Don't fall. Don't fall.

"Eleanora?" His voice seems to hover, warbled and hollow.

"I can't." That's all I can force out before my throat compresses. Panic rushes through me like a stampede and once again, I'm helpless against the monster inside. Tears flood my lids as I collapse. Still awake but in another world outside my body where reality doesn't exist. Where I don't exist.

Gentle arms wrap around me. "What can I do?" he asks.

"Nothing." Not a damn thing.

What if this never stops? What if this is how it ends, me in an episode carried to an asylum. Oh, God. Make it stop.

I nestle my face into his chest. His soft shirt and peppermint tobacco are like hands reaching into my hysteria to pull me back to normalcy. His heart beats against my cheek. Solid. Safe.

Like a gift, the panic recedes, leaving a trembling shell filled to the brim with embarrassment. I tuck to recoil, but Miles pulls me close. He rests his cheek on my forehead. "You're safe."

Tears fall silently down my cheeks and stream down my neck. "What's wrong with me?"

"Nothing, Nora. Nothing is wrong with you."

With his warm breath against my ear, my body no longer revolts. Who knew a touch could heal? I certainly didn't. As is the cruelty of my fate, I mend my panic just as hysteria looms.

CHAPTER EIGHTEEN

Eleanora

I can't go back. I danced however the hell I wanted to. On stage. In front of people. Now come the consequences handed down from Price and all I can think of is how I'd do it again.

"Eleanora, that was magnificent!" Sadie squeals when the girls find me pacing the wardrobe room post-episode.

Zelda places her hands on her hips. "You might just show me up, Miss Eleanora. I don't know how I feel about that. Just kidding. I love it!"

Ruby studies my face but doesn't add to the conversation.

"I don't know what I would do without you all."

Sadie smiles. "The world is already against us. Nothing left to do but love each other."

Zelda throws a silk scarf around her neck with a flourish. "Star Girls today, sisters forever."

The way their eyes glisten reminds me of spinning in the misty nights with my mother, eyelashes dripping and skin damp, loving someone so much that joy lights you from the inside. I thought I'd lost that.

Ruby walks arm in arm with me to the dining room for an afternoon cup of coffee. "Tell me the truth. How do you feel?"

"I'm sure Price isn't happy. I ignored the approved routine."

"That isn't what I asked." She stirs her teacup of steaming coffee using a tiny gold spoon. "You performed in front of the entire troupe. And you did so by breaking all the rules."

I examine the ceiling molding around the dangling light in the shape of a rose. "I had a breakdown backstage. A bad one."

She grimaces and places her teacup on the saucer with a soft clank. "I should have been there. I'm sorry."

"Miles helped me."

She raises her eyebrows. "Miles Price, our spoiled director helped you through an episode?"

"Why do you act like he's awful? He's been kind to me." I flinch inside, remembering how vulnerable I was against his chest.

"He isn't awful. He's just Winston Price in training. Money and status above all else. He won't stand up to his father and he's the only one that could make him listen."

She's right, but Ruby doesn't understand the losing battle of loving someone trapped in their own selfish obsessions. Her mother sacrificed everything for her while mine nearly killed me.

"Will you keep training with magic?" she asks. "Keep pushing the limits and pissing off Price?"

A tornado of thoughts crashes through my mind. I shouldn't. I won't. But I want to. I dare to mutter my worst fear. "What if that decision pulls me under and I drown?"

"Yes, it might."

"Well, that's encouraging."

She places her hand on mine. "But magic might also set you free."

"Is there such a thing?" I slide my hand from hers.

"In the mountains, we drew boundaries and kept secrets. Folklore and mountain medicine makes sense to us. Nobody questions that I can build waterfalls with my music. But outside our cabins, our ways mean something devilish and wrong."

"Nothing about you is wrong."

Her eyes wander to the frosty window. "Life was simple when the lines were clear. Before they arrived with torches. Protect yourself, and inside your own world, no one can take that from you."

But I barely know how to access this thing inside me, let alone control it. I'm about to say just that when a commotion outside grabs our attention. From the window, I count ten women gathered under the marquee.

"They're holding a banner." I strain to see the writing when they turn in a circle, fists pumping in the air. "Bring Safety Back to Seattle. Arrest the Star Girls."

"Don't those ladies have some Bible readings to host?" Ruby scoffs.

"Their husbands and sons toss girls like us into prison cells at their behest." I lean my forehead against the window. "Women who participate in our destruction are a special kind of wicked." I can't see their faces, but I imagine them as skeletal figures with dark eyes.

Zelda bops in, grabbing an apple on her way to the window. "What are we looking at?"

"Protestors," I say.

"They look like they've just come from a funeral. We should throw some feathers and shimmer on them. Draw some rouge on their dour faces."

"That's probably why they hate us," I say. "We're shiny and loud. All things women shouldn't be."

"The Luminaire has given the outcasts a stage. They've dressed us up and showcased our oddities and rewarded us with alcohol. Their hate for us runs deep." Zelda bites into the ripe apple and wipes the juice from her chin.

"It's just a little elemental magic," I say. "Fire and water and light. Some levitating." I realize the ridiculousness of that thought as soon as I say it. Magic isn't simple. Not in our world.

"It isn't the magic they hate," Zelda says. "It's the freedom. A fact Price never lets us forget."

Ruby scratches behind her ear. "No one likes when the witches enter daylight."

"They don't like when the fat girl gets attention, either." Zelda forces a smile.

The room heats, as if ten fires rage around me.

"You're flushed, Nora. Are you alright?" Ruby reaches for me.

"Yes, fine." *Keep it together.* I can't have two attacks in one day. It might kill me. I rub my face a few times, hoping to focus my attention on this conversation but my heart still races, and my vision stays blurry. "I'm going to get some air."

"I'll come with you."

"No, Ruby. I'm fine. Really." Please don't follow me. Please don't watch me fall apart.

I hurry out the door looking for anything to bring me back. The textured wallpaper, the fading light of a wall sconce. The sting of my nails against my forearm. Nothing helps.

My last hope is a shot of cold air from the December rain. I'm holding onto my mind by a frayed thread. Darkness threatens its grasp around my throat. Please, stop.

Out the alley door, I take a deep, harsh breath of freezing air. A sheet of ice floats on a puddle near a grate. I slam my heel to break it and reach for the shards. I rub the ice on my face, my neck, and my forehead. A shock of reality to save me from falling. If I were near the ocean, I'd dive in. I just need the panic to stop.

The ice melts against my hot skin, dripping a cold trail down my spine. With a shiver, the panic recedes. Sanity beckons. My body welcomes me home.

A cloud of smoke rises into the afternoon sky as screams bounce from First Avenue. They could have set a fire on the street and I can't care. I'm too busy trying to breathe.

Forehead against the rough bricks, I let the sensation of failure wash through me. The thing I need to be is what will end me. Destiny. Unfair destiny.

***

I wait for Iridessa in our rehearsal space, avoiding news of an arson attempt under our marquee this afternoon. Apparently, the protestors stuffed a sack and decorated it as a witch on the stake, setting fire to the pathetic thing at our door. I can't let that in right now. Fear landed on me in the misty nights of my youth and has clung to my heart ever since. Now I must rehearse.

"You think you're clever."

Price. I don't want to look at him or talk to him, or even admit his existence. So I stare at our reflection in the mirror. "Not at all."

He steps inside the rehearsal space, his sleek black Oxfords clunking against the floor with purpose. "You know the rules here." He hovers behind me, staring down at my reflection. "We choreograph. We design costumes, carefully craft routines." His gaze lowers to the top of my head. "You comply."

Unable to tolerate his scorching stare, I whip around to face him. My hands are already turning numb. "You don't understand us. Since our first magic swell, we're taught to hate our bodies. Shame our elements. We spend our lives apologizing for things people like you deemed wrong."

Why is my mouth so quick to act when my mind screams to slow down?

His chest puffs to double its size. "If it weren't for me, you'd be scrubbing dishes, wasting your last speck of magic in a dingy speakeasy. Your mother was a pain in the ass, but she brought crowds larger than I've ever seen. She was spectacular. You've yet to perform once."

The only thing stronger than my attitude is my painful fragility. "You do love to threaten us."

"I make the rules here. If you don't like it, you are free to walk outside right now. Return to your small life dreaming of all the things you're too afraid to fight for." He rubs his mustache a few times. "Or you could be a good little girl and perform the act written for you."

A good girl. I'm beginning to see how powerful my mother really was. She threw this man's bravado right back in his face.

When I say nothing, Price nods. "Wise choice." He steps away but spins on his heel back toward me. "Just think. You could have everything you've ever wanted. Protection, a family, stepping into the spotlight your mother left behind."

"You know nothing of what I want."

"I know you don't want to end up like her. Follow my rules and you could live like Iridessa. Safe."

"Dance like a good little girl and avoid a painful death. What a deal." Once again, I must ignore who I am and live by someone else's rules.

He points at my reflection with a long, tense finger. "If you disobey me again, I'll throw you out to the old bats at the Temperance League. They fund the asylum in town." He waits until I react, then he drops his hand and struts away.

I can't summon the tears that sting, so I tap hard and fast until a blaze of fire shoots from my palm and singes a feather boa black. The panic resting in my chest recedes, but my anger still bubbles below the surface like hot oil.

Iridessa floats into the room. "You were magnificent today." She says the words, but no joy lives in her voice.

I open my eyes. "Are you upset I didn't follow our routine?"

"No. I expected as much."

"How could you know? I didn't decide until I was mid-spin."

"Because it's who you are, Fire Girl. You don't take well to instruction or orders for how to dance and summon elements." She touches my chin just as my mother used to do. "You're so much like her."

"Not enough." I stretch my toes, rocking my feet back and forth.

Tears pool in my lower lids. "Free dance shouldn't be cause for all this fear. But people love to loathe me. They'll make me the poster child for magic run amok."

"People believe nonsense." She closes her eyes, her brows tight with a seemingly painful memory. "They still think we're witches."

"Witches," I scoff. "The power to cast a spell would be a hell of a lot more useful than rings of fire."

"I grow wings and cast rainbows. It's as close to the devil as this world will see."

"But you made it. You're here, dancing for us. Training us to be like you."

She steps forward, cane gripped in her fist. "I do not train you to be like me."

My spine stiffens. "Understood."

"I guide your dance skills, but you decide how far you'll take the supernatural." She shakes off her frustration as a coat of red shimmer dusts from her shoulders. "Use your power. But there *will* be consequences."

"Our ancestors lost spouses and children. Died in prison and at the stake. Withered away in asylums. I don't see much power in that."

"No, but there is in living honestly." Emerald toe shoes appear on her feet. Six pirouettes turn the room into shining green lights. She comes to rest in a graceful croisé derrière through a whoosh of thin, celestial air.

"There's a part of myself I've been ignoring, and I can't turn away anymore. But I don't know what to do about the horror inside me, and all the things I've seen out there." I motion above us.

"The horrors have been there for decades, bubbling below the surface. We were only safe until the wrong person found a system for targeting us." She waves her arm and with a blink, my slippers settle onto the wood floor like soft sand. "Remember what I said, Eleanora. No one decides for you. Especially not the audience."

I nod, remembering all those years I wished for my mother's talent to bleed into me, desperate to avoid dancing on my own. I've always known this moment would arrive.

"Now," she says, "let's dance."

I take position and follow Iridessa's instruction with one giant question lingering. How can I decide my fate when I can't trust my own mind?

CHAPTER NINETEEN

Fiona

Daylight has become insufferable.

One month of spinning fire at the Milk House has made my magic unruly. My body temperature grows hot even in the cooling fall temps. I beckon fire and smoke at the slightest initiation of movement. The more fire dance I do, the more fire dance I want.

I pace the basement with a smoking, trembling hand, watching Eleanora dance with the girls. She's come a long way with their help, but if I suggest an improvement, her magic dries right up.

I flick my ring finger and tap my foot waiting for the first show of the night, though that's two torturous hours away. The jazz dancer has taken a liking to Eleanora. She's a cheerful girl with sparklers constantly shooting from her palms. "Fiona, did you see her spins?" she asks.

I wave at my daughter. "Beautiful, Eleanora!" She's holding back. Her body is rigid, her fire is weak. By this age, her tap shoes should cause explosions. Holding back will only cause problems.

Eleanora taps over to me. "I'm getting better, Mama."

"Yes, you look wonderful."

Her arms drop. Her frustration snuffs out the hazy ring of fire around her head. "You don't think I'm good enough. I can tell."

"What? You're dancing every day. Flames shoot from your tap shoes at your will now. It's lovely."

She tightens her lips into a thin line. "You think I can't tell when you're disappointed?"

I want to remain calm but this heat in my belly burns something fierce. Heartburn stings my throat, and a fever simmers on my skin. "Eleanora, please." I take two long drags of what's left of my cigarette.

"Tell me. Go on."

"I'm so proud of you." She won't let up, I can tell. "You'll get there. But you're holding back. If you'd let me show you—"

"No."

One last inhale of tarry smoke to fill my lungs. "Why do you fight me so much?"

She grabs the cigarette, snuffing its burning end in an ashtray on one of the tables. "All this is so easy for you."

"Because I've worked at it." I wiggle my toes and stretch my shoulders, but nothing extinguishes this need inside me. "I can help you."

"I don't need your help. I have her." We look back at the perky jazz dancer. I don't even know her name.

"I'm glad you have a friend." I go behind the bar to grab the pack of cigarettes, but Eleanora slaps them from me. "Hey, you may hate me but I'm still your mother."

"Being your daughter is like living with the moon. I can't do anything when you're hanging there all giant and bright."

I'm growing tired of her excuses. "I'm worried about you."

"Why? I have friends. I dance. Someday I'll be on this stage. What do you want from me?" She pulls her braids over her shoulders and tugs.

"You hold your magic in so tight, it's going to ruin you."

"Stop expecting me to be perfect!" Her cheeks glow bright pink. "I push as much fire as I can. Besides, you practically vomit fire at all hours of the night, and it's done nothing but turn you feral."

A monster. A beast of fire who can't rein in her universe of magic. She hates that I won't stop dancing for her. "Listen, baby." I reach for her, but she yanks away. "If I stop dancing, I will die."

"Five performances a night, seven days a week has only made you hungry for more."

"I'm working toward the Luminaire. I'm *trying* to build us a safety net."

She turns away from me, beckoning the jazz girl. "Let's grab a malt."

The girl skips toward us and off they go. She's barely eighteen, but she's probably the mother Eleanora really wants. Fizzy and light with thready magic that no one seems to care much about.

Lady struts out of her office. "You're flushed."

"I'm dying to get on the big stage, Lady."

"I've never met anyone like you. A well of magic so big it swallows you."

I wriggle, hot and uncomfortable. "Eleanora and I had a fight."

"You two tend to do that." She pops a bottle of beer from her favorite wildcat brewery and slides it over. I guzzle the cold bubbles and hold the bottle to my neck. "This is just how mothers and daughters are."

I stare at her, wondering for the first time what the hell her backstory is, then I throw my hands up. "I'm doing it wrong. She wants me to stop performing, stop being so, well, me."

"You can't stop, Fiona." She pops her own bottle and clinks it against mine before gulping down half in one swig. "You're teaching her to own her magic."

"But she's so terrified. If I could take my fire away, I would, but it's like asking me to change my height. And dancing alone just to burn off the energy leaves me with an aching emptiness I can't crawl out of. Am I being selfish?"

She slams the bottle to the bar. "You listen to me. That girl needs someone to look up to. You keep being true to yourself."

It's nice to have someone believe in you, especially when you question every decision you've made. "What's the story on the Luminaire?"

"Still working on getting you an audition. They're inundated with magic girls begging for a shot. The owner and his son won't give me the time of day. But I'll get you there, I promise."

"Thanks for being here."

"I may not be a magic girl, but many in my family are. I'm tired of these idiots saying you all are wrong. You're the most interesting things in this world."

They say we inherit magic like we do eye color. Some daughters get it, some don't. "Part of me wishes I didn't give this to Eleanora." I shrug. "But this is who I am."

"You be strong for her, even if she doesn't see it."

The jazz girl bops back in. "I got Eleanora set up with dinner and a malt."

"Thanks." Eleanora can't be here when patrons arrive. Too young to be around all that booze and sexy dancing. "Let's get ready."

Lady preps for the night. We get ourselves dolled up and sip coupes of champagne in the backroom. A dozen performers circle through here every night with a handful of regulars like me. We're dancers, aerialists, and singers. It's a good thing this room is made of stone with eighteen-foot ceilings. It's barely enough to contain our elements.

By the time the patrons arrive, I'm already drunk and feverish. I knock over a makeup tin and fumble to pick it up. The girls help steady me as my insides threaten to explode.

I jump in place while waiting for my turn on center stage. A man I usually dance with slinks up behind me. "Hey, doll. Looking sleek tonight." He grabs my hip and a rush of heat swells in my belly. I push him against the wall, kissing him, hard, then slap his hands on my thighs and force him to squeeze. I bite his lip. I've avoided men since Chicago, trying so hard to be the mother Eleanora needs. I've made myself a woman about to implode. I shove him away and catch my breath.

"Thanks, honey." I wink, ready and focused to take the stage. Two fire dancers join me tonight. We hold hands and move to the jazz beat. Our hips pop side to side, and around in circles. Our clasped hands shoot tiny flames, a teaser. My fever cools. My head stops thumping. We move in unison, led only by our intuition. Bonded by things we don't say, we kick and slap our thighs, squealing as fire rages from our palms and feet. The stage erupts in flames. We stomp through the circle, lit with energy hotter than the sun.

Pure joy. Freedom beyond measure. We shake our heads and spin on our toes, pirouetting as red-hot flames shoot from our feet. We hit our last note, arms up and full of fire. Then, my moment. The silence. The only time I feel truly alive.

I wait for applause but all I hear are screams. Fire evaporates. Chaos everywhere. Policemen grab the girls by their wrists, not caring about screams or tears. Lady beats one of them with her fist but he shoves her to the ground. Then he comes for me.

Teeth bared, face hot, he grabs my wrist hard enough to burn. He cuffs me and bends me over to slap me on the ass. "Okay, you little slut. Time to cool off in jail."

I yank myself up, arms pinned behind me. "See that ass you just slapped? Well, you can kiss it, you toad." He drags me by my hair through the insanity of people fleeing. "You won't arrest the people paying us, only the women offering them magic, huh?" I buck against his fist over my hair and knuckles pressed against my scalp, but he just slaps me when I do. As I finally succumb to my first purity raid, I look up to see Eleanora in her pajamas on the stairs, tears streaming down her face.

She will never have a normal mother. As the heat already rises in my chest, begging for a way out, I know with certainty, someday soon she may not have a mother at all.

CHAPTER TWENTY

Eleanora

Tonight, as rehearsal wraps, the girls bounce down to the Sapphire Bar but all I can think of is how I embarrassed myself with another episode, and vow to hold on to my sanity at all costs.

Young men grab the Star Girls by the waists, nuzzling in their hair and smelling their perfume. Zelda and her boyfriend sway together, lips grazing, as our musicians play a zippy tune. Ruby's fiddle creates blue light in all corners of the room.

"They all look so happy, don't they?" Miles's voice appears behind me. I stiffen against the doorway, wondering if I can run away.

"Yeah."

He steps closer, his breath warming my neck. "You should join them. You deserve to celebrate too."

Heaven help me, I'd rather stand here, close to his deep voice. "I don't think I do."

Zelda climbs on a chair and backflips across the bar, her hair turning to glass. Everything about her shines. It's too much to take in all this beauty knowing we're all going down in flames. Some quicker than others.

"Excuse me." I turn to walk past him, but my breath catches when I meet his eyes. Miles steps out of the way, a gesture that makes me weak. "I'm mortified, you know." All those years Mother instructed me to toughen up, be bold, and step into my birthright. Here I am, blatantly cold to cover my hidden, wounded magic.

"I can't imagine why. You're human. That's nothing to cause embarrassment." He rubs his arm and holds it tenderly, draped across his chest. "Much like an acrobat who can't tolerate heights."

I step closer, my body pulled to his. I know he's using me, but I don't care. Mesmerized by his golden eyes, I find myself saying, "Dance with me."

"Rehearsal is over for the night."

"Not to practice. To *dance*."

A smile tugs at the corner of his mouth. "Lead the way, Diamond Nora."

We make our way to the quiet theater, sneaking glances at each other through the hazy light in the hallways. "Wait for me there."

I step onto the cool stage, stare into the darkness, and wait.

With a loud clunk, one spotlight floods me in a warm glow. "Something changed in you on this stage the other day." His voice appears from behind the intensely bright light that washes out any view of the audience.

"Yes, it did." I knew the consequences, yet I took the leap anyway. I made star stairs and danced upside down. If I could summon that again, I'd be unstoppable.

"Why are you scared?" he asks.

I search the theater but still can't find him. "I'm heading face first into a mental breakdown fueled by fire. What do you think?" I crack my knuckles one at a time until they're all out of pops.

"I think you're here now, stable and strong."

Somehow, it's easier to talk with a faceless voice. "There's this power inside me. Like rage and anger and love swirl in a cyclone, pressing out against my body."

"You can't control it?"

"No. I'm completely at the mercy of my emotions. Magic Dance is the portal to all things magnificent and devastating. I never know which will prevail." The other girls aren't quite as intense as me. My mother wasn't afraid, and that's what killed her.

"Coming back here meant failure." His shoes tap through the aisles in the dark. "Seattle, this theater. I couldn't breathe here."

"What about your mother?"

"She died when I was young. Since then, this place is the only thing he cares about." He sighs. His steps halt. "I didn't want any of it. I wanted to dance and perform, not sit in an office and pay bills."

"And you did that. In London."

"Until I failed. No one would hire me after that. Hell, I get queasy at the top of a flight of stairs now. My acrobat days are over."

"Come on stage where I can see you."

"I was dying a slow death back here with my father." Tap, tap. His shoes make their way into the spotlight. "Until I discovered Fiona's daughter hiding out at a speakeasy near us. You turned out to be a miniature version of her with black hair, gray eyes, and the same attitude. But you hold more wisdom. You ask more questions."

"I ask too many questions." Oh, Mother. I miss you with the ache of a rotting tooth. "What do you remember about her?"

"Fiona and Iridessa trained me. They'd sneak me into rehearsals and show me every dance and acrobatic move my little boy heart desired. Father would have had their heads if he knew."

He knew a side of her I never did. "You just wanted to dance, but you have no magic to offer your father. He asks to serve in a different way."

Dust motes flitter around us in the illuminated circle, like flecks of gold. "Something like that," he says in a quiet voice.

The tension is too strong. The only cure for the weight of the universe right now is to press my cheek to his. "We came here to dance."

He slides close, head tipped to the side. "We are dancing."

I don't tell him how fear once forced me out to the streets where I learned to fight the dark monsters in the night. "My feet haven't moved."

"What is dance other than a conversation between souls?" He reaches for me. I want to hold his soft hand. To sway to the rhythm of invisible notes and trust that the Milky Way won't drop me into the abyss.

"Sometimes," I hesitate but decide to reach for his hand. "I think the thing I'm most afraid of is the thing that could set me free."

Loose strands from his ponytail quiver in the drafty air. "Ah, yes. I know that battle well."

Electricity shoots through our connected hands and warms my palm. "But I can't get past myself."

He presses his chest to mine as his hand slides behind my back. He lifts my right hand. A duet ready to set a rhythm across the stage. "You take a lot of blame for being human," he says.

My stomach drops so hard and so fast I drop into his arms like a near-faint. Men swell our emotions and try to dull that which they pulled to light. I hear your warnings, mother. I just don't want to listen.

But mobsters save us from lawmakers which simply trade hands of power over our bodies. Audiences laugh and swoon and spit vitriol all in the same night. Blades slice open flesh to cut out the magic that eats up our insides.

"Eleanora?" Miles waits for me to come back to the moment where our bodies touch and sway to an invisible beat. "You want to get out of here?"

"Yes."

***

The frosty December night reddens our cheeks. The city breathes with danger and potential. Among the homeless and prostitutes, the rich scurry between hidden bars, searching for a magic girl to stoke their yearning for danger.

"Look at them. The underground city is like their playground," I say.

Miles looks through the smattering of couples stumbling in secrecy. "Speakeasies are everywhere."

"So are magic girls." I shiver with the realization of how many hide away. My curled hair sits in soft tufts at my chin. Sadie swiped charcoal in my eyelids, and the red lipstick I borrowed from Zelda should keep my lips stained for the next week. I'm a Star Girl now.

"So, Miles Price, director extraordinaire. Where will the night take us?"

"I have somewhere in mind." His eyes twinkle under the silver moon.

"Do tell."

"I think the stage does something to you," he says. "Tonight, I want you to laugh. Let everything go and be in the moment."

"There is no *in the moment* for me. My mind is a wasteland of terrifying thoughts and potential dangers." Why did I just tell him that?

He runs the back of his finger along my chin. "It's a good thing you're with me then."

"Why is that?"

"My mother was unwell. I'd comfort her when her cries filled the house, and I sat with her at the window when she was too afraid to venture outside our walls."

That could be why his chest feels like home.

"I don't want to bring up the past." He straightens up, shaking off his earlier moment of vulnerability.

"What do you want?" I ask.

He spins me in three tight, fast twists and lands me in a dip, his face hovering over mine. "I want to dance."

Miles takes me across town. Away from the underground bars of the city center, the night turns quiet. Nestled in a dark, rundown neighborhood, we approach a mortuary, dark and gothic with its scrolled iron gates and steeply pitched roof.

"You want to dance with the dead?"

"Saddle up those tap shoes, Eleanora."

We walk through a creaking front door into a Victorian parlor with faded lace curtains and cracked glass oil lamps. "Definitely some ghosts here. Do you think they like the waltz?"

We walk down the hall, over an ancient maroon floor runner. Framed pictures of women in lace line the hallway, their silhouettes seeming to glare at us as we pass.

We step into a stark room packed with caskets. "Pick one," he says.

"Well, this is a first. Are you going to stuff me inside with a corpse? I do like a cozy, dark bed."

He lowers his chin as shadows dance across his cheeks. "Pick one and you'll find out."

"This little game of yours is very unsettling." Still, I play along. I point to the closest casket. Shiny and black.

Miles unhooks the lid as I try not to grimace, looking in the satin lining of a death box. "Ah, wonderful choice, Diamond Nora."

I peek over the edge, making sure not to get too close. Tucked in the glossy white cushions are bottles. Dozens of them. I pick one up and read the label. "Glenmore Bourbon."

"Just in from Vancouver." Miles tosses the bottle in the air then catches it. "Shall we?"

"Caskets of booze. What's next? Are we going to drink embalming fluid?"

He holds my hand and leads me through a kitchen and a pantry, leading onto a spiral staircase. It's dark and I'm grateful for his hand. I've never explored the speakeasy circuit, but this night calls for a little danger, it seems.

Jazz music greets us in the stone cellar, a smoky haze wafting over a singer in a black dress, a crown of jewels dripping down her forehead. She waves at Miles and puckers her lips before draping herself over the piano.

Miles smiles at the bartender and hands him the bottle of bourbon.

"I'll take champagne," I say.

The bartender raises his eyebrows. "Oh, she likes the expensive stuff."

A wry smile hides the fact that I've never tasted the good stuff. I've only ever had flat, overly sweet, once sparkling wine that occasionally enters the Milk House. Swill. All I've ever had is swill. Until the Luminaire.

Miles lights a cigar. The bartender tilts his head, examining me. "You're new."

I swipe the cigar and puff the leather-scented smoke out in circles. The darkness and musty scent of booze fill the room in a dreamy haze.

"How many ladies do you invite to rummage around your caskets, Mr. Price?" Am I doing this flirting thing right? Some women make this look easy.

He smirks. "None, if I'm honest. So few see the fun in casket humor like I do."

The bartender hands us our drinks and Miles guides me to a table in the corner. He slides over the coupe of champagne. "Go ahead. Enjoy."

"These secret bars are dangerous for me." I throw back the entire glass of champagne. Fizzy bubbles tickle my throat and instantly make my head float. "I've never seen an underground show that didn't make me question everything in my life." The Milk House included.

"They're magnificent." He swirls his glass of amber bourbon. "Sultry and dark. When dance is forbidden, everyone wants it more."

The curvy singer breathes pink mist into clouds that gather on the ceiling.

He rolls the cigar between his first finger and thumb, tilting his head to examine me. "This mortuary is the perfect front for bootlegged liquor. Caskets hide bottles and a hearse delivers them all over the city. No questions asked. And down here, girls perform on their own terms. Price Enterprises supplies the money, and they supply our booze."

The singer rolls her shoulders as the beads on her sleeves turn to clinking prisms that bounce light all over the dance floor in silver and green. She glides her hips in a figure eight, swirling the colors into a kaleidoscope.

"She's so beautiful," I say.

"Why the stage name Diamond Nora?" he asks.

"Ancient Romans believed diamonds were splinters from falling stars. Seemed appropriate."

"You do love the stars."

Mother told me to look for her there. I've always known I'd live without her, and she gave me hope that someday I'd hear her whispers if I listened hard enough.

He stares into my eyes so intensely, my breath hitches. I don't turn away for fear that this night will soon end, and I'll never again experience his eyes upon me like this.

Miles leads me to the dance floor. No one even looks at us. By flickering candlelight, I sway to the sultry drumbeat. Miles steps behind me. My breath catches again when he slides his hand around my waist, resting his fingers on the front curve of my hip. He presses into my back, left hand gliding my arm up like an eagle's wing. "Just let go."

I sink back into his touch, my body aching for more. I remember those early days when I could stare at the moon for hours and dance barefoot without a care in the world. This moment is mildly reminiscent of those childhood magic swells where the rush felt safe.

With pressure at my hip, he guides my leg back with his and sweeps our toes together in a giant circle. Our feet point together like pencils about to write poetry, and he leans me back.

He touches his lips to my ear with an exhale. A groan escapes my lips. He pulls me tall and raises both my arms above my head, trailing his fingers along my arms and torso, evoking chills along my skin.

He spins me to face him with a quick stop when I'm near enough to see the gold ring in his eyes. Still, no one cares to watch us. "Why aren't they staring?"

"Don't think about them. Just dance."

I lower my arms as my hands float to his shoulders. To the curve of his muscles until my hands buzz. I can't tell if it hurts or fills me with pleasure. "It's too much."

"So, take a breath," he says. "And let yourself enjoy the moment. Not everything is as big as the sky."

The buzzing in my hands turns into an ache. "For me it is."

He hasn't moved his hands but breaks into a half-smile. His fingers lace with mine, hands grasped firm as we tremble together. "You dance," he says. "I'll follow."

"You should always let the man lead," I say with a cheeky grin.

"I don't believe that and neither do you." He winks, sending my entire body alight. Maybe I can be brave.

I walk behind him just as he did with me. I grab his hip and pull him into my chest, raising his arm to the side as I guide his leg out with mine. He leans back into my breasts, a deep inhale pressing us close. I twirl him to face me, throwing my top hat to the wall where it hovers like a black moon.

He glances out the corner of his eye. "Dancing in the moonlight? How romantic."

Here, dance is whatever I want it to be. I wrap my leg around his waist and move his hand to grab my thigh. He shifts, dipping me, his hand firmly against my low back.

"Just look into my eyes," he says.

I nod, unable to force a blink. I want to taste every second of this magic. He spins me out, catching me by the hand. The floor clears. "Tap," he says.

Quick ball change.

He mirrors my steps, toe to heel as fast as lightning, not missing a single beat. We shuffle across the floor in and out of silver light. My hat spins, spitting light like a sparkler. Under my feet, the floor turns glass, a different gemstone color with every tap. Miles dances with me. We glide across the glass floor, cracking silver tap shoes into shards of chrome light.

Something in his eyes tells me to let go. Maybe I'm brave or naive. Or maybe I'm just tired of holding the universe together with my bare hands.

I laugh wild and free over a floor of flames, my body having turned lights on from somewhere deep inside. I wrap my hands behind his neck, my fingers gliding through his hair, aching to taste his kiss again.

Until I remember the day. Wednesday evening crossed into Thursday morning while I danced in a speakeasy. I forgot about Aria. Again.

CHAPTER TWENTY-ONE

Eleanora

A burst of tangerine light wakes me as the sun creeps into the sky. My body, warm and strong and grounded, revolts against my mind, warning that we've broken through a barrier that can't be repaired. And I don't want it fixed, ever again.

How can something so dangerous ignite me with the burning sense of being so completely alive?

Aria needed me and I disappointed her. I quickly dress and slip outside into the frosty morning as guilt rips through me. The sky has turned to slate clouds about to gush rain. With Christmas on its way, the city breathes its own kind of magic. Bells jangle on horse-drawn carriages and children skip past window displays of toys.

The last few winters alone at the Milk House were enough to carve a hole in my gut that may never heal. In the corner of a window display, a clean, new Kewpie doll stares onto First Ave. Her eyelashes are thick, and her blue dress reminds me of Aria.

My pay from the Luminaire covers the cost, and I even buy a blue ribbon to tie around her head. I hope she forgives me.

Once again I find myself at the Milk House. Inside, Lady sips coffee, black makeup smeared under her eyes. "Eleanora." She nods, as if she's been expecting me.

"Have you seen Aria?"

Lady sucks on her cigarette between sips from her chipped teacup. "No."

"I should have met her last night, but I forgot."

"You forgot her?" Her eyes widen. "That's interesting."

My hand grips tight around the doll's porcelain body. "What does that mean?"

"It's just," Lady considers if she wants to keep talking. "You think she needs you, but I'd say you need her more."

"Please. I've lived this long on my own." She doesn't need to know about my newfound craving for Miles or how much I love waking up with the troupe every day. And how those things scare the wits out of me.

"We all need people, Eleanora." A drunk couple stumbles out from the speakeasy, releasing a cacophony of laughs and burps, squinting when they glimpse the morning light.

"What's Price up to?"

She plucks feathers from her fallen curls. "He'll turn on you, that's for certain."

I can't speak, as my voice might remind me how painful it all is. "How bad will it be?"

"I was going to tell you when I knew more, but he's gathering all the nefarious men in the city and threatening the rest of us. Your New Year's Eve show will be more than just a debut." Her cigarette glows red as she inhales long and slow. "He's kept the specifics under wraps."

"I don't suppose you're going to do anything to stop it."

She picks a fleck of tobacco from her lower lip. "You made your choices, Eleanora."

"As did you. You wouldn't want to disrupt that hustle you've got going on, would you? Supply the Luminaire with bodies of magic girls. Who cares what they do to us once inside."

She clanks her cup against the saucer hard enough to shatter. She's left with the curved handle attached to nothing but air. She drops it to the floor and sucks the drop of blood that's sprung from between her thumb and forefinger. "I never forced you to do anything."

"I did what I had to. I couldn't stand to live in the shadows anymore."

"Your mother didn't live by shouldn't and can't." She walks around the edge of the bar, approaching with reddened cheeks. "She lived in a world where the only rules that matter were the ones in her heart."

My palm sweats against the doll's pale blue dress. "I never did understand you. You manipulate all the rules in Seattle. You smile at the men who wrong us and pour whisky in their filthy, lying mouths. And you dare explain my mother to me."

She points her two fingers at my face, a trail of smoke spiraling up from her cigarette. "I sleep soundly at night knowing I've stayed true to myself. I hope one day you experience that too."

The morning sun filters through the windows. I stare at the doorknob, willing myself to turn it and run away. Eyes pooled and voice shaking, I say, "There are ghosts here. I needed a new stage and a fresh start." I hand Lady the doll. "Please give this to Aria. And be nice to her for Christ's sake. She's just a kid."

I slam the door behind me, heaving in the crisp air as icy tears spill over my lids and dampen my cheeks. I'll be strong enough. Panic won't grab hold. The men in charge won't break me.

Price will not win.

***

Midnight under a cloudy sky usually breathes with possibility. On the Luminaire rooftop, I lie on my back, wrapped in a wool blanket just as I've done countless times before. But tonight, before clocks all over the city mark the beginning of a new minute, a new hour, a new day, the inky December sky bleeds a warning.

In ten days, my life will change. Midnight at New Year's Eve, Diamond Nora becomes real, like a princess.

A door clicks open as Ruby and Sadie tiptoe over. They cuddle next to me as Sadie pops the cork on the bootlegged bottle of California sparkling wine and takes a swig. She bumps her shoulder into mine. "Are the stars very talkative tonight?"

I sigh, hoping beyond reason that they'll someday surprise me. "No."

Ruby after a gulp, asks, "You seemed a bit off at rehearsal today. Is everything okay?"

The thought of a lonely porcelain doll with the blue ribbon only adds to the pressure building on my chest. "I disappointed someone who needed me, and I'm angry with myself."

Ruby, seeing straight through to my soul, says, "We all make mistakes, and sometimes we hurt people."

Was it a mistake when I danced with Miles instead of keeping my promise to her, or was it a willful choice? I no longer need a hazel-eyed shadow to calm my frazzled nerves, as a theater of friends now play that role. Why Aria chose to idolize me, I'll never know.

"What are we searching for?" Sadie asks, her mouth hung open, searching the sky. "Like, a meteor shower or something?"

They lie back on either side of me, cuddling into my shoulders. Touched from both sides. "The Milky Way. It's a band of stars that slides across the sky like a silver rainbow."

"I saw it back in Texas a few times. Does it mean something to you?"

"All my troubles seemed to fade during midnight dances under a clear sky or a blood moon, or the intense blackness of a crescent. When the Milky Way would appear over us—I don't know. It was a feeling."

Ruby's wild curls tickle my ear. "What did it feel like?"

"Like magic fell from the sky and sprinkled on us like rain. Like moonbeams and the infinite knowledge of the universe was mine. Nothing else mattered."

Ruby tucks her knees toward her chest. "Maybe the answer isn't up there. It could be deep in your toes connected to the Earth. In the truth of magic." She bumps my arm. "Perhaps you're making this all harder than it needs to be."

"Easy for you to say. Both of you are gorgeous and fearless. I'm a struggling tap dancer who battles her worst fears every time I step onto a stage. And only rarely wins."

Sadie places her hand on my elbow as a shiver runs through me. "You forget how magical you are." Her wheezy breath sounds painful.

"It's hard to see all that when panic rules my life."

"I need to tell you something." Ruby lifts her fiddle. She sits cross-legged and plays a stretched tune. The music levitates the glass bottle, spinning it above our heads. "You know I talk to the dead, right?"

Sadie sits up. "Um, no." We exchange worried glances, knowing some Appalachian folklore is about to get passed down and leave us with all kinds of chills.

Ruby keeps playing, soft enough we can hear her words. "Babies born at midnight have the power to talk to ghosts." Her curly hair seems to dance, floating from her shoulders like a puff of wind has graced only her.

"What do the ghosts say?" My breathing speeds up, fear gushing through my limbs.

"To listen to the animals." Ruby's freckles glow. "Ravens fluttered into my dream last night. When the sun rose, a crow stood on the window of the sleeping porch."

Sadie scratches her neck. "What does it mean?"

"Something's about to change." Ruby closes her eyes and draws out the last long, sharp note from her fiddle, sending the bottle spinning. "A crow means change. A transformation. The ghosts tell me things before they happen." The bottle lands in the center of our circle with a thud.

After a long, painful moment, I say, "I want to perform. But I don't want to change who I am to do it. I'm afraid Price will never let that happen."

"Don't crows mean death?" Sadie slaps her hand against her mouth, instantly regretting the words.

"It could mean an end of one thing and a beginning of another," Ruby says.

"It can also mean literal death," I gasp.

Ruby squeezes our hands and closes her eyes. "I talk to the dead and they help me change the world around me. Sadie, your breathing difficulties disappear when you dance with water, and Annelise sings poetry from a sightless world."

"Zelda uses her big body to take up space like the beautiful star she is," Sadie adds. The whites of Sadie's eyes turn to reddened veins like lightning. "The thing that makes us miserable is the reason we can do magical things?"

A warm bubble of pressure rises in my chest, like I could go weightless any second. "We aren't broken. We're chosen."

"Listen to me, Eleanora." Ruby leans on her knees. "A disaster is about to bring our world crashing down. Whatever's coming, we face together."

I'd secretly hoped someone would lead me to the spotlight. I've spent too much time walking in my mother's shadow and couldn't see past her looming presence, even after her death. I lift my gaze to the silent, starless sky, begging a faraway notion of home to settle in my heart. "Together."

CHAPTER TWENTY-TWO

Fiona

I've twisted myself so tight, the fire threatens to burn me from the inside. All night I've tried to dance in this cell, but the guards come in and backhand me. With my hands gripping the bars and my breath caught in a snare in my chest, I look up to see Lady through blurred eyes. Holding my fire will hasten my decline.

"The guard is completing the paperwork. I'll have you out in a minute."

I rock back and forth, trying to calm the panic. "I can't be in this cage for one more second."

"I know, I know." She grabs my hand. "Hang on."

Tears grip me. I can't breathe. My vision goes black. "Shit."

Lady whispers, "Hurry. Dance now."

I release the bars and force myself to move. Dance feels foreign, but I still spit a few bursts of flames. They could smell smoke and beat me again, which sends me to the cold floor. Lady screams at the guard but I don't hear her words. My heart may thump a hole in my chest.

A clink and grating slide of the cell door, finally. She grabs me. Lifts my wasted body and drags me out. "Keep moving."

I want out of this hellhole, so my legs walk against their will. On the way out, the policeman who arrested me puckers his lips for an air kiss. Lady slaps him with her handbag. "Shut up, Carl. I'll tell your wife about what you do in my storage closet."

His smile fades. She drags me outside and down the street, hugging me so tight I lean into her embrace. Once at the Milk House, she yells at the decoy bartender. "Make me some tea." She takes me to her room, helping me to the sofa and pulling a blanket over my trembling body.

Through chattering teeth, I force out the only thought I want to say, "Don't let her see me this way."

"I won't." The bartender appears with a tray. Lady takes it and shuts the door. She gathers ice in a towel and dabs it on my forehead. "This will help bring down the fever." She fusses for a while, tightening the blanket around me on all sides and rubbing balm on my busted lip.

My heart settles as I sip the lavender tea and finally, my limbs stop shaking. "Thank you."

"It's nothing." She checks my forehead like my mother used to do. She never had magic either and despised my grandmother for her wild ways. I was an enigma to her until she died from pneumonia. I was ten. "This is life, isn't it?"

"What do you mean?" she asks.

"We hurt and we cry, and once in a while, we dance."

She looks off into the distance as she slides to the floor next to me. Her hand still rests on mine. "Yeah, I suppose it is."

"Lady?" She looks down at her lap. "The Luminaire?"

"Why do you want something so risky? You have a family right here. On that stage, you'll have no power, and your decline will come much quicker."

"Lady, I just broke down in a prison cell because the police thought they could beat the fire out of me. I have no power now."

"Fair enough." She turns to me, her eyes heavy and cheeks swollen from fatigue. "You have an audition tonight if you want it."

Life filters back into my body. "How did you manage it?"

She reaches under the couch and produces today's paper. A picture of me handcuffed, skirt up to my waist, fire blasting from my mouth. "You're a headline now."

My palms burn like I've touched hot coals. My body has started to turn against me, just as I knew it would. Our lives are short and bright, usually with a devastating end. "I want it."

"You could stay here and have a few more years with Eleanora," she says with a tilted head.

"Or I could build something that will protect her as she navigates her own decline in a few years." I gulp the rest of the tea so hard my throat stings. "Fuck, I hate this legacy."

***

The Luminaire flickers with light. Shining and brilliant, it's everything I've dreamed of. I push past protestors and arrive in the lobby. Velvet curtains. Crimson carpet. Grand staircases along both walls. At the top of the stairs, a man appears. Not young, not old, but lost somewhere in between.

"Fiona?"

"Call me Celtic Fire." Play the part. No time to waste.

"Go through that door," he says with a subtle side nod. "Meet me on the stage."

Though my legs tremble, I force a prideful walk through the side doors into the massive theater. Damn, it's the most elaborate thing I've ever seen. Gold balconies bright as sunshine with seats of tufted velvet. I walk up the stairs to the stage, every step echoing around me. Empty seats. Quiet space.

A light thuds on and I find myself in a spotlight. Without waiting, I dance. I dance to save my future and quiet the boiling fever inside. Eleanora will never forgive me. I don't stop. I can't. This will be my end, and I will do it my way.

I don't even have to think. My fire explodes into the giant space and produces a ring that drops from the sky. I twist my body and extend my limbs in ways that no woman should be able to do. The fire burns away any pain.

My skin ignites in a fire so hot my brain ceases working. Nothing but air and disappointment. I let go of the ring, plummeting toward the stage in my white fitted leotard. My dance sequence often summons this outfit, perhaps to offset the flames. Where once I performed with confidence, now I dance with desperation, thirsty and raw.

My flames evaporate, and my feet somehow land safely on the stage. The man appears on the balcony as if lifted from darkness. He removes his spectacles, mouth wide, eyes aglow. There's no question he sees dollar signs on this stage instead of a human. "You're hired."

Safety from the police, from purity raids. "I can't live here. I have a daughter."

"You'll take your chances out there. I can only protect you inside these walls."

My dance moves outside of me. My body is in transition to become my enemy, but I don't care. Eleanora needs a future. Money. A legacy. "When do I start?"

"Tonight."

CHAPTER TWENTY-THREE

Eleanora

Dress rehearsal has arrived.

Today I must perform Price's approved routine with contained magic. A curated, perfectly sharp line carved by my director where elements start and stop on rehearsed command. Everything dictated by a father and son cornered by the society that built them.

Dessa arrives at our rehearsal space in the basement, appearing in the reflection behind me. "You're beautiful," she says.

"Price chose our outfits to match our elements, didn't he?" I run my hands down the sleek line of gold silk on my skirt. I turn sideways and glance over my shoulder. Delicate straps cross my back in a web of diamonds.

"Everything must create a sensation." Dessa, ever the composed ballerina, doesn't so much as twitch despite her words dripping with irony.

"Miles choreographed my dance with more freedom than his father would want. Mr. Price directs my facial expressions. You sharpen the lines in my extension and turnout. But where am I in all this?"

Iridessa cracks a tiny smile. "That is an answer only you can discover."

My makeup is perfect. Diamond encrusted pins stud the finger waves in my hair. My tap shoes sparkle gold. "Everything about me shines. Why then, do I feel so very invisible?"

"Your mother loved to leap across the rooftop in her undergarments and a feather boa."

I can't help but laugh. "Yes, that sounds like her."

"I couldn't contain her any more than I could catch the stars in my hands," she says. "You don't have the same wild streak. There's nothing wrong with that."

I fiddle with the jewels dangling from my neck. "Once the country told her she was wrong and illegal and dangerous, something lit up inside her. I think she quite liked the idea of unbridled fire." No amount of stretching seems to loosen my tight shoulders.

Iridessa smooths my hair and straightens my diamond and gold necklaces. "First they blame us, then they attack us."

I touch her hand softly. "Then we find our family."

Dessa drops her long, graceful arms. "New Year's Eve is a few days away." Her dark skin shines more golden than my dress. Her cheeks are bronzed and naturally high, like light fills her from the inside. "I can't wait to watch from the wings."

I find the strength to turn from my reflection and stand eye to eye with Iridessa. "Price is planning something that could sabotage me, isn't he? Allow me to think I'll shine but send in the police to rip me from the spotlight."

She drops her to her sparkling ballet slippers. "Mr. Price hasn't always been this way. Neither has the Luminaire."

"But here we are." I shrug.

"I've remained safe. An anomaly among our kind with a sharp mind and years of ballet magic still ahead of me, even as an old lady."

Regret is always an easy identifier in someone's eyes. Like they can't tolerate the sight of someone staring back at them. "He isn't your responsibility, Dessa."

"No, you are. And your mother was, as is every girl who dances under my tutelage. I've remained healthy because I had to for all of you, but—" She grimaces hard enough to wrinkle her forehead, a sight I rarely see from her radiant skin. "My protection came at the sacrifice of fighting for what's right."

"You think you could have stopped all their hysteria? It's in our blood, Iridessa."

"No, it can't be." Her hand lays gracefully across her chest. "I've waited for my mind to crumble for decades now, yet here I stand, watching you face your future, and wondering how to stop another catastrophe."

She doesn't cry like I tend to do. She remains tall and in control but very, very sad. "None of this is your fault," I tell her.

"After Fiona, I kept you all closer. Trained you with a firm but loving hand. And now her daughter faces the same fate, and I've not stopped a thing. It's only grown worse."

A spray of red mist falls from her arm as she extends into fourth position. The scent of rose fills the air. "None of us could have saved Fiona. She accepted her destiny, come what may."

She exhales, long and slow, as her eyes glisten and look up at the hanging clock. "Almost show time." She walks away, waiting to exit the door before wiping her eyes as if I can't see.

I join the Star Girls backstage, each in our glittering gowns and leotards. My hands tremble uncontrollably as we wait for our final dress rehearsal.

Ruby holds my hands and leans her forehead to mine. "Star Girls today. Sisters forever."

Sadie hugs me from behind and Zelda wraps herself around the three of us. Even Annelise crawls her hand through the dark to find my shoulder.

"You can do this, Eleanora." Ruby smiles.

Hope and love flow through me as I beg the universe for one speck of my mother's talent to find my performance. Later, we'll dance under the moonlight, and everything will feel whole.

"Uh, girls?" Ruby holds the curtains open, startled.

We crowd around to see what causes her eyes to grow so wide. The audience is filled with men in suits. Dozens of them. They smoke cigars and drink whisky, multiple showgirls draped over their laps.

"Who are they?" I ask.

"I'm not sure." Sadie coughs twice, wheezy and tight.

Zelda pushes her way forward. "That's every speakeasy owner in the city. Every mobster and hustler with money."

"How do you know that?" I ask.

"I frequent them all. Both the speakeasies and the men." She winks.

I step over to Ruby, who stands stoically by herself, eyes closed. "Ruby, what is it?"

"They're here for something more than a dress rehearsal."

"What?"

She shakes her head. "I don't know." She paces a frantic circle in the blackness of backstage. "This is the death the ghosts warned me of."

I stare out at the audience again. Men hang from the balcony and dance with showgirls in the aisles, while Miles gazes toward his feet in the corner. "Did Miles do this?"

"Welcome, gentlemen!" Mr. Price steps on stage like the King of Seattle. "The Luminaire has gathered you here today for something special. You are all the most successful and cunning businessmen in the city." He paces left to right. "My son Miles had a wonderful idea to bring us all together in solidarity against the unfair laws that threaten every one of us."

"He did do this," I mutter.

"If the Luminaire falls, we all fall. They'll dictate what we drink, how we live and breathe. Our every choice will disappear at the hands of a few radical extremists. Miles knew we had to fight back. And that's what we'll do."

The men erupt in cheers, guzzling their whisky and wrapping the showgirls in tight embraces. Price clasps his hands behind his back and waits for a hush of attention. "We have a special feature we've been keeping secret. A dancer the world will want to see. Who they'll demand to see."

All eyes backstage turn to me.

"This theater once controlled the city. Our shows were so powerful and outrageous, we wrote our own laws. Ran things as we saw fit." He nods several times. "Over the years, we've bowed down to the lawmen who only line their own pockets. We're losing power every day."

Our future is now dictated by the men who can't have magic. Does he not see the irony, or does he not care? Miles rubs his eyes, collapsing against the wall under the balcony.

"It's our turn," Price says. "We will take back our rightful place in this city, and we'll do it together. We'll cultivate a world of magic and booze so popular the city will have no choice but to bow down to us."

"Anyone else feel like a bull in Spain?" Sadie says. "Prodded and cornered. Released to fight, knowing we'll end up stabbed?"

None of us answer.

"The Luminaire has something special planned for New Year's Eve," Price says. "A feast for the senses where theatergoers won't know whether to be terrified or exhilarated. And it all starts with someone special."

Please don't call me. *Please.*

"Welcome to the illustrious Luminaire stage, daughter of the best Star Girl of all time, inheritor to the famed Celtic Fire, Eleanora Cleary!"

Applause erupts from every corner of the theater, with hoots and hollers, waiting for this magical dancer to step into the spotlight. I'm barely me, just the stand-in for the most infamous woman in Seattle.

"No."

Zelda touches my arm. "Go on, Eleanora. This is your moment."

"I don't want this moment." My head thumps. "I want my own moment in the spotlight, not one crafted by Winston fucking Price the Third."

The applause dies down and Price, exasperated, motions to throw open the curtains. The heavy velvet parts, revealing the Luminaire troupe, glossed in metallic hues, stunned into silence.

Price walks toward me. In a hushed whisper, he says, "Get on stage."

"No."

He curls his lips and presses his front teeth together. "You wanted this, Cleary."

I turn to stare at my star sisters with their sad eyes. Miles appears behind his father. "Give me a minute with her."

Price snarls but agrees. He steps back a few feet. Miles grabs my hand and pulls me to center stage. "Eleanora—"

"You orchestrated this? All these men here to judge me?"

His glimmering eyes meet mine. "Yes. But it's not what you think."

"It looks to be exactly like what I think. You promised your father a spectacle and the girl who panics makes for something interesting. Dammit, I should have seen this coming. You came looking for me and handed this whole idea to your father to save your inheritance."

"No. I brought the men here to invest in us. To join forces and change these ridiculous laws." He runs his thumb along the back of my hand. "To give you the freedom you deserve."

I slide my hand from his, distracted by the dozens of businessmen staring at us. "They're just more men to control us. Don't you see that?"

"They're meant to watch the entire troupe. I didn't know my father would single you out."

"Then you're naive."

Miles wipes his hand across his mouth and down his jaw. "Maybe I am." The room fades in and out as my eyes scan the crowd of blurry men. Miles places his finger on my cheek to turn me back to face him. "Do you want this?"

What I want mixes with what I can't have to form one giant mess in my head. It swells and grows until I can't breathe.

"You don't have to hurt yourself to prove anything." Miles's voice is soft and gentle. "Walk away right now if you want."

Men swell our magic but dull the shine. They leave us in hysteria. Yet, his gaze warms my insides. I want—perhaps stupidly—to believe him. I step back, confused and wheezing. My gilded shoes tap against the stage until I back right into Mr. Price.

Never without a scowl, I'm convinced his down-turned lips are scarred that way. "You'll ruin this for everyone," he says.

Shaking, I run off stage and out into the alley, and I don't stop until I realize my bare shoulders are slick with rain and my hands have turned blue. Hovering under a fire escape in an unknown alley, I slide to the dirty concrete and cry in my shining gown of gold.

CHAPTER TWENTY-FOUR

Eleanora

I can't face the Star Girls, but I'll freeze into an ice block if I stay out in the December rain. By the time I step into the Milk House, my limbs have stopped stinging, too numb to hurt.

Lady takes one look at me and rushes to my side. "You're blue."

"Blue is lovely next to Gold." My voice hitches in a forced laugh.

"Come on." She finds a blanket and walks me in her arms to her apartment upstairs. She holds up the blanket while I fumble to remove my dress. I wait near the fireplace, wrapped in wool while Lady draws a bath.

On the mantel, a beaded frame holds a picture of my mother. She's dressed in a fringe dress and matching headpiece, alive and happy. It's hard to believe she's been gone for seven whole years. I catch my reflection in the mirror. Wet hair stuck to my cheeks, snow white skin and lips the same hue as my eyes. Fear tightens every inch of my face.

"Hurry up," Lady says. "You're positively frozen."

I shuffle toward the bathroom and drop the blanket on the tiles. My slip still hugs my body, and I'm shaking too terribly to untie my brassiere, so Lady helps me manage, holding my arm as I step into the hot water that stings my tender toes.

I slip into the tub, the intense memory of failure heavy on my chest. Lady leaves the towel over the radiator to warm. "Will you be alright?"

I nod, having trouble meeting her eyes. "Lady?" She stops, looking at the door instead of back at me. "I panicked tonight." I'm certain there's a halo of gold around my head for the way my eyes well with tears. I don't wipe them away. I'm so tired of hiding my swells.

She lays the dress over her arm with care, then glances over her shoulder. "Life is much messier when you brave the thing you fear the most."

I uncurl from the tightened ball of failure, stretching out and staring at my legs under the water. "This has been my home for years. I didn't leave because of you. I simply needed more, and I couldn't find it in the kitchen."

"I know." Lady freezes, taking several slow breaths. "I'm sorry we live in a world that invented purity raids. I'm sorry I couldn't help you through your fear of the stage. And I'm very, very sorry I could never take care of you the way you needed."

"But you aren't sorry for pushing my mother to perform." I pick at a crack in the porcelain tub.

"Sometimes people we care about do things we don't agree with, but we support them anyway."

"I don't accept that."

"I know. And I hope that doesn't unravel you." Lady checks her scarf in the mirror and runs her hand along her aging cheek. "You'll always have a home here." She clears her throat before walking out.

The door shuts and I'm left to my lonely bath and even lonelier tears.

Once dressed and back in my body again, I step into the living room, where Aria sits cross-legged on the rug. "You're back!" She runs to me, arms wide. "I'm never letting go. I'll move in if Lady lets me."

"Aria, I've missed you."

"Yeah?" She looks up, flashing me a teary smile. "Seems like you forgot about me."

"I'm so sorry. I got swept up in all the wrong things." I hold her hand and walk her to the bar where Lady waits with a mug of hot cocoa. "You got one for my sidekick?" I tilt my head in Aria's direction as if to say, *She's right here. Be nice.*

"Fine." Lady prepares another mug, sliding them toward us.

"What about you?" I motion to the cocoa.

"I don't touch the sweet stuff." She reaches for a faux can of pineapple and gulps from the triangle cut in the lid. "Now, tell me. What did Price do?"

"He put me on display for every mobster in town. He's exploiting my name."

She waves me away. "Aria, what say you? Should Eleanora keep trying for her dream on a big stage?"

Aria smiles. "I vote for dreams."

"I panicked. I couldn't even tap. The threat was just too big. All those disapproving eyes. I completely failed."

"We all have our own definition of failure," Lady says.

"What's yours?" I'm not sure why I ask. It's not like I've ever cared before.

"To be what someone else dictates of me. That is failure with a capital F." She motions to Aria. "And you?"

Little Orphan Aria with her blue ribbon around her hair says, "Failure means never trying at all."

I take in their words as the door bangs open. Ruby and Sadie. "Thank God you're here," Sadie stumbles in. "It's terrifying out in those streets!"

Lady throws a rag over her shoulder. "We'll wipe the smudges from glasses. Come on." She motions to Aria, and they disappear behind the curtain.

Sadie wipes the rain from below her eyes. "Homeless men and the Temperance League protesting on every corner. What do people see in this mess of a city?"

"Potential," I say. Mother loved the cool air to offset her fire.

Ruby shakes her wild hair loose of raindrops. "We don't like to leave the theater. Too risky."

"You don't leave? You just stay inside those walls? Forever?" I ask.

Sadie shrugs. "Yeah. It's more and more unsafe out here. But we had to find you and this little cream house of yours."

"Milk House," Lady shouts from behind the curtain.

"Right." Saide holds my hands. "Come home."

"I don't know if I belong there, Sadie." I roll my mug of cocoa around in my still chilled fingers.

Ruby purses her lips. "Of course you belong."

"But this morning. All those eyes on me, and I just gave up. I ran away."

"It isn't New Year's Eve yet," Sadie says. "Give it one more week."

"Why would I subject myself to more embarrassment?"

They link arms and lean their temples together. "Because we're lost without you."

"I know the feeling." Aria shouts.

"Miles put me in that situation. I trusted him." My face warms and I wish my vulnerability would retreat. "I feel so stupid."

"About Miles." Ruby scrunches her nose. "I think he wants to make it up to you."

"How?"

"Come with us and find out," Sadie says.

Searching for my mother's whispers has only led to a deep silence. It's time I fill the space with something real. "Okay."

***

Back in the Luminaire, Ruby and Sadie both smile then immediately disappear down the endless hallway. Alone at the foot of the staircase that will welcome ravenous crowds in less than a week, I take in the soft lights and the scent of freshly oiled wood.

Miles descends the stairs toward me. He's dressed in a jazz suit and top hat. I don't speak as I'm not sure what to say.

"Hit me," he says with an assured tone.

"What?"

"Punch me hard, right in the nose. Make me bleed. Go on."

I glance in all directions for some catch. "No."

His eyes fill with a glassy sheen. "Why not?"

"Because we're all prisoners here, including you." Against all reason, I reach for his cheek. I rub my palm across his cheekbone and my fingers through his hair. His deep brown eyes catch the light.

"Your halo is showing," he whispers. "A gold crown." He pulls me into his chest, his lips nearly touching mine.

"I should be furious. But right now, all I want is to tap my way into the night with you."

"I'd much prefer to dance right here, on solid ground, but I know you need to feel the stars." He hooks his soft fingers around mine.

Everything seems safe. All the horrors of tonight fade in the flame of his eyes. "Show me."

He leads me up the winding staircase, past the balcony and through the gallery, up another two flights of stairs toward the only door left at the top of the Luminaire. "The rooftop?" I ask.

As he creaks open the door, a sea of glittering lights shines from every direction. Hundreds of string lights, candelabras, dripping candles, and lit faux trees from set design. "Woah," I walk past him and step into the galaxy of light.

He presses himself against the door, panic gripping his face. "It's your stage."

I step to the elevated wood floor to the center of flames of light. A swell unlike any other rises inside me. This one doesn't feel untamed. It feels full and soft.

Still pressed to the wall, Miles swallows nervously. "Our famed Star Girl deserves her own stage."

"Why here?"

He slides his feet away but keeps his palm firmly on the wall. "City lights resemble the stage."

"You did this for me?"

"Well, the other girls helped. The ones who aren't afraid of heights." His nervous laugh lightens my worry over what happened today. "Go ahead," he says. "Try it."

I take position in the center of the makeshift stage, lights encircling me. The chilly night air trills against my skin like music. Dance flows through me, my peep toe heels following the rhythm of the flickering candles in the wind. I spin and leap and tap and shuffle without a thought of choreography. The cold wind tousles my hair against my chilled neck, locks sticking to my rouged lips.

My fingers extend overhead to the hazy moon, but my eyes settle on Miles. "Dance with me?"

He smiles, until he remembers he's seven stories high. "No, I... I'm too afraid to move."

"But you want to dance?" I ask.

"With you?" I can see his heart pounding from here. "More than anything."

The scent of melting beeswax mixes with peppermint tobacco. Without a hint of panic, I summon my magic. With every tap, a cloud of gold dust billows from my feet, growing like steam from a boiler. My feet create a rhythmic tapping, but my eyes don't leave his.

No panic. No hysteria in sight.

He watches as gold puffs skitter toward him. He closes his eyes and nods his head. Flecked with blue raindrops, the cloud of sparkles carries him until we're face to face. "Tell me when I can open my eyes," he says.

I reach for his face. Wrap both my hands around his neck and lean my mouth to his ear. "Do you trust me?"

He slides his hands across my waist and balls the back of my blouse in his fist. "Yes."

Our arms glide, matching each other's movements. Miles's eyes remain closed, but his moves are flawless. He reaches for my hand and spins me out and back to his chest.

The cloud grows beneath us as we levitate together. Miles's body goes rigid, but he pulls me close.

"I'm right here," I say.

"Stay forever."

When our chests touch, I gasp, wanting his hands on me for the rest of time. We hover in the air, above the city in a cloud of dust. "Don't let me go," he whispers. The cloud surrounds us as we dance together, embraced in elongated twirls and backbends.

"Open your eyes," I say.

He cracks his eyes open to find me in crystal trousers and a beaded blouse. He's in a matching tuxedo. We're encased in an orb of twinkling stars, the city spread out below us.

"Don't look away," I say. "Look right here." I stare into his eyes as warmth spreads through my limbs.

He leans to me, stopping just shy of my lips. His hand spreads across the curve of my back and he pulls me tight. His eyes remain on mine, fear gone, replaced with a sparkle of light reflected in his mirrored eyes.

When his lips touch mine, a different kind of magic flows through me, twirling my insides like its own galaxy. He runs his fingers through my hair as his tongue tangles with mine and we spin into the sky, surrounded by gold light. He pulls me into a tight embrace, our hair flying to the air around us in slow motion.

He slides his hand down my leg and behind my knee, leaning me into a backbend. His kiss flips me upside down and inside out, though our bodies remain in a dip, frozen in space.

He lifts me back to standing as the orb descends us to the rooftop, our feet landing like pillows on the makeshift dance floor. A strong wind blows out the candles, but the twinkling lights remain to light the night sky.

He smiles as he runs his fingers behind my ear, along my halo that lights his arm like a lightning rod. "What's it like to have magic?" he asks.

"Like the world is endless and so am I. I hold everything tight because I'm afraid of spinning away into the unknown."

"You're afraid of flying away, and I'm afraid of plummeting to Earth."

"Maybe they aren't that different, our fears."

The world quiets. We kiss again, deeper and fuller. Feet grounded to the rooftop and head in the stars, I lean into his kiss where neither of us fear the fall.

CHAPTER TWENTY-FIVE

Fiona

One month as a headliner. The city has adopted Celtic Fire but has decided Fiona Cleary must die. Perhaps they wish to cleave me in two and fight over the halves. As I stand in Price's office, waiting for him to respond to my straightforward question, I wonder how deep his lies go.

"I don't know, Fiona."

"You do know." I'll ask him again. "How can we protect the Milk House?"

He rubs his temples, avoiding my gaze. "I'm barely hanging onto my exemption. I pay the cops. I pay the mobsters. Someday this will all fall apart."

"Someday isn't now." I press my hands into his desk, leaning so far forward my arms ache. "I'm a sensation. I pack the house every night."

"I'm aware," he growls.

"Double your prices. Set the place on fire and have one of the water dancers spray them down." I slam my palms on his desk. "Just fucking protect my kid."

Price ignores his own teenager wandering through this place. I've taught the boy how to tap when his father isn't looking, and Iridessa has him practicing ballet. He can't see that his own son wants the stage, not the big desk with all the responsibility.

"Pay them to stop the purity raids?" The man has the audacity to roll his eyes.

"Only at the Milk House." I cross my arms. "Do it or I walk." It may be a bluff. I can't quite tell how far I'll take this.

"This was your plan all along, wasn't it?" he asks. "Make me indebted to you."

I shrug. "People are predictable. If they make me the enemy they love to hate, they don't need to look at their own lives."

"You're comfortable with this?"

"I've never been comfortable a day in my life." I hate this man, but I understand him. Holding on to the one thing he has and ruining everything in the process. "What would you do to keep Miles safe? I know you want him to carry on this thing you've built. I'm no different."

He considers me. He knows if I walk, he loses the frenzy and then, the money. "Fine. I'll figure it out."

"Do it now." I head for the door with a skirt flip just to take my last stand of female power. "I need to blow some fire before I vomit."

I leave him sweating, wondering how to pay for all this. He'll probably have to dip into his coffers. Not my problem.

Fever rising, eyesight fading in and out. It's become an hourly ritual now. Once again, I blast into the gymnasium in the basement and start dancing. My limbs fatigue, but fire releases with ease. Flames from my eyeballs are new, but thank God, they release the wicked headaches.

Destruction has begun.

I collapse on the ground, heaving and choking. Iridessa floats down next to me in attitude. Her ruby mist fills my nose with sickly sweet rose air. "Why do you do this to yourself?" she asks, settling into first position.

A few dry heaves and I find my voice. "It's my destiny."

"None of this is set out for you."

"Have you ever met an old fire dancer? No, we don't exist." I pull a flask from my bodice and swig until the pain subsides. "We burn bright and die young. Might as well do the thing I love and leave all the ugly in pieces at my feet."

"You're pushing too hard."

"Just hard enough." Iridessa doesn't know what we endure. I guzzle enough whisky to seize my throat for one terrifying moment. "Why withhold the wicked when I'll die in terror anyway?"

She lowers to the wood floor, sitting tall and pristine next to my hunched, twisted body. "For more time here. With us, with your daughter."

"Stop." I taste the last drop from my flask. "You help contain these girls. You teach them to ignore their instincts."

Her spine remains so unnaturally straight. "I am a ballerina."

"With no fire." I stumble up, looking down on her lean, controlled body. "I won't let anyone control me. I do this my way."

"I know." And she rises on her toe shoes like a wisp of wind. "I don't want you to get hurt."

"Too late."

"When you first arrived, you danced with joy. Your naked leaps on the rooftop were something new. Please, just work with me."

"I don't take orders, even from the best ballerina in the biz." Iridessa wants to protect us, I know that. But you can't protect a wild thing. "I have to go. The ugly comes up fast these days."

I don't wait for her response. I'm out the door and past the protestors, focused on my one good hour. Several women shove me, though I've learned they mostly stop there. Sometimes I shove back. Better for publicity anyhow.

At the Milk House, I find Eleanora cleaning the bar top. "Mama!" She throws her arms around my waist, and I squeeze tight.

I gasp, pulling her back to check her new look. "Your braids are gone."

She taps the bottom of her bob with both hands. "Same as you."

"You look so grown up." A sweet ache gnaws at my chest.

"Lady says I can debut here at sixteen, but I can't taste the booze for a long while. Not sure I'd want to."

"How's the dance?" I ask.

"Better. I think I'm starting to let go."

"Well done, sweetheart." Heat rises in my throat. Not yet. I should have more time before my damn fire returns. I'm not ready for my end.

"Are you alright?" I shake my head and force a smile. "Lady lets me wash dishes so I can watch the acts. Isn't that great?" she asks, full of excitement.

"It sure is." I reach behind the bar and open the first bottle my hands come across. Just a quick guzzle. The girls are lined up looking haggard and nervous. "What's up with them?"

"They're scared." Eleanora takes a deep breath. "One woman started showing signs of hysteria yesterday. She's only twenty-five. I just keep remembering that you've made it, so I bet I can too."

She thinks I've avoided my tragic end. Oh, sweet girl.

Men bang through the door. A bunch of thugs with night sticks and bad haircuts. They knock girls over in yet another purity raid. "Mr. Price will deal with this. Please, stop."

One grabs me by the dress. "I'm Celtic Fire." He grunts, shoving me aside, knowing legally I'm safe from their brutality. He reaches for Eleanora and something in me breaks open. I grab him by the hair and knee him in the groin. This unleashes a fit of screams and beatings by the police. I shove Eleanora into the kitchen. "Put on an apron. They won't care about a dishwasher."

My begs mean nothing. They slam their sticks on the girls' legs and cuff every one of them. Lady waves a pile of cash in their faces but it's too late. They finish their sweep. Unconscionable bastards.

I run into the kitchen and check Eleanora. She's standing at the sink, apron half tied around her waist, watching the jazz dancer shake and cry. Sparklers flicker from her palms as she slides a blade down her forearm without a fleck of hesitation.

"I don't want it anymore," she says through tears. Blood gushes over her arm and drops on her pretty shoes. Eleanora's face turns ghost white before she faints into my arms.

CHAPTER TWENTY-SIX

Eleanora

December 30.

The staff at the Luminaire is hard at work preparing for tomorrow night's showcase. String lights dangle from pillars in the lobby, with a veritable forest of illuminated Christmas trees in every corner. Pines with bursts of electric lights, feathers, and silk roses. At the Milk House, we strung popcorn on thread for decorations. Here, strands of pearls and crystals reflect every glisten of light.

The Star Girls gather in the Sapphire Bar, exhausted from another day's rehearsal. The hours have grown longer as New Year's Eve approaches. Mr. Price greets us with a feast of smoked ham, broiled potatoes and cheese, cakes, and powdered butter cookies. Even the cocktails flow from a blue champagne fountain.

"Welcome." Price sounds boastful. "Please grab a drink and gather around."

My muscles are tired, but I drag myself into the bar to catch a glimpse of Miles standing behind his father.

"You've all worked very hard to get this new show off the ground. I know we've pushed you, so tonight, we celebrate." He snaps as a line of well-dressed men in masks sashay into a circle around us. "These guests are here to dance with you all night. You have carte blanche in the theater. I've instructed these men, and some women, to entertain you. Dance, fly, spin magic. Fall in love. Our orchestra is situated all over the theater, hiding in every nook to create one magical night."

"This is odd," I whisper to Ruby.

"Offering us dance partners all night? Yeah, it's weird."

The girls mostly smile, their eyes lit up with the enchantment of a night of Magic Dance with partners and no choreography. I lean toward Ruby. "Bleed your magic now so you have less for tomorrow."

"This is what your lives could be if this theater wins. If we fight hard enough and dance so spectacularly, the country will be forced to see you. They'll want to accept you."

Miles still hasn't said a word.

Iridessa floats in from the door in a cloud of colored dust. "A little fun for our hard-working girls." She stomps her foot which lights the wood in prismed glass in every shade of the rainbow.

"Enjoy," Price says.

"Whatever he's serving, I don't want it," I scoff.

Zelda pushes her way past me. "Speak for yourself." Her hair turns translucent, and her eyes clear into glass orbs, as she grabs a man, spinning him into a dip.

The girls let loose in a frenzy of drinks and screams as magic erupts in every corner. Fireballs explode from breath, swings made of vines creep from the ceiling, and a waterfall of cobalt water rains from behind the bar.

Ruby clinks her glass to mine. "Since men don't have magic, they'll never understand how lucky we are."

"Do you get the sense we're all broken, and gifted this magic as a way of balancing the sadness?" My episodes may well be a fault line through my soul.

She shrugs, watching the room dance and laugh. "I think we're magic in an unfair world. Simple as that."

I wrap my arms around her in a hug as she cries on my shoulder for a few brief seconds. "I'll never let the torches near you, Ruby."

"Yeah?" She forces a laugh. "How are you going to stop them?"

The Sapphire Bar teems with life as girls spin with color. "I'm going to blow the roof off at the showcase. I'll teach Seattle there is nothing wrong with magic dancers."

"You aren't afraid of fire anymore?"

"Oh no, I'm terrified. Of magic, of Price, and most of all, myself."

I think of my mother getting dragged away, her eyes wild and frantic. Lady telling me about the botched surgery, and the sensation in the papers for weeks after. But then I hold Ruby's hand and remember her world of greenery and Iridessa's content, stable mind. Miles floating in the stars with me high above the city, and Aria loving me when I failed to love her back.

"I suppose I'm ready to be more than a dancer scared of her magic."

Ruby winks, the sparkle back in her eyes. "I'm going to play my fiddle at the mezzanine."

"Don't you want to dance with one of the masked men?" I force back a smile.

"I'll take the fiddle, thanks."

Heat rushes up my neck when I turn to see Miles. "You're missing a room full of men and champagne fountains," he says.

"The Star Girls might burn the place down, but they'll have a hell of a time doing it." I smile, getting lost in his eyes.

He steps close, the back of his fingers brushing against mine. "You helped me fly last night," he says.

"Were you scared?"

"Yes." He pulls my hips toward his. "But your touch softens the screams in my head."

"I'm afraid nothing quiets my screams."

He drops his hands from my waist. "The Luminaire I inherit will not place limits on the Star Girls. My theater will be free, and so will everyone in it."

"You don't stand up to your father."

"I know." Miles breaks the slightest hint of a smile. "I want you to dance your heart out tomorrow. Screw him." He shakes his head and when he opens his eyes, I've moved within inches of his lips.

"What kind of director tells their dancer to ignore everything they've taught?"

"The kind who can't keep fighting the man who refuses to hear me."

"Your father will kill us both if I let loose tomorrow night." I rest my palm on his cheek. He leans into my hand. "He's guilting us with an evening of freedom," I say. "So, let's fly."

Hand in hand, we run through the theater, along hallways and sliding down banisters, a cloud of stars dangling around us. Gold spits from my shoes as I tap along the mezzanine, spinning around Ruby's clover-covered balcony. I land in Miles's arms in a golden burst of laughter. A swell of love to eclipse the darkness.

In the costume room, I hide behind a mirror and gesture for him. He drags me by the hand into the empty space surrounded by mirrors. Shuffle ball change. Sidestep. I point my hand to the instruments stored in the corner. Ivory keys plunk out a light tune. I spin my palm up and wiggle my fingers.

He smiles, then taps with me. Stamp clap, shuffle ball change, chug. I match his movements. Basic steps, but he's setting the rhythm. I combine heel step, scuff, and paradiddle until the floor has turned to a giant prism. Miles matches my choreography, swaying his way through the music my magic has created.

He holds my hand, spins me against his chest, then unravels me into a tight spin. Gold light spits off my fingers, spraying fire-lit diamonds into the mirrors. I've never let magic fly quite like this.

I hesitate in a moment of fear, but Miles slides to me, arm around my waist. We tap together, palm to palm, his eyes settling any fear rumbling deep in my mind. He nods once, then pushes me away.

My tap shoes transform into Oxfords. My dress flutters into a tuxedo as the beat hastens. A top hat appears on my head, sparkling bright enough to cause Miles to squint. When I kick, the ceiling turns to stars. Fire spits and I whisper, "No turning back."

My body spins so fast all I see is a whir of shining light. When I come to a halt, I slam my foot into a pool of silver, causing it to bead like mercury. Chest heaving, sweat on my brow, my body settles like after an episode. Free, clear, and powerful. I push Miles into the closest mirror and press my lips to his. Our mouths taste each other, slow then fast, our tongues exploring a dance of their own.

He runs his mouth along my neck and unbuttons my jacket and blouse, his tongue soft and warm on my skin.

Magic swells inside me and around me as he cradles my head in his hands. His deep stare into my eyes stirs my halo, but I rein it back in. I pull him to the ground, now a wave of sapphire gems, hungry for his body on mine. He lowers his chest over me.

I pull him closer until his weight presses onto me fully, like a warm blanket. I throw my top hat in the air as it hovers above our heads—a magic umbrella to shield us from the falling stars plunking around us.

"Miles, I could decline any minute. You need to know what you're getting into."

"I know exactly what I'm doing." He kisses me hard, holding his lips against mine. He unbuttons my blouse while kissing along my sternum. My stomach. He whispers, "Are you prepared for things to get dangerous?"

"My life started dangerous. I think things are just getting interesting."

With that, we kiss and press our chests together in a heat-fueled tangle of bodies.

Danger be damned.

CHAPTER TWENTY-SEVEN

Eleanora

The Luminaire Re-opens after Hiatus!
Droves of Protestors Petition Grand Re-Opening
The Star Girls Get a New Look!
Fiona Cleary's Daughter Fights Mania for a Shot at Stardom

If nervous energy could kill, I'd be face down dead in a pile of diamonds and makeup. Alas, panic hasn't offed me yet, and my fire demands to burn.

Damn Price leaked headlines for the papers while hosting our free-magic extravaganza. Jerk.

The dressing room is a hive of movement. Loose feathers flutter through the air as gems plunk on the floor, and the scent of powder and perfume is enough to choke the remaining air from my chest. Price chose only five tonight, leaving the acrobats and showgirls to watch from backstage. Why, I don't know, but I presume we're about to find out.

Zelda stands on her chair, one foot propped on her makeup desk. "Each of you are glorious, my dear friends." The room stops to smile at Zelda's inspirational speech. "We are magic dancers, meant to dazzle crowds of all ages." She creates diamond dust as she glides her hand through the air. "If any of you doubt your place on this stage or in this world, just remember, the Luminaire would be nothing without us."

Tears prickle the backs of my eyes. She's right. Price needs us. This crowd needs us. They're here for magic. To see if Fiona's daughter fails as spectacularly as she did.

"Eleanora, are you alright?" Ruby's voice holds my panic sturdy, like an anchor.

The room—a dizzying circus of Star Girls and lights—closes in on me. "I can't."

I pull from her hand and force my way out the door, desperate to get away from all the noise, all the pressure in my head. My shoulder bumps right into someone.

"Shit. Sadie, I'm sorry." Crystals and blue shimmer powder line her bright eyes. Her hair is slicked back like a wave, weaved with blue ribbons. "You look beautiful."

Sadie tilts her head. "This leotard and ice blue ballet skirt are sewn with crystals so I shine on stage. It's not my choice, but nothing ever is."

"Okay," I say through quick breaths.

"It's an act, Eleanora." She turns to a mirror which reflects the darkness backstage. With a pirouette, she creates a spotlight toward us. "This is how I get through the madness of it all. I remind myself that none of it is me."

"An act." I repeat the words in my head. "That could work."

"If I could dance for myself, I'd be dressed in black and crimson, twirling to a dark stage, lit with a thousand candles."

Sadie turns me to the mirror, now framed with pearls and gold roses. The backstage has disappeared, the chatter from the filling audience has quieted. It's just me and Sadie in the reflection. "What do you see?" she asks.

The seamstress agreed to adjust my outfit since my last rehearsal. Beaded gowns don't fill me with power, the opulence simply leaves me exposed. "I see black tights. Real tap shoes with heels and shiny straps. A drop waist dress of black and gold fringe. Makeup garish enough for a clown."

We both laugh, magically lightening my panic.

"Those curls aren't you," she says. "This headpiece with gold leaf and diamonds wrapped around your head probably gives you a headache, right?"

I nod. "Yes."

She rests her hands on my shoulders. "We protect ourselves by giving the audience nothing of ourselves. Your body might tap a circle of stars, but the real you remains protected, right here." She points to the center of my chest.

"Sadie, I need your help."

"Anything." The spotlight fades, a roaring crowd once again competing with the orchestra on the other side of the curtain.

"I need you to find a little girl and let her in. She's probably outside with the beggar kids." I promised myself I wouldn't forget her this time.

"Okay. How will I know which one she is?"

"You'll know. Blue dress, matching ribbon in her hair. Annoyingly hopeful smile."

"Yeah. I'll go right now."

"Thanks. I need to do something before the show starts."

Sadie flits into the darkness and I take a slow breath to gather myself. I search backstage, around props and loose swatches of fabric hanging from hooks on the wall. Miles is where I expect him to be. Stage left, staring at the set he designed.

"Do you wish you were up there with us?" I ask.

"No." He scratches his thumb to his brow. "I don't like the audience. The pressure of it all. The gasps that undoubtedly come when you make a mistake." He adjusts his top hat and coattails. "I love the beauty of dance and acrobatics. The heartbeat between dancers." He swallows but doesn't meet my gaze. "I don't need the show."

"Then why are you our emcee?"

His lips tighten. "Father requires I prove myself worthy."

"Miles, do you think I can do this?" I stare at the glittering stage.

"I know you can."

Our bodies turn toward each other, our faces nearing a kiss. I gently lay my fingers on his chin. "Regardless of what happens tonight, will you still dance with me?"

He finally breaks a smile. "Forever."

Just then, the lights flicker, and the orchestra tunes their instruments. Something lifts me from my despair, my unending panic. I have a family here. My sisters in dance, the man who sends me into a swell of magic I never want to escape from. A home. I have a home. And I'll ruin everything if I perform how my body wants to.

"I'll be here waiting for you," he says.

He squeezes my hand before skipping out to center stage with arms wide. "Welcome, ladies and gentlemen!"

The audience erupts in cheers and laughter. When the sound dies down, a faint drumming occurs outside of stomps and chants. There must be hundreds of protestors out tonight. Reporters and cameras. Even a few policemen.

"Welcome! A show awaits you unlike any you've ever seen. Here, magic and dance create the most magnificent show of all time. Libations are served in the lobby and thrill is served right here in this room."

More cheers and applause, louder and slightly frantic.

"We have a special evening planned for you tonight. All elements on display, the magic of performance will dazzle this theater when our illustrious Star Girls take the stage." He meets my eyes and smiles. "Something special waits for you at the final act of the evening. Sit back, relax, and enjoy the show."

He retreats behind the curtain. Up first, Zelda. Spotlights light up a black stage. Resting on her forearms, she smiles at the audience, her body in a backbend over her head, and her toes pointed to the stage in front of her. She rolls forward in the most unnatural way and pops to her feet, diamonds spitting from her palms.

I could watch her defy expectations all night, but Ruby tugs at my arm. "I heard something."

"What?"

"Price. He was talking with his new buddies from the speakeasies right before curtain call.

"Were you eavesdropping?"

"Of course I was." We duck into a dark corner. "His little band of merry idiots? They're protected. The police are raiding every other speakeasy during our show. Price will have all of them arrested, their alcohol stashes confiscated, and dancers sent away."

"Away? You mean, asylums." The word causes my head to spin.

The audience jumps to their feet in whoops and cheers as Zelda balances on one hand on the tip of a giant glass star, her legs in a perfect split above her head.

Ruby's cheeks flush, her freckles lit like sparklers. Miles announces Ruby. She sneaks past me, her black flowing dress waving at her feet. She steps into the spotlight as her lonely fiddle wakes the room from silence. Fog forms around her head like a veil, wrapping her in an ethereal glow.

Her music grows in speed and volume, coaxing tufts of grass to appear at her feet. Cobwebs dangle from her elbows and skulls drop to the stage beside her.

Ruby is more than a witch, but all this audience will see is a girl with wild hair who casts spells.

Miles appears beside me. "Are you ready?"

"Although I can control magic, it mostly controls me. Colors and light seem to appear on a whim, and I never know whether it will be a black night or a meteor shower."

"To survive here, one needs to play by the rules or shatter them to pieces." The man winks like a secret between the two of us. Which direction do I choose? Miles's path of freedom, or his father's of protection? Which gives me the most control?

Ruby takes a bow and hands the stage to our acrobats. As they flip and spin to the beat of our orchestra, Miles pulls us chest to chest. "Did you mean it when you said I was a prisoner here just like you?"

"Yes," I say. "What's left for either of us but our one shot at infamy?" Together, we can create the theater my mother never had.

"Eleanora, when you're up on that stage, I want you to remember our dance in the stars. I felt safe with you. Like you were made to tumble in the sky and breathe starlight. Don't let anyone take that from you."

"I'll try." Even as I say the words, my body begins its revolt, starting in my toes as they curl into my shoes.

"Good," he says. "Because it's your moment." He kisses my cheek then smiles before bounding onto the stage.

"What a night!" He raises his arms to the balcony. The audience grows wild. "As promised, we have a special act for you tonight." He pauses, turning just enough to wink at me. "Born into theater life with magic in her blood, our next act brings with her a legacy of performance. The woman you've been waiting to see. Daughter of the great Celtic Fire and tap dancer extraordinaire, please welcome, Eleanora Cleary!"

He nods and backs away as I take my spot. Breathe. One, two, three, four...

The curtains fly open and here I stand, in the spotlight as Diamond Nora, teetering on a new life at the stroke of midnight. While I debate what to do in my swirling mind, visions pour through my memory. My mother's manic smile. How she had whisky for breakfast and men for dessert.

People grumble, unsure whether my panic is part of the act. Play a part, Eleanora. Protect yourself.

Then, from the corner of my eye I glimpse a waving hand. Aria.

I've never been so happy to see that red-cheeked kid. I sigh, thankful Sadie was able to find her. Aria lifts her doll so I can see it and she mouths, "You're amazing."

Eyes on her, my heel taps in place, soft at first, then louder. My body sways with my feet and the music begins. The audience sighs with relief. Their money hasn't been wasted tonight.

I tap, hard and feverishly, grinding deep into the stage, gritting my teeth with resolve. The music crescendos, and bam! Silence.

This is it. The moment my life transforms.

I know which I'll choose.

The stage goes black while two balls of fire appear in my palms. They burn bright enough to light the stage. Shuffle. Shuffle. Flames erupt in ripples around me.

The stage explodes in a carpet of flames as I hover over them. I tap in place on a square of stars, rolling the balls of fire in my hands, swirling my arms in waves to leave trails of light.

I did it. I followed the routine. My chest tightens when I see faces form in the audience, but one glance at Aria squashes all my fear.

I hit every move, every line with precision. I don't think, I just dance. Let the music move through me and swallow my worry.

With five forward flips through rings of fire, I land back on the stage where my mother's Irish dance shoes appear on my feet. I never wanted these shoes. Price insisted. I'm here to revive the glory days of the Luminaire.

I dance her Irish jig through sickness roiling in my stomach as I light up this full room with Celtic Fire.

I am Fiona Cleary's ghost. And I want to cry.

With every hesitation aside, I evaporate my fire, return my shoes to taps, and hold a galaxy of stars above me. This was never in the performance, but I need something of my own. Somewhere, Mr. Price is cursing my name. But I did it. I conquered my fear.

Hysteria doesn't win. Not tonight.

The audience erupts as I taste victory.

One final bow with my troupe, and I can call myself a Star Girl. I earned it. I hurry to my spot on the stage, my sisters beside me. Ruby smiles and whispers, "Wow."

Filled with glee, I wait for the curtain to rise and the audience to shower us with approval. They do, and it's glorious.

Mumbles disrupt the cheers, and I can't figure out what's changed. The audience stops clapping. They gasp. I turn to see Miles off stage, shocked with wide eyes. "What?" I mouth to him. He shakes his head with frantic eyes, as if he's having trouble breathing.

From a microphone deep in the orchestra's belly, a voice booms. "Tonight is more than a showcase. Tonight is the introduction to a new

Seattle. One where we decide our future. Here at the Luminaire, magic is our greatest asset. It's who we are."

Ruby turns to look above my head. Curtains drop over us with lighted signs. Above Sadie, *The Crystalline Asthmatic.* Annelise, *The eyeless Starling.* Ruby, *The Outcast Witch.* Zelda, *The Giant Tumbler.* I turn back to mine, horrified to find, *The Hysterical Daughter.*

Mr. Price continues, safely hidden in the orchestra. "Can the Star Girls overcome their greatest defects to fulfill their magic destiny?"

What the hell has he done?

"Pick your favorites and place your bets," he says. "It's 1926 at the historic Luminaire. Welcome to the world of enchantment and magic. Welcome to the Star Games."

CHAPTER TWENTY-EIGHT

Eleanora

The Star Games. I did not see that one coming.

Will they kill us in some star-themed Gladiator performance? Burn us like witches? A bloody fight to the death to escape an asylum? My fear just ratcheted up a thousand notches.

"Who does he think he is?" Sadie paces the kitchen. "That coward disappeared right after the show last night. It's a good thing, or we might have ripped that mustache right off his face."

Last night Price dropped a bombshell on us. When the curtains closed, the Star Girls gathered in shocked gasps and desperate questions. We hugged in a circle, our heads down. Miles approached but when I shook my head, the troupe created a wall between us. Zelda stepped forward and said, "She doesn't want to see you. None of us do, so get lost."

We haven't slept, and here we are, waiting for answers.

This morning's newspaper features Zelda, leaping over a glass stage, her arms covered in a sheen of silver stars. Under her image reads the headline: *First Ever Magic Competition Kicks off at the Luminaire. Star Games Seeks to Change History.*

Our front-page feature on *The Seattle Times* should be thrilling, but no one is celebrating.

Ruby throws the paper down, then paces, twirling her strawberry red curls around her finger and pulling them taut so they bounce back to her scalp. "They're taking gambling bets on us."

Sadie shrugs. "Yeah, they've opened a betting counter around the backside of the theater."

"We're nothing more than glittering racehorses who'll be shot when our speed falters," I say. "Except we're forgotten the moment we're kicked offstage. Racehorses are beloved for years."

Zelda stretches into the splits and touches her toes to the back of her head. "Forcing our troupe to compete against each other. It's cruel."

Protestors scream at the theater and anyone who approaches. Here we are, pit against my sisters in a competition none of us signed up for.

The truth forms in my mind. "He needed me to create a sensation. He brought together investors with a promise to eliminate their competition and create a show with so much hype, the government wouldn't dare shut us down. These men are going to own us and create a world so hostile we wouldn't dare leave."

Squeals bring my attention back to the window. Frozen rain pushes the protestors out of the streets, but they wait under awnings and in doorways for their chance to spew hate once the ice stops falling.

The worst of it all? Minimizing us to our one physical trait, the thing we struggle with. Asthma or blindness—or hysteria. Price capitalized on our weakness.

"Welcome to the greatest show in the world," I say through tears. "The same reason people pay to see a bearded lady or a seven-foot man. They want a glimpse of something spectacular and bizarre. But we aren't to walk among them."

"Prison inside the Luminaire, or prison outside," Ruby says. "Take your pick."

It doesn't matter that I did what Price asked, followed his stupid rules. It didn't save me. My world has turned sideways, and there's only one person who can bring me back upright.

***

The Milk House is dark. A pool of icy liquor gathers at the door among shards of glass where illegal goods were extracted. Booze and magic girls were thrown from the theater like contraband.

I walk around back, knowing the alley is my best shot to find Aria. The back door to the theater is open, half broken on its hinges. A cold draft accompanies me into the makeshift theater which is now torn to shreds. Shattered bottles and broken chairs lie in piles all over the floor. Torn curtains hang from the stage, and a giant X has been painted on the floor near the soda counter.

Peeking out from behind the piano on its side, Aria waves.

"Are you okay?" I ask.

The tears in her eyes shimmer brightly in the dark. "Lady's gone. The speakeasy is gone. What am I going to do?"

"You go back to your orphanage and forget this place ever existed."

She rubs her fists into her eyes. "This was your home too. Aren't you sad?"

The once spinning cutout of a cow now lies in pieces, his cartoonish face busted in half. "Everything right now makes me sad."

She steps onto the red X and runs her scuffed Mary Janes along the paint. "I thought you were beautiful on that stage."

Performing someone else's act in my dead mother's shoes. "Thank you. I'm really glad you got to see me perform."

She pretends to perform a shuffle ball change, which is nothing of the sort. "The Star Games doesn't seem so bad."

"Not so bad?" I kick a pile of splintered chair remains. "Someday, you're going to have to venture out of this place and enter the hellscape of the city."

"And how do I do that, Eleanora? I'm an orphan. A nobody. The only people I dare to love never love me back. Now the one place I felt safe is gone."

Huh. All this time, I thought the magic made me lonely. Aria has no magic to speak of and she's just as frightened. "Orphan life doesn't define you."

"Funny thing for you to say." She crosses her bony arms with her hands tucked into fists.

"What does that mean?" I don't need to be lectured by anyone right now.

"You never asked for magic, or a love of tap dancing. And you certainly never wanted your mother to die." I ball my fists to prevent fire from scorching its way through my skin. "Yet you can hardly stand your image in the mirror. You fear everything. Hysteria, applause, love."

"Hey, I'm out there trying, which is more than I can say for you. You hang around this place hoping for crumbs." All it takes is one stream of tears down her cheek to make me see how terrible I've become. How venomous my words can be. "I'm sorry, Aria. Really, I shouldn't have said that."

"I *am* trying." She collapses to the floor.

I sit next to her and wrap my fur jacket around her shoulders. What a jerk I am. "Hurt is a funny thing," I tell her. "If I could have stepped onstage without passing out, I could find home. Then I got to the Luminaire and thought, if I can dance with freedom, I'll find security. Now I've done both and have neither."

"I don't understand."

"We convince ourselves that it will be better, just around the corner. One more step or one more ladder to climb and then we'll be happy. That's a big, giant lie."

Aria shoves me with both of her tiny hands, as if she can knock me over with her featherweight body. "Stop it!"

"Stop what? This is life, kid." I will myself not to run. I can't leave her crying alone in the dark.

"Stop telling me I can't ever be happy. I cried happy tears when I saw you on stage last night. It was the best moment of my life. It made me believe in myself." She struggles to get the words out over her heaving chest.

"The Star Games, Aria. I'm stuck in a competition I don't understand, where the only prize is loss."

"But you danced." She wipes her eyes, but tears continue to fall. "You held your dream in your hands."

I heave in unison with her sobs. Why do we hurt the ones who admire us?

I wrap her in my arms. She falls into me, her teary cheeks glistening under the lone lamp. "I'm tired of being sad," she says.

"I know." I pull her close and wrap my hand around the back of her head as she trembles. "We were born into an unfair life, you and me."

"Someone else's failures will give us strength, if we let them," she says.

I pull back to look into Aria's eyes, knowing full well she wouldn't have come up on that on her own. "Where did you hear that?"

"Lady tells me that all the time. She says it to you too, but you never seem to listen."

Someday I'll have to let her go and face this ugly world all on my own. I sigh strong enough to form a cloud of white in the cold room. "Let's get you back to the orphanage. I'll walk you."

One step into the alleyway and I realize I've never asked where she lives. She seems to sense my confusion. "This way." She holds my hand and won't lighten her squeeze even when I try to wiggle my hand free. I should have given her more attention, but I've been so busy needing her.

Newspapers litter the alleyways, along with streamers and popped balloons. Sad remnants from last night's celebration that turned dark. We hold hands as I wind through the streets, following this little sprite of a girl. My fur jacket drags at her feet. Only five blocks away, we stop in front of a two-story brick building with freshly painted white columns. A fancy copper sign is embedded in the brick wall that reads, "Thorpe Home for Children."

"This doesn't seem so bad," I tell her.

"Yeah, well. A home is more than clean floors and a coat of paint." She lets go of my hand with a wistful smile and walks toward the alley. "I'll go in how I usually do. Up the fire escape."

"What should I do, Aria?"

Her smile fills her face with rosy happiness. "About the Star Games?"

"I've found the family I've always wanted. Maybe even fallen in love. But everything is a mess."

"Why do you think I chose you?" she asks.

"You chose me?"

"Sure. I watch and listen to everyone. You can do that when you're forgettable." She forces a laugh. "You have a gift."

"Please. Plenty of girls tap dance."

"No." She shakes her head with big turns side to side. "Your gift is sensing things in a way no one else does. Like you see invisible things and emotions." Her nose reddens as if she may burst into tears. "But you ignore me over and over, only running back to me when you need a friend."

Damn. She's right. "I care about you, Aria. I'm just very, very bad at showing it." I bite my lip. "How does this relate to the Star Games?"

"I don't know, honestly. I'm just a kid." She spins three times to watch the fur flutter in the breeze. "Here." She hands back the jacket and folds her arms over her chest. "Lady once told me that all girls have more power than we give ourselves credit for."

"She told me that too. Good night, Aria."

She slips her doll out of her pocket and hugs it tight, reminding me she is, in fact, just a girl looking for love.

CHAPTER TWENTY-NINE

Fiona

I don't do rehearsals.

While the rest of the girls take direction from Price, I'm sitting alone in the Sapphire Bar drinking enough whisky to flatten me. My cigarette is all I see against a backdrop of blue glass. Sizzling paper, gray ash. The hysteria has taken hold now, but booze quiets the fire. Just weeks ago, I still laughed and enjoyed this place.

Just as I drift off to nothingness, someone shakes me awake. "Leave me alone." My bottle is gone. Smooth, cold bar top under my palm, but no drinks.

"Fiona."

Shit. "Leave me alone, Price."

He stands behind the bar, face down at my level. "How are you gonna perform tonight like this?"

I lower my cheek back down to the bar. "I don't care."

"This isn't a game." His voice trails off as the darkness swallows me. I hear grumblings, then a splash.

"What the hell?" Cold water wakes me. A bucket of it. I'm soaked. My eyes are open, my heart's racing. "Price, you asshole."

"It was me."

I wipe my eyes to see Lady, hands on her hips. "What are you doing here?"

"Someone has to talk sense into you."

Drops of cold water run down my cheeks and plop on the bar. "You threw water on me."

She tosses a towel in my face. "I'll dunk you in an ice bath if I have to."

Price fumes next to her. "I called her."

"What do you want from me?" I do my best to wipe my face dry. "I perform. I bring the house down. I make you money. I'm holding up my end of the bargain." The cold jolts my memory. "Did you get those girls out of the slammer?"

His face drops. "They were already taken."

"Taken where?"

"An institution."

I could slap him. He doesn't even appear sorry.

Lady slides a cup of coffee over to me. "The jazz dancer had to be taken away."

"Eleanora's friend?" I suddenly remember how she sliced her arm. "She bled all over the floor."

She points to the coffee again and I acquiesce with a forced sip. "The hospital stitched her up, but they deemed her unstable. We'll never see her again."

All I can think of is my daughter. "Is Eleanora alright?"

"She's safe. But I'm worried about her."

I force down more coffee, but only so I have something warm to hold. "Why should I try? We're all going down."

"Fiona," Lady says, "We need you. Eleanora is doing some things that concern me."

"She'll be fine. She always is."

"No, she needs her mother. She's scared of everything, and some things she says worry me. She's not doing well."

Price slams his fist on the bar. "I did not bring you here to ruin me, Fiona Cleary. I brought you here to make headlines and create a sensation."

"Which I've done." I pick up my cigarette, but the burn is long gone, so I flick the butt to the floor.

"You're out of control," he says, as if he understands Magic Dance.

"Yeah, well." I catch a glimpse of myself in the mirrored walls. Black makeup smeared down my cheeks. Bloodshot eyes. "This is what you asked for."

"I asked for a performer. What I got was a drunk."

"So, fire me then." I drain the coffee cup and withhold a wave of nausea. "That's right, you can't. I'm too sensational." I wish my hands would stop trembling.

Lady grabs my wrist with such force I gasp. "Your antics bring crowds. But you don't need all this to be sensational. When you arrived at the Milk House, you were full of magic and love for dance. Love for your kid. You were enough."

"*Was* enough." I yank my hand away. "Neither of you have this beast inside you. You can't understand. It's destroying me and all I can do is drink to quiet the noise in my head. The fire burning my insides." My breathing speeds up. My hands go numb. "I can't stand who I've become."

Price walks up to me. He opens his arms like he may hug me, but his face suggests he's angry enough to slap me. I wince before he nears. "I'm not going to hit you."

"Are you sure? Most men do."

"Listen to me." He lowers his tall frame until he's eye to eye with me. "This theater is my entire life. No one is worth losing what I've built. Certainly not some unstable fire dancer who can't get through the day without booze, and cares nothing for those around her."

"Don't act like you care, you bastard." I shove him away. "You have some strange allegiance to this place. It drives you as mad as I am."

His chest twitches. As if he has a heart beating somewhere in there. "This place is more than a theater, Fiona. Just like your dance is more than a performance." He tosses a handful of bills at my face. "Get yourself together and you can stay. If you pull this nonsense onstage or threaten my exemption, I'll have you hauled off to the closest asylum, and I'll cuff you myself."

Once he's gone, I resist swiping the bills off the ground. "Bring that money to Eleanora," I tell Lady.

"She needs you, not cash."

Those words settle on my skin like needles. "I know."

"Come back. Hold her. Tell her you'll do anything to make things better."

"Lie."

She takes a deep, annoyed breath. "It doesn't have to be this way."

"Yes, it does!" And the fire begins once again. Flames spit from my hands now without dance. I assume this is end-stage hysteria. "Why make her watch me die? This is her future too."

Lady holds my hand. "I don't believe that."

"What the hell are you on about? This is our destiny. The most unstable of all the magic. Only girls get this tragedy, and I passed it onto my beautiful, gentle daughter." I squeeze her hand so tight, though I want to fall far and deep and never wake up. "I hate myself."

Her eyes fill with tears. "Maybe that's what has ruined you all. Not the hysteria or the fire, but the way the world makes you believe you're wrong. You aren't."

"Tell that to the Milk House girls getting meds shoved down their throats right now." I want to hug Eleanora and dance like we used to. I want to feel strong again. It's too late for all that. Fire magic attacked me like a plague, and I've welcomed the rats to feast.

CHAPTER THIRTY

Eleanora

I stand across the street from the Luminaire where ice and sleet coat the sidewalk. The terrible weather isn't enough to stop the new billboards gracing the theater. Framed gold images of each Star Girl, with security stationed to prevent protestors from ripping them down or splashing them with red paint.

The first is already in place. A picture of Annelise drawn like a svelte, curvy woman with bold red lips. She isn't. She's a skinny girl who doesn't enjoy makeup. She loves to sing, but also loves the hush of a quiet theater. *The Eyeless Starling.*

She has eyes. Beautiful brown eyes. She sees with her voice and her words. They've named her. Reduced her to the parts of her they can sell.

That strange sensation returns, where I'm not sure if I will faint or fight. I'd run, but the ground is slick, and I have nowhere to go. My chest tightens enough to remind me I'm still here.

Careening toward panic, I do the only thing I know how to. I decide to find someone to yell at.

When I burst through the door to the instructor's lounge, teacups rattle on saucers. They all turn to me. They're dancers and acrobats who've earned their secure place in the Luminaire by aging out of performance and now train the next generation to step in line, finding themselves useless while none of their pupils made it to the Star Games.

"Where's Iridessa?"

"This lounge is for instructors only." I hear the voice but don't stop to see who it comes from.

"Go ahead. Try to kick me out and see what happens."

"I don't think you're understanding the rules, dear."

"Get her or I'll set this entire place to flames." My throat stings from screaming.

Over the years, I've learned how to fight the constant fear. Beat it with my fists until I'm left bloody if need be. Bruised and crying is preferable to whatever hysteria waits in threatening silence.

"It's fine, ladies."

Iridessa's calm, steady voice rattles me further. I turn to face her, close to breaking into tears at the thought of her betrayal. "What did you do to us?"

"Come with me, Eleanora."

She reaches her elegant hand for mine, but I won't take it. Trust is for fools, and I've been played too many times already.

She nods, presumably acknowledging that my anger is louder than anything else in my head. "Come to my room. Please."

I follow her through the lounge, into a long hallway with bedrooms on each side. It's not as extravagant as I imagined it would be. Her room has a lonely brass bed against a floral wall. One nightstand, one mirror, a sink. Soulless.

"I can imagine how angry you must be," she says.

"No, I don't think you can." I run my bottom lip under my teeth. "Yes, I was naive enough to trust Miles, but my stupid heart is to blame for that one. I trusted you. How could you not tell me about the Star Games?"

Iridessa rattles her hands above her head as bells clang and rainbows light the room.

"Stop that," I yell. "You're using magic to manipulate me."

She tilts her head and drops her hands to her sides. "Is that what you think dance is for?"

I could curl over from the gnawing pain in my stomach. It makes it hard to hear her words.

My legs grow wobbly as the room fades. Iridessa catches me and lowers me to a chair. I tuck my head between my knees and breathe, counting the wavy lines in the floorboards.

"Better?" she asks.

"Yes, but I'd like to stay here and brood for eternity, thank you very much."

She lifts my shoulders. Color returns to my vision as I notice every detail of her concerned eyes.

She lowers gracefully to the bed. "You know I worked with your mother."

A fact that makes her betrayal sting that much more. I don't acknowledge her question.

"I tried to contain her wild ways. It was useless. Fiona was only happy when she set the stage on fire. Literally."

Everyone thinks they knew her. No one did. Not even me.

"I wanted to keep her safe, just as I want to keep every one of you safe now. Price is up against some very dangerous people, and all of us, including you, cannot stop the freight train that has collided with this theater."

"You could have warned me. Let me decide for myself if I wanted to jump out of the way of that train."

"If you leave, I can't protect you."

"You can't protect me now!" I stand but soon realize my legs still hold the strength of a wet spaghetti noodle. Back to the chair I go.

Iridessa stares out her tiny window to the building across the street. "Fiona stood up to the resistors. Those in government that executed Prohibition and pushed for complete eradication of our kind. She threatened them with fire and even burned a few."

"I'm certain they deserved it."

"Probably." She smiles but it quickly fades. "But they made her pay, didn't they?"

I find the strength to walk to the window. "The stage terrified me long before I lost her." I lean my temple to the cool glass. "Fire always felt like flirting with death."

Iridessa walks over to me in her soft ballerina way. "Fiona became the symbol for all the things they hated." She swallows with a wince. "They're coming for us again and this time, they won't stop until every magic dancer is locked away. Price is fighting for us, in his bizarre way. So is Miles. I've always believed that this place will save us."

"What will happen in the Star Games? Please tell me the truth."

"I promise you, he told me nothing until after the show. I would have tried to talk him out of it. But here we are now and he wants you to perform out in the world. Force the city to face you. Our only hope is to make our theater strong enough to withstand their fire. We turn this place into a show of force."

"This show will divide us. The competition will turn us against each other. This can't be good for anyone."

Her heavy eyes suggest she's swimming in as much helplessness as the rest of us. "I don't know how to help you, other than to keep you under my care."

"Stand up to Price."

"Miles tried. It's too late."

We're the closest thing to children she's ever known. She's keeping us close, teaching control. It's how she's survived this long. "How will this end?" I ask.

"I hope it will end with a revolution. Where the world demands equality for dancers and churchgoers alike."

"That's a lofty hope, Iridessa."

"What else do we have but hope and each other?"

I want to hug her. I'm overrun with guilt that my showcase led to the death Ruby predicted. To save my family and every magic girl in the world, I must prove myself in the Star Games without letting the pressure crush me.

Magic on a string like a marionette, and I'm the conductor. If only I had any idea how to control anything.

CHAPTER THIRTY-ONE

Eleanora

Price summoned us to the theater after allowing a two-day cooling off period. None of us have cooled. We're only enraged and trapped.

Our banners still hang from the ceiling, mocking us with caricatures of our true selves. Our oddities have been made digestible for the masses. Miles stands off to the side, his eyes steadily on me, but I don't meet his gaze.

"Despite what you may think," Price says. "I've done this all for you."

"I think I'm going to be sick," Sadie murmurs.

"We've created a powerful group of men in this city to protect our Star Girls. We're forming a sensation so big, the government will be powerless to stop us."

Us. He means the men in power with the Star Girls as pawns. Our needs were never considered.

"The Luminaire made money on New Year's Eve. A lot of money." He draws out the sounds mo–ney. "Enough to buy power in this city. Every one of you could have riches and comfort beyond your wildest dreams."

Ruby, who grew up eating whatever critters her family could scour from the forest, lowers her eyes when Price speaks. She cares little for money, but with that word comfort, he hooks her. Sadie glances at us, shame spread across her face. She likes the endless parties and attention. I can't blame her. We all handle loneliness in our own way.

"We have a few people to thank for this opportunity." He extends his hand toward me. "Eleanora, join me on stage." I shake my head, pressing back into the chair.

He clears his throat, a threat of rage bubbling below the surface. My troupe's hopeful eyes bore straight through me. I can't be the one to take away everything they've dreamed of. With legs heavy as lead, I stand and make my way to the stage opposite Miles.

Mr. Price turns to admire my banner. *The Hysterical Daughter.* "This young lady made this all happen for you. She has faced her fears and learned to triumph on stage. I'll even forgive your little slip in approved choreography." I wait for the backhand that's surely about to smack me. "Eleanora has fought her bloodline. Her hysterical destiny."

There it is. The slap of an insult wrapped in a compliment.

"We are privileged to watch you fight this battle to maintain your sanity, Eleanora. Because of your name, and your sensational performance, your sisters will have anything their hearts desire." He grabs my arm and leads me closer to Miles.

"Nora." Miles whispers so softly my heart flutters in response.

"Don't."

"From here forward, we will face many challenges." Price paces the stage, drawing out his soliloquy. "Protestors will scream at you and the government will fight to hold you down. But together, we will ensure a stable life for us here at the Luminaire."

"What happens at the Star Games?" I make certain my words are clear and strong.

Price's eye twitches. "A public showcase of each member of our troupe."

Not satisfied, I narrow my eyes at him. "What happens at the end?"

"We enjoy the spoils of a battle hard fought."

He actually believes this will end in our favor. My mother understood the risks. She'd rather let her mind spin into the stars and never come back than live by someone else's rules. I'm not sure which prison I'd rather be locked in.

"Cut the shit, Price," Sadie says. "Give us details." As If on cue, her breathing turns whistly.

Outside these doors droves of protestors chant about our witchy souls. Any speakeasy that would allow magic has now either been shuttered or is owned by Price. The world is hostile toward our kind and the only place we're safe is in Price's greedy hands.

"Don't be so dramatic, Sadie. No one is dying."

"Easy for you to say." I force my voice not to waver.

"It will be an extravaganza. A celebration of your oddities. Perform better than you ever have and you'll all be fine. Now, get to work in the gymnasium," Price says. "Tonight, you will all celebrate with a grand feast. Welcome to the show, ladies."

Perform better? The only way to do that is to give us our dance back. In our clothing, to our music.

The troupe thins, walking out of the theater one by one. Price struts down the stairs, presumably off to his office to hatch more evil plans.

Miles and I linger in the empty theater after the last door slams shut.

"I never wanted any of this," he says.

"Yet here we are."

"I knew Father was planning the games, but I tried to stop him. I promise you, I tried."

"Okay." I count the plaster stars on the balcony, biting back tears.

"I want this place as much as my father, but for different reasons." He walks around my shoulder where our eyes meet. "He's in it deep. I don't know how to get us out."

Miles may care for me but he's fighting to keep his father safe too. "I'm tired of being pulled by all sides."

Miles brushes the backs of his fingers against mine as soft as a whisper. "We can do this on your terms."

"Somehow this has all fallen on me. The hysterical daughter fighting a legacy of mania."

***

Dressed in a cloche hat hung low over my eyes, I call on every prison in Seattle. The weight of money in my purse is a sensation I'm not familiar with and can honestly say, I never want to go without.

I could do anything with my Star Girl stipend. Another string Price uses to hold us in place. If we leave, we'd have nothing on our hands but a fight with the world. So why, I wonder, do I use my dollars to pay bail for the woman I left behind.

I'm certain there's a deep answer for this, but right now I simply want Aria to have a home again.

A compact officer greets me at the front desk of the third station I enter. "Afternoon, miss." He flashes me a smile, no idea I can tap dance fire bolts through those dark blue eyes.

"Yes, hello. I'm here for Lady. She ran the Milk House."

He puffs his lips. "You aren't caught up in that illegal stuff, are you, sweet thing?"

Sweet thing. His words make my skin crawl. "Yes." I'm not sure what's come over me, but he stares at me like a juicy piece of fruit, and I want it to stop. "If you wish to arrest me, you can come do so at the Luminaire." My boss pays off all these swindlers and somehow that makes them see us as property.

"Oh." His eyes crawl over my body as a twisted smile reveals crooked teeth. "You're one of them witches." He's part offended, part aroused. What an off-putting combination.

"I'd like to pay her bail."

The man rests his hands on either side of his belt and sucks air through his front teeth. "Blood money?"

"It's money just the same."

"Hold on." He sighs, reluctantly walking out of the room.

Far too many hours sit between me walking in and the moment they walk Lady out from the back. Her hair is disheveled, and her dress torn, but her eyes are as bright as ever. "I didn't expect you," she says.

"They handled the bail money. You should be free to go." I hand her a cigarette. Lady leans to the policeman who escorted her. He lights her cigarette and tilts his head. "Keep peddling contraband and you'll end up in here again. One of these days, we'll find a long-term solution for you."

"It's been a pleasure for me too, sonny." Lady pushes past me with instructions to follow.

The squirrelly man from the front desk blocks the doorway. "Don't think you witches will get away with your spells and black magic. We're coming for every one of you."

Instead of yelling, which I yearn to do, I simply hiss. Long and slow, holding the air between my tongue and front teeth until he steps away.

I run to catch up with Lady, who's fixing her hair on the move. "Lady, wait!" I catch up to her, but she doesn't slow down. "You're going the wrong way."

"Wrong way for what? There are a few speakeasies left that resisted Price's raid. I'm going to find one of them."

"You can't give up."

"The Milk House is gone, Eleanora."

"It's just torn up. You can rebuild."

She ducks under an awning to light her cigarette. "Why did you bail me out?"

"Because you were in jail and I'm certain it's terrible in there."

She blows smoke from the corner of her mouth. "Not buying it. Come on, fess up."

"Fine. Aria needs you." I don't expect her to care.

"Aria isn't my responsibility. I only gave her a job to make you happy."

My hands tremble, shaking my arms when I ball them into fists. I turn my back, frantically searching the sky for guidance. Newspapers flutter. Rain plunks on brick. A gentle breeze whistles past my face. "I can't forgive you. Mother didn't have to die that young."

"After all this time, you still haven't seen it?"

"Seen what?"

"I begged her to come back for you." She inhales so deep on her cigarette the paper burns down by an inch. "Everything that happened to Fiona was her doing."

I shake my head to force away the memories. "I could have had her another month or another year. Magic will be our end and performing fire will claim me the same as it did with her, screaming and crying."

"If you really believe that, what are you doing at the Luminaire?"

CHAPTER THIRTY-TWO

Eleanora

"The entire city is Star Girl crazy!" the broadcaster says with a frenzy in his voice. "What will become of us once the witches cast their spells over Seattle? We may all be doomed but we seem to welcome the horror with open arms."

Even the radio programs can't stop airing salacious pieces on us and taking bets on who will falter. Ruby clicks the dial off. "I hate this."

The troupe halfheartedly sips afternoon tea as spoons clink against teacups and we collectively try to forget the broadcaster's quips.

"This is ridiculous." I stand and scan the room. "We're magic dancers. We don't belong in a tearoom, cloaked in silence for fear of ridicule."

Annelise clears her throat. "Speak for yourself."

Their defeated sighs ignite something in me. "Everyone up."

The girls glance back and forth, waiting for someone to speak. Zelda shoots up, breasts bouncing and eyes glistening with excitement. "I'm in."

"You don't know what I'm asking," I say.

Zelda shakes her hair free. "I don't care. I'm in."

"I want to be us without the rules, without the need for applause. I need a night to spin barefoot under the stars until the sky drops gold on my lashes."

Annelise perks up. "The stars can do that?"

"They haven't for me, not for a very long time." I think about what Lady has said before. How magic dancers need each other in a way regular folks can't understand.

Zelda pulls her dress down to reveal the top curve of her cleavage. "I don't dance on the freezing cold ground. But if we could find a speakeasy that's still open, I can tumble across the room until I find a handsome boy to kiss." She winks.

"You do this all the time?" Ruby asks.

"All the time."

I raise my hand. "I know a place."

***

The mortuary is darker than I remember. The girls gather behind me in a pile of heat, whispering about my poor judgment. "Are there real dead bodies in there?" Sadie asks.

"As opposed to fake ones?" Zelda knocks her hips into Sadie's.

"Follow me."

I take the same path Miles showed me through the creaking door, past the caskets and creepy paintings of Victorian families.

"Why do we need to do this?" Annelise grips Sadie's arm, trusting her to lead her safely.

"To prove that Price doesn't own our bodies or our dance." Ruby smiles with a confident nod.

"Exactly." Down the spiral staircase and into the hidden bar, the Star Girls arrive with a flourish. Dressed in theater garb with shining layers of stage makeup sparkling across our eyes, we stand in a line like glitter witches before an exile.

Though the entire bar has stopped to stare, the bartender recognizes me. "Champagne, right?"

The music restarts and the mumbles once again bounce through the darkness. The girls scatter through the bar, finding a drink or a companion, or both.

I lean against the wall, taking in their joyful faces. They dance in a circle, kicking up metallic dust and levitating above a stage of spinning diamonds.

Something blows in my ear.

"What the hell?" I brush the air away from my ear and spin on my heels. *Miles.*

"What were you thinking bringing all of them here?" His face attempts to twist in anger. It's annoyingly adorable.

"We needed a night to let loose, and I'd say, you owe me." I poke my finger to his sternum.

"Now the entire troupe knows about my secret escape and it's only a matter of time before my father acquires this place. I like having somewhere to go that isn't his."

Both hands on his shoulders, I press close to his chest, our lips close enough to graze. "We're even." I grab his tie and drag him to the dance floor, where he spins me to a swell of jazz music. In the flash of one thrilling moment, we've crashed into an intimate dance, hearts and bodies flushed with heat.

My back slams into his chest hard enough to send my hair loosened over my eyes. The wispy tips of a few locks stick to my lipstick. Miles's hand grabs my hip and gathers my dress in his fingers.

I reach back to grab his hair as he kisses the sensitive skin on my neck. "I never said I forgive you," I whisper.

"Same here." Another spin and we're chest to chest again. Peppermint tobacco lingers on his lips, but before I can taste the sweet smokiness, we're off into the tango. His strong frame leads me in all directions with ease. Back, back, slide. We lean backward, eyes intensely on mine.

Miles glides me across the dancefloor to hoots and hollers from the Star Girls. My stomach pressed to his, his hand splayed across my low back, he says, "Show me your magic, Diamond Nora."

Ruby shoots me a warning glance, but I'm too far in it now. I shove Miles away and tap with bent knees and burning thighs as diamonds rain down around me. I spin fast enough that the world blurs. When I crash to a halt, I'm dressed in my glittering silver tuxedo, top hat in hand.

Far away, through a tunnel of sound, my feet, as if on their own, tap a rhythm once again in time to my thumping heart. Light and energy rush through my body like a waterfall. The ceiling has now turned into a sky as clouds part. A shining, clear Milky Way draws itself through the slate sky, leaving a trail of stardust.

I step forward to see the galaxy. To ground me back to this moment. To keep me from exploding into a thousand tattered pieces. I finally understand the safety of a speakeasy.

Mother appears from the ether, her pale red eyelashes blinking through the mist. "Nora girl."

"Mother?" The speakeasy is gone. It's just me and my dead mother. "I miss you." I reach for her but my hand waves through her cloudy body.

"My dear, Eleanora." Her smile is calm, with no mania shooting from her eyes. "You've crossed into a new world now."

"What do you mean? A new world where the Milky Way speaks to me, like you said it would?"

"A world where panic becomes part of you. Hysteria will settle in your bones and become one with your soul. Just like it did for me." Her eyes turn dark as black blood drips from an incision that appears across her forehead.

"No."

The once soft stardust turns to hail, and I lift my hands to protect my face. "Don't leave!" My voice fades to a whisper.

With a crash, I land against Miles's chest, his hands cupped around my face. The Star Girls stand around me with hands of illumination that shine on us like spotlights. He smiles and releases a soft exhale. "That was magnificent."

Breathless and frantic I say, "Did you see her?"

"See who?"

The ceiling is once again a dark speakeasy with no stars to speak of. But I saw her. I *felt* her. Was she real or an apparition? Either would mean I'm changed forever.

Miles envelops me in a warm embrace as applause surrounds us.

A bell rings from above the bar, prompting Miles to whisk me off the dance floor. "Hurry. The lookout sees the cops."

Miles opens a closet and slides open a false door to reveal a tunnel with low lighting. The girls hurry in after me. Footsteps thunder through the ground floor above us, quickly circling the spiral staircase. "Hurry!" He smooshes the girls in just as the bartender pulls a switch. The framed pictures flip to more Victorian creepers with strange eyes and another door opens in every wall as all the night crawlers disappear into the walls.

Miles slips inside the closet and shuts the door just as the police burst into the bar screaming, "Where are the devil girls?"

He holds his hand up for us to follow. It's a square tunnel, braced with plenty of stones and wood beams. I lean against the cool wall to let the troupe past me, hiding the way my mind wanders to collapse. Rubble. Stuck alive and alone underground until I die.

The tunnel seems to constrict around me. Miles appears. "Nora, I'm here."

I throw my arms around his neck and hold tight, breathing frantically in his ear.

Shit. I saw my mother.

He flinches but hugs me tighter. "Let's get you out of here."

My legs tremble so intensely I worry I'll fall. There's no room for embarrassment while panic swells inside me like a hot air balloon. My skin warms enough to hold in the fire.

Once we climb a set of stairs, a door clicks open and we're above ground. I gasp for air like we've just surfaced from the depths of the ocean. Ruby grabs my arm. "What happened?"

"Nothing, I'm fine." I force a smile.

We're in a storage facility that holds hundreds of crates and a dozen cars. Zelda runs her hands along a cherry red Packard roadster. "There's no hiding in this beauty."

Miles shakes his head. "We'll have to walk back to the theater."

"All this," I say. "For what?" Cars that cost more than each Star Girl will ever make. Booze piled high as the ceiling. "How much money does one person need?"

Miles rubs his neck. "Money is power, Eleanora."

There's a sneakiness in his eyes that grows bright as he looks at the illegal stash. "This is yours, isn't it."

His eyes glow with purpose. "I've been stealing money from the business. I needed something of my own that he can't ruin."

"You have money? Use it to stop the Star Games."

"I tried. Once he joined forces with the mobsters and speakeasy boys—" He backs away. "They're too big now."

He opens the metal door and leads the troupe out to the chilly night. While the policemen search the mortuary, the Star Girls huddle together in the cold, returning to a theater with an unknown future.

Ten blocks later and the hangover has set in. The girls yawn and complain of headaches. Miles unlocks the front door but waits on the sidewalk while they shuffle in. "The cops followed reports of magic dancers. You risked my entire operation."

I step close, chest to chest with him. "I'm sorry. We needed that fun tonight."

"I know." His eyes move from my eyes to my hair and down to my mouth. "I'm sorry I haven't been able to stop this."

I want to kiss him and hold him and go back to the underground where we danced, and I sensed a future. Until my mother came to me in my magic. Now I can't see anything but fear. Was it a sign?

He reaches for me. "Eleanora, I know this is frightening."

"No, you don't. If this all fails, you'll return to your mansion and find another way to get your inheritance. You aren't risking what we are."

"I'm a failed circus performer who believes in what this theater started as. A place of acceptance and joy. We can get back to that."

"I don't see how." I let my fingers slide from his, ducking into the theater and shutting the door between our locked gazes.

Oh, Nora. You lured him into your manic world. No one wants to live there, not even you. I miss his touch already.

While the girls tromp up the back stairs to the sleeping porch, I stay behind. Alone in the Sapphire Bar, I take a shot of whisky to burn away all the memories from tonight. The bleeding head, the black eyes. The hazy glow softens all the fear.

One more shot.

And another.

Finally, the pain lightens, and I can breathe. I lay my head on the bar, drifting into a sleepy haze. My forearm rests in front of me. Before I drift away, I scratch my nails down my arm hard enough to sting and sharp enough to slice open my flesh.

Magic bleeds out of the wound into an amethyst pool under my cheek.

Good night.

***

I wake with the sunrise to a loud gasp I suddenly realize is my own. My arm. The slice. I stumble away from the bar, terrified of what I'll find.

Two long, red scratches mar my forearm but there's not a drop of blood in sight.

I wait for my breathing to steady while I hold my arm to my chest. Tears fill my eyes. I've crossed the line I never wanted to find. Where dreams and awake are one and the same. Where nightmares bleed into consciousness.

Tears spill over and dampen my cheeks. Iridessa steps into the bar, coffee cup in hand. "I thought you could use some company."

I wipe my eyes and nose and check my forearm one more time for blood. Still clear. "I'm fine." Besides this wicked headache and the need to vomit.

"You don't look fine."

She hands me the coffee. The milky, bitter liquid is a taste of normalcy. "When did my mother begin losing her mind?"

"Hard to say, really. I'm not sure she ever did."

I stretch out the tightness in my shoulders. "They threw her in an asylum."

"They throw lots of people into asylums. So few did anything to warrant drugs and institutionalization." She smooths her hand across the bar. "I think the alcohol ruined her. And the hate this city had for her."

"I let my magic take over last night."

"And, what happened?"

A wave of nausea ripples through me. "Nothing good."

She nods. I sip more coffee. Even though it turns my stomach, I keep drinking, hoping it will soothe the sickness pounding through me.

"It's my fault," I say. "I didn't follow the rules."

"Which rules?" she asks.

"Controlled dance. Someone else's choreography. Stay within the limits of this theater. I didn't realize they protect us as much as they protect everyone else."

"I used to think that."

"And now?"

"After years of the same restrictions, I think all they do is convince people we should all dress and smile and dance the same." She steps closer. "We were never meant to be the same."

"No, we're meant to put on a show."

"Price doesn't have the answers any more than we do." She grabs a rag and wipes down the bar, rubbing over and over the same spot, even after it gleams. "I regret a great many things in my life. I've lost every man I've ever loved. I left my family. I regret never having a baby in my arms." She keeps rubbing in a slow circle, staring ahead at the filtered blue morning light through the glass windows. Until she locks eyes with me. "But I've never once regretted life as a magic ballerina."

"Aren't you angry at what they've done to us?"

She drops the rag and walks around the bar to meet me. "I'm furious."

Iridessa reaches for my hands. She's not one for touch, something I've always appreciated. "Your sensitive nature and your ability to see things that others don't is a gift. You hear me?"

"What kind of gift makes me black out and see my dead mother return with a warning of impending mania?"

"You saw your mother?" she asks.

My non-response answers for me. She pulls me into a hug and doesn't let go. She lets me cry and my hard edges fade as I hug her back.

"I don't know what it's like to tap dance on stage with an offensive banner above your head," she says. "And I certainly don't know what constant panic does to a person." She slides my disheveled hair away from my eyes. "So, I won't tell you how to fix this. But I will remind you of this: the things that make our dance unique can plague us with pain, and pain hides our gift."

"What plagues you?"

"Childhood rheumatism." She extends her bony fingers. "The day I burst into tears because my knees locked like steel, I saw my colors. I knew right then, sitting stiff-legged on the bathroom floor, this was my life. For better or worse."

"I want to be that strong."

"Oh, my dear, you already are."

CHAPTER THIRTY-THREE

Eleanora

Star Games. Tonight!
Join Downtown Seattle in a Battle Between Elemental Dancers.
Who will Falter and Who Will Fly?

We dress in frustrated silence, preparing for an evening we never asked for in a battle none of us want.

As we gather in the lobby, the nervous energy is enough to level me. Sadie wheezes next to me. "We dress as they want, dance as they request, and play their little game. What's in it for us?"

"I think we're all questioning that same thing," Ruby says.

Annelise has an even tighter grip on Sadie than usual. "At least we aren't out there fighting the masses."

The tension is too much. "No, we're fighting them from the stage," I say. The way our magic needs to perform has ruined us all. As mother used to say, *Our fire cannot burn without applause.* It's our damn legacy, every girl born with magic swirling in her blood, and we're about to pay the price.

Footsteps click into the lobby. We turn to find Miles in his top hat and crimson coattails. None of us smile, including him. He licks his lips and clears his throat. "They're about ready for you," he says.

The girls see me as the Miles Whisperer. As if I understand anything that's happened between the two of us. "I don't want to do this," I say in a voice as strong as I can muster.

"You can refuse," he says. "Walk away right now."

The entire city knows my face. I'd find myself in a police car before I even reached Third Avenue. "So could you." We hold silence until it's uncomfortable. This is who we are, for better or worse. "What's going to happen out there?"

"You'll showcase your acts one by one. The crowd will either love you or hate you. Probably both." His words are dry and forced. No emotion anywhere.

"Any moment, we'll be put on display," I tell the girls. "Ridiculed and applauded in equal measure." They glance at each other, some with tears in their eyes. "This man will march us to a makeshift stage in the freezing night where we will perform our hearts out to prove our worth to a city who sees us as witches."

In the Luminaire, we attracted patrons of dance. Purveyors of magic. Out here, anyone with hate in their heart can cheer for our demise.

The doors open. Camera bulbs flash and pop with blinding light. We lift our hands, trying fruitlessly to block the flares and shrieks that await us outside. In the doorway, Mr. Price stares at his troupe as cold as I've ever seen him. "It's time."

I step out first and close my eyes. No turning back now.

Shouts erupt. So many, it's difficult to make out the words. A little girl waves at me, and I relax enough to release a slight smile. One step forward and a tomato flies past, splattering onto the framed picture of Zelda, *The Giant Tumbler*.

I don't react. Not even when the crowd laughs. Mr. Price looks away. I carry on, glancing back to make sure the rest of the girls aren't taking a cabbage to the head. Police are everywhere. They glare at us, doing nothing to stop the mob yelling, "Kill the witches."

We walk one block down the street to where a makeshift stage takes up the center of two cross streets. In the middle, Miles waits, diamond-studded cane in hand. I wait for him to notice me, knowing he can't avoid me for much longer.

Through the policemen-lined narrows, we tromp through throngs of screaming, picketing hecklers. Some carry silver cutouts on sticks with our caricature. They've chosen their favorites, it seems. Prepared for a battle of witches.

I lead our troupe up the stairs as Miles comes into view. He lowers his eyes and stares at the ground. We cluster onstage like a multicolored dandelion. People aren't just in the streets. They're hanging from fire escapes and dangling over balconies.

I lift my chin and face Miles. "Here we go."

A stinky head of broccoli lands on my belly. It's amazing how a softened vegetable can pack such a sting. Miles picks up the broccoli and winds his arm back, searching for who threw it. His father grabs his arm and instructs him with only a gaze to let it go.

Price extends his arm to a life-sized metal birdcage dangling from a crane by a thick cord. A staircase leads to the open door of a velvet-lined prison.

"No," I say adamantly.

From every building around us, scrolls drop along the bricks, a giant flag for each contestant of the Star Games. The crowd stomps and chants, "Lock them up. Lock them up."

"We've done nothing wrong," Sadie says to Miles.

"I know you haven't."

I rub my face, probably smudging my makeup beyond repair.

Price turns to whisper to us. "If you don't get in, this crowd could storm the stage. Many of these cops will look the other way." He swallows, a grimace taking hold.

Old man Price is running out of answers too.

Fireworks burst through the sky and the Luminaire's sign lights with a new marquee. *Vaudeville Royalty Eleanora Cleary fights For Sanity. Can she Overcome her Demons?*

"I'll make sure you stay safe," Miles says.

"It's a little late for that, Mr. Emcee."

"I'll throw myself between this troupe and anyone who tries to hurt you. A few shows and we win over the city."

"I admire your optimism."

Against a backdrop of manic spectators, I walk up the stairs. The crowd absolutely loses their minds with excitement. The rest of the Star Girls follow, poorly hiding their worry.

I grasp the bitterly cold stair rails in my sweaty palms and inspect the sky. Cloudy, with remnants of firework ash. Not a star in sight. Up, up we climb. In the distance, I glimpse the Milk House's roof, where a crowd once gathered to watch my mother nearly jump to her death with her fourteen-year-old daughter.

What's most terrifying about this memory is not watching my mother spiral beyond help, but the realization that I would have let her take me with her. I would have died to avoid breaking her heart.

Her eyes shined that night. Wide and bright and clear. I followed her without a word, desperation begging for a few last moments with her. She mumbled at first, then once we stood on the rooftop, two stories above the street, the sky lit up with stars, her voice rang clear.

"We're going home, baby." I knew our bodies would shatter, but I closed my eyes anyway and prepared for the hit.

Until Lady grabbed my dress and shoved me to the ground. I tried to crawl to my mother, but policemen had already swarmed the rooftop. I was supposed to die with her.

The click of the lock on our cage thrusts me back to the moment. My forearm shines. Pale, pristine skin welcomes the closest blade. I want off this ride.

"It's like some twisted version of the Colosseum out here," Zelda says.

"Are you frightened?" Sadie asks her.

"Nah. I was born without fear. Even standing here in this cage, I really can't summon anything but an interest in where this night is going to take us."

Ruby steels her face. She's backed against the rails, hyperventilating. "My fiddle. It's on stage. I don't have my fiddle."

I rest my hand on her arm, our bodies shaking to the earthquake of the swaying crane. Miles, a crimson dot on center stage, shakes his head.

"Seattle," he says without much gusto. He tries again. "Seattle." Finally, the entire world seems to collectively lose all decorum. "Welcome to the Star Games!"

I lower my head, devastated that he's really going through with this. Sadie slides to the floor of this contraption, heaving for breath. Her wheezes set my head to throbbing. It's as if my panic has bled out to every one of my sisters. Except Zelda. Her confidence is something to be studied.

Mania fizzles through the air as Miles paces in a circle. "We've gathered the finest in entertainment for you tonight. The cream of the crop at the Luminaire, these Star Girls are truly magnificent." He stares up at me, this animal in a cage who lured her pack to the slaughter.

"Tonight, we begin a battle for the spotlight." Miles's voice echoes through the microphone into the misty night. Lights bounce off umbrellas as men with their families point and laugh.

"What sort of battle do we have in store?" Miles looks up to the pattering raindrops and the people hanging off balconies like creeping houseplants. "Well, the audience decides which star will kick off the evening."

Spotlights point to our flags one at a time as Miles assesses the audience's reaction. Every time the light shifts to another image, my heart jumps.

I cough a little too loudly to force calm back to my chest. But no, my body still revolts against my mind as I prepare for a breakdown of epic proportions.

The crowd narrows their choice to two. Me, the hysterical daughter, and Annelise, the blind girl with a voice born of magic.

"The Star Girls may be dancers and singers and acrobats and musicians, but they are so much more." Rain pelts his jacket. He commands attention as if the sun shines directly on his face. "These young women have pierced the secret veil of magic and brought back a collection of stars. They spin color and light into the most spectacular show of our time."

"Keep those witches off our streets!" A man's voice screams.

Annelise leans into the girls, reaching for their hands. "It's dangerous to sing for them," she says.

Miles keeps calm. "These are no witches, sir. They are performers."

The man leaps on stage, followed by two more carrying signs that read "Lock them up. We must protect our children!" He spreads his arms wide, as if giving a sermon. "I demand you remove these occult heathens from our midst." The ones holding signs turn toward us and stare, hate boiling from their eyes.

Sadie gulps air through wheezing breaths. "What if we just do as they ask? We can dance and then go back inside where we're safe."

I grind my teeth. "We aren't any safer inside the theater. Price changed the rules on us and there's no going back. No one can protect us now." I believed I could change my own fate, but I never stopped to think of how I'd be ruining everyone else's.

The only thing that matters right now is Annelise, who shivers in her long-sleeved, crimson velvet gown.

The men are removed, and all eyes turn to our cage. Annelise whispers, "The spotlight, it's on us right now?"

"Yes," Sadie says.

The door to the birdcage flies open. Somehow, magically, through a fit of panic deep enough to knock me to my knees, I step onto the staircase. A man holds out his hand to guide me. I take it, simply because I need to feel something other than cold.

The staircase glides with the wind as thick chains clatter between the metal planks. An unsteady step causes my heel to catch. I crumble to the metal stairs, prepared to crack a few bones on the way down, but the man catches me before I tumble.

"Thank you." Tears sting my eyes.

Once on the stage, I stand next to Miles but turn away as he leans to me. His breath audibly hitches but he carries on, as emcees do.

"Bring down our next girl."

Annelise approaches the door. She smiles at the crowd, and for a split second, I believe we can do this.

The man takes Annelise's hand and shoves Sadie back inside. Everyone gasps but by the time the girls have reacted, the door is once again locked. Annelise cries, "Girls?"

Two men dressed in tuxedos grab her around the waist, ignoring her cries. They carry her down the steps to laughter from the audience. Sick, evil laughter.

Pain rushes to my face. My head thumps something fierce.

Miles calmly addresses the audience. "We fear what we do not understand," he bellows. "Tonight, you get your first glimpse of the magic beyond our earthly understanding. There is nothing to fear, my friends. Only wonder to behold." He tilts his head and meets my gaze, a deep sorrow in his eyes.

I wish I held his beliefs that we could change minds and hearts. Alas, I've never trusted anyone that much. Least of all myself.

"Our first exhibition is a Star Girl with a voice that rings from the heavens. What she cannot see is reflected in the magic that is her voice. Please welcome the Eyeless Starling!"

Annelise taps her feet in place. She sighs, as if exhaling the collective fear from every one of her sisters. The eerie silence after screams die down sends shivers up my spine. Raindrops ping on the wood stage. The crowd grumbles in anticipation. Silence makes it appear as if the world has stopped. Our entire future rests on our Annelise. I can hear her chattering teeth from here.

"Come on, girl. You can do it." Ruby says loud enough for her to hear.

Annelise breathes out a whisper of mist. Her chest heaves and her fingers fidget with her dress.

"Do something, you worthless witch!" A man yells from the crowd.

Miles lifts his hands to the crowd. "Patience." He turns to Annelise and whispers, "You can do this." Annelise whimpers, as tears gather in her lower lids.

A woman stomps her spool-heeled shoes in a puddle. "Liars! You're all liars. There's no magic here. Just swindlers and floozies!" The whole of downtown laughs and screams like an interactive melodrama.

Annelise flicks her eyes around, tears streaking her cheeks. "Eleanora, I can't do it."

I lead her to Iridessa's extended hand.

Miles nods slowly. "A challenge to the opening act!"

Confused excitement thunders into the air, as if we planned these theatrics. As if our lives are a stage.

I step next to Miles, smiling as wide as my cheeks will allow. I extend my arms and bow, waiting for the city to erupt like the spectators of any blood sport do when pain is on display.

"I hope you're happy," I say through a forced grin.

"I am many things right now," he says. "Happy is not one of them."

"Then get the hell off my stage."

I stomp out a rhythm as music begins. My feet morph into Irish light shoes. My mother's feet take over, though the true me remains stuck in a pool of mud about to drag me under. It was always going to end this way.

Miles backs away and I sense her. Mother. Her presence creeps into all parts of me. I let her dance and shine as she's meant to do while I simply watch her ghost inhabit my limbs, my heart, and my mind.

Can anyone else see her, or feel her the way I do? No, I don't suppose anyone without hysteria understands the hell I live in. The sharp decline of another Fire Girl. I continue this conversation with myself as my body moves about spitting fire and sending rockets of flames into the sky. It isn't my body. All of this is her.

I hear only empty blackness when I stare at the crowd, though their mouths form shapes of screams. Are they happy or frightened? Truthfully, there's very little distance between the two emotions. As Fiona Cleary's act comes to a fiery end, my sisters dangle in a cage high above our Seattle streets. They watch in awe, though Ruby is the only one who meets my eyes.

All at once, a searing pain shoots through my chest. I fall to my back, head thumping against the hard ground. A galaxy flickers above, a cluster of milky blue light and purple at its center like cracked earth. The rain soaks my clothes as the galaxy disappears once again behind the clouds.

I turn my head to the audience, my cheek pelted with rain and my limbs absorbing the air to cool my fever. The only faces I see are Lady and Aria, holding hands. They don't smile, but they do offer me their most sympathetic frowns, and it hurts like hell.

None of this is me. I never wanted this. I only wanted to rejoice in dance and find a way to love myself.

Sadly, it's too late for regrets.

CHAPTER THIRTY-FOUR

Eleanora

I don't remember leaving the stage. I have a vague memory of Miles lifting me in an embrace, and the Star Girls released for the finale. But one image is seared in my mind. Lady's face. I finally danced wild and free—so much that my mind left my body. She should have been proud.

Back inside the theater, I wake on a tufted couch in the lounge as Ruby pats my forehead with a cool washcloth.

"They put us in a fucking cage!" Sadie paces back and forth, her face fire red.

Iridessa hands me a glass of water. "They'll do it again next Friday, and the Friday after that. The crowd will choose two Star Girls to compete for the crowd's approval."

"You're awfully calm about this, Iridessa," Sadie snaps.

"I hate every second of these games." She glances around the room of tearful girls. "None of you deserve this."

Zelda squeezes her breasts high to her chin. "If they're going to use us, I'm at least going to have a splendid time drinking their booze and dancing with their men. To the Sapphire Bar!"

The troupe follows, except for Ruby who hasn't moved from my side. Iridessa soaks the washcloth in water and wrings it back into the bowl.

"Dessa?" I sit up against a foggy head. "Why are they doing this?"

She pauses then keeps twisting the rag though no water drops loose. "Why do you think? Money. Power."

"No. We're missing something. Price maybe, but Miles? For all his faults, he doesn't seem to care about money."

"Miles needs his father's approval," Dessa says. Her voice is steady, but her fist clenches at her side. She drops the rag back in the water. "He'll do anything to get it."

"Why do we do dangerous things for the parents who don't seem to love us back?" Damn those tears for appearing again.

Ruby stands between us. "Iridessa, we can never go back to the way things were, can we?"

"I doubt it." She glances back and forth between us. Her eyes redden but she squeezes them shut hard enough to stop the tears. "We've all lost control." She drops her arms, walking back to her room with shoulders slumped. What an odd sight.

Ruby focuses on me. "What happened tonight?"

She's probably the only person I can trust with the truth. "I was the hit of the town, that's what happened."

"It wasn't you," she said. "Nothing about those movements or attitude came from you. Even your halo looked different."

I scratch my fingernails through my hair and pace around her, searching for the words that press against my throat. "Ruby, how do you know if you're losing your mind?"

"Oh." She understands everything in an instant. I know she does.

"I see things I know aren't there. People I know aren't real." Oh God, this is happening. I'm admitting fire hysteria. "I drew blood that never actually appeared and spoke to ghosts."

I want to hide in the dark and never come out.

"I speak to ghosts and I'm quite well."

"I'm scared, Ruby."

"Look, we've all developed some unusual ways of dealing with this mess of a life. If you retreat into some fantasy to get through the pain of it all, that doesn't make you sick. It makes you really fucking strong."

"I'm strong enough. I want to be happy."

"What will make you happy?"

"I don't know. Can you mix up an oil or herb to fix my panic? That would be a good start."

"Let me tell you something. Back at home, after the torches, I mixed up a potion and made a spell. I was going to rid myself of magic and everything that made me a witch."

"You didn't do it, did you?"

"I started. In the mix of river water, chicken bones, and a drop of my blood, I glimpsed a life without magic."

"What did you see?"

"Without magic, without witchery, I am not me. The Ruby you know would cease to exist without the good and awful that brought me here. I didn't want to lose any part of myself, and I don't want you to either."

"I just want to cut out the parts that hurt."

"It doesn't work that way."

I wipe my face with a towel. Scrub away all the stage makeup. The sensation reminds me how much I ache to escape, just like I did as a dishwasher. When will I live a life I don't need to escape from?

"I'm going to see Miles."

"I'm coming. Let me grab my fiddle."

"Why would you need a fiddle at the Price mansion?"

She winks. "We always need our magic."

***

Ruby stands next to me, both of us in awe of the size of the columned stone Price mansion with enough stained glass to pass for a church. In the heart of the city, it could pass for an entire apartment building.

"Why does he need more money, again?" I ask.

"You'll probably need to ask him."

"Is this stupid? He recruited me for my name, convinced his father to headline me, and coaxed the fire to the surface."

"You give him too much credit." She smirks. "What does your heart tell you to do?"

"To go back in time before this mess all started."

She lifts her fiddle to her chin. "Since you can't do that, why don't we start by dealing with Miles. Look. He's right there in that window."

Miles paces back and forth, rubbing his chin, completely unaware that we're watching from the street.

"Hold on." Ruby slides the bow across her fiddle in a sweet tune. Leaves appear on the concrete, growing as large as elephant ears under my feet. Vines lift me off the ground. Cradled in a soft web of greenery and Ruby's mountain music, I float up to the window and wait for Miles to see me. When he does, he falls backward over a chair. He rushes to the window but stays on his knees as he slides it open.

"Nora, I can't see how you're up this high, so please just come inside before I pass out."

I climb through the window as the vine recedes.

"Told you," Ruby says with a smile. "We need our magic." She blows me a kiss before sauntering away into the night.

I shut the window, so Miles doesn't panic. "I'm fine. Stand up."

He slides the curtains closed and collects himself. "You were amazing tonight."

"Until you had to carry me offstage."

"I was worried about you, but Iridessa held me back. Told me you were better off without me." He bites his bottom lip and slides his hair back into a low ponytail. "She's probably right." He runs his fingers along his desk with drawings of our city stage.

"It's too late for better off."

His eyes widen, regret washing across his face. "I've tried to get my father to sign the place over to me, but he won't. He refuses to let me see the financials and insists things are too tenuous. I wouldn't have allowed any of this."

"Your father can offer you the theater. Money, your inheritance. I get all that. But at what cost?"

"Listen. We all do things we don't want to do. Your act tonight was incredible, but it wasn't you. It was Fiona's dance from years ago that you resurrected."

"I've done everything you've asked of me." I turn away, focusing on the bookshelves that line his walls. "I danced your choreography. I watched them lock my troupe in a cage while I gave the audience what they demanded." Iridessa was right, I should never have let any of them decide my limits.

Miles takes a hesitant step toward me. I can tell by the slide of his shoes. "Can you imagine if you dance with the freedom I saw the first night at the Milk House? I still believe that's our way forward."

"*Our* way?" Did he do this to me, or did I do this to myself? I spin slowly, afraid to meet his gaze. "The world knows me as the Hysterical Daughter. That's all I'll ever be."

"Not to me." He slides his arm around my back and presses me into him.

Our lips find their way to each other. Despite my confusion and anger, I need him. The way he touches me makes all the hurt disappear. He kisses me deep and hungry. His hands in my hair and body pressed to mine, I can't breathe, but in the best way possible. I slide his ponytail free and run my hands through his hair, gripping it in my fist and pulling him to kiss me more. Faster.

He unbuttons my blouse and slides one shoulder down, kissing my neck and arm and earlobe until I can't take it anymore. I remove my blouse and drop it on the floor.

I slide my hands up his shirt, along his chest muscles. "I choose my future, not you."

"Understood." He grabs my face in his palms. "Listen to me. You can walk away from the Star Games. I can't."

"The Star Games could go on for years. New Star Girls. A horrid Seattle tradition to last through the ages. And you're going to stand by your father through it all. What power does this man hold over you?"

He reaches for me, his teary eyes like the sun reflected off diamonds. "My mother danced with me every night."

"What?"

"Before she died, she danced with me in secret. Through these halls and around the furniture. We'd slide down the banisters." He doesn't let go of my hand. "Father didn't approve. He wanted me to be a businessman, not a performer."

"What happened to her?"

"She died on my tenth birthday. She set the curtains on fire. We think she knocked her head on the ground and the smoke—." His face flushes. He swallows the memory that seems stuck in his throat. "I was at the theater with Father. By the time we arrived home, they'd put out the fire, but she was long gone."

I pull him close, tucking his hair behind his ear. "Miles, how did she set the curtain on fire?"

He shakes his head, stuttering as he tries to speak. "I'm not supposed to say."

"You're a grown man now. You can say anything you want."

He leans his cheek into my hand. "She had fire dance."

I can't quite understand how Price can manipulate and use us when his wife was one of us. "Did he ask you to keep that a secret?"

"It's part of my inheritance, which I don't care about anymore. But I grew up believing secrets were necessary. I had to protect her image. Her safety. It was my job to keep her safe."

He failed her, at least, in his own eyes. "It's who she was, Miles. You were a kid." Pain twists in my chest. A sudden awareness that I didn't understand the world like I thought I did, and I certainly didn't understand Fiona.

"Father always told me the world wouldn't understand her. They would hurt her." His knees buckle. We lower to the bed where he leans his head on my shoulder. "I should have been there."

"I'm so sorry, Miles." I know the pain of a mother slipping from your grasp. The guilt that rips through you when you can't save her.

"I think she wanted to die. Her episodes were growing worse. Hysteria was taking her fast. My father treated her like a fragile doll who couldn't leave the house. She was broken, and he was going to fix her."

"This theater isn't about your father at all, is it?"

He sits up, hair dangling over his eye, lips parted. "I want to build the world she never got to see."

Oh, the way my heart flutters. "One where we aren't afraid to be who we are."

He reaches for me, his hand drapes gently around my neck. "I don't think it needs to end the way it did for our mothers. The magic didn't kill them, society did."

"It's easy for you to say. You don't have the threat of death by hysteria."

"That's exactly why I can believe in a better theater." He pulls me into a kiss. He pulls my body close.

"Miles?" I run my hands along his cheeks. Through his fine hair. "I'm afraid to hope. All I've ever known are the legends of women who came before me. It never ended well for any of them."

His fingers settle on my throat, his palm warming my chest. "Then we'll have to make a new legend."

He kisses my neck and chest. I fall into the closest thing to bliss I've ever known. We tear off each other's clothes and taste every inch of skin. We kiss and sigh and share a moment of unending hope. My halo doesn't appear. All that time crushing down my emotions, and all I had to do was make room for them. This swell brings me closer to the thing I've always dreamed of... a place I belong.

***

I've lost track of the hours we've laid together, hands and limbs and mouths entwined. Miles begins to fall asleep, but I wake him. "I need to go back to the theater. Ruby will worry about me."

As I dress, my body wants to scream with joy. I'm alive and whole and not at all frightened. How a man's touch can do such a thing makes me instantly regret judging my mother. I'm hungry for this feeling too.

Miles wraps me in a hug and kisses me long and slow. "I'll walk you downstairs."

He holds my hand down the carpeted staircase toward the grand entrance. Off in the distance, I hear voices from a flood of light at the end of the hallway. Miles's shoulders tighten. "That's my father's office."

I lean against the wall and slide toward them, eager to hear the chatter, as Miles follows with an unapproving pout. We hide in an alcove, behind a bronze statue of a mustang.

"It was a good start, Price," a man says.

Mr. Price stutters, his usual bravado long gone in place of a nervous old man. "I'll get there, I promise. Look at the sensation we've created."

The sensation. A damn birdcage and fruit tossed at our heads.

"I like what I'm seeing," the man says in what I recognize as a Chicago accent.

"You don't need to worry about me," Price says. "You know I deliver."

Awareness wiggles through me, and I can't believe what I'm hearing. Miles rests his hand on mine.

"This girl, the one whose mother lost all her marbles and got sent to the nuthouse?"

Oh, if I could summon Ruby's witchery and turn that man into a warted toad right now.

"Eleanora Cleary," Price says. I'm surprised he knows my real name.

"She made quite the impression."

I count three Chicago accents of different tones. Three mobsters pushing Price to push me. How did I not see it? I thought Price was rich enough to fund the Luminaire with his own fortune. I've seen plenty of mob men through different Vaudeville stages.

There's a reason Vaudeville stars are the highest paid women in the world. It's why my mother never let anyone own her. Realization hits. That's why she moved us so much.

I believed Price was the evil ringleader, but he's merely the pawn, just like me.

"You approached us, Price." Grumbles, a chair shift, but no response. "If it weren't for us, that little Prohibition exception would be revoked like that." Snap. "You've made your living peddling magic girls

with great legs and the best martini this side of the Columbia River."
He sounds as if he lowers his hands to the desk. "Would be a shame to
lose it all."

"And I'm very grateful for all that you've done." Price clears his
throat.

"Don't stop now. Just do as we ask."

"Our deal." Price's voice shakes. "You promised me you wouldn't
bring him in."

"Things change, my man." A hard slap and what sounds like a
punch sends me leaning into Miles's arm. I cover my mouth to prevent
any wayward gasps. "Your son is a brilliant emcee. The crowd loves
him. And he loves that twisted little dancer."

Miles closes his eyes. This is why he can't walk away.

"The city wants a love story, and we know this will end in tragedy.
Just look at the girl's bloodline."

"No. This is my responsibility," Price says. "My son is off-limits.
You promised."

A chair breaks, what sounds like a kick from one of the men. Price
thuds to the floor as they proceed to pummel him. Miles doesn't move.
I suspect he's seen this before.

"Promises are meant to be broken," the Chicago voice says. "Just
like bones."

"Take me," he says. "Break my legs. Take my money. Just don't
involve Miles. He did nothing wrong."

"This little show of yours was a great idea, Price. Brilliant, in fact.
Now, we need to take it beyond Seattle. Make the country sit up and
take notice. Miles, the failed acrobat falling in love with the headcase
who might explode at any moment? It's too good to pass up. Like a train
wreck. Just think of the speakeasies we can build around a traveling
show. Those silly Star Girls can be our bait. We'll turn them against
each other like hungry, caged tigers."

Price clears his throat. "You'll threaten the Temperance League and
the church wives? Take away their power?"

"We hate those bitches too," the man says. I take silence as they've reached a deal.

No end in sight. No turnover of the theater. I can't breathe or move or even feel my hands, so I close my eyes and wait for the panic to tumble away.

"If you don't get Miles and Miss Hysterical on board, we're coming for you. We want the kind of meltdown the Celtic broad had. Public and messy."

I form a plan, right here behind this horse's bronze rear. They're about to get the fire dance that not even I've ever seen. I'd rather burn to a crisp in a wall of my flames than let them own me.

I hear you, Mother. Wild as the Stars.

"We'll pick off every magic dancer while the country watches. Imagine. Every Star Girl in an asylum. Widespread panic. Don't think your little band of idiots from a few speakeasies can stand up to our power."

"Yeah. We'll sacrifice that tap dancer and make your son watch. Then we'll come for him."

Destruction with no way out. Now all I have is the magic that may end me, and the surprising acceptance of what may come.

CHAPTER THIRTY-FIVE

Eleanora

The sun is about to rise. I've wandered the Seattle streets since leaving Miles two hours ago. The stakes seem to grow higher by the minute, like a ticking clock about to break. Here I am, a scared woman searching for the lights from the bottom step of the orphanage so a literal kid can ease my worry. Every window is dark. If I ring the doorbell, I'll wake the headmistress who already dislikes Aria.

A bell rings behind me. I turn to find a woman wrapped in scarves and chains of jewelry that bounce against her chest. She drags a wagon down the lonely street with one hand, a sizzling cigarette in the other.

The woman stops in front of me and examines my face. An uncomfortable moment of silence passes. When I open my mouth, she lifts her hand to show me I'm not to speak.

She waves her cigarette toward me. "You have a gift."

Very impressive. My image is plastered all over the city. "Big surprise. I'm a fire dancer."

"No, not dance." She writes something in the air, watching the trailing cigarette smoke write some invisible words. "Stars. Gold. You see things."

"All I see is a fortune teller trying to make a few pennies. Move along." I turn back to the orphanage and decide I'll have to wait for an appropriate time to ring the bell.

"You're waiting for whispers that won't come."

I don't turn around. I count my breaths.

"The answer was never in the stars, young lady. It has always been in the place you fear."

She knows nothing. I whip around to tell her to get lost, but the street is empty, save for an early morning fog heavy over the streets. Not even a jingle from the bell on her wagon.

"Eleanora?" Aria peeks out a second-floor window with sleepy eyes. "What are you doing?"

"I'm sorry to bother you. I just—Will you come down here?"

"Yes!"

The window shuts and a few minutes later, Aria stumbles around the corner in her nightdress, a ripped jacket, and untied boots. "I'm here." Her giant smile soothes my weary heart.

"How did you know I was out here?"

"I don't sleep much. I often stare out the window and count stars or trace the moon. I'm so happy to see you."

Even sleep is hard for her. How she maintains a smile I'll never know. "Will you get in trouble?"

"No. The headmistress sleeps like the dead. I slipped out through the kitchen. Are you okay?"

"Yes." I force a smile, but her face drops and I know I can't hide it from her. "No, I'm not."

"There's always a solution just on the horizon. That's what the radio program I listen to says. I think they're right."

"I'm not sure there's any way out of this predicament I'm in. The worst part is that I brought all of this on myself and risked everyone I care about." As hysteria creeps into my life, I fear what comes next. I can't control my haunted brain.

"I get my hand slapped for stealing cookies every week."

I'm tempted to laugh at the ridiculous comparison, but I force seriousness. "Yeah?"

She nods. "But I do it anyway. I don't know, I'm hungry, and I like the thrill of stealing. But I accept the sting because it's worth it."

"It is?"

"Sure. There used to be this old lady around the corner. She'd bake cookies and pies and cool them in the window. I learned that every Sunday she'd have something baked, and I started sneaking what I could from the sidewalk."

"She must have been angry."

"I did this for years. Until one Sunday I arrived to find a note under a rock. It said *I'm sorry I won't be able to bake for you anymore. I'm moving to a home for the elderly.*"

"That's sad."

She tightens her jacket. "No way. It's the kindest thing anyone's ever done for me. She was my gift. Like clockwork, I had something to hope for. I still steal cookies and get slapped because it reminds me of her. Whoever she was."

"Why are you telling me this?"

"I'm twelve! My only life experience is cookies and growing out of shoes every month."

I laugh. A deep, hysterical belly laugh that brings tears to my eyes. She laughs too and together we gasp for air, me doubled over and her rolling on the wet pavement.

Once I collect myself, I stare at her wild, happy eyes. "I'm teetering on losing everything and you can still make me laugh. How do you do that?"

"Easy." She sighs and grins so wide her cheeks glow. "You know I'll love you even if you fail."

All the laughter I felt just a moment ago has dissipated and left me with a cold, painful ache in my heart. "I don't deserve you."

Aria walks to me with her arms out. We stand toe to toe. She leans her fragile body against mine and her cheek against my shoulder. This hug is painfully real. From her musty hair and her too thin ribs, to the way she trusts that I'll love her back. It's so real I have trouble breathing, but I can't let go.

"Fire dance may ruin me."

"Please don't leave." She pulls back, staring through red-rimmed eyelids.

"I can't leave." How true that is. I'd disappoint everyone. Better to stay, where I only disappoint myself. "Besides, I can't let you have all the fun around here. It makes it easier when I see you in the crowd."

She flashes a pitying smile, as if she knows more than I do. "I'll be there for every show. As long as you ask me."

That's an odd thing to say. She must be feeling needy, like I am. "Thanks, kid."

She yawns, which I've never seen. "I'm kind of tired. Would it be okay with you if I went back to sleep?"

"Of course. I'm glad I found you tonight."

"Me too." She skips toward the corner but stops before she disappears through the kitchen door. "Nora, I forgot to tell you about the last part of the note from the cookie lady."

"What did it say?"

"You're never alone."

CHAPTER THIRTY-SIX

Fiona

The stage means nothing to me anymore.

Midnight show on a Saturday. The house is packed. They station cops outside the theater now and I can't leave for fear the mobs may beat me senseless. Everyone wants me gone, including Price. The papers have deemed me a nasty witch. I don't care.

I take the stage to both cheers and boos. Rolled up papers hit my flank, as do a few tennis balls. Nothing I can't handle. The crowd still needs me, even if it's more hostile than adoring. My body goes through the motions of dance. Fire erupts, yet I feel nothing. My mind has cooled. Maybe it's all the whisky. No, I suppose it's accepting the rising hysteria, because I'm tired of fighting.

By my first step offstage, I'm already holding a cigarette and bottle of booze. One of the Star Girls shakes me, spilling whisky on my hand. "Stop it," she says.

Lost in blissful numbness, I stare at her red lips. She's the new star. I'm a parody of the once great Celtic Fire. "Back off."

"You're ruining everything." The disgust in her eyes hits me like a familiar heartache.

"Yeah, so what." I suck against my gasper until the sting swallows any pain. "You sound like Price."

"You're gonna set the place on fire. Did you hear how the crowd screamed?"

"Yeah, I heard it. That means they're having fun."

"They're terrified of you!"

A swig of booze burns through my throat. "Close enough." I stumble past her, getting drunk already. Thank God. I'll lose my mind shortly, lost in memories of Eleanora and her beautiful eyes. Back when she adored me. By the time I come to, I'm standing in the lobby amongst the audience as they shuffle out.

I don't know how I began yelling, my words come out like a screaming slur. "I'm not a witch, you assholes."

The crowd seems both terrified and amused. Good. I'm done hiding. Let them see what they've done to us.

"She'll set us all on fire!" A man pulls his wife away.

Yes, I know. I'm a monster. I've fought it for too long. Now I've finally grown my tail and thickened my scales. "You used to love me." Oh no, pathetic, drunk Fiona has taken over. I hate her. "Now I'm nothing to you all."

"Leave!" A woman shouts but I can't see her. "Go back to the forest, you witch."

"Ah, but if I could. I wish I were a witch. I'd put a spell on you to choke on your tongue in your sleep." I open my mouth as fire bursts forth. Anger takes over and sadness fuels the flames. I breathe until the curtains catch fire, filling the room with screams. People run out in a panic while I drain my body of every bit of heat. Not dissimilar to retching, the pressure chokes me, and my eyes leak with tears.

Someone grabs my arm. I turn with a jerk, coming face to face with Iridessa. She lowers her shoulders. "Fiona, come back."

"No way." I yank away, so angry at myself for not hugging her instead. "I'm spoiled goods," I say with a teary smile.

The flames die out. The heat dissipates. I tumble down the stairs, a floppy, broken mess of a human. By the time I land, I'm having trouble breathing. The cops have taken me, dragging me through the wall of flames. I finally vomit on the cop's shoes. He throws me into his car. While I lie on my stomach on the backseat, wrists cuffed behind me, I see crowds gather around the windows. They hate me and pay to watch my demise.

A flash hits me. Maybe I did this on purpose. I couldn't handle the spotlight anymore, so I became their villain. They can hate me on my terms. What is love anyway, but hate wrapped in sadness? This will ruin me soon enough.

I drift to sleep and just before the blackness hits, I hear madness calling me home.

CHAPTER THIRTY-SEVEN

Eleanora

Another Friday, another competition.

The troupe waits in our familiar spot just inside the door to the Luminaire. An empty lobby doesn't warm my body the way a full one does. Ghosts seem to hang from chandeliers and peek out from behind statues, casting memories like cobwebs.

Ruby holds up this morning's front page. "Trash." I snatch the newspaper from her tightened fingers. A cartoon of Ruby dressed in a pointed witch hat, holding a broom, a snake wrapped around her fingers.

"They really don't understand what a witch is, do they?" I rip the paper in two, then in fours. I keep ripping until my hands are full of shreds. Once I tap a few steps, my top hat plunks onto my head. When I slam my heel to the carpeted floor, fire erupts from my palms, igniting the pulp balled in my sweaty hands. They turn to dust and disappear. So does my top hat and fire. "Don't let those bastards break us."

Sadie wraps her arm around Ruby. "Who's ready to be locked in a birdcage? No one?" She puffs out her lip to mimic Price. "Well, my little devils, perhaps you need to work harder. Give me magic or give me death!"

My heart lurches into my throat when the door opens.

"Line up." Price's voice is flat. I can't sympathize with him, though I know the truth. Price is a prisoner too. He's too far in now and risks his only son.

I wouldn't dare tell the girls how we're all on the menu for the mobsters feasts. Once they know, they'll be in misery with me, with no way out. I stand at the threshold, unwilling to move. Price growls at me. "Now."

I complied on New Year's Eve. I obeyed last Friday. We let him lock us in a cage, mock us, and throw us one by one for the city to consume like raw flesh in a pack of wolves. I've hidden away in a kitchen to avoid what I've always known, but there's no more hiding.

The crowd stomps their feet in unison loud enough to resemble an earthquake. They chant, "Bring the witches" in a high, low beat. A count of four followed by four stomps. Over and over, louder and louder, they chant.

I shake my head. "I bleed Magic Dance, and I'll fight to the bloody death to protect it."

Price hovers over me. "Then get your magic ass on stage and fight."

"As deeply as you're fighting for your son, for your wealth and security, you can't imagine our struggles. We fight for our bodies. For our right to exist." I meet his eyes. "I avoided theater life and passed out on stage and withdrew from the world because—" I breathe through the realization. "That was my way to protect myself from people like you. And people like them." I point to the crowd. "All of you killed my mother."

Price bares his teeth. "I don't have time for your little crisis right now."

Little crisis. I'd laugh if it weren't so painfully real. Anything that doesn't affect his status is little. Meaningless. We glance at the Star Girls as they hold each other, relying on each other's smiles to shield their insecurities against the brutal world around them. I doubt this man will never know true family.

Price grabs my arm hard enough to make me wince. "Get on that stage or I'll throw you in the nuthouse myself."

The fear in his eyes tells me he means it. Wouldn't that be poetic? He kills my mother and sends me for the same fate. Once again, I obey. This isn't about me anymore.

By the time I reach my troupe, I've already decided what must be done. "Tonight, we give the people what they want. Tomorrow, we climb out of this mess."

We march up the stairs to center stage, hands linked like a chain. The crowd surrounds the circular platform on all sides. A barricade has been knocked down to make more room for spectators, which brings them too close. Signs shoot into the air with cutouts of each person's favorite Star Girl. Ruby's has a witch hat. Annelise's has a knife stabbed through her eye with fake blood dripping down her face.

People chant and scream. It's so volatile, I can't decipher any of it. In the shadows, Miles appears. His hair hangs in his eyes. He holds his top hat at his side while punching his thigh.

The orchestra begins. As if I can ready myself for what comes next, I harden my face and tighten my ribs.

A voice from above announces, "Seattle. You asked for more and we delivered. Welcome to day two of the battle for magic. The fight for the spotlight. Welcome to the Star Games!"

People crowd the stage, but policemen keep them from climbing toward us. Every rooftop and balcony overflows with people. I search the audience for Lady or Aria, but with so much commotion and twirling lights, I can't see a thing.

I squeeze Ruby's hand.

The curtain falls. Miles stands in the spotlight, the gems glittering from his tuxedo. His face is shiny and red.

"What's the matter with him?" Sadie asks.

"He knows what's coming," I say.

"Well, Seattle. We meet again." Miles's voice is so low and contained, the crowd quiets to a near-silence. Everyone looks around, confused. "Tonight is somber for me. I'm afraid I'm not in the mood to razzle dazzle." He finally acknowledges the troupe dressed in gowns, shivering from the cold. "Girls, to your spots."

"What the hell is he talking about?" Sadie asks.

The stage lights up in six spotlights, our faces painted on each one. We release hands to take our spot on the stage.

"Turn and face the audience, please." Miles steps around the stage aimlessly.

We turn to face the sea of strangers. So many expressions. Everything from fear to excitement. So much shouting.

"What do we think?" Miles asks the crowd. "Do we love our Star Girls?"

Nothing but applause and adoration. A giant lie.

The stage moves and shifts. I bend my knees and lift my hands to steady myself against the rattle as a circle breaks free, turning me to face the center. One circle lifts higher, rising above the others. It holds Ruby.

"Tonight, we see if the witch will entertain us, cast a spell on our wicked souls, or blow the audience to pieces with her black magic."

More chants mixed with laughter, squeals, and plenty of gasps.

An egg flies from the audience, landing straight in Ruby's face. With a crack, the egg oozes down her face. She hardly twitches but wipes the goo away and flicks her hand to the side.

"Die, witch!" a man screams, followed by a ripple of laughter.

Miles steps behind me. I can smell his tobacco. "Nora, I'm so sorry."

I stare forward. We both know what's at risk here. "Go on. Do as you must."

He brushes past me, stopping to whisper in my ear. "I wish there was another way."

Tears rush to my eyes, so I shut them tight, which only makes the noise grow unbearably loud.

Tonight is different. They've separated us. By the time I realize it, the stage is moving again. Something drops from overhead. Everyone looks up. Above me, against the black sky, metal circles descend from a crane. Fireworks spark and lights spin in colored circles. I can't make out what they are. Suddenly, they descend around each performer. We're all in cages. They lock in place with a click.

Ruby stands in the center with her fiddle and a face full of desperation.

"From the mountains of Appalachia to our shining theater, this girl knows a thing or two about sadness. Watch in wonder as our outcast witch battles for approval and love."

It's so much worse than I imagined.

"Get the witch!" their chants aren't original or interesting.

The circle platform spins Ruby slowly, as all spotlights converge on her. I grip the icy bars around me, watching her soar above the crowd. I want to blow the restraints off and fly us all away from here.

Her hands shake ever so slightly, something only the troupe would notice. As she plays, greenery and sticks climb the pole holding her up. Wind chimes, a pan flute, and organ rise from the orchestra.

Nothing here is about us, except, everything hinges on our very souls.

Her magic produces a blood moon which drops stars on silver threads that dangle over the audience. They reach for them but their hands only wave through like a mirage. Ruby grabs the moment, creating music with passion.

If this is how well she performs on Price's orders, imagine what her true magic could do?

The energy shifts. Fear rattles deep in my bones.

The lights disappear and Ruby's music fades to silence in the black night. Spotlights settle on the Luminaire rooftop. Teetering on the edge is Miles.

"I am but a lonely emcee. A director at the great Luminaire. I have a secret to share with you all."

A hush descends over Second Avenue. I suddenly miss the chaos.

Miles's knees shake. He hugs the pole that holds him in place. His father put him up there, knowing it's his worst fear. "I am in love with a girl who may never love me back."

The wind picks up and Miles catches himself on the grate that holds him on the rooftop. Gasps fill the crowd. "Don't jump!" one yells. "She's not worth it!"

"Which one is it?" they yell.

"I'm unsure I can save her from magic's wicked ways." His voice catches, as if he's about to cry. "Can I ever really tame a hysterical daughter?"

Lights flood my cage.

I pull away as the crowd howls. As if I'm the villain.

"Play for me, witch! And cast a spell on our unstable tap dancer so I may finally save her from her hysterical mind."

He actually did it. I didn't want to believe it, but of course he could. I would have done worse for my mother.

Lights fall on myself and Ruby. She plays through tears, her eyes unwavering from mine.

Suddenly, a group of men rush the stage. One taunts me with a straitjacket that dangles from his thick fist.

"Lock her up!" The crowd joins the chant.

More men storm the stage. They push past policemen followed by rings of light. "Oh, God," I say. They're carrying torches.

I shake the cage until my arms ache which only makes the men with the straitjacket go wild. "She's feral!" They laugh with such freedom I want to rip them to shreds with my teeth.

Perhaps I am feral. I could burn them right now and not regret it.

The crowd chants *Celtic Fire* over and over.

The men with torches surround Ruby, screaming, "Witch!" as a ring of fire blazes like a bonfire below her. They pummel her with eggs. Dozens of them. She loses her balance while I scream her name.

Ruby falls. She catches herself on the platform and now dangles by her hands, her feet dangerously close to the fire where her fiddle crashes into pieces.

I couldn't stop the torches.

Lights shine on me as I tap feverishly, full of anger, my magic swelling against my insides. I shoot fire at the rails, but the flames only bounce back at me, blasting my face with heat. When I fall to a heap on the floor of my cage, the men point and laugh.

Ruby screams. The Star Girls yell. Iridessa appears onstage attempting to shove the men back.

I've hit my head. Dizziness swarms my mind, but I rise to my knees enough to scream, "Help her!"

Fights erupt and policemen club anyone onstage, slamming their night sticks into backs and thighs, backhanding women so hard they fall face first to the wood floor. Ruby makes her way to the pole and slides down, running to help Iridessa open the cages. The audience turns hysterical, and I know, we can never return to the safety of the Luminaire we once knew.

CHAPTER THIRTY-EIGHT

Eleanora

Shattered glass still litters the streets from broken bottles and windows. Crumpled posters flutter through alleys and eggshells have now frozen to the ground. Blood splatter decorates storefronts from fist fights. Only a few hours ago, the city damn near lost their collective minds, and it was carried out by the Prices. One place of safety remains in my world, so I find myself back again, where it all started.

Red paint marks so many doors in the city, it appears there were more speakeasies than people. Then there's the Milk House. I stare at the rickety building I called home for years, where I waited for star whispers but settled for an empty, ghost-filled room.

The door is cracked open, so I push on the painted X to let myself in. Dark, decrepit, and shattered into pieces, the makeshift stage now resembles a junkyard. The bar still stands despite gauges and holes punched along the sides. The burn mark from one of my swells still exists. I scratch my fingers along the ridges of scorched wood that still smells of smoke after all these years.

"That was quite a spectacle last night," Lady says.

My heart leaps into my throat. "Ruby survived, but she's shaken. She might never be the same."

"Price got what he wanted."

My stories live in these walls. "For years, my mother would wake me early in the morning." I'm still too afraid to look at her, so I count the remaining jars on the shelves in groups of four. "Still dark, she'd sit on my bed and tell me stories of my ancestors. How to prepare myself for what's to come." I take one final scratch of the burn mark and bring my fingernails to my nose. "She smelled of fire and I pretended not to see the flask she sipped from that eventually made her pass out on the floor next to me."

"I don't take favorites in my speakeasy, but Fiona held a special place in my heart. She always will. And so will you."

Something inside me locks up every time she tries to reach me. "You fed her booze and handed her to Price. You made her believe fire dance was her legacy."

"That's exactly what fire dance was."

"And to lose her sanity?" I've finally found the strength to face her. "Was her destiny to die in an asylum at the hands of people who wanted to cut out part of her brain while her only daughter cried herself to sleep?"

Lady doesn't react. She seems to give space for my outbursts, which makes me even angrier at myself. A memory floods my insides with panic, bursting to the surface, refusing to stay in the deep. "I heard you. One night I came down the stairs, ready to heal her scratches and burns. Her hair was cut to the scalp, chopped and uneven. Her neck glowed with bright red fingernail scratches." My brain seems to chop the memory off right there.

"You heard me tell her not to run away." Lady slides her feet toward me, but I flinch away. "Things were getting dangerous."

"You gave her a wig and makeup to hide her wounds. I wanted to fix her, and you only cared about keeping her addicted to the pain." I try to force tears to release this tight expanse in my chest, but my eyes remain dry.

"I refuse to tell people they cannot be who they are meant to be." She coughs back a sob, something I've never witnessed.

"Danger found her anyway."

She collects herself. Forces a return of her steely demeanor. "You could have done anything with your life, but you stayed with the theater."

"You think I wanted this mess?" I snap.

"You auditioned for the only legal magic theater in the country. You're just as wild as her."

The air thickens, like I'm about to float out of my body to get away from this terrible pain inside. "I'm not strong enough."

"Why did you decide to go?" Lady asks somewhere deep in my soul.

Why, why, why. So many questions that might never find answers.

As though she hears my inner thoughts, Lady steps closer still. "Why the Luminaire?"

I stumble back but the bar catches me with a sharp jab to my ribs. "I had to."

"Why?"

"To fix what broke her!"

My vision turns wobbly and pale. Lady stares at me with sympathy, which causes me to crumble to the floor in a ball and cry until I can find the air to speak. "Maybe, if I could be the best parts of her, I could stop the worst parts from ever existing."

Lady, in all her frustrating honesty, simply nods. "There was no Fiona without all the parts. Good, bad, and downright terrifying."

"I don't want magic to break me."

"I'm not sure it will, Eleanora." Lady slides over a rickety chair next to me and sits with a loud sigh. "But I know something that might."

Heaven help me, I actually play into her life lesson. "What's that?"

"Fire dance is in your blood. Tap dance and a love for the theater is who you are. A legacy of incredible performance and hysteria might not be what you want, but it's inside you. You don't need to let it win."

"I don't want panic and fear. Constantly at war with my mind." I rub my face to clear away the tears. "I'm afraid of everything, Lady. Look at the Star Games. With incredible performance comes too much danger."

"Did you leave your body?" she asks. "Retreat to somewhere in your mind where the fear is even worse than the reality?"

I peek up from my hands. "When I fire dance, that's what happens."

Lady removes her scarf. She slides the fabric from her silver curls to reveal a scarred burn mark on her scalp.

"Did my mother do that to you?" I ask this, not sure I want to hear the answer.

"No." She closes her eyes. "My daughter did."

I stare at the webbed flesh long gone of any hair. "Your... daughter?"

Lady leans her head back to stare at the ceiling. Then she places her scarf back on her head. "I lost her years ago. Long before she died, she fought this life with the strength of a warrior."

"Was she a fire dancer?"

"Fire gymnast. As beautiful as your mother. As troubled too. She would lash out with her fire or bare hands, but I never fought back. I wish I would have."

"Why didn't you ever tell me?"

"Tell you what, exactly? My beautiful, strong, unstable daughter succumbed to her worst impulses, and it was all because this world made her believe she was wrong for how she was born? She never asked for magic or fire or hysteria, but that's what my bloodline gave her. My grandmother had the gift too."

"You knew what was in store for her. Why would you want the rest of us to meet the same end?"

Lady rubs her eyes. I wonder how often she cries herself to sleep too. "The magic didn't break her, Eleanora. She fought to live magicless, and all that did was make her life intolerable. I know in my heart, had she been encouraged to accept the things this world didn't understand, she'd still be with me today."

"You tried to save all the Milk House performers in the same way."

She shrugs. "I failed at that too. But I'd still do it the same ten times over."

So many people have loved fire dancers, and we've hurt them all. "Lady, can I sleep in my old room tonight? I can't go back to the Luminaire."

"It's always here for you."

Her soft voice nearly breaks my long-held grudge. I walk on crunching glass and step over splintered wood toward the staircase behind the stage. But at the red X on the floor, I face Lady who hasn't moved from her memories. "Goodnight."

The stairs creak in the same spots and the top step still bows with my weight, but my door appears smaller. I turn the knob and, as expected, the door won't budge without a hard yank. All the quirks of my old life I took for granted were sounds that remind me of happier times. I couldn't hear them when I was too focused on moving on and growing up.

Nothing amiss. The same mouse chatter in the walls. The same rickety bed under a pitched roof. I wrap myself in the rosebud blanket, lying on my side to the same view of the brick buildings and a peek at the winter sky.

Mother would wrap her arms around me on chilly nights, her skin hot as a fever. Magic Dance flushed her for hours, her heart thumping hard against my back when we'd cuddle under this same blanket. She'd mumble to herself and whine, fighting the swell that refused to pop.

I would take a fire bolt to the face if it meant she'd return to the woman I knew back in Chicago, even if for just a few moments.

As her fame grew, her hysteria spiraled low and deep. She heard voices and mumbled in the corner. I cried alone in the bed, not knowing how to help her. Some nights the screams were shrill and others as quiet as a whimper. I kept holding on, waiting for those few moments when she'd smile again. Then she stopped coming around.

I've loved someone in the throes of hysteria, and it ruined me for life.

I throw off the blanket and sit at the bedside, bare feet on the cold floor, while my throat fights the restriction it knows so well. I could conjure a full episode and breakdown right now.

If I run away, which my body screams to do, I risk the safety of everyone I care about. It's my mind or the lives of my theater family. An impossible choice. I fight for my sanity with everything I have, warding off an episode by hanging on by my fingernails.

And I do that by saying the words, "I am the hysterical daughter."

CHAPTER THIRTY-NINE

Fiona

By the time the hangover fades, I'm in the throes of a feverish tremble. Sweat runs down my forehead into my eye. I reach to wipe it away, but I can't move. My wrists are cuffed to a bed. My chest thumps so hard I'm certain I might die. Do hearts explode?

I panic, kicking against my restraints. "Get me out of here." Rattle. Stretch. Nothing works. "I can't be here."

A nurse looks down her nose. Her lips purse so tight, I wonder if she has any. "Calm down."

"I'm tied to a bed. I can't calm down."

"I've given you some medicine. When you decide to stop fighting, I'll see to it that your restraints are loosened."

Calm down? My skin itches like hot sandpaper. "I'm Fiona Cleary."

"I know who you are." Her face tells me she wanted to throw in insult after that statement. "You're unwell."

"Oh, and you're going to help me." My teeth chatter and every muscle in my body seizes. "Is this the booze leaving my body?"

"In part." She reaches her hand for my throat. Without thinking, I turn to bite her, so she scratches her fingernails down my neck. I don't dare scream. "Don't try that again. This is your fire taking over."

"What the hell does that mean?"

"We treat fire here. You'll be tied up until we can perform your procedure."

No. This isn't happening. "You can't. I belong at the Luminaire. I'm supposed to be safe."

"The only way to keep you safe is to cut out the diseased part of your brain. The part that holds fire."

I could kill her. Right now, with a blast of fire. Just as I consider it, she walks away. Okay, okay. Think. I look around the room. My eyesight blurs, but I can make out a hospital room. No windows. A tray of blades. Jesus Christ, I'm in a nightmare. All I can think of is Eleanora. This is not how I leave her.

Time passes. Painful quiet where I recall every mistake of my life. Why did I threaten the audience? Finally, a doctor opens the door. I force every bit of calm I can muster. Play nice. Make them believe you're sane.

"Miss Cleary." He doesn't even look at me. "Quite the damage you've done."

"I made a mistake."

He laughs. "It isn't your fault. Your fire has ruined you." People like them have ruined me. "Take her to the ward," he says to an orderly.

A tall man unlocks my cuffs. "If you try anything, I'll slice your neck open without hesitation," he says.

I lie still, not sure what to do.

"That's a good girl." Oh, how I want to hurt him. He lifts me to standing and slips on a white jacket. My arms are pinned to my chest in a crossed pattern. I'm suffocated and hot. Tears stream down my cheeks.

He lowers me to a wheelchair. As we roll out the door and down the hall, I imagine the fire building inside me, burning like a furnace about to explode. He pushes me into a room with a dozen other women. They're all in white jackets. Some are drooling, others mumbling to themselves.

I recognize them. They're all magic dancers.

This is it. It's my end. They'll drug me and cut out the fire and then I'll be nothing. They will own me. There is no worse fate.

I slowly stand and begin dancing. The orderly's eyes flare with rage. "Stop that."

Why leave my legs free? They assume the fire comes from our minds. Mine lives in my bones. In my eyes and skin. It's everywhere. I dance so hard and so big that fire erupts on my face. Explosions send the jacket flying right off me in a fiery mass. I turn toward him and breathe fire which knocks him over in a cloud of smoke.

I run for the door but stop to stare at the room of drugged dancers. I want to save them all. Swoop them in my arms and carry them to safety. It's too late.

I run through the halls, knocking over nurses as I run toward the exit. Something grabs my hair, so I turn around just as a palm smashes against my cheek. I land my fist right in their face.

The doctor. He stumbles, stretching his jaw. "You shouldn't have done that." Just as he launches toward me again, I spin, shooting fire spurts directly at him. Some land in the glass and shatter the door to pieces.

I stand over the top of him. "The fire was never meant to hurt you. Stop trying to tame it." I duck through what's left of the doorframe, blinded by the early morning light. They see something different and think it's dangerous. We never wanted to shoot fire at them. They made us who we are.

***

I arrive at the soda fountain of the Milk House, body trembling, and tear-streaked cheeks. My lip burns from where the doctor hit me. Lady steps toward me, arms out. "Come here."

I fall into her arms and cry like I've never cried. I heave for air, releasing something akin to fire leaving my body. Her arms are strong yet soft. Like the mother I used to be for Eleanora. "I'm so sorry." I've never cried this hard.

"Shh." She rubs my hair. "It's alright."

It's not alright. It's all imploding and I can't stop it. But I don't speak. I simply hug her tighter. I suddenly notice that my hair isn't falling over my eyes. I reach for my head. "They chopped it off."

"It's just hair. You're safe now."

By the time I meet her eyes, I've accepted the end. I know with certainty I won't let them take me. "I can't stay. They'll come for me."

"Don't run. Stay here. We can fight together."

"Do you hear yourself?" I can't imagine what that would look like. "Eleanora can't see them take me away."

She holds my hands. "I lost everything because this country decided magic was evil. Because Prohibition made those I love illegal. I should have fought harder."

Of course. Her daughter. She couldn't fix her, and she can't fix me. "It's too late."

"No, it isn't." She cups her hand to the side of her head like she always does. "I'd die for you and Eleanora. I'll fight for your right to dance free. Just please, don't leave us."

I look past her to see Eleanora standing on the bottom step, peering around the corner with her big blue eyes. "Mama? What did they do to you?"

"Come here, baby." I summon a smile.

She wraps her arms around my waist, placing her cheek against my sternum. "I'm scared."

I hate this with every fiber in my body. I wanted to be more for her. Break the shackles and create a sensation the world would have to acknowledge. Make them fall in love with me. The one thing I never accounted for is myself. "I know I look a fright, but I'm just fine. Really." I rub her hair, missing those long braids under my fingers. "I've messed up, baby. I wanted to make everything better, but I've made it worse." I cup my hands around her cheeks. "Please know I tried."

"What's gonna happen to you?" Her eyes glow like a silver sky.

"I will make this better."

She hugs me so tight tears gush from my eyes. As if she knows this is the end. "Don't leave me again."

Maybe I shouldn't have told her about our destiny. I wanted her to be prepared. In control. All I did was frighten her. What a horrible mother I've been. "I love you so much, Nora Girl."

Her breath hitches. Lady cries in the corner, not saying a word. I'd like to leave her with one parting memory. Something beautiful and good to make up for the hell I've put her through. "After I'm gone, look for me in whispers from the Milky Way."

CHAPTER FORTY

Eleanora

Pressure on my shoulder. I'm still in a deep sleep, but I sense a gentle hand on my arm. Against all reason, I wake expecting to see my mother returned from the dead. Through blurry eyes, reality comes into focus. "Iridessa?"

"Hello, Eleanora."

I turn on my side away from her. "Leave me alone."

"Ruby wanted to come, but I asked if I could visit you instead."

I ignore her by tracing the wood grain in the wall which I know so inherently it might as well be part of me. "I'm in hell and there's no way out."

"I'm sorry it turned so quickly last night."

I cover my face under the pillow and release a garbled, "It was always going to end up this way."

"I didn't expect it to go so far." She lifts the pillow, and I finally look at her, knowing my pale face and red eyes reveal just how deep that show cut me.

Those words bring me an odd sense of comfort. "We knew it would."

She rests her dainty hands in her lap. "I expected a competition. Some laughs and a bit of mocking. I didn't expect. That."

"I really can't imagine how, Iridessa." I sit up and face her. Directly in the eyes. "After everything you've seen, how can you expect humans to do anything other than hurt each other?"

"Because I see past what people do." She stops, apparently considering her words. "Price is misguided and desperate. He's mean and truly ignorant with emotions."

"Not seeing the positive here."

She smiles. "He thinks he's protecting you. All these years, he's fought off policemen and lawmakers. He's had purity warriors carried out these doors and tossed into the streets. He cut off one of his donors for attacking a Star Girl years ago."

"It's not for protection. He does that so no one else can control us like he can."

She stares at the rainy morning. "Much like Miles, he digs himself deeper without realizing how many people he'll drag under. It's an awful cycle we're stuck in."

I tuck my legs close to my chest and rest my chin on my knees. "Worse than awful."

"I've been around the theater long enough to learn a few hard truths. You will mourn the death of your favorite shoes because no other will compare. Some nights you will be off and there is no salvaging the performance regardless of how hard you try."

"And?"

"Nothing aches worse than ignoring the dance that begs to be set free."

As if we have a say in the things that make us ache. "That's life at the Luminaire. Dance for Price and his cronies or die trying."

"Like any troupe, individuality is sometimes sacrificed for uniformity of the ensemble." She sighs. "But you aren't in an ensemble, are you?"

I sit up and cross my legs. "We dance individually."

"Yes. Which means you could perform in any way you choose."

"But there would be consequences."

"There are always consequences." She gazes out the window as light snowflakes flutter from the sky. "Theater is a business, and the government has tried to control it since its inception. We're wild and creative. We signify the extremes of society and push boundaries the world would rather ignore. We are art."

I suddenly understand her quiet resistance. "No one seems to understand us."

"Dance is part of me. Rainbows and fairy wings and light that warms my core. I would die without it."

"Which is why you teach us to play by the rules. Do as they ask to avoid getting hurt."

She lays a hand on mine. "I was trying to protect you by teaching you to make the same choices I did. After last night, I see I've been as wrong as Mr. Price. Cruel sacrifices and disappointment are so innate to me, I hadn't stopped to think things could be different someday."

I stand and pace the room, confusion marching its way through my every thought. "Do you know who owns Price?"

"Yes. Mobsters from Chicago own everything illicit. Alcohol sales, Magic Dance. Anything the government has tried to shut down."

"And do you understand that if I fight, they could throw me in an asylum or beat me in the streets?"

She rises, her tall frame like a willow tree gliding toward me. "I'm not telling you what to do. Only you can decide what's worth fighting for. But I believe in you."

"Did you believe in my mother too?"

Her eyes lower. "You need to understand, Eleanora. Your mother was magnificent in every way. But she was sick. Her mind needed support in a world with no options to help her."

"Just like me."

"You are not the same person." Words I know, but they resonate when I hear them aloud. "It hurts to ignore who you really are. And that, I sense, is a betrayal you'd never recover from."

"Okay, so I tap dance to my own rhythm and create my own act. How does that solve anything?"

She flashes a sad smile. "Your mother's mental state worsened when the audience turned on her. She couldn't let them win. I admire her for that."

I rub my temples with both hands. "That doesn't make sense. She was revered for Celtic Fire. Everyone wanted more."

"They wanted more on the stage. In life, every man left her, and every director fired her. She was a product of the greedy needs of every money-hungry and attention-seeking man who crossed her path. Every time she tried to act the *correct* way, her hysteria blew up."

My poor mother just wanted to be accepted for who she was. A spectacular, beautiful, complicated dancer with a personality of fire. "Everyone asked her to burn bright, then tried to extinguish her flames."

As soon as my tears flow, Iridessa wraps me in her arms. Her hug is like a warm blanket, a cool breeze, and a spotlight, all in one.

"I love you, Eleanora. So do your sisters. And I suspect Miles does too. Although you don't want to hear it, Lady loves you too. You have an entire universe who adores you just as you are."

I pull away but still hold her hands. "Mother told me we came from the stars. I've been holding onto a fairytale as if it were truth."

"I've been told we're descended from a long line of healers. Women who danced to cure sickness and speak to the dead. Hundreds of years ago, townsfolk declared healers witches and exiled them for their sorcery. Through dance, they developed elemental responses to release the magic they held inside."

"We aren't from the stars?"

"Very much from the Earth."

I'm not prepared to let go of the stars, or my mother. Or my dreams. "Mother lied to me?"

"She told you the truth she knew."

"I've been listening for whispers that would never come." If my theater family has taught me anything, it's that Magic Dance—when on my terms—is nothing short of perfection.

"We all make our choices, Eleanora. My hope for this troupe is that somehow, the world sees us for what we are. Dancers who color the world with light."

Iridessa touches her hand to my cheek. The morning sun sends rays through the window, warming the patch of room where I stand. Snow still falls, but the flakes seem to flicker like prisms through a slice of amber light.

"Iridessa, I have a wild idea. It might ruin me. It probably will. And our troupe by extension. But to make it happen, I need you and every Star Girl. Will you help?"

She rubs her neck, presumably sore from standing rigid all these years. So much unnecessary pain. When will it stop if we don't fight for change?

"You walked into the Luminaire to prove we can all be free," she says. "You helped create a world that hadn't existed before. One where Ruby, Zelda, Sadie, and even me, look forward instead of back."

"Is that a yes?"

"If it involves my troupe stepping into their power then yes, I'm ready. Where do we start?"

"The Luminaire rooftop. Midnight."

CHAPTER FORTY-ONE

Eleanora

A clear, sharp night on a Seattle rooftop should fill me with terror. I almost plummeted to my death on a night like this. As a kid who watched magic from afar, I envisioned a flight into the stars with no belief I could actually touch them.

Iridessa is the first to arrive, a few minutes before midnight. She's wrapped in a fur coat and hat, her dark skin smooth as silk under the silvery moonlight. "The girls will be here shortly," she says.

I pick up a paper Ruby cutout that somehow landed on our rooftop. "Did I do this to them?"

"No." She tightens my coat with a firm hand. "The investors did. Price leveraged the theater with some shady fellows a long time ago, and it spiraled out of control."

The door clicks open, and the girls run over to hug me.

"We were so worried about you, Eleanora!" Sadie checks my face and hands. "Are you alright?"

"I'm fine. Thank you."

The girls huddle together to stay warm, just as they did in the birdcage, while I step away to gather myself. Iridessa nods to encourage me to speak.

"My mother turned this place into a spectacle and Price has been trying to manage the madness ever since. I've made everything worse by bringing back my name and all our drama."

Ruby shakes her head. "We wouldn't change a thing."

Love swells in my chest, which turns my palms fire hot. "But the horrid stage names they gave us."

"I don't care that they call me giant," Zelda says. "I *am* big, and I tumble better than anyone out there. So what if I'm fat? I take up space on the stage in a big, joyful body, and I won't break myself down because my thighs jiggle."

"I wish I could be like you, Zelda. I don't see hysteria as something joyful."

"Maybe it isn't," Ruby says. "Like everyone's oddities, it's both joy and pain wrapped together in all the things that make us human."

Sadie bumps her hip. "Says the Appalachian witch."

She smiles. "Yes. I'm a witch. I love the dirt and leaves and worms and butterflies and sunshine. I thank the herbs that heal us and respect the monsters that crawl the mountains at night. I also fear those with pitchforks and torches."

"I'm so sorry I couldn't protect you."

Ruby wraps her arm through mine. "I hate the city for doing this to us."

Snowflakes turn to a light mist in the dark morning. A sea of stars splashed across the blackness disappears into the gray dawn. "We've been dancing for the crowd. Wowing them with our talents. But we've missed the most powerful gifts we have."

They glance at each other with gratitude in their eyes. "That, right there." I point to Sadie and Ruby. "The connection we have. That's our superpower."

Zelda arches into a series of back walkovers, lighting the rooftop under her hands with prismed rainbows. "Sorry, had to keep warm. Carry on."

"We've always taken the stage one at a time. It's time we worked together."

"I make ice when I tumble," Zelda says. "If you light a fire next to me, together, we could produce water. And Sadie, what happens when you're around water?"

"I can breathe." Sadie's eyes light up.

"Exactly. The key is to perform together like a symphony," I say. "Just the right mix of elements to make something together we could never make alone."

Iridessa grins "I think we could do it."

"Of course we can." Zelda clears her throat. "I have no fear, remember?"

"I have enough for both of us." My hands still hum with heat, and I imagine what my mother felt near the end when her fire went wild.

Ruby plays her fiddle, breaking the silence. Trees sprout around us, their knotted roots lifting us from the rooftop. A pool of starry water glistens inside our circle, its ripples forming a wavy image. My reflection stares back at me in a sequined black tuxedo and top hat, my lips crimson red.

"We show up Friday for the next installment of the Star Games," I tell the girls. "But we do it our way." I lift my arms as my sleeves gleam under the moonlight.

"No more separation," Sadie says. "We fight together."

Annelise hums a nervous breath. "What happens if we fail?"

They all look at me as if I have answers. "Then we fail together. But at least the world won't own us anymore."

Annelise sings and we admire the mountain scene she's created. The pool and trees disappear as roots shrink into the rooftop. Bubbles float from her mouth with every note. Inside each one is a snow globe. A swirling universe of snow and stars. They combine to form one large golden orb of iridescent metallics. When Annelise stops singing, the orb falls to the stage with a pop as light splatters like oily paint.

"We risk a shuttered theater and eternally banned Magic Dance," Iridessa says. "But we also won't change a damn thing unless we try."

Iridessa told me we come from healers, not from the stars. If this is true, our purpose is much larger than saving a theater.

"One week to make this happen?" Zelda asks. "I do love a challenge." She places her hand out, palm to the sky as a glass heart spins in the air. "Look at that. I'm not moving. Seems like a sign."

We all raise our palms as elements appear. A garnet over Dessa, an emerald light over Ruby, a black icicle over Sadie. My hand remains empty.

"Eleanora?" Iridessa points to my torso.

I lower my head. Gold light shines from my chest. Somehow, beyond reason, I've found a family of women who understand me. Who won't leave me. Alone, I'd never have the strength to control the stage, but together, we have the full weight of magic. No more hiding.

CHAPTER FORTY-TWO

Fiona

You don't need alcohol to numb the pain once you've decided magic wins. Sure, it will kill me, but death will be on my terms.

By the time I arrive at the theater, I've hidden from cops and ducked between rioters. Lady's wig and makeup do a bang-up job hiding the real me. I climb the fire escape but stop to look down on the streets that crawl with outrage. The mob that wants me dead. One thought of those restraints sets my heart pounding. I'll never let them take me again.

The place is quiet. No rehearsals or screams or laughs. I suppose they're shut down to repair the fire I set. I walk through the empty halls and find myself in the grand theater. When it's quiet, I can appreciate the details. The gilded moldings and velvet-lined balconies. I sit on the edge of the stage, feet dangling, as steps approach.

"You shouldn't be here." Price steps out from backstage and surprisingly lowers next to me.

"I never noticed how beautiful this room is."

"You were too busy setting the place on fire."

"True." I inhale the scent of leather and perfume. "What is it about this place? Why do you risk everything for a theater?"

He growls but there's an acceptance in his tone. "It's not just a theater."

"Then what is it?"

He crosses his arms. "I don't owe you answers."

"No one owes anyone a damn thing. But I see what others don't. You aren't a monster. You're heartbroken." His jaw stiffens, the only indication that I've hit a nerve. "Who did it?"

He rubs his forehead hard enough to wince. Then he hangs his head, collapsing after a deep sigh. "I built this place for my wife."

Hard to imagine.

"She had the fire dance, just like you."

Price married to a wild dancer? Wild. "Did she perform here?"

"God, no." His eyes bulge at the notion. "We were kids when we met. Fifteen. I fell in love the second I saw her big dark eyes. They turned gold when she swelled with joy."

"Not a halo?"

"No. She'd trained it to stay inside. She could close her eyes to hide her emotions." The way he twitches makes me sad for him. "Her parents taught her to hide. By the time I found out about her fire, I was already so in love I would have died for her."

"It's wild what love can do."

"Have you ever—"

"No. The only person I've ever loved is my daughter."

He nods once, glancing over to meet my eyes. "Probably better that way. My family shunned us. High society ladies were awful to her even though some of them had hidden magic."

"Rich ladies are the worst. They could have changed the world with their power but no, they had to help their husbands turn us into witches and whores. Those same husbands are the speakeasy's best customers."

"The way they treated her." His face turns hard. Bitter. "She danced in secret, curtains drawn. I made a fortune in Vaudeville theaters and built this. It was her dream to perform onstage."

"A fire dancer who never performed? Tragic."

"She was too afraid after everything they did to her." His arms straighten, locked against his sides as if holding the stage in place. "She performed for us. Midnight when the theater had closed. I kept a headline spot for her, but she could never do it."

I stand on weak knees as heat rises in my forehead. A paltry spin causes a spit of fire. Nothing, really, yet it's enough to send me to the floor. Price turns but I hold up my hand. "Leave it. I'm fine." I'm not fine. Magic is slowly killing me. The pressure never leaves my chest now. I lie on my back, staring at the paneled ceiling as it glitters against the stage lights. "What happened to her?"

"Miles wouldn't leave her side. He was dying with her. I couldn't take it." He stands, walking around to examine my tired body.

"Is that why you won't let the boy dance?"

"Miles will train for business." He walks away but I can't turn toward the noise as exhaustion presses the dead weight of my limbs against the wood stage. Tired but peaceful. I may be ready to leave this world.

Price bends down next to me. He lifts my shoulders to help me long sit and hands me a glass of water. I take a sip, though it's hard to lift my head. "Thank you."

He sits with purpose, cross-legged next to me. "She set the house on fire. Killed herself. She could have killed Miles but thankfully he was with me."

"You know, our fire isn't as dangerous as people think it is."

"Your little performance the other night suggests otherwise."

I grimace, knowing I took that too far. It was all the booze and fear. The mania of needing the next hit of audience adoration. "The way people treated her. That's what drove her mad. We're taught to hate ourselves from our first swell. Hide. Swallow. Pretend. Until one day, you just can't anymore."

"Is that why you need the audience?" he asks.

"The stage is the only place anyone has ever loved me. Even when they hate me they love me." I lean toward the glass, but my arm won't cooperate. Price peels my fingers from the glass. He holds it to my mouth while I sip. A gentle, surprising moment.

The glass clinks as he sets it down next to me. He extends his hand. I take it, surprised that I feel something close to admiration for this man. He helps me stand as I gain my footing.

He nods, beginning to walk off so I can't look in his eyes. "I won't rest until those Temperance ladies burn," he says.

"I hope you ruin them."

"Yeah." He doesn't move. We remain for a long moment, backs to each other. "I bought protection for the Milk House. There won't be any more raids as long as your daughter is there."

I could cry. "Thank you."

"You can't stay now that you've risked my exemption. But you've also given this theater power by way of infamy. I guess I owe you."

"Consider us even." It would be disrespectful to turn around now. To see his tears when he's worked so hard to hide them. "If hate brings this hysteria to an end, then so be it." I want Eleanora to know a better world than I did. To love herself and find the family that's eluded me.

After he walks away, I stand in place, in the cool of a stage without a spotlight. Without fire. I hope Eleanora finds her way here someday and blows the roof off—not for the need of applause, but for the power within her.

CHAPTER FORTY-THREE

Eleanora

Six days until we fail or change the world.

While the Star Girls work with Iridessa on new routines, I stare at Miles's office door. By the time I finally find the nerve to knock, I realize the office is empty, so I go in search, finding him in the lobby with his father. They examine the new sign being installed outside while I slide into an unlit alcove to listen.

"We have no choice, Miles."

"No, I have no choice. I force Nora to dance with me on stage and coax out her fire until she breaks. I won't do it."

Price balls his fists. "Son, if you don't, they're gonna beat us both to a bloody pulp."

Miles throws his head back, sending his caramel locks loose around his shoulders. "I won't ruin either of you. I can't."

"You brought her here."

"I know. And I think I love her."

There goes that swell in my chest again. And a burning in my hands. I want Miles. I *need* him. Like the magic brewing inside me I can no longer ignore.

"This *is* how you protect her. These men will come for her next, you get that, right?" Price closes his eyes in a surprising show of regret. "You know I'd give it all up to save you, but we're in too deep. These men own us."

My hands tremble. Our troupe won't just be up against the audience, we're up against the mob, the policemen, and every dollar they've invested to control us.

"I'm sorry, son." He lays his hand on his shoulder. "Stand on stage with her and show the audience she's dangerous, but you love her anyway."

"I did that during the last show and it damn near killed me."

"Do you think this is the man I set out to be?" Price drops his arms. "I still want the people who hurt our family to pay. But somewhere along the way… shit." He scrapes his fingers through his hair. "We all lost."

He steps outside to yell at the workers who drop the corner of the new sign. Miles kicks the bottom step then notices me. "Oh. Um, how much did you hear?"

"All of it."

He hesitantly steps into the alcove. His eyes glimmer in the shadows. "I won't do it. I won't put you in danger."

Somehow, his frustration is just as sexy as his brooding. "What if I can perform without breaking?" I ask. "We could show the world a romance between a Star Girl and an Earth Boy." I reach for his face. Touching him ignites my light but leaves the fire cooled. "Show them we aren't dangerous."

He leans into my touch, closing his eyes for a long pause.

"We're not so different." I close the space between us, leaning my lips close to his. "I'm haunted by my past. But I don't want panic to rule my life anymore." I touch his lips with my trembling fingers. He slides his hand along my waist to press my body into his.

He presses me against the wall in the dark, holding my cheeks in his hands as his kisses lighten from hungry to soft. His hand slides up my thigh, gathering my dress up to my hip.

"I can't watch the city turn on you again." He kisses me once, softly. "Those torches were too much."

If I risk nothing, I'll never discover what my life could be. "Dance with me on stage next Saturday. I think I can do this."

He buries his face in my neck and pulls me into a tight embrace. His chest rises and falls at a quickened speed. "No."

I try another angle. "If you don't dance with me, they'll come after you and your father. Then they'll come after me. The troupe and I have a plan. Please, trust me."

"I do trust you, Eleanora." He drops one hand and steps back, leaving his other hand trailing slowly away from my waist. "Which is why I can't hurt you."

"I wasn't ready before, but I am now."

"These men won't stop. They only want more until they discard you for the next scheme. Hurting my partner ruined me. They could send you to an asylum." His touch is gone. "No."

My heart sinks. The exact opposite of a swell, it's like the magic has dried up, ground to powdery dust. "I can fix this."

"I hope you do," he says. "But it won't involve me."

"Miles, please. Don't go. I need you."

Tears line his eyes. "I'm sorry."

I step out of the dark to watch him leave, holding back the desire to beg. I tried that with my mother, and it never worked. So, I watch him walk away as my heart rips in two.

I can do this without him. I just don't want to.

***

As far as Price knows, we're polishing our acts until they gleam. When he throws open the door to the gymnasium, all he sees is Iridessa counting out a beat with her cane and Zelda in a spin on her golden rope. By the time he leaves, we all exhale and drop our plastered smiles.

"Dammit!" she says. "My glass has only turned to ice a few times and I don't know how to summon frozen water."

"Forget what you've always known," Iridessa says. "Try it again."

She drops to the stage and pushes everyone away. With a deep breath, she flips into four consecutive back handsprings and then launches into a double layout. When her feet thump into the floor, she's holding two icicles that drip from her hands. "It worked."

Sadie jumps onstage. "My turn!"

She flutters her hands, leaping across the stage. A droplet grows to the music until she holds a giant globe above her head while in pointe. Her long, lean arms like bird wings change the shape of the water as it undulates with a galaxy of stars.

"Beautiful," Zelda says.

Sadie throws her arm to the side as the water forms a circle around her. She leaps and spins over and over, water spinning around her like a hurricane.

"Sadie, careful," I say. "You don't usually tumble like Zelda."

"Must push harder," she yells. She buckles under the weight of the water. We all gasp but she recovers and floats off the ground. "See? It's fine."

The bubble bursts. Sadie recoils and the water show of light sprays in all directions. She thuds to the slick stage, smashing her cheek with a horrific thunk.

"Sadie!" We swarm her but Iridessa holds us back. She examines the welt on her face and asks where it hurts.

"I'm fine. Help me up." Zelda and Ruby lift her, one under each arm. Sadie drops her foot and screams. Her ankle swells right in front of us.

"Carry her to the medical room," Iridessa says.

"No," Sadie says, breathless. "Zelda made me ice and I want to dance in the water and make a reflecting pool for Ruby. I want Nora's idea to work." She cries, heaving for air. "It's too perfect, using our powers together. I can't miss it."

My idea won't work if we lose one of us. All or none. "Sadie, you need a nurse. Go on," I tell her.

The girls carry her backstage where Price will call in a doctor. We have perks here, I suppose. I step through the watery mess from Sadie's magic. Her injury stopped the swell. She wasn't ready. "I will tap like my life depends on it," I say. "It nearly does."

Ruby joins me in the puddle. "No. You'll dance without restraint. With nothing but joy."

"I'd like to think that's possible. But Miles is gone. Sadie broke her ankle. You fell from the platform in the last show. What the hell am I doing?"

"You're standing in bravery." Iridessa spins and leaps toward me, her magic drying up the water as she dances. Her wings flutter like the ring of tiny bells when she comes to a stop in front of me. "I was wrong."

I meet her eyes. "Wrong?"

"Yes. I can't protect you any more than Miles could. The mobsters will continue to attack us because society thinks we're weak. They use our magic while making certain we never taste any drop of the power we hand them."

"I want to show the world how beautiful we are. How much joy we can bring when we aren't stifled. If I fail, we're all in serious trouble."

"Okay, so don't fail."

"Why didn't I think of that? You're a genius, Iridessa."

"I can tell by your tone that you're mocking me. Remember, I am a Black ballerina. I may seem soft spoken, but I've seen things you can't imagine. I've danced in pointe shoes through blisters and ripped toenails. Strained backs and boos and hisses." She points the cane at me. "I've auditioned for perverts who want to catch me in the changing room, and I've been rejected so many times the word no has lost all meaning. Passed over for younger, thinner, faster, louder, quieter. Whiter." She spins her cane in giant circles. "Too soft, too short, her nose is too thin, her eyebrows too thick. Her hair too shiny and her ass too round. It's a butt. It's supposed to be round!"

Iridessa has clearly lost composure, and I'm enjoying the show. "You're not your usual buttoned up ballerina self."

"Oh yes I am." She rushes toward me.

"Again with the cane?" I duck from her giant swings.

"Because we have flawless posture doesn't mean we aren't fierce. I love you girls with every fiber in my body and I can no longer tolerate looking away. Let the Star Games showcase our talents. Let them throw fruit because I will throw it right back."

"What about the mob?"

"You know how you bring a brute to his knees?" She hands me her cane. "You hit him with a giant stick when he turns his back."

"Now I just have to find the right stick." I have no idea how to take out these scoundrels, but I know someone who might.

CHAPTER FORTY-FOUR

Eleanora

Tomorrow! Star Games Showcases Witches as City Fights for Reform
Star Girls Battle for Their Place on Seattle's Only Magic Stage
Magic or Wicked?
The Luminaire Has Gone Too Far

The headlines grow more sensational by the day. The Gazette led with *Seattle's Star Girl Crumbles Under Pressure*. There's only one person who'd leak the story of Sadie's broken ankle.

Price.

I knock three times on his office door, a room that fills me with rage. He answers a grumbled, "Yes."

With a steadying breath, I open the door to find him staring out the window. I can't even hear the chanting anymore, but Price's face is pressed to the glass, practically counting the number of protestors.

"Oh, Cleary. What do you want?"

"I'd like to speak with you."

"I'm very busy."

"This will only take a few minutes." I pull the chair out facing his desk which creates a horrible scrape across the floor. I sit politely, hands clasped in my lap, waiting for him to face me.

"The Star Games was a necessary evil," he says. "The cage and the posters. It had to be done."

"You think there's no way out."

His face reddens like a sunburn. "You know nothing of the world. You've been protected and coddled."

"Is that what you think?" I can't withhold the laugh that bubbles to my throat. "I wasn't the one born in a mansion, Mr. Price."

The protestors' chants grow loud and angry. Beads of sweat appear on his brow. "I've funded this lifestyle, Cleary. I made your mother famous and gave her everything she ever wanted."

"You never listened to what she wanted. You used her and let the world spit her out." The question I really want to ask sits like a boulder in my chest, warning me I might not want to know the answer. "Did you send her to the asylum?"

His eye twitches. "How dare you ask that?"

"She died getting her brain sliced open and I need to know."

"You've waited this long to ask me?"

"I didn't want to believe it. How could anyone who met her have believed she needed to be locked away?"

Price dabs his forehead with a handkerchief. "I've done some awful things, Cleary. I've made a mess of everything in my life. I kicked her out, but I didn't send her to an asylum."

Relief, I suppose. Though I wanted to blame someone.

"Come here." He waves me over and points to the protestors. "Every one of those people tell themselves they're doing the right thing. Prohibition started because men drank too much and beat their wives. Booze came first. Then magic."

"They took away alcohol and magic instead of teaching men not to beat women. It's no wonder my mother fought the whole thing."

He rubs his chin, just as I've seen Miles do.

"My wife had episodes," he says. "Like yours."

"Miles told me."

He clears his throat a few times before closing his eyes. "She was the most sensitive, kindest woman in the world. She cared so deeply for people it ruined her. She stopped leaving the house, so I brought everything to her. Filled our mansion with fresh baked goods and evening gowns. Jewelry and custom hats."

"You bought evening gowns for a woman who didn't leave her house?"

Surprisingly, he cracks a smile. "I loved her the only way I knew how."

"By building her a pretty jail rather than helping her break free."

He slides his hands in his pockets. "It's what I do." He sighs, almost like a regular human with feelings. "The Milk House hasn't gotten a purity raid in some years."

"Not since my mother died."

"The night before they took her, I agreed to protect you. I've paid to keep you safe."

Suddenly, the azure crack in the sky means very little. The galaxy of magic isn't the thing that breaks my heart. My mother made sure I was safe because she couldn't do it herself. Her final sacrifice.

"I should thank you." Somehow that seems like enough.

"Miles looked up to Fiona. He found out Fiona's daughter was hiding out in a speakeasy. I suppose he wanted to give you the chance I gave her." His neck tightens into rigid bands of muscle. "I didn't want you here because I knew how this would end. Not because you aren't good enough."

A bubble of hope pops inside me. "Did you care for my mother?"

"Beyond all reason, yes. We both wanted something so hard we ruined our lives for it. I chose revenge. She chose you."

I remember her smiling, dancing and free. Before Prohibition stole our lives. I'd always thought she could have sacrificed for me. Turns out, that's what she was doing all along. "Revenge took away all your power. Now you risk everyone, including your son."

"I see the irony of that." A sad acceptance washes over his eyes. "Listen, Fiona knew how to work a crowd. But you're a better dancer. I'd tell you to run and hide but I believe Fiona would want you to finish what she started."

A cool breeze blows past my shoulders though no window is open. "I think you want me to stay because it helps you."

"True." He shrugs. "But this is the last night of the Star Games. After this, mobsters will take over. The country will turn you into a sideshow, and I will have lost everything. What else do we have but to play small and stay safe?"

"We can play big, just like Fiona did." In a strange twist, we share a smile. "Be careful what you ask for, Price." I stand and smooth my skirt, remembering my mother's unending audacity. "We're headed for a wild night."

"If you make things worse for me, I will make you pay." His words hold a minor threat, but they seem to have lost their teeth.

"It's my destiny." As I reach for his door, I catch his reflection looking like an angry, proud father who hasn't yet learned his lesson. "And also, because—fuck 'em."

CHAPTER FORTY-FIVE

Eleanora

The night before the big show, the girls gather for a free dance. A few hours in the gymnasium where no one thinks of choreography or blocking. But I still have work to do.

Back in the Milk House once again. Today though, my chest doesn't tighten, and sadness doesn't swallow me. Today, I just want to find Lady. She isn't in her apartment and the bar is empty.

As I approach the door behind the stage, a flash of that jazz dancer's slashed arm grips my heart. I stay in that image for a moment, producing something I haven't remembered before. After she realized what she'd done, she looked up and mouthed, "Help."

I shake myself, suddenly realizing how completely sick it makes me. With a turn of the handle, I face the staircase. Down a narrow flight of stairs and through a brick tunnel with yellow sconces, through a false cabinet that's been left open, I step into the forbidden speakeasy where I once spent many lonely nights.

"Lady?"

A vast room with a stage in the center and a high ceiling. Shining paneled walls with inlaid mirrors that now lay in pieces on the ground.

"Eleanora." Lady appears carrying a crate of empty bottles from the storage room. "What are you doing here?"

"I need help."

She sets down the crate on the one remaining table and leans her elbow on the bar. "Okay."

I spin around, examining the empty shelves and busted plaster walls. "I'm glad you're rebuilding."

"The girls needed space to spin and leap, so I'm cleaning up what I can." She points to a smattering of divots in the ceiling. "See that? Your mother shot fire above her head and each flame turned into gems. It was beautiful."

I point to the stage. "Why did I wash dishes when I could do this?"

"You weren't ready."

I'm still not. "Lady, Price got us into trouble with the Star Games. Mobsters own his theater, his money, and now they own us. If I don't dance with Miles tomorrow and showcase what they'll bill as *A Dangerous Love*, I risk everything. Every person I care for, every hope I have for freedom. *Everything*."

"So do as they ask. You know now you can dance without panic."

Do I? "Miles refuses and the girls have put their trust in me to perform our show, our way."

"You're planning a revolution for tomorrow? After all this time I really have rubbed off on you." Her eyes glimmer. A moment of pride. Like she's been waiting for me to show up.

"I want the city to see our talents and our beauty. I don't want them to fear us anymore."

Her eyes shine with tears. "Well, that sounds like a show I would very much like to see. What do you need from me?"

"How do I get these men what they want so they don't break any bones? How do I take away their control?"

"Only one way. You offer them something bigger than what they already have."

"They want to create a traveling show with me, the unstable tap dancer and Miles, the lovesick director fighting my sanity. Traveling speakeasies will spring up in every city. They'll make a killing showcasing me falling apart."

Lady wrings her long pearl necklace as she thinks. "I know every shady character in this town. Only the weak ones agreed to get on board with Price's mafia protection. The rest of us prefer to go at it on our own. But I could convince them of an opportunity."

"What kind of opportunity?"

"You let me figure that out. Just go out there tomorrow and perform the show that would make your mother proud."

Did everyone know her better than I did? Sometimes I feel like an outsider in my own life. "All I could see was you not fighting for my mother. Now that I understand about your daughter, I see you were fighting for her the entire time."

Lady wraps her arm around me in a rare moment of affection. I lean into her shoulder. "I'm so sorry."

"Don't be. Growing up is hard, and when you have special powers like Magic Dance, it's damn near impossible."

I bite back tears and pull away. "Hey, let's say a farewell to the dishwasher life. It will be fun."

"What are you talking about?"

"My apron, it has to be here somewhere." I search behind the bar and open drawers.

"No, Eleanora, don't do that."

Nothing but papers and castoff clothing and jewelry in this place. "I need a good laugh. Let's burn it with my fire." I laugh until I slide open the last drawer to a familiar sight. "What's this?"

Lady tightens her lips, her hands shaking. "Nora, please listen."

My heart stops. I hold up the Kewpie doll in the blue dress with a ribbon in her hair. "Why do you have this? Did Aria leave it here?"

Her face falls. "No, sweetheart, she didn't."

"What happened to her?" I spin in circles, wondering if she's hurt. "Did she run away? Aria?"

Lady places her hand on my shoulder. "No, she didn't run away."

Something's wrong. "Does she live here now?"

"She's always lived here, Eleanora."

The lights flicker ever so subtly. Is it the bulbs or my eyes? "What? No. She lives in an orphanage. They're terrible to her and she escapes to this place even though they punish her."

Lady's eyes soften. Her gaze suggests she understands more than I do. "When did you meet her?" she asks.

"A few years ago. What does that have to do with anything?"

"Tell me more."

"What are you getting at?" I pace, my palm sweating onto the blue dress of the doll. "The day they admitted my mother to a sanatorium. The very last time I saw her alive."

"I couldn't be another person who hurt you."

"What are you saying?" My voice shakes wildly. Hysteria. This dangerous world. My need to escape to where I'm safe. My breath trembles like rustling leaves. No.

"Aria never lets you down. She's the voice who will love you forever and always. She is everything good you wanted to see in the world."

The divots on the ceiling now appear as hollow pockmarks instead of remnants of gems. The shining walls reveal themselves for what they are, gin-stained, fire burned hunks of wood long forgotten underground. "You're wrong. She's my friend."

Lady reaches for me. Her touch may as well be fire for the way I recoil. "You needed her." Her voice is raw, real. But I can't believe it. Nothing makes sense. I need her.

Aria.

She's always been there. And no one else saw her.

"You let me believe she was real." I scratch my scalp hard enough to sting. "Why didn't you help me? Fix me? Dammit, Lady."

"I didn't know how."

"The voices my mother heard. Did she have an Aria too?"

"I don't know. When you slept in the streets for a few weeks, you came back with her. I tried to explain how she wasn't real, and how you didn't need her, but that only sent you into terrible attacks. You didn't leave your room for days and your mother wasn't doing well. You weren't eating. I played along. If Aria gave you some sort of comfort, who am I to tell you she wasn't real?"

Worse than the moment I realize my mind has lied to me, is the moment I understand... she's gone. My optimistic little sidekick will never again smile and cheer me on. My best friend never existed.

"I can't breathe."

Lady reaches for me, but I shove her away. I stumble up the stairs and through the main floor, out to the freezing air. Please no attack. Please no.

I run. I pound the pavement in my heeled shoes, unafraid of slipping. My body needs to thunder through the streets and shed the fear of hysteria. It lives in me like a parasite. I don't want you anymore! I scream the words in my head.

Drops of evening mist settle on my cheeks. I double over to slow my wheezing breath. I want Aria back.

The orphanage is shuttered. The window where Aria sits is black. The sign that once read "Thorpe Home for Children" is now a copper plate covered in dust. I climb the stairs and wipe the sign with my purple hand. The words are so faded I can't read them, but in the front window a sign reads "No Trespassing. Building Unsafe for Entry."

The gleaming white columns are nothing more than chipped paint and yellowing plaster. Holes in the walls allow me to see through to the mess of wood and bricks inside.

This was never an orphanage. I created what I needed in my wild, untamed mind.

The Hysterical Daughter.

CHAPTER FORTY-SIX

Eleanora

After they dragged my mother away, I lived on the streets, leaving for days and returning when I needed food or clothing. A doctor sliced open her brain, and she never woke up. The hurt was too immense, so I slept on concrete until my fingers turned blue, walking like a shadow through haunted nights. Once, the temperature dropped enough that my mind turned upside down.

That's when Aria came to me, sitting with my freezing body and hugging the panic away. Once my brain warmed in the spring daylight, I couldn't let her go.

Tonight, on the eve of the most important night of my life, I find myself back on the streets I once slept on. As truth seeps into my mind and rattles my bones, I realize how dangerous loneliness has been. I'm stuck with memories so painful, their whispers carved lines on my heart like blades. This is the corner where Aria first flashed a smile and told me I looked like a dancer.

Could she really have been a creation from a broken heart? Of course she was. Maybe I've always known. I told myself not to fall for those troublesome whispers that ruined my mother. But when the world is full of haunting eyes, a little girl with a big smile is near impossible to ignore. She loved me and I knew it. She filled a hole so deep and sharp I welcomed her in and asked her to stay forever.

She told me to return to Lady under my own rules. Aria was the only whisper I wanted to hear because her voice never hurt me. Performance hurt me. People disappointed me.

Without Aria, I don't think I'd be here today.

The truth hurts. The Milky Way is nothing more than silent stars and Aria was a way to escape the hurt. Mother died. Lady loves me more than I could tolerate, and Miles left. My life has been one lie after another.

I lie back to absorb the harsh world around me. Tears roll out the sides of my eyes, cutting a cold trail along my temples. "I miss you so much," I say to the stars.

They don't whisper back.

***

By morning, I'd slept a few hours, surrounded by quiet breathing of my sisters. After the shocking January night, I slid into my warm bed, dreaming of my moment on stage. By the time I yawn my way awake, the sleeping porch has cleared. A glass vial sits at my bedside. Filled with green liquid, a written label reads, Courage Potion.

Ruby brewed me a courage perfume. I slip the bottle in my pocket and get dressed, realizing this might be my very last morning on this porch and my sweet-voiced security blanket won't be there to talk me through an episode.

I can't do this.

On the way down to the basement, I take in the luxury of the theater. The way the chandeliers rattle from the thundering protests outside. The bitter smell of coffee in the dining hall and stale gin in the bar.

The gymnasium is quiet and dark. "Iridessa? I need to ask you something." Maybe she knows if something like Aria happens to all fire dancers.

One giant spotlight illuminates a circle around me. Ten feet away, another spot appears like a halo around Ruby. "I've made you a potion,

Eleanora, though I don't think you need it. You've already taught us how to be courageous."

Ruby lifts her fiddle, playing long, warbly notes that spin her high in the air on a beanstalk freckled with purple flowers. Her dress transforms into overalls and a blouse. She's barefoot. Her hair is big and wild. Vines from the stalk travel across the floor, growing electric toadstools that burst with red light. The vines dig under the wood and disappear, as another spotlight floods an empty circle.

Tiny green tendrils spiral through the cracks in the wood and shoot tall to the ceiling. They grab a hold of a platform of glass holding Zelda, contorted like a pretzel. Zelda drops into a dive, but the vine catches her by the ankles. Her hair turns to glass as she spins, her fingernails translucent.

"I've learned to find a new talent because of you, Eleanora. You've taught me to keep learning and never give up."

She throws a handful of glass shards into the air. They turn to icicles and melt over yet another spotlight where Sadie whips the water like a ribbon while seated in a wheelchair. Dressed all in black with white hair and red lips, she could pass for a movie star. "Eleanora, were family now."

And through the center of our spotlights, Iridessa joins us. Her wings grow expansive and colorful. Her toe shoes now a soft rosy pink. She spins toward me, sharing the light. "We may not change the world tonight, but you've changed us forever."

I lift my arms as the troupe moves toward me in the outfits of their dreams. Dancing to the rhythm of their magic. We wrap ourselves in an embrace, and sway to the comfort of sisterhood.

Iridessa drops her arms. "Eleanora, what did you need to ask me?"

We have our routine. We have a family. "Nothing important." Nothing important at all.

CHAPTER FORTY-SEVEN

Fiona

I slip in through the fire escape, into our old room in the rickety old ice cream house that hides magic. The home we've built from the ashes of my fire dance. Eleanora sleeps soundly, alone but near enough to Lady next door. She's safe here.

I can't leave without saying goodbye.

I smooth her hair back, brushing my fingers against her soft skin. A deep, devastating pain takes over my body. Something worse than fire. Uglier than loneliness. "I'll miss you so much," I whisper. She half-stirs. "God, you're beautiful. And kind and loving." She's one of the only good things. The best thing. "You make me proud."

She drags her lids open, still half hanging over unfocused eyes, moaning with fatigue.

Salty tears stream down my cheeks. Some roll onto my lips. "I'm going home, baby."

"Home?" she asks.

"Yes. They want to take me in and I...I can't." The image of restraints cut off all words. I'll do anything to prevent institutionalization. "You're safe. Lady will take care of you and there will be no more raids at the Milk House."

She falls back asleep. I crawl in bed with her and cry. I hug her so tight even though the fire in my belly causes such pain and cramps I can barely breathe. I'm not well. She's better without me. "Staying here is dangerous. I need to protect you."

She slides her hand over my arm. A gesture that tells me I'm doing the right thing. I need her perfect, sensitive heart to remain intact. Mine is too far gone.

After a long while holding her, I do what I know I must. A mother's love sometimes necessitates brutal loss.

I close the door, catching every second of her sleeping face. It's just a few months. The heat is too much. A furnace inside turning my body to charcoal. I climb the stairs and step onto the rooftop. Blissful cold cools my skin.

I spin out a succession of flames, each weaker than the last. I'm so tired. I walk to the edge of the roof, watching my toes dip forward and back over the edge. If only I could fly home to somewhere free. Eleanora thinks the Milky Way is magic. It's simply the stars. But I needed her to have something real. Beautiful. Something that will always remind her of our happy times.

We aren't from stardust. We are simply flawed humans with fire inside.

"Mama?" Her tender voice breaks me. I can't say goodbye again.

"Sweetheart?" I look over my shoulder but stop when the sirens arrive. Cops flood the entrance to the Milk House.

"Take me," she says.

I flash my gaze between the street below and the door inside. Maybe the fire escape. "I won't live without you anymore." She rushes to my side, grabbing my hand in hers. "Let's go."

"You can't."

I check below as the fire rises in my throat. It burns heat through my forehead and presses out on my skull like a watermelon about to pop. They're coming for me. More restraints. Drugs. Needles. They'll cut out my magic and kill me in the process. I squeeze her hand and force a smile.

In a panic, I point up to the sky. "Look at the beauty up there. Listen for the whispers of how I love you. In the stars, we are free." It's nonsense, but I have nothing left to give her. The lights flicker on the police cars as they thunder through the Milk House looking for the dangerous fire dancer who threatened hundreds.

Lady shoves the door open. Eleanora doesn't see her. She's too focused on staring up at me. I can't tell if she wants me to save her or if she's trying to save me. The voices begin inside.

Lady says, "They're here."

I stare once again at the ground as my vision turns wobbly. My heart thunders. My skin prickles.

Lady nods once. Police appear in the doorway, forcing flames to erupt in my head. I can't see straight. One more look down. I smile at Eleanora. Lady reaches for her hand just as I shove her back with all my might.

Eleanora falls into Lady's arms.

All it will take is a step. One breath. I'll float free where fear can't hurt me. Where my fire has cooled. A pool of water glistens on the pavement. I close my eyes and breathe. No more hurt.

I lean forward, arms out, but before I can fall, their hands are on me, dragging me away, screaming from the ledge. I reach for Eleanora, yelling I love you so loudly my throat stings. Watching her cry for me may be the worst moment of my entire life.

This is not how I will leave this world. I collapse limp in their arms as they drag me to an asylum. They will drug me and tie me down, cut the diseased spot of my brain. But inside, I will churn a fever so hot it will end me before they can.

My terms. My fire.

I love you, baby girl.

CHAPTER FORTY-EIGHT

Eleanora

The electric night pulses around me. Fireworks and music blare as kids clang pots on fire escapes. People gather on rooftops. They flood the streets in anticipation of the Star Games. Panic no longer owns me, but still swirls in my belly like a tide pool. We gather behind the curtain in our Price approved costumes.

"Did you use the potion I made?" Ruby asks.

"Yes. I dabbed it behind my ears. I smell like a gimlet."

Despite her nervous energy, she still laughs. "Where's Miles?"

"Gone." I smooth my dress. "His office is empty." I won't think about how my arms ache for him.

"I really thought he'd show up for you."

Price marches toward us. "Where's Miles?" he says in a tone that could crack glass.

He's using me because he wants to save his son. We do desperate things in the name of love. "He left us both, Price. It's up to me now."

He doesn't respond. The audience stomps their feet and screams. People sell cigarettes and popcorn while every spectator waves a miniature flag featuring their favorite Star Girl. Vendors sell rotten fruit and eggs to throw at the ones they hate.

A woman breaks through the barrier around the stage and runs toward me, fist high in the air. "Witch! You're a witch!" I widen my arms to protect the girls. Her snarl reminds me of a feral cat. "We will eliminate your kind!"

Just then, Mr. Price grabs her wrist hard enough to make her wince. "Back away, hag." He motions for the police to drag her away. He hates them, but maybe he cares some for us.

Price grabs a microphone and trails it out on stage. Cheers mix with boos as screams offset growls from the audience. Each member of this audience would have a different answer for who is the hero and who is the villain.

"Good evening, Seattle." His voice is hesitant, though I doubt anyone notices. "Welcome to week three of the Star Games." He waits for the crowd to settle as he searches for his son who will not appear. "Tonight, we will showcase something new and exciting."

"He's really going through with it," I say.

Sadie grabs my arm from her wheelchair. "Through with what?"

"Lovers doomed by a magic dancer's unstable mind." The familiar wave of panic hits my chest. "He's making a spectacle out of his son and the girl he loves, knowing he won't be here."

"Why would he do that?" Zelda asks.

"To save him."

Price throws the cord away from his feet. "A love story for the ages." He glances back at me, sorrow in his eyes. I think he may change his mind but that hope instantly dissipates. "A hysterical dancer unable to control her magic. Driven mad by her own hunger for fame. And the lovesick emcee who risks everything to save her."

The audience absolutely swoons with excitement. Everyone loves to watch someone fall.

Zelda grabs my arm. "He's going to make you the public's favorite villain."

"I think I already am."

Tonight, we hoped to show the world our Star Girls are nothing to fear. I'm too busy thinking of Price's monologue, Miles's absence, and the mobsters ready to swoop me offstage when this show is over. I stare at my empty hand. I'll never have Aria with me again. I'll have to face panic episodes on my own.

With no options left, I must do the one thing I've fought this entire time.

"Please welcome the Luminaire's own hysterical daughter and her troupe of broken dancers!"

"Bastard," Sadie snaps.

I step on stage, my tap shoes clicking against the freshly shined wood. A rotted head of lettuce hits my cheek, and grains of rice pelt my arms. Men sweep the food from the stage with a flourish, something the crowd finds hilarious. I assure the troupe as best as I can with a smile and a nod. They drag themselves onstage behind me, holding hands in a semicircle, ready to surprise everyone with our group routine.

Price attempts to shush the unruly audience. He places his hand over the microphone. "I'm sorry, Eleanora."

"Go on then. Do what you must."

He shakes his head but carries on. "Now, to dance for her opportunity to prove her love to our emcee, here is Eleanora Cleary." I step forward to face the crowd, holding back tears. "Can she overcome her mother's legacy of mania to win the heart of the man she loves?"

More fruit smashes sticky pulp onto my dress but I remain calm.

The stage lifts me high into the air. The crowd gasps, screaming "Don't hurt me, witch!" The city has created a melodrama over my life, where I'm the monster.

The girls take their places, prepared to dance together and overthrow Price's plan. I could join them. Move ahead with our grand vision to teach this unruly mob not to fear us. Perhaps Ruby's potion has seeped into my skin, but I know what I must do. It's me the crowd wants to ruin, not them.

I spin so fast I lose count. Gems fly from my dress and clang to the stage below. I come to a stop and take a breath. I must save them all by ruining myself. I think of my mother's breakdowns. Morning whisky to calm her nerves. Miles refusing to share this stage with me. Never again dancing with my troupe. The swell starts in my belly and ripples through my limbs.

And just like that, flames.

Fire shoots into the sky in all directions, much to the crowd's enjoyment. I turn to face the troupe. They've taken positions. Ruby lifts her fiddle. Zelda prepares to somersault her way into a ring of glass.

I nearly shatter when I look at their faces. With a shuffle ball change, I shoot fire toward the troupe. Explosions light the stage and everyone in the city screams.

I've created a ring of fire around the girls. A cage of flames to hold them and prevent them from saving me.

As the flames burn, I swan dive off the elevated stage. In a freefall, I imagine what broken bones might feel like. But then, Ruby yells, "Sisters forever!"

I tuck into a ball and somersault seemingly a thousand times and land in a lunge, my strappy gold dress billowing in the breeze. Applause erupts despite more food thrown my way. I face the audience, tears streaking down my face. "The emcee cannot save me," I yell. "Hysteria is an unfair beast that drives away everyone I love."

Ruby is right. Performing a lie might be the worst feeling in the world. So I stop lying.

"So here I stand, in my gown and my dance shoes, a hysterical daughter of the great Fiona Cleary, asking the man I love to dance with me." I hold out my trembling hand to the cold air where no one will take it.

The crowd laughs. Joy at other's pain, what a disgusting form of entertainment.

Silence descends over the city except for a few pops and hisses from my flames that still burn bright.

No Miles. Just as anticipated.

Tears spill over my lower lids and my breathing grows tight. Not now. Please, not now. I thought I'd beat this.

My hand shakes so severely I drop it to my side. My arms set my body quaking, and a scream escapes my crimson-tinted lips. My vision warbles and I fall to my knees. Camera bulbs flash. I can't do this. I can't have an episode while the world watches.

Almost against my will, I spin in a gold orb that lifts me high above the stage. Protected in my luminescent shell, I'm safe and protected, where no food or screams or laughter can hurt me.

Suspended, frozen in my bubble, I hover and scan the crowd. Every face is a different shade of gray. Their shouts and screams are gone, blocked by this protective wall of my own making. Not a fleck of color exists outside my happy, comfortable, faraway place.

Gold flakes dance around me like a snow globe.

I finally see it. I've been pulling myself from this painful life to exist in a world where no one can hurt me. Where my mother doesn't die, and my heart never risks the threat of failed love. Where I can exist without hurt.

I also can't share in the joy of my sisters' smiles and warmth of their hugs. In here, I'm safe, but alone and very, very empty. If I avoid hurt, I'm not living the good stuff.

After a long hard blink, I open my eyes to find Aria inside my bubble, smiling.

"What are you doing here?" I want to throw my arms around her in a hug and never let go.

"I've always been here, Nora. Inside this space, I've showered you with love and protected you from all the evils out there." She gestures toward the audience. "I was never meant to live outside your heart."

"But if I leave this happy, protected space, I'll lose you."

"You don't need me anymore. You've discovered how much love the world has for you."

My chest swells and aches at the same time. "I don't want to say goodbye."

"You don't have to." She holds my hands. Her dark hair turns to a wave of gold light. "You see what you've long known in your heart. I'm part of you."

"Can I call you when I need you?"

"Of course. I'm yours. But you'll find you may no longer need the things you created years ago to get you through a very sad life."

Tears spring to my eyes. My breathing hitches as strangled sobs force their way through my throat. "I need you."

"I will always love you, regardless of what mistakes you make. But you know the truth, Eleanora. To change this world, you can't block out the hurt and fear." She turns my shoulders to the audience. "What do you see?"

"Gray, colorless shadows. A terrifying sea of angry people."

"Look again," she whispers.

My orb, like a magnifying glass, dilates a flicker of gold like a spotlight in a little girl's chest. The silence outside breaks as one high-pitched bell rings in my ear. "She has episodes, just like me."

"Yes."

Another gold spotlight shines from a man in the third row. An angry one who can't stop shouting. Three more people light from their chests. A woman with a cane and a baby in his mother's arms. A teenager on a balcony dressed in a tuxedo and top hat.

"I'm meant to find them, but I was too frightened to look. I'm here to teach them not to be afraid of the panic, aren't I?"

She smiles. "And you can't do that when you're in here with me."

I wipe the tears streaming down my face. "How do I—"

But she's already gone.

This bubble suffocates me. It's tight and too quiet. I tap my foot through the bottom. My orb bursts into gold light as I plummet to the stage. When I land, I'm dressed in my glimmering black tuxedo and top hat, a swell of love in my chest. I wipe away the tears and begin to tap. I dance, free and wild, with no need to summon fire.

Jeers compete with screams, but they don't stop me from dancing for myself. For my own joy. Magic begs to join me, so I shoot a gold star from my hand, which lifts me above the city streets as if hanging from the moon. With sharp focus, I send shots of fire, igniting every flag depicting our Star Girls. These aren't us and I love watching them burn.

I release the star and land on a sea of starlight. This is my moment. My one chance to say what's in my heart.

"You all just watched me panic." The crowd seems to hush, and I know now what power lies in the things we're afraid to say. "I have episodes. Some call it hysteria, but I call it life. It's my life and I'm no longer afraid if you see it."

Sadie screams, shooting water at the flames I built around them. They run, arms linked behind me. Ruby says, "We do this together."

I nod and for once, sadness doesn't make me want to cry. "This is something I've always lived with and will always be with me. No more hiding. See these hands?" I hold them up to face the crowd. "When I get scared, they tremble but grow so numb it's like a part of my body has fallen off or disappeared into the abyss of black closing in around me. And this hair?" I lift locks on either side of my head. "I grab it when I panic. Pull so hard I sometimes rip strands from my head."

The audience has quieted, my honesty somehow disarming them. It no longer matters what their reaction is. I'm done hiding.

"My chest swells with fear and joy and everything in between. This occurs independent of my magic. Do you understand what I'm saying?" I pace the stage, facing the people who launched moldy fruit at my face. "Manic dance, panic episodes, and fear live inside me, but so does love."

I won't tell them about Aria. She's just for me.

Ruby steps forward. "I'm a witch." It's no surprise when the audience screeches. "All that means is I'm connected with the land. I make oils to help with headaches and heal wounds. My fiddle reflects who I am, one with nature." She plays her music softly as vines lift her into the air.

Piano keys tap a light tune from somewhere in the sky as Ruby's violin pulls an elongated tune like a loose thread. We gather in a circle around Sadie.

"We fly together, or we fall to the depths as one." I speak to the girls with a smile.

Annelise exhales. She reaches for my cheek, exploring with her fingers until she finds my temple.

Our feet stomp to our own rhythm, drowning out the boos and jeers. Even Sadie uses her good leg to join our thumps. Ruby draws a lingering crescendo of notes, as if an orchestra leader sets our tone. Our stars pulse and glitter like a conversation in the night.

Zelda throws icicles by tumbling across the stage. "See these boobs?" she yells. "They're large and round and bouncy. Just like my ass. I love my body, and you should too."

Everyone laughs and a few even applaud her sass.

Her icicles drop onto a sea of ground cover spun by Ruby's creations while Annelise's song creates a rainbow wall on the sides as the makeshift aquarium fills with water.

Sadie nudges me. "Watch this, Eleanora." Her bubble lifts her from her chair and drops into the water where she smiles. The rainbow wall turns to glass. All our elements mesh together to form something new.

I step back, realizing she can breathe underwater. Her asthma disappears when she's submerged. That's why she dances with water and why she's held that secret close. Once the crowd realizes it too, they applaud with such fervor, I no longer hear the shouts of protestors.

Ruby motions me forward, nudging me to be Diamond Nora.

"Who among us hasn't felt ashamed?" I ask the hushed crowd. "Who hasn't felt that something inside of us is wrong? You all have faults. Yours might not come with elements, but they are oddities just the same. Some of you cut yourselves just to feel something. Some drink at speakeasies until you wake up in an alley alone. Others have panic episodes just like me." I stare at the grandmother holding a cane. Tears fill her eyes.

I hold hands with my troupe. We smile, accepting whatever comes, because we've spoken our truth.

"Freedom lies in honesty," I say. "We welcome you to join us."

"I failed miserably." We turn to find Miles, standing on stage behind us, hands fiddling at his sides. He steps forward, to the middle of the Star Girls, right next to me.

"I became an acrobat in a circus. I loved the performance and lights and applause," he tells the audience. "Until I dropped my partner. She broke both legs. Now I can't sleep without hearing her screams. I can't climb stairs without panic." He holds my hand. "I'm afraid of heights and I'm afraid of losing someone I care about. I'm no longer your emcee. This stage belongs to the Star Girls."

Annelise breaks into song, leading the audience to sway their arms in the air.

Miles wraps his arms around my waist. "You came back," I whisper.

"If you're brave enough to tell the world your fears, so am I."

"What about the men from Chicago?" I grab his sleeves in my fists. "They'll own us now."

"About that." He motions to Lady who's in the front of the audience smoking a cigarette. "We've come up with a plan. We've offered them control of the speakeasies in town that were shut down by my father, and a few other interested parties. They get to open if they bring in gambling halls and a host of other illegal goods, including Magic Dance."

"We're free of them?"

"I told them they wouldn't get much out of our love story. We've already found our happy ever after."

I wrap my arms around him and kiss him. "And the Luminaire?"

"I gave up my inheritance. It's my father's now to do as he wishes. I no longer live at the mansion, so I guess I'm homeless too. But Lady has a lead on an abandoned school. We could all start over there together, in a school for dance and performance where we teach magic girls to thrive."

"That sounds amazing." I exhale, terrified. "I see things sometimes. Things that aren't there. You should know that I struggle with my mind and hysteria may still take me."

He reaches for my cheek. "It's a new day, Nora." A sweet smile proves he's not afraid to love me. "I'm here. Through it all."

I know Aria is there whenever I need her, but I say a silent farewell to the panicked girl who listened for whispers. The terrified teenager who couldn't let go of her mother. I'm not the helpless daughter of fire.

I pull back and ask loud enough so the crowd can hear, "Miles, will you dance with me?"

"Forever, Eleanora."

We tango and spin, dip and kiss as the crowd cheers and my troupe dances around us. I don't know if the crowd is happy or angry, but I no longer care. Iridessa appears to spin us into the air in a rainbow. "I'm so very proud of you both."

Miles still winces at lifting from the stage, but I'm here to hold him through fear. I kiss him as the world watches. I won't always win, but now I can try with my whole heart.

Lady smiles wide enough to light her entire face, and struts away into the night. We float back to the stage where our troupe takes a bow.

"We're stronger together," Ruby says.

Sadie wraps herself in a blanket, hair wet but her smile big. "Star Girls today. Sisters forever."

And then we dance. To our own music in our own costumes, letting our magic set the rhythm of our hearts. We move and smile to the whims of our bodies because they are finally ours.

My silver and black tuxedo shimmers in the night and I shade our faces with my top hat so Miles can kiss me in private. Maybe the crowd cheers, maybe they scream. None of that matters anymore.

The Milky Way spreads across the sky as I hear the whispers I've longed for. They were always inside me.

ACKNOWLEDGEMENTS

Some have heard of Vaudeville, though few realize that the performers of this variety act circuit were some of the highest paid women in the world. As I read about the wild theater lives of these women, an idea took hold: a speakeasy tale of Vaudeville royalty left out of the spotlight. As my stories tend to do, the original concept twisted and turned, and never stopped reconfiguring until I found the deeper reason these characters came to me.

Wild as the Stars tells a tale of dark theater, legacy, fame, and power, but at its heart, it's a story of loneliness. I threw myself into the examination of mental health while crafting this world, unpacking my lifelong struggle with anxiety and panic disorder. I so rarely see panic attacks discussed in books, and I wanted to explore the insecurity and intense loneliness that results from anxiety.

My writing community has always been a pillar of my success, but this story especially necessitated a collaboration of trust and kindness. I found that in my writer friends and critique partners, who lovingly carried me through the writing, editing, and revision process that eventually (eighteen months later) ended in a creation that I am incredibly proud of.

To Jen, Sayword, Lisa, Samantha, and the authors of the Eleventh Chapter, thank you for being my friends and always helping me find the story my heart wants to tell, but my head so often stands in the way. These women act like guides, offering a circle of encouragement where I can always find my way home.

My husband's support for my dreams has never wavered. He encourages my passion (obsession) with writing, standing right beside me through every story and every page. Thank you, Mike, for being my best friend.

I too often see mental health narratives passed over in publishing. When I pitched this idea to Black Rose, they were ready to dive in with me. They encourage curiosity and exploring new genres, unafraid of the magic twist I wanted to take with historical fiction.

And thank you, dear readers, for picking up this book. Your support allows me to keep writing and exploring the wild ideas that float around my manic brain. I wouldn't be here without you.

ABOUT THE AUTHOR

Kerry Chaput is a multi-award-winning historical fiction author who writes of daring women with loads of adventure and a splash of magic. Born in California, she now calls the Pacific Northwest home, where she spends her days hitting the trails, chasing historical rabbit holes, and feeding her addiction to espresso and doggy cuddles. Explore more stories from women's history at www.kerrywrites.com.

OTHER TITLES
BY KERRY CHAPUT

NOTE FROM KERRY CHAPUT

Word-of-mouth is crucial for any author to succeed. If you enjoyed *Wild as the Stars*, please leave a review online—anywhere you are able. Even if it's just a sentence or two. It would make all the difference and would be very much appreciated.

Thanks!
Kerry Chaput

We hope you enjoyed reading this title from:

www.blackrosewriting.com

Subscribe to our mailing list – *The Rosevine* – and receive **FREE** books, daily deals, and stay current with news about upcoming releases and our hottest authors.
Scan the QR code below to sign up.

Already a subscriber? Please accept a sincere thank you for being a fan of Black Rose Writing authors.

View other Black Rose Writing titles at
www.blackrosewriting.com/books and use promo code
PRINT to receive a **20% discount** when purchasing.